Priceless Treasure

Dominic sat back on his heels and his gaze fell on Elspeth lying naked before him, her hair spread like a glowing tawny escutcheon on the red plaid of the tartan. If he lived to be a hundred, he knew he would remember this moment and the gifts she was offering him. Beauty, love and courage—precious gifts every one. And after he had taken her, he knew that he would not let her go again. The love she offered was even more priceless than the irresistible draw of her body.

He couldn't promise her permanency or even stability, but if he tried to make her happy in the moments they had. . . . But he had to do more than that. He had to find a way to protect her if anything happened to him. He had to keep her secure and security meant money.

The Kantalan treasure.

He stared unseeingly into the darkness, turning over in his mind the possibilities offered by the legendary treasure offered for the woman he loved. . . .

This Fierce Splendor

Iris Johansen

BANTAM BOOKS

TORONTO • NEW YORK • LONDON • SYDNEY • AUCKLAND

THIS FIERCE SPLENDOR

A Bantam Book / February 1988

ISBN 0-553-26991-7

Published simultaneously in the United States and Canada

Bantam Books are published by Bantam Books, a division of
Bantam Doubleday Dell Publishing Group, Inc. Its trademark,
consisting of the words "Bantam Books" and the portrayal of a
rooster, is Registered in U.S. Patent and Trademark Office and in
other countries. Marca Registrada. Bantam Books, 666 Fifth
Avenue, New York, New York 10103.

PRINTED IN THE UNITED STATES OF AMERICA

KR   0 9 8 7 6 5 4 3 2 1

Prologue

❧❧❧

Kantalan, Mexico
Summer, A.D. 1517

The Sun Child was trembling.

The motion beneath Sayan's sandals was a mere quivering that vanished almost as it began. She would never have noticed it if her senses had not been tuned to exquisite sensitivity by the knowledge of what was to come.

Her hand tightened on the stem of the silver goblet. She was also trembling. She hadn't expected to be this afraid. She had thought once she had accepted her fate, she would have the courage to meet it with dignity. After all, it would not be a cruel death. She would drift peacefully to sleep, never to awaken. At least, never to awaken on this plane. There had been something in the flames, a promise. . . .

She lifted the goblet to her lips and quickly swallowed a large draft of potent maize wine. It was strong and smooth as it slid down her throat, leaving warmth in its wake. She was not quite so cold now, and she would be able to meet her fate as a *clairana* should. She moved slowly to the polished brass mirror affixed to the far wall. The mellow golden circle reflected the scarlet blossoms in the white jade vase on the low table in front of the mirror and beyond it her own image. She had dressed very carefully tonight to forestall this very terror and give her confidence. She wore her favorite ceremonial robe, the cloak of sunrise. A sunburst of fine silk pleats fell from the shoulders of the garment in a cascade of gold and ivory and rose and was fastened at her

1

throat with a large yellow-diamond clasp whose facets sparkled in the soft candlelight. The ivory silk gown beneath it was a mere slip of material, and it revealed the full thrust of her breasts and the clean line of her thighs. At least she looked like a *clairana*. She mustn't have these doubts. When the time came she would have the courage she needed. Probably the isolation of the last few days had been more painful than her death would be.

The priests had been very wise in their punishment. They had snatched none of the riches that were the accoutrements of her position from her. They had taken away only their belief in her and the companionship to which a *clairana* was accustomed. She decided it was the terrible loneliness making her so cowardly. Everyone was alone within their soul, but a touch, a word, would have been a comfort as she released her essence to the—

"You look splendid."

Sayan whirled to face the man standing in the doorway. "No!" she whispered. "I told you to leave. I begged you to leave and you promised you would. Why are you still here, Dalkar?"

"I lied." He strolled into the chamber, moving with grace and athletic coordination. His sandals made no sound on the marble tiles. His white teeth were gleaming in his bronze face as he smiled at her, and she felt an eddy of warmth cascade through her that was more heady than the strong wine she had just drunk.

He was the one who was splendid. Strong and superbly muscled like a giant jaguar, his dark eyes shining with humor and vitality. He was naked to the waist as was his custom. The single swath of a dark brown leather *chanton* girdled his slim hips, leaving his muscular thighs as naked as his hair-roughened chest. The cords of the sandals that crisscrossed his ankles and lower calves were also leather. A beaten silver necklace imbedded with turquoise encircled his strong brown throat; the center medallion, inscribed with the cross of the four rivers, hung directly between his breasts. His features were not at all handsome. His nose was too short and blunt and his cheekbones too broad. It made no difference. He drew women to him like the great lodestone in the temple of Ra. He was all male virility and joyous laughter. Sayan had heard the whispers that followed him before he had even approached her, and knew he was not a man she could trust to keep his distance. That, too, had made no difference. His body had seduced her with its strength and heated masculinity, but it was his laughter that had enchanted and won her.

He was laughing now. "You should have known better than to trust me. Any man who would dishonor a *clairana* is capable of any crime." He picked up the graceful silver pitcher from the black marble table and poured a small amount of wine into a goblet. "I knew you wouldn't stop arguing unless I told you I'd leave Kantalan." He lifted the goblet in a toast. "And I had no intention of leaving either you or Kantalan. If you stay, I stay."

"I don't want you to die. I want you to live. It *will* happen, Dalkar, believe me." Her eyes glittered in the candlelight with the tears she refused to let fall. "Please believe me. I saw it in the sacred flames. It was a true vision. Ra didn't take away my powers when I committed the blasphemy."

He stiffened and his smile faded. "It was no blasphemy. It was beautiful. Just because the priests have declared us outcasts doesn't mean what we did was wrong. If you hadn't been the *clairana,* I would have been allowed to take you as my lady. We were right to ignore those pompous fools and their outdated superstition and seize the joy that was our right to know."

She shook her head. "No, we were wrong. If I hadn't betrayed my vow, our people would have believed in me and fled Kantalan. They would not be climbing the Sun Child tonight to give sacrifice."

He frowned. "You have regrets?"

Her eyes widened. "Of course I have regrets. The

greatest civilization that has existed since we left the homeplace is going to be destroyed." Her despairing gaze searched his face. "You don't believe me either, do you?"

He shrugged. "I'm a soldier, not a mystic. I believe what I can see, what I can touch, and what we are together." He smiled. "Is that enough for you, Sayan?"

"No, you *must* believe." Her voice was vibrant with urgency. "You must leave Kantalan, Dalkar."

"Shh." His fingers touched her lips gently. "It doesn't matter what I believe or don't believe. If I thought Ra was going to rain fire down and destroy the world in the next instant, I would still be here."

"There will be no fire." She closed her eyes. "Not this time. Not until the four who come after walk the streets of Kantalan."

Dalkar felt a cold chill in the hollow of his spine. He had always been a confirmed skeptic, but her utter certainty shook him. Then he moved his shoulders as if shrugging off a burden. He had always lived for the moment, and Sayan had given him the most exquisite moments in his life. He had learned these last few days when he had forced himself to stay away from her that a future without her would be meaningless. It was not a future he could comtemplate. If Sayan's prophecy proved true, then he could have no more beloved a companion with to whom spend that final moment. Yet it was against his nature to accept even the possibility of death meekly. "I could take you away. We could make a life for ourselves somewhere else."

"I *can't* go." She opened her eyes to reveal a sadness that made his throat tighten with empathy and love.

Love. He hadn't realized until this moment how much he did love her. She had been a passion, an obsession, a challenge. He had always been tempted by any challenge that presented itself, and Sayan had posed a most difficult and exciting one. He didn't honestly know whether he had set out to seduce her because she was forbidden or because he was truly captivated by her. She was undoubtedly a great beauty, with her perfect features and huge dark eyes, but her solemn mystical temperament was foreign to his easygoing nature. Well, it no longer mattered how they had reached this point; their future was bound inexorably together. Of that he was sure.

His fingers moved from her lips to caress the hollow of her cheek. "Then I can't go either." His hand dropped away. "Now, stop protesting. You're too intelligent a woman to waste your time with futile arguments." He smiled with gentle raillery as he took her goblet and placed it with his own on the table. He took her elbow and propelled her toward the doors of the balcony. "Particularly since you're convinced we have so little time left. Why don't we watch the procession up the Sun Child? It will be quite a spectacle. Our being outcasts has one advantage at least. We don't have to climb to the sacrificial plateau for the ceremony. We can watch it from right here." He drew aside the heavy drapes of filigreed silver and stepped aside for her to precede him. "Perhaps their sacrifices will pacify Ra into forgiving our sins."

"Don't joke." She heard the soft metallic rustle as Dalkar released the silver curtain and it fell into place behind them. She crossed to the stone balustrade to look out over the city. It was hot and utterly still tonight, the air heavy and difficult to breathe. "It was a sin. I don't think Ra considers it a sin against him because he gave me the vision, but it *was* a sin against our people. I should have been more responsible. I should have obeyed the law."

His arm slid around her slim waist beneath the pleated cloak and his lips grazed her ear. Her dark waist-length hair caressed his naked chest and the delicate woman scent of her caused his head to swim and his groin to tighten. "There's no one more responsible than you, little Sayan, and it was a law meant to be broken."

She could feel the strength and warmth of his

heavily muscled arm through the thin ivory silk of her gown and caught the scent of leather and musk that was innately his own surrounding him. She leaned back against him and sighed. "I love you so. Why did I have to love you?"

She obviously didn't expect an answer, and he gave her none. His gaze was fixed toward the south at the lower foothills of the Sun Child, the highest mountain in the chain that encircled the city. The trail leading up the mountain was dotted by thousands of torches as the citizens of Kantalan wound their way to the plateau halfway up the peak.

"I love this city." Sayan's words were only a thread above a whisper. Her gaze was not on the mountain but on the deserted city below them. Stately pyramids and flat-roofed marble edifices sat side by side in faultless harmony and the four rivers dividing that exquisite harmony of architecture shimmered in the silver moonlight like the inscription on Dalkar's medallion. "Could anything be more beautiful than Kantalan?"

"No." He experienced a surge of the same pride he had heard in her voice. It surprised him. He was a man who needed to struggle and build, and the perfection of Kantalan had always grated against his basic drives. But what else could he expect? He had chosen to become a soldier in a land that revered peace. Yet tonight, for some reason, he was responding as he had never done before to the serene beauty of his birthplace. "Nothing."

She was silent for a long time. "Perhaps it will be easier for us than for Cadra. I don't know if I could bear to leave this place and live among the barbarians."

"You've sent Cadra away?"

She nodded. "He, at least, believed my vision. He didn't want to leave me, but I told him it was Ra's will and there had to be someone to tell the tale of Kantalan and summon the four who come after."

"Where did you send him? Tenochtitlán?"

"Do you think I'm mad?" Her voice was suddenly harsh. "You told me yourself Montezuma made over five hundred human sacrifices last year. He has forsaken the true way of Quetzalcoatl. Do you realize he would have had me buried alive for the offense I committed? We were right to cut off all communication with that colony when the blood sacrifices started. I will not give them Cadra or Kantalan to sacrifice on their altars."

He chuckled. "So fierce." His lips brushed her cheek again. "Where did you send him?"

"To the north. It is better that he live with the primitives than with those monsters who have forgotten that civilized cultures cannot be founded on earth soaked with blood." She drew a deep shaky breath. "We have accomplished so much here. Legend says the homeplace was better but I cannot believe it. Kantalan is—" She paused, searching for a word. "Ra."

"Now, your humorless priests really would consider that blaspheming." His breath was warm as he laughed softly in her ear. "I think I'm jealous. I don't want you to be thinking of Kantalan while I'm holding you like this." His arm tightened around her. "And I'd like you to tell me you love me again. Will you do that, Sayan?"

"Why should you doubt it? After what—"

He could feel sudden tension stiffen the muscles of her spine. "What's wrong?" His own body tautened in response, his gaze searching the streets below for some unknown danger.

Sayan realized he hadn't felt the trembling beneath their feet, yet it was far stronger than the tremor she had noticed earlier. Her gaze fled to the Sun Child's peak framed against the moonlit sky. Nothing. No sign of even a whiff of smoke issuing from the mouth of the volcano. Not yet. They still had time.

She turned in his arms and buried her cheek against the warm smoothness of his naked shoulder. "Please go. Please leave me, Dalkar."

"Be quiet." His voice was rough as his fingers

tangled in her shining dark mane as he tilted her head back to gaze into her eyes. For once there was no laughter in his own eyes. They were direct and grave and so loving, she felt as if Ra had flooded the night with sunlight. Her entire being was floating on that stream of light. "I don't know anything about your visions or your gods. All I know is what we have together. I could no more leave you now than I could change what I feel for you. Do you understand?"

"Yes." He would not leave her. Pain, joy, regret. The emotions tumbled through her in a wild cataract of feeling. "I understand."

"Good." The gravity vanished from his expression and he smiled down at her. "Now will you tell me you love me?"

"I love you. I will love you until there is no sun, no moon, and no homeplace on this earth."

He kissed her lightly. "My solemn little Sayan, you are nothing if not extravagant. I would have been content with a promise involving the rest of our lives."

He still did not believe her, she realized sadly. She would waste no more time trying to convince him. Time was far too precious now. Her lashes lowered to veil her eyes. "Will you lie with me?"

A flicker of surprise crossed his face. "You wish to merge?"

She shook her head. "I'd like to lie in your arms." Her lips were trembling as she tried to smile. "We have never lain together without merging. I would like very much to hold you with gentleness and love."

He didn't answer for a moment, and she could sense the waves of emotions emanating from him with the same clarity as she had sensed the trembling of the Sun Child. He stepped back. "I would like that very much also, my love." He held the silver curtain for her. "Though I won't promise we won't merge before this night wanes."

"I ask no promises." No promises were necessary. The time was near. She unfastened the yellow-diamond clasp of her ceremonial cloak and draped its brilliant folds across the backless chair against the wall. She moved across the room to the golden-hued cushions of the couch in the center of the chamber. He was there before her and held out his arms to draw her down into his embrace.

"Just hold me, Dalkar."

He was gently stroking the dark tendrils of hair at her temples. She was no longer afraid. How wonderful that love could banish fear. She knew a stab of poignant regret, and then that also faded away. It was not the end. Love did not end and there had been the promise . . .

Her gaze fastened dreamily on the silver filigree drapes at the balcony door. The curtains were glittering in the candlelight, the fretwork forming lacy patterns against the indigo of the night sky. She heard the faintest tinkle of sound, as if the heavy draperies were being stirred by an errant gust of wind. But there was no wind on this hot summer night . . . not the slightest breath of a wind.

1

June 12, 1870
Hell's Bluff, Arizona Territory

"**R**ein in! This is a holdup!"

As the deep-voiced command had been preceded by four gunshots, one of which skimmed the brim of his hat, Ben Travis decided it behooved him to obey . . . and fast. He glanced with longing at the shotgun beside him in the boot of the stagecoach, then reluctantly pulled up the horses just short of the lone bandit standing square in the center of the road ahead.

A thrill of panic darted through Elspeth MacGregor, and her hand unconsciously tightened on the black grosgrain reticule she carried. She mustn't be forced to give up the little money she possessed. If Dominic Delaney wasn't still at Hell's Bluff, where her father had last made contact with him, she would have to search for him. Heaven only knew how long it would take and how much it would cost to find him.

"Do not be frightened, mademoiselle."

Those slightly accented words were the first the plump young man across from Elspeth had spoken since the stage had left Tucson. Her fellow passenger had appeared to be dozing continuously since their early morning departure, and Elspeth had felt relieved to be ignored by him and left to her own thoughts. Now, however, the man's dark eyes were blazing with excitement.

"I've read about these desperadoes," he said, "and they have a certain code. The would never tamper

10

with the virtue of a respectable lady such as yourself. They want only our money."

Only! Elspeth came close to laughing aloud. Women as plain as she seldom had problems with would-be ravishers, so she hadn't a fear on that score. But she did fear being robbed; she *had* to have money on which to live until she could find Dominic Delaney. She had a little gold secreted in her trunk, but most of her remaining funds were in the reticule she was clutching so desperately. "Do you have a weapon?" she asked her plump companion. "We could try to overpower them. We cannot just let them rob us."

He blinked. The woman facing him was small, quite fragile-looking really, and her voice was sweetly melodious despite its urgent tone. The mere suggestion from her of trying to overpower even the weakest of men seemed ludicrous to him. Deciding fear was robbing her of good sense, he said soothingly, "I do not think it would be wise to challenge these fellows. They're probably very dangerous." He shrugged his shoulders and the fine biscuit-colored broadcloth of his fashionable coat scarcely rippled. "Naturally," he said forcefully, "if you weren't present, I would confront these outlaws."

"Naturally," she echoed dryly. He appeared to be accepting this robbery with equanimity, even a certain amount of pleasure. Judging by the beautifully crafted leather boots and expensive clothes of this calm individual, she suspected he could easily afford to lose the money he carried with him. She could not. "Do you have a pistol?" she asked.

He looked slightly affronted. "Of course I have a pistol. A very fine derringer."

"May I borrow it?"

He blinked again. "Do you know how to fire a pistol?"

"I haven't the slightest notion how to do so, but at least I can threaten those bandits with it." She straightened briskly and held out her small, gloved hand. "Please."

Clearly astonished at what she wished to do, he blustered, "I do not think—"

His sentence was interrupted by a string of curses shouted by the driver of the stage.

Elspeth frowned. She'd overheard her father and his students using some of the milder oaths on occasion, but many of the curses the driver spouted now were utterly incomprehensible to her. She cocked her head, listening carefully as the man called Ben Travis went on.

"I could have blown you to kingdom come with my shotgun, you young jackass. It would have served you right."

"Now, Ben, where's your sense of humor? My horse threw a shoe and I needed a ride into town."

The deep voice of the bandit, no longer low and ominous but jocular, confounded Elspeth for a moment.

"You're always telling us what a boring run it is from Tucson to Hell's Bluff, Ben, so I decided to liven things up a little for you."

"By holding up the stage?" Ben Travis's voice dripped sarcasm. "What do you think your granddad will have to say about this?"

"How else could I get you to stop? You always go flat out the last few miles into Hell's Bluff. I had to find a way to get your attention."

Elspeth's tension ebbed. Apparently there was no threat here after all. That young man had played some sort of bizarre practical joke.

"My attention?" the driver thundered before loosing a fresh string of curses that mingled with the younger's man's rich laughter. "You've got feet," Ben said. "You could have walked to town, you know."

"When did you ever know a cowboy who would walk when he could ride? Even this rattlebone coach of yours is better than walking."

"Rattlebone! This is the finest coach that ever came out of Concord, and only a half-weaned, bowlegged cowpuncher wouldn't be able to appreciate her."

"Sorry, Ben." There was still an undercurrent of

laughter to the man's voice as he apologized. "Can I have a ride to town in the finest coach that ever came out of Concord?"

"Hell, no!" There was a pause, and then another curse. "I guess if I leave you out here, you're loco enough to try the same fool trick on one of the ore wagons. But I don't want you up here with me. Tie your horse to the baggage rack in back and get in the coach, where I don't have to look at you."

"Thanks, Ben."

"And you behave yourself with the paying customers. We've got a lady passenger today."

"A lady going to Hell's Bluff?" The deep voice was chuckling as it came nearer. "You sure your eyesight isn't going bad, Ben? There are ladies and then there are . . ." He trailed off as he opened the door of the coach and caught sight of Elspeth. He quickly doffed his hat. "How do you do, ma'am. Sorry for the commotion. I hope I didn't frighten you."

Elspeth stared in surprise. Why, he was only a boy. He couldn't have been more than eighteen or nineteen in spite of the hardened muscular body that made him appear older. The afternoon sunlight danced over his chestnut-colored hair, revealing its red highlights, and his dark-brown eyes were still sparkling with remembered laughter. No, not remembered, but present once again as he smiled easily at her. He was so *alive*. She was used to being around boys his age, but she had never seen a young man quite like this one. "How do you do?" she asked faintly, thinking that if his chin had been less firm, the slight depression in its center might have been termed a dimple.

"Not so well. My horse threw a shoe on the way back to my ranch." He climbed into the coach and settled his long slim body in the seat across from her and beside the portly man in the biscuit-colored coat. He stretched his denim-clad legs out in front of him. "Which means I'll have to take him to the blacksmith in Hell's Bluff and not get back to Killara until tomorrow." He made a face. "My grandfather is going to skin me alive."

She found herself smiling sympathetically at him. She had an idea most people found themselves smiling when confronting this young man. "I'm sure he'll understand that it's not your fault."

"Permit me to introduce myself." The plump man sitting next to him was gazing in fascination at the auburn-haired cowboy. "I am Count Andre Marzonoff, heir to estates in Vlados and recently arrived from St. Petersburg. I am delighted to meet you."

The cowboy gazed at him blankly for a moment. "Well, howdy," he said, and Elspeth was sure his eyes were twinkling. "I'm Patrick Delaney, heir apparent of Killara, but since I share that honor with a sister, a cousin, and five uncles you may think it tends to lessen my importance a trifle."

Elspeth stiffened. Delaney. It couldn't be a coincidence. Now here, so near to Hell's Bluff.

Andre Marzonoff nodded. "I, too, have an older cousin who holds the purse strings. Perhaps we have other things in common."

"Perhaps." Patrick Delaney's glance drifted from Marzonoff to Elspeth. "And what kingdom do you rule, Princess—?"

"I am Miss Elspeth MacGregor."

Patrick Delaney tilted his head as if listening to pleasant music. "You're Scottish, aren't you? I ran into a fellow in a saloon in Tucson who sounded like you." He grinned. "Well, not exactly like you. Your soft little burr is like harp chords and he sounded like a stomped-on bagpipe."

She smiled. "I'm from Edinburgh, Mr. Delaney, and I'm afraid I'm heiress to very little. My father was a professor of antiquities at the university and scholars rarely acquire more than the wealth of knowledge." She hesitated. "I wonder if you could be related—" She stopped speaking as the coach lurched into motion, pressing her back against the leather seat. She heard another round of curses from the driver that were mild in comparison to the ones previously heaped on Patrick Delaney's head. Evidently the man couldn't open his mouth without an obscenity issuing from it.

"He doesn't mean any disrespect," Patrick said quietly, his gaze on her face. "He's just not accustomed to having to watch his language. I'm afraid you're going to find we're all guilty in that respect. We don't get many ladies in Hell's Bluff."

"I'm not offended, just a bit surprised." She looked searchingly at Patrick Delaney's face. "I wonder if you know a man I'm going to Hell's Bluff to see, Dominic Delaney."

The boy's indolent position didn't change, but Elspeth had the impression that he had suddenly become alert. He crossed his legs at the ankles, his gaze on the dusty toe of his boot. "Everyone in Hell's Bluff knows Dominic."

"You have the same surname. Are you perhaps related?"

"Dominic Delaney." Andre Marzonoff's eyes were wide with surprise and excitement. "The gunslinger? He's in Hell's Bluff right now?"

"Dominic is no gunslinger." Patrick enunciated each word carefully. "However, on occasion he's been known to have permanently removed a few gentlemen, who have displeased him. I happen to know one of the things that displeases him most is to be called a gunslinger."

The underlying menace in Patrick's voice seemed to make little impression on the Russian. "I will be discreet. Will you be so kind as to give me an introduction?" he asked with enthusiasm.

Elspeth stared at him in amazement. How very curious. The count had just been told Dominic Delaney had actually killed a number of unfortunates and yet he was behaving as if the man were a god from Olympus. She shifted her gaze back to Patrick Delaney.

He was studying her with the same, cold analytical keenness she had seen on her father's face a thousand times when he was studying a hieroglyphic—or lecturing her on one of her faults. Patrick Delaney no longer looked like a boy but seemed suddenly fully mature and vaguely threatening. "And do you need an introduction, too, Miss MacGregor?" he asked softly.

She moistened her lower lip with her tongue. For a fleeting moment she was swept back to the past. She was a child standing before her father's desk, crushed and bewildered, flooded with that familiar unreasoning miserable sense of guilt. "Yes," she stammered. "I mean no. I mean . . ."

Patrick felt as guilty as if he had kicked a puppy. The woman had appeared so cool and assured, but now he saw she wasn't a woman at all. She was little more than a girl, just a few years older than he and his twin sister Brianne, and a hell of a lot less confident. She was peering at him from behind the thick lenses of her spectacles as if he were a wild animal suddenly let loose in the coach.

She must have taken him off guard with the question about his uncle or he wouldn't have been so damn suspicious. He, as well as the rest of the family, had become accustomed to protecting Dominic over the years, but he realized that Elspeth MacGregor could pose no possible threat to him. No one in his wildest imaginings could mistake her for a Delilah hired by one of Dominic's enemies.

She wasn't even pretty, though the flush now coloring her cheeks made her look more attractive than he had first thought possible. Her features were regular enough, her nose small and straight, her lips pink and well shaped. It was the lack of expression and vitality that robbed her face of real interest. She was as pale and controlled as the statue of the Madonna in Manuela's chapel at the ranch. He thought her eyes must be a shade of brown, but it was difficult to be sure, as they were masked by the round thick lenses of those damned spectacles. Her hair was light brown also and pulled severely away from her face and bundled into a bun on top of her head. That silky black high-collared gown she was wearing was too loose to reveal much of her tiny, fine-boned figure, but he had an idea it was as unispiring and lackluster as her face. No, definitely, no Delilah. And certainly not one of Dominic's women. Dominic had no taste for respectable women these days, much to Gran-da's despair. It was clear Elspeth MacGregor was not only respectable, she was vulnerable.

He forced himself to relax and smiled gently. "Dominic is my uncle and I'll be very glad to introduce you, if you're not acquainted with him. May I ask your business with him?"

He was being kind to her. Patronizing and indulgent and very kind. Elspeth could feel the tears of frustration and self-disgust sting her eyes. She had meant to be so adult and coolly businesslike, but at the first hint of intimidation she had reacted with a regrettable lack of composure. Patrick Delaney was only a boy and nothing in the least like her father. What could have triggered the memory that had caused her assurance to melt like ice in the sunshine?

She would *not* behave like the helpless nonentity her father had thought her. This was a new life, a new Elspeth MacGregor. She drew a deep, steadying breath and lifted her chin. "I would appreciate your help, Mr. Delaney. I have a business proposal to make to your uncle and he's a stranger to me. I'm sure he'll remember my father, however."

"Hell's Bluff isn't the kind of town that can offer a lady any of the amenities. Your father would have done better to come himself."

Elspeth lowered her eyes to the reticule on her lap. "My father died four months ago."

So that was the reason for all that overpowering black. "My sympathy. There was no one else who could make the trip?"

She shook her head. "I'm alone now." She lifted her eyes and met his gaze. "And even if I weren't alone, I would have come anyway. In case you hadn't noticed, women are becoming very capable of handling their own affairs. In fact, I understand in your territory of Wyoming they have already won the vote. I don't need anyone to shelter and protect me, Mr. Delaney."

No more than a newborn calf in a snowstorm,

Patrick thought while he carefully kept his expression from revealing that judgment. "I can see you're very capable, but perhaps you'll let me escort you to the hotel and get you settled, if that wouldn't compromise your principles too drastically." His lips twitched in spite of his attempt at solemnity. "I promise I won't tell the ladies in Wyoming."

He was laughing at her. She should have been annoyed but somehow she found that impossible. There was something in his manner that was so genuinely sunny and caring, she found herself smiling again. "I believe I'd be willing to risk their disapproval, but I'd prefer to see your uncle immediately. I may be able to conclude my business with him this afternoon. Is he staying at the hotel?"

"Well, not exactly." Patrick had a sudden vision of the last glimpse he'd had of Dominic when he'd stuck his head in Rina's room this morning to say good-bye. Rina had evidently decided to be generous; there had been a golden-haired beauty on one side of Dom in the big double bed, Rina herself on the other side. The thought of this little owl named Elspeth invading that scene of bacchanalian debauchery might be amusing, but he doubted Dom would think so. "It would be better if I brought Dom to you. He moves around a lot and has an interest in one or two claims out of town."

Elspeth frowned. "If that's the only way I can see him. Claims? You mean gold mines?" She had known Hell's Bluff was a boom town, one of those fabulous places that had sprung into being when gold had been discovered. It was rather like Athena springing full grown from Zeus's head, she thought. She should have guessed that Dominic Delaney was still here because of the gold being found in these parts. She experienced a swift rush of dismay. She had nothing to offer him but the potential for great wealth. What if he were already a wealthy man? "He owns gold mines?"

Patrick shook his head. "He grubstaked a couple of miners for a percentage of their claims, but they haven't brought in more than a few sacks of dust yet."

He shrugged. "There's plenty of gold here in the Santa Catalinas all right. It's probably only a question of time until Dom's miners make a strike."

Elspeth released the breath she hadn't realized she'd been holding. She still had something with which to bargain, then. "We've heard of your famous gold rushes at home. Hell's Bluff must be a very interesting town. Do you have one of these claims, too, Mr. Delaney?"

He made a face. "I have all I can do on Killara. My gran-da keeps us all too busy to go prospecting."

"Except your uncle Dominic?"

"I heard he shot two men in Carson City," Andre Marzonoff broke in. "He faced them in the street and they both emptied their guns while he walked toward them. He didn't fire a shot until he was within range and then gunned them both down. Is it true he's being hunted by the Texas Rangers?"

Elspeth had almost forgotten the Russian was in the coach. Now she saw he had been drinking in Patrick Delaney's words with an avid thirst that was faintly repulsive.

It was clearly repulsive to Patrick Delaney as well. "No, Dom's not wanted by the law any longer. He was given a full pardon by the governor five months ago." He lowered his voice to a dangerous softness. "And questions regarding a man's past aren't encouraged out here, Marzonoff. If you want to stay healthy, you'd better observe our primitive customs."

For a moment Marzonoff actually appeared indignant. Then he smiled ingratiatingly. "I meant no offence. I admire you westerners very much. You bear a resemblance to the Cossacks of my own country. My cousin, Nicholas, is related on his mother's side to Igor Dabol, the most powerful tribal leader in the steppes."

"How interesting," Delaney said politely. "I'm afraid I've never heard of him." He looked down and Elspeth noted a gleam of pure mischief in his hastily averted eyes. "We Delaneys have a few well-known relatives ourselves. Have you ever heard of the James brothers? Jesse and Frank?"

Marzonoff's eyes widened. "Jesse James?"

"Cousins," Delaney said. "On my mother's side, of course." He was scrupulously keeping his gaze from Marzonoff's rapt face. "And then there's old Joaquin Murrietta. You might say he's the patriarch of the California branch of the Delaney clan. Of course, I guess Uncle Bill is probably more famous."

"Bill?" Marzonoff was almost stammering with excitement.

"Bill Hickok. However, there are those who say he's more infamous than famous. But not to his face. Uncle Bill is very careful of his good name."

"Wild Bill Hickok," the Russian repeated dazedly.

"And the Daltons and the Youngers are second cousins on my . . ." Delaney trailed off and Elspeth saw his shoulders begin to shake, though his expression was still bland. She was forced to smother a laugh herself.

Patrick Delaney's voice was a little choked as he continued. "I think I'll take a little snooze. All that walking has made me plumb weary." He put on his stetson and tipped it over his eyes, ignoring Marzonoff's obvious disappointment. "I'm afraid I'm not as rough and tough as my kinfolk."

Elspeth didn't know about his toughness but she was sure the young rascal could far outpace his "relatives" in sheer deviltry.

She settled back on the seat, shifting her gaze between the two young men opposite her. They were a strange blend of contrasts and similarities. The plump Russian was the older, she judged, close to her own age of twenty-two years. His fine city clothing should have given him the advantage of inner confidence over the auburn-haired cowboy, but such was not the case. Patrick's tight denim trousers were shabby, his brown shirt and tan suede vest dusty, and his black stetson was sun-faded in spots. Yet his wide shoulders and narrow hips, the careless grace of his strong body, gave his attire an elegance Andre Marzonoff could never hope to bring to his clothing. Patrick's speech was puzzling. His words sounded as educated and cultured as any of her father's students, and yet they were flavored by a lazy and quite unusual drawl. This young Delaney was something of an enigma, she thought.

She glanced out the window. The Santa Catalina mountains were very beautiful but as stark and rugged as the rest of this wild country. How different they were from the mist-shrouded mountains of her native land. She shifted restlessly, suddenly tired of the scenery. She felt as if she had traveled years instead of weeks since she had left Edinburgh. She was growing terribly impatient now that she was so close to her objective. Her gaze returned to Patrick Delaney, and a tiny smile lifted the corners of her lips. She closed her own eyes and tried to relax.

The young cowboy was a complete scoundrel. Her father would have disapproved of both his attitude and his background, yet she was delighted to have his assistance when she arrived in Hell's Bluff. Her smile brodened. Yes, she was perfectly delighted.

Dominic Delaney moved with utmost care down the carpeted stairs. His head felt as if it were being struck by the sharp point of a miner's pick with every step. He stiffened the muscles of his neck as well as his entire upper body in an attempt to keep that blasted hammer at bay.

Red. Damn, why did Rina have to have such a fondness for red? Why didn't she listen when he pointed out to her that a whorehouse didn't necessarily have to look like a whorehouse. The flowered paper on the walls of the foyer was garish and rolled before his eyes as if he were seasick.

The front door opened and he flinched as slanted rays of afternoon sunlight hit him squarely in the eyes. He squinted against the glare and recognized the tall, familiar silhouette framed in the doorway. It didn't improve his temper. "Shut the goddamn door," he said in a growl as he reached the bottom of the stairs. "Are you trying to blind me?"

"Sorry." Patrick's voice was cheerful as he entered

the foyer and closed the door. "You look like hell. You ought to stick to singles if you don't have the stamina for Rina's little games. You're not as young as you used to be, you know."

"I'm young enough to take on a runny-nosed kid who doesn't know better than to smart off to a man in my condition." Dominic turned away and walked slowly down the corridor toward the kitchen. "And it wasn't Rina or her games, as you call them. It was the whiskey. Lord, I've got to get a cup of coffee. What the hell are you doing here? I thought you were going back to Killara." He turned his head too quickly and cursed softly as pain stabbed his temples and behind his eyes. He gave Patrick a sour look. "Don't think you're going to stay in Hell's Bluff. A Saturday-night spree now and then is all right, but whorehouses and saloons are no good for a man in the long haul."

Patrick's lips quirked. "You didn't have to go to all this trouble to furnish me with proof of the wages of sin."

"You go back to Killara tomorrow," Dominic said flatly.

"If you're so convinced Hell's Bluff is the road to destruction, why don't you come with me to Killara?" Patrick met Dominic's gaze. The laughter had vanished from his face. "Come home, Dom. Why do you think Gran-da doesn't give me hell for coming up here so often? He wants word of you. More, he wants you to come home, where you belong."

Dominic averted his eyes and felt an ache somewhere within him that had nothing to do with his overindulgence of the previous night. Belonged. How long had it been since he'd belonged anywhere as he once had belonged at Killara? There had been times during the last nine years when he'd missed his home with a ferocity that had been sheer torture. "Someday."

"When, Dom?" Patrick asked softly. "You're not on the run any longer. You love Killara. Maybe more than anyone but Gran-da. Times aren't good now. Killara needs you."

Dom flinched as if he'd been struck. "And whose fault is it that times aren't good? For God's sake, I've practically destroyed Killara. Do you want me to come back and finish the job? You know damn well why I can't come back to the ranch. Now drop it, Patrick."

"Dom, I—" Patrick broke off and slowly shook his head. "You're wrong. You're a Delaney. You know we protect our own." He paused. "Gran-da just wants you home."

Dominic's lips twisted in a mockery of a smile. "And what if protecting me ends with Cort or Sean or you dead or shot up? Will he want me then?"

"Yes," Patrick said. "I think you know that, Dom."

Yes, he knew his father wouldn't count the cost when it came to any member of his family. It made the situation all the more painful. "Well, I'm not about to let any of you pay that kind of a price. I've cost Killara too much." He violently pushed open the door to the kitchen.

Li Tong turned away from the stove with a wide smile as they came into the room, took one look at Dominic's face, and nodded shrewdly. "Coffee," he said with certainty, and hurried toward the cupboard, his pigtail bouncing. "Sit down, Mr. Delaney. I get."

Dominic dropped into the wooden chair at the large round table covered in blue-checked gingham. He gave Patrick a sardonic glance. "Tell Da I'm doing fine. Who could ask for anything more? I make a decent living playing poker at the Nugget. I can sleep all day and spend most of the night pleasing myself."

Li Tong placed a steaming cup of coffee in front of Dominic and looked inquiringly at Patrick. When Patrick shook his head he moved silently across the large room toward the large woodburning stove.

Dominic deliberately changed the subject. "Speaking of pleasure, how did you like Dulcie?"

"Very talented," Patrick said, his thoughts still far away from the playful redhaired strumpet who had shared his bed the night before. Then his frown disappeared as he grinned at Dominic. "Maybe you ought to try her. You wouldn't need exotic variations to revive your flagging manhood if you concentrated on quality instead of quantity."

"Flagging manhood!" Dominic took a sip of coffee before he turned his gaze to Patrick with the faintest flicker of a smile. "When you get a little older, my lad, you'll find a true man has to challenge himself on occasion." He grimaced. "And last night was definitely a challenge."

"Were the ladies satisfied?"

"I don't remember." Dominic rubbed his temple. "But I think I was. And I'm sure Rina will let me know when she wakes up if she wasn't."

Patrick chuckled. "I agree. Rina's not shy about voicing her displeasure." Not that Patrick could recall a time when Dominic had had a problem pleasing Rina Bradshaw. The madam seemed more than happy to have Dominic's company in and out of bed as often as possible. Patrick rocked the chair onto its rear legs and pushed his stetson to the back of his head. "Maybe you're right. Could be this isn't such a bad life after all."

Dominic took another sip of coffee and looked straight ahead. "Don't even think about it. You're going back to Killara first thing tomorrow morning."

Patrick raised a quizzical brow. "Oh, am I, Uncle Dominic, sir? And just what would you say if I decided to stay and join you in a life of decadence?"

"I'd knock you on your ass, tie you on your horse, and send you packing to Killara. Then I'd tell everyone in Hell's Bluff if they allowed you in a saloon, a whorehouse, or even in the general store, they'd have to face me." He smiled with a gentleness that was more menacing than anger. "Would you care to call my bluff, Patrick?"

Patrick gave a low whistle and shook his head. "Not at the moment. It would be a waste of time, as I have every intention of going home tomorrow. In fact, I would have been home tonight if my horse hadn't thrown a shoe about five miles out of town."

"You could have told me."

Patrick grinned. "And missed the chance of goading dangerous Dominic Delaney? You have things too much your own way here, Dom. You need someone around to whittle you down a peg."

Dominic suddenly smiled with engaging warmth. "You do a pretty good job. I'm lucky you aren't around all the time, or I'd be whittled down to the size of a toothpick." He finished his coffee. "Well, as long as you're here you might as well enjoy the fruits of corruption for a little longer. Do you want to come over to the Nugget with me and see if we can get up a game?"

"Maybe later. I thought we'd go over to the hotel for a meal." Patrick paused. "There's someone there I want you to meet. She arrived on the stage this afternoon."

"She?" Dominic smiled faintly. "Dulcie couldn't have been as good as you say if you had to go out and find another ladyfriend so soon."

"It's nothing like that. You're the reason she's come to Hell's Bluff. She said she had a business proposition for you."

"Maybe Rina has been telling the world about my skills," Dominic drawled. "Do you think she wants to hire me as her fancy man?"

Patrick frowned. "I'm not joking. She's not like that, Dom. She's kind of . . ." He shrugged. "She's a lady."

"Evidently one who has impressed you considerably." Dom was studying him speculatively. "Pretty?"

"Good Lord, no." Patrick shook his head. "She looks like the schoolteacher we had living at the ranch after Rising Star came. Spectacles and prim and proper as they come. She said you knew her father, Professor Edmund MacGregor.

"Christ, I thought I'd shaken off that little bastard."

"You did. The lady said he had departed this world for a better place. Who was he?"

"A very persistent and unpleasant gentleman with the hide of an armadillo and the narrowmindness of a preacher's virgin daughter."

"Some of them aren't all that narrowminded,"

Patrick protested. "I ran into one last year in Tucson who was neither a—"

"What does she want with me?"

Patrick shook his head. "You'll have to ask her."

"The hell I will." Dominic leaned back in his chair and rubbed his cheek. He could feel a slight stubble, but he wasn't about to shave. At the moment he couldn't stand the thought of anything harsher than a feather against his skin. "Tell her I'm too busy to take on any new business ventures and put her on the stage back to Tucson tomorrow morning."

"See her, Dom. She's come clear across an ocean and an entire continent. Why don't you let her tell you what she wants?"

Dominic reached into his shirt pocket for the makings and began to roll a cigarette. "I have a good idea what she wants."

Patrick's brown eyes glinted with curiosity. "What?"

Dominic ran his tongue over the thin paper and reached for matches. "The same thing her father wanted. What everyone in Hell's Bluff wants. One good strike that will make them king of the hill."

"Elspeth MacGregor is no prospector."

"We'll see." Dominic lit the cigarette and drew deeply. "Or, rather, you'll see. I have no intention of talking to the lady."

"I wish you would, Dom." Patrick's brow furrowed. "It wouldn't hurt to be polite to her. She's sort of . . ."

"Sort of what?"

Patrick hesitated. "I think she's a little owl who believes she's an eagle."

Dominic burst out laughing. The hardness and cynicism disappeared from his face, and for an instant, he looked as young as Patrick. "God, how poetic. Rising Star couldn't have put it better."

Patrick looked a little sheepish. "Well, it fits anyway. A little owl won't be any trouble for you to shake off. See her, Dom."

Dominic's expression had softened miraculously as

he gazed with affection at his nephew. "If you're wrong about your little owl, you're going to wish you'd never come back to Hell's Bluff today even if it meant crawling to Killara on your hands and knees. You say she's over at the hotel?"

Patrick nodded. "She said she'd wait in the parlor."

Dominic pushed back the chair, shuddering as the legs screeched on the floor. "I'll go upstairs and get my hat."

He paused at the door to glance back over his shoulder. "How is Rising Star?"

Patrick's expression became shuttered. "Fine. She's in her seventh month now. She's very happy about the baby." He looked down at the tablecloth and began to trace one of the blue squares with his index finger. "It shows. She kind of . . . glows."

"That's nice." Dominic started to say something but changed his mind. What the hell could he say that would do any good? he asked himself. Abruptly, he turned away. "I'll be right down."

2

❧ ❧ ❧

"**M**iss MacGregor, may I present my uncle, Dominic Delaney?"

Dominic Delaney was not what Elspeth had expected. He was not the uncouth barbarian described by her father nor did he bear significant resemblance to his nephew, Patrick, standing beside him inside the parlor doorway.

She supposed he could be considered quite beautiful by those in thrall to the slightly wicked appeal of the likes of Byron. The last rays of the setting sun streaming through the window highlighted the shining darkness of his neatly barbered hair and revealed the tiniest hint of a wave in its thick crispness. His long sideburns accented the high cheekbones of his slightly elongated face, and the hollowed line of his jaw and deeply bronzed skin gave him a faintly Spanish look. His attire had the same Latin air: a waist-length black suede jacket, a shirt of fine white linen, and a black string tie.

He inclined his head. "Miss MacGregor."

The two men stepped closer. Patrick and Dominic Delaney were of a similar height, a trifle over six feet, and both were slim. At that point the resemblance ended. Dominic Delaney had none of Patrick's loose-boned elegance. He was in his early thirties and his physique was more mature, his chest wider and deeper, his shoulder broader, the muscles of his thighs heavier and clearly delineated in the black trousers

28

tucked into polished black boots. Even the way he walked was different from his nephew. He moved with a restless grace as if suppressing a powerful and volatile energy. Still, there was nothing to indicate there was anything particularly intimidating about the man.

Then, as he drew closer, Elspeth abruptly changed her mind. The eyes gazing into her own were a queer blue-gray shade that appeared warm, almost soft at first glance. It was only when she realized the keenness with which his gaze was holding her own that she became aware of how cold they were. A shadow of a stubble darkened his cheeks and the cynical smile curving his well-shaped lips could never in a hundred years be described as soft. The gun belted low on his hip was curiously unobtrusive and then, with a little shock, Elspeth realized why. It was unobtrusive because it was as much a part of him as those icy translucent eyes. Yes, she could see now how her father would think of him as a hard and relentless man.

She was experiencing a strange breathlessness as she held out her hand. "Thank you for seeing me, Mr. Delaney. It's very kind of you to take the time." Oh, heavens, her voice sounded like a child's. She took a deep breath before going on. "It was most important or I wouldn't have bothered your nephew to bring you. I did offer to go to you."

For an instant there was a flicker of humor in Dominic's eyes as he shot a glance at Patrick. "I'm surprised he didn't see fit to take you up on your offer. It might have saved us all time and trouble if he had." He could just see this prim little miss being escorted into the parlor at Rina's place. One look at the negligee-clad Dulcie lolling in half-naked splendor on the cushions of the horsehair couch would be enough to send her running for the next ship to Scotland.

He took her small hand and pressed it politely before releasing it. "I'm afraid you've gone to great trouble for nothing, Miss MacGregor. I can't help you."

"My father thought you could." She steadily met his gaze. "If you wished to do so, that is. Won't you sit down?" She gestured to the striped couch a few feet away and was gratified to see Dominic take a seat. "I have no intention of giving up and going home as my father did, Mr. Delaney. You're going to have to stop this foolishness and be sensible."

There was a faint explosion of breath from Patrick, who had remained standing. "I believe I'll leave you alone to discuss the matter and get a bite to eat in the dining room. I'll see you later, Dom."

"No." Elspeth's command stopped Patrick at the door. She had felt a sudden sense of panic, realizing only when the younger Delaney was about to leave how much his presence had bolstered her confidence. "I mean . . . there's no need for you to go. After all, you are related."

The color ebbed and flowed under Elspeth's clear silky skin, and Dominic found himself watching with something close to fascination. A little owl, Patrick had called her. Wide, solemn eyes, a quivering rustle of black plumage. He could see the rapid throb of the pulsebeat in her delicate temple. He felt a sudden urge to reach out and touch that pulsebeat, to run the pads of his fingers over that silky skin. He glanced away hurriedly. Christ, what was the matter with him? For a fraction of an instant he had actually felt the hot thickening in his groin that signaled intense lust. Certainly Patrick's little wide-eyed owl couldn't inspire lust. "Yes, stay, Patrick. This won't take long."

He was angry, Elspeth realized in bewilderment. She could sense it in the coiled tension radiating from him. Perhaps she should try to pacify him. Oh, dear, she was wobbling again. These Delaney men appeared to have a dreadful effect on her confidence. She supposed it wasn't surprising she should have relapsed when that confidence was still a puling infant. She crossed to the couch and sat down next to Dominic. She kept her back very straight and she tucked her feet in their high-button boots under the hem of her gown. "It may take longer than you think, Mr. Delaney. I'm not a woman to give up easily."

Her Scottish brogue was very evident in the words and Dominic found himself listening to the soft, rhythmic cadence rather than the words themselves. What the devil were the color of her eyes behind those spectacles anyway? Brown, he had thought at first, but now he was sure he had caught a glint of green in their depths. "You're not?"

Patrick raised a brow in surprise at Dominic's absent tone as he propped himself in a half-leaning position on the windowsill.

Elspeth shook her head. "Not when my purpose is such an important one. I've spent nearly every pound I have on this journey." She drew a deep breath. "I want you to be my guide to Kantalan, Mr. Delaney."

He stopped trying to pierce the thickness of those annoyingly distorting spectacles and glanced away. "I thought you did."

Patrick gave a low, disbelieving whistle and sat up straighter. "Kantalan? That's just a myth."

Elspeth shook her head, her gaze fixed desperately on Dominic. "Surely you see you have to take me? There's so much we can learn in a city more ancient than Montezuma's Tenochtitlán."

"A legend," Dominic said flatly.

"It's *there*," Elspeth said with an intensity that caused her voice to tremble. "My father was sure of it, and so am I. He spent over fifteen years studying legends and stories from the Indian tribes of Mexico and this territory. All of the tales were vague and unreliable except for one. A legend originating in an Apache tribe in this area. A legend that was handed down from generation to generation as a sacred trust. The general knowledge became known to everyone as myth, while the true and detailed knowledge was entrusted only to the medicine men of the tribe. They alone learned the exact location of Kantalan and its true history."

"I've heard all this before and I told your father I had no intention of going on a wild goose chase. There are hundreds of legends of lost cities full of riches." He shook his head. "I don't believe any of them."

"The legend says Kantalan's treasury contains a fabulous fortune in gold and jewels," Elspeth said crisply. "It would all be yours. My only purpose is to study the ruins and gather information. I have enough money to outfit a small expedition and you could become a very rich man with very little effort on your part."

"Providing Kantalan actually exists," Dominic said caustically. "And providing we could find it."

"It does exist. I couldn't be more certain." She leaned forward, her folded hands trembling on her lap. "Ever since I was a small child I've heard my father speak of Kantalan. I did a great deal of the research for his last expedition and I've pored over everything written about the ancient civilizations in this part of the world. I'm not merely mouthing my father's words, Mr. Delaney. He was forced to give up his dream of finding the city but I canna do that. Kantalan means too much to me."

Patrick spoke suddenly. "Why was your father so sure Dominic could help?"

"White Buffalo, an Apache medicine man, refused to give my father any detailed information. He told him only enough to tantalize him. He did say there were two people who had the knowledge to help him. One was Dominic Delaney. He wouldn't give him the name of the other person."

"White Buffalo." Patrick looked startled as he turned to Dominic. "Isn't he the medicine man of Rising Star's tribe?"

Dominic nodded.

"And do you know—"

"I don't know anything," Dominic interrupted roughly. "The only time I ever talked to White Buffalo was during the week I spent in their village when Joshua married Rising Star, and that was fourteen years ago. He muttered something about the four links coming together and gave me a sort of blessing. Kantalan was never mentioned."

"He must have told you something else," Elspeth insisted, her gaze never leaving his face.

Something flickered in Dominic's eyes and then was gone.

"Why? White Buffalo was an old man and my father kept the fire water flowing pretty freely during that week-long celebration."

Dominic Delaney knew something he wasn't telling her, Elspeth thought, and the relief she experienced made her feel dizzy. For a moment he had almost convinced her that her only lead was a false one. "It wasn't the liquor speaking. He *did* tell you something. Why won't you help me?"

"Go home, Miss MacGregor. There are no seven cities of gold, there is no Eldorado, and there sure as hell is no Kantalan."

She smiled. "I don't know about Eldorado or seven cities. For all I know they may be real. I'd like to try to discover the truth about them someday, but right now my whole purpose is to find Kantalan. And we can find it together, Mr. Delaney."

Lord, she was stubborn, Dominic thought, trying to smother the spark of admiration tempering his feeling of annoyance. He rose to his feet and inclined his head politely. "Good afternoon, Miss MacGregor. This is the last time we'll be having this discussion. I've had my fill of the MacGregors, father and daughter, badgering me. I want to make my position crystal-clear: I won't see or talk to you again. If you speak to me, I won't reply. I hope you have an enjoyable stay in Hell's Bluff because I promise it won't be a fruitful one." He turned away, glancing at Patrick. "Coming?"

"Not right now." Patrick's gaze was fixed with sympathy on Elspeth's face. "You go on. I'll join you at the Nugget in a little while."

Dominic felt a jab of exasperation and another emotion which he refused to examine too closely. "Suit yourself," he said curtly.

Elspeth watched him stride out of the room, her hands clenching ever more tightly. "He's so hard," she whispered.

"He's had to be. He's been on the dodge for almost ten years," Patrick said. "He had to get tough or get

killed. A man named Durbin has had gunfighters on
his trail since he left Killara. Durbin wasn't satisfied
with making sure every lawman in the Southwest was
looking for Dom."

"Durbin?"

"Charles Durbin. When Dominic was about my age,
he shot and killed Durbin's son in a gunfight. It was a
fair fight but Dominic was just a little faster."

"Then why wasn't he acquitted?"

"It never came to trial. Durbin is a banker in Tucson
and has enough money to buy whatever he wants." He
shrugged. "He bought three witnesses who swore the
Durbin kid wasn't armed when Dom shot him. If Dom
hadn't run, they would have hung him."

"Why are you telling me this? I don't care if your
uncle's a desperado or not. It doesn't affect me. I need
only one thing from him."

He smiled gently. "That's why I'm telling you. So
you'll realize you're not going to get from him what
you're asking. The kind of life Dom's led has whipped
most of the softness out of him. He does exactly what
he wants to do these days." He paused. "And he
doesn't want to go searching for any lost cities."

She was silent a moment, her teeth gnawing at her
lower lip. Then she rose briskly to her feet. "He'll have
to change his mind. I'll just have to find a way to wear
him down. Where is he staying? I'll go to see him
tomorrow morning."

He shook his head. "You can't."

"Of course I can. Where is he staying?"

"It's not a place a lady can visit." He shifted
uneasily.

She stared at him in puzzlement.

He sighed resignedly. "Dom rents a room in a wh—
house of ill repute."

"Oh," she said blankly. "I guess it would be awkward for me to go there."

His lips twitched. "Yeah. Awkward."

She brightened. "Well, he can't stay there all the
time. I'll see him somewhere else."

"What good would that do? He said he wouldn't talk to you or see you."

"He may choose not to talk to me at first, but he will do so eventually." She smiled with considerably more confidence than she felt. "And there's no question that he'll see me. I'll make certain of it. Thank you for your kindness to me, Mr. Delaney."

"Patrick," he corrected her solemnly. "Formality is out of place when a gentleman has recently stuck up a lady's stagecoach."

She nodded. "And you must call me Elspeth. Will I see you tomorrow also, Patrick?"

He hesitated before slowly shaking his head. "I have to leave before daybreak for the ranch." He stood up, his expression troubled. "I may come back next Saturday night, but I imagine you'll have left Hell's Bluff by that time." He hoped so. He didn't like the way this situation was developing. Dominic's temper was very finely balanced these days. He wouldn't allow himself to be pushed far before he turned and savaged any aggressor, and it was clear the little owl was planning on being very aggressive indeed. "If you change your mind, I could arrange for a seat for you on the coach tomorrow morning."

"I'll be here when you return next Saturday," she said firmly. "Thank you, again, Patrick."

"My pleasure." He bowed. He had done all he could do. He only hoped Dominic wouldn't be too rough on her. "Until Saturday."

She kept a smile pasted on until he had left the parlor. It vanished the moment she could no longer see the back of his fiery hair. She closed her eyes and drew a long, quivering breath. Her knees were shaking and the palms of her hands were moist and cold. This interview had been more difficult than she had imagined it could be. Independence would become easier for her in time, she assured herself desperately. It wasn't simple to break the habits of a lifetime, and she'd had the bad luck to pit herself against a man like Dominic Delaney in her first real attempt. She had found herself breathlessly nervous and unsure

from the moment he'd walked into the room. Even
before he'd bluntly refused to consider her offer, she
had detected an antagonism in him that had height-
ened her physical responses to a near painful level of
sensitivity. Why had he been antagonistic? She had
felt his gaze moving over her face as though trying to
see beneath the flesh. What on earth had he been
looking for?

A weakness perhaps. She didn't fool herself that
there was anything about her appearance he might
find attractive. Her father had been very careful to let
her know that men would never look at her with
anything but indifference. No, Dominic Delaney had
been searching for holes in her armor in order that he
might more easily rid himself of her unwelcome
presence.

"Are you quite well, Mademoiselle MacGregor?"

She swiftly opened her eyes. Andre Marzonoff stood
in the doorway. He had changed into a beautifully
tailored coat in a shade of pearl gray; it was even less
flattering to his girth than the biscuit-colored one he
had worn previously.

However, his concern was obviously sincere and she
forced herself to smile. "I'm just tired. I think I'll go to
my room and rest."

"Perhaps you should have something to eat. I would
be honored if you would join me at dinner."

"I'm not hungry." Her stomach was fluttering and
the very thought of food made her a little ill. Yet he
seemed so disappointed, she added, "We could have
breakfast together if you're not engaged."

His face lit up and he shook his head emphatically.
"I would be delighted. I know no one in Hell's Bluff."

"Then why are you here?" she asked curiously.

"It is a most exciting place. In Tucson they told me
it was the toughest boomtown in Arizona. I thought I
would meet many interesting people here." His tone
became carefully casual. "Perhaps you could introduce me to your business associate, Dominic Delaney, when you have finished your transaction?"

"I'm afraid you'd better rely on someone else for an

introduction." She wrinkled her nose. "Mr. Delaney wasn't pleased with my proposition."

His smile faded. "Oh. Well, perhaps I can strike up an acquaintance somewhere else. I hear he is a professional gambler."

"When he's not shooting people, you mean?" she asked dryly.

His brow furrowed. "Oh, he's not really a murderer. It is the custom here. A gunfight is as honorable as a duel is in Europe."

She stared at him in disbelief at his enthrallment with the West and its gunfighters. Suddenly, though, she realized there was something quite vulnerable, even a little pitiful in his childlike excitement. "I see," she said gently. "I hope you're able to arrange to meet Mr. Delaney. I believe he was planning on going to a place called the Nugget when he left here."

"Thank you." He looked eagerly at the door. "I hope you rest well. Shall we meet in the dining room at nine?"

She was surprised he even remembered their proposed breakfast appointment. It was obvious he couldn't wait to go in search of Dominic Delaney. "That will be fine."

His reply was barely audible as he hurried from the room.

A few minutes later Elspeth breathed a sigh of relief as she closed the door of her room behind her. She could relax now. There was no one to see how weak and insecure she felt. This America was such a strange place with its brash and fast-moving people. Every time she turned around there was something new and different with which she had to cope. She had traveled extensively with her father both on the Continent and in the Far East but under very different circumstances. Her father had made quite sure she was kept too busy doing his research to have time to experience the practical and emotional difficulties of existing in a foreign land, a fact that had both disheartened and relieved her.

Even this hotel room was strange. The small cham-

ber was clean, but it bore no resemblance to other
hotel rooms in which she'd stayed. And, of course, it
was nothing at all like her bedroom in the narrow
two-story brick home in which she had grown up. The
rough pine boards of this floor were covered by bright
rugs in a bold design reminding her of a picture of an
Aztec mosaic she'd seen in a book in London. The
double bed across the room had no headboard and the
springs were sagging slightly; the spread covering it
was no more than a shabby patchwork quilt. A
mahogany nightstand was adjacent to the bed and a
rocking chair with a woven straw seat occupied the
corner of the room to the left of the window. The
mahogany armoire against the other wall was
chipped and scarred and the flower-sprigged China
basin and pitcher on the washstand next to it were
permanently stained. It was a totally depressing and
impersonal room, she thought in discouragement. If
this sort of room was all that was available to rent, it
was no wonder Dominic Delaney chose to live else-
where.

Then the color stained her cheeks as she realized
how naive had been her thought. A man like Delaney
didn't live in a bordello for the quality of the bed but
for the quality of the women in it. Elspeth was quite
aware of a man's physical needs and his casual way of
satisfying them. Indeed, a by-product of studying
antiquities had been the gain of a good deal of
knowledge about hetaerae and the services they
rendered. *Services*. The word was inappropriate when
used in connection with Dominic Delaney. It sounded
bland. Mechanical. That hardly applied to the man
whose every movement was intense and radiated
vitality. Even when he was still she had been conscious of something waiting to break free. Did it break
free when he was with one of those women who lived
in the bordello? She could imagine his face dark,
intense, as he—

She straightened hurriedly and walked quickly
toward the single window across the room. What was
the matter with her? What did she care how he

behaved toward the Hell's Bluff version of hetaerae? She pushed aside the rose-colored calico curtains and stared out the window. There was little to see. The window faced the back street, and any view of the grandeur of the mountains she might have had was marred by the white post supporting the balcony and the flight of stairs leading down to the hard-baked dirt of the street. The only attractive thing within sight was a huge stately oak tree at the end of the street. It looked old, very old, and had an air of reassuring permanence in this town that seemed appallingly new.

She let the curtain swing back into place and turned away. The view didn't matter. She'd probably be in this room very little in the next few days. As soon as she was rested and had recovered from her encounter with Dominic Delaney, she would have to concentrate all her time and energy on convincing him he must give her what she asked. Dear heaven, how was she to do it? How did you persuade a man to do something he didn't want to do when he'd sworn he wouldn't even talk to you? Well, she would think of something. But it didn't have to be right this moment.

She was so very weary. She would curl up on that uninviting bed and try to nap for an hour or so. She would forget Dominic Delaney. Instead, she would think of the exciting search to come. And, perhaps, she would dream of Kantalan.

3

Patrick stepped squarely into a pile of manure. He gave a low exclamation that both identified the substance and expressed his ire at discovering it. He then proceeded with a derogatory tally of Charlie Bonwit's ancestors. It was damn dark here in the yard of the livery stable. He had told Charlie he would be leaving early this morning, and the least the blacksmith could have done was leave a lantern burning outside the barn. He extracted his foot from the pile and stepped carefully around it, trying to wipe the sole of his boot clean on the hard-packed dirt of the stable yard. Christ, he must look like a horse, himself, pawing in the dirt.

"Patrick?"

He whirled to face the deeper shadows of the smithy's lean-to on his left and automatically reached for his gun. Then he relaxed as thought caught up with instinct. No threat. His name had been spoken in a soft, uncertain voice shaded with a strong burr. Elspeth MacGregor. His hand fell away from the handle of his gun as he tried to steady the hard pounding of his heart. "You scared the bejiggers out of me. What the devil are you doing here?"

"I've been waiting for you." Elspeth moved forward out of the lean-to. "I think I've been here for hours. I didn't want to miss you. I had no idea what time you meant by 'before daybreak' and I—" She stopped and tried to get her breath. She mustn't sound nervous. It was just that it had been so *dark* waiting here alone. "I know it's a great imposition, but I have a favor to ask you that would have been most awkward for me to ask anyone else."

"You shouldn't be out here alone," Patrick said sharply. "Wait here. Charlie usually leaves a lantern hanging on the post just inside the barn. I'll go get it." It took him only a few minutes to locate the lantern, light it, and come back to the stable yard. Elspeth was standing where he had left her, her face pale above her black gown. One small, delicate hand was nervously clutching her reticule.

She was frightened, Patrick realized. Frightened and trying desperately not to show it. His annoyance ebbed. "You shouldn't be here," he repeated more gently. "Let me walk you back to the hotel."

She shook her head. "I've made a decision. I believe the reason your uncle dismissed me so lightly was that he didn't realize how serious I am. I have to find a way of making a statement of my determination and let him know I won't be ignored." She moistened her lips with her tongue. "It was very cowardly of me to reject the idea of pursuing him to that house of ill repute. It was just that I'm not accustomed to thinking in quite those terms and—"

"Wait just a minute." Patrick held up his hand. "I don't like the direction this conversation is taking. Why are we suddenly talking about Rina's place?"

"Is that its name? We're talking about it because I've decided I have to go there. I think once your uncle realizes I'm prepared to go to those extremes, he'll treat my request with more respect."

"You want to go to Rina's?" He was staring at her, dumbfounded. It was one thing to toy with the amusing image of Elspeth at Rina's, but the reality was something else again. "No!" he said positively. "A lady does not go to wh—to a place like that under any circumstances."

"I know that. I'm hardly an ignorant ninny. But there are times when propriety must be put aside, and this is one of them. Your uncle Dominic must be made aware I'm an antagonist worth his mettle."

"Not this way. Think of something else."

"You needn't feel concerned. I wouldn't think of involving you in the matter." Her brow knitted in a thoughtful frown. "I decided it would be more practical to go see him quite early this morning. It seemed to me that the establishment would be least populated then. Isn't that true?"

"Yes," Patrick said weakly.

"I thought so." Her expression brightened. "My problem is that I don't know where this place is located. If I'd asked anyone else, it could have been misunderstood. So I thought you might be kind enough to give me directions."

Patrick shook his head in amazement at Elspeth. Too nervous to ask directions, but planning on walking into Rina's place in search of Dominic. The woman before him aroused both his amusement and his protective instincts. "I don't think you've thought this through. There's every possibility your reputation could be damaged beyond repair. Your presence at Rina's might definitely be . . . misunderstood."

"Why should that bother me? I'm a scholar and an explorer and I couldn't care less what people say about me." Elspeth added simply, "not when gossip is balanced against Kantalan. Nothing is more important than Kantalan. Now, will you please tell me where to find this Rina's place?"

He stared at her helplessly. There was implacable resolution in her expression. Christ, she was going to do it. "I can't talk you out of this, can I?"

She shook her head. "I thought about it a long time last night. It wasn't an easy decision. I'm not really very courageous, Patrick."

"You could have fooled me. Have you thought how you're going to find Dominic once you're inside the house? He told you he wouldn't see you."

"No." She frowned. "I guess I'll just have to go looking for him."

The thought of Elspeth searching diligently through the rooms occupied by Rina's girls and their customers brought a fleeting grin to Patrick's face. "That's not very practical, Elspeth. We'll have to think of something else."

"We?" She shook her head. "I won't ask you to help. I have to learn to take care of these matters myself." Her expression became distressed. "I hope you don't think I was hinting you go with me?"

He knew very well the little owl was incapable of such machinations. "I didn't think that." He decided to make a final effort. "I could try to talk Dom into seeing you again."

"It would be of no use. He seemed quite determined."

Patrick was of the same opinion, but he couldn't just ride off and leave her, dammit. She would get into all kinds of trouble at Rina's before she managed to rout Dominic. And when she succeeded in doing that, she might face the biggest mountain of trouble any woman had ever faced. Dominic might go off like a fire cracker on a Chinese New Year. Patrick went still. Then he began to laugh softly. He would do it! Lord, Dominic would be furious, but it would be worth it.

"What in heaven's name is so amusing?" Elspeth asked, affronted. "I assure you I'm quite serious."

"I know you are." His brown eyes were dancing in the glow of the lantern light. "And yes, I've just had a very amusing thought. I believe I've solved a portion of your problem. Come on, I'll take you to Rina's." He raised his hand when she attempted to speak. "Don't worry, I'm not going to interfere." He chuckled again. "I promise I'll let you confront Dominic on your own." As long as he was standing watch close by, he added silently.

She gazed at him doubtfully. He had the same wickedly mischievous expression he had worn in the coach when he had told Count Marzonoff those outrageous lies. "I suppose that would be all right."

He took her elbow. "Fine. Now, come along. It's starting to get light in the East and I want to be at Rina's place before dawn."

"Is it far?" She had to half-skip to keep up with his long stride.

"Far? No, it's only at the other end of town. It shouldn't take us more than fifteen minutes to walk there." He smiled. "But we have a stop to make on the way."

"Where?"

"Sam Li's bathhouse. There's something I want to pick up."

"Firecrackers?" Elspeth eyed with alarm the stack of slender sticks linked with long fuses. She had been curious about the large blanket-wrapped bundle since Patrick had picked it up from Sam Li's shack, but she had never imagined it contained anything as exotic as firecrackers. "What are we going to do with firecrackers?" she asked again.

Patrick was busy tying the fuses together. "You said you wanted to get Dom's attention and make a statement of your determination." He looked up and grinned at her. "This will make a very resounding statement, I guarantee."

"I'm sure it will," she said faintly. She glanced at the large whitewashed house across the street. It was a fashionable two-story wooden building; eaves and cupolas abounded and a long, gracious porch ran the entire expanse of its front. The candles in the two decorative lanterns on either side of the door had burned low, and all the windows were dark. "But I had a more sedate statement in mind."

"You want Dom jerked from his lair and forced to confront you in the fastest possible way." His nimble fingers moved to the second string of firecrackers. "This was the only way I could think for you to do it."

"The only way or the most interesting way?" she asked dryly. "I think you're planning on enjoying this."

"Sure, I always did like a good show." Patrick started on the third string. "If you can think of a more effective idea, we'll drop this plan and go on with yours."

Elspeth certainly wished she could think of something else. She had an idea Patrick's plan had elements more explosive than the firecrackers. "Your uncle is going to be very angry."

"Yep."

"But he'd probably be angry at my coming here anyway."

"Uh-huh."

"And it's really his own fault for being so narrow-minded and uncooperative. This is a very important undertaking; it can add greatly to our fund of knowl—"

She was interrupted by his low chuckle. "I think you're trying to talk yourself into something."

She grinned back at him. "I think I've done it." She knelt beside him. "Let me help you."

He sat back on his heels. "They're all done." He glanced at the sky that was growing lighter by the minute. "And just in time. Li Tong gets up at day-break and we don't want him seeing us and raising a hullabaloo."

"Li Tong?"

"Rina's houseboy. Here, you take these two packets and run them from the front door down the steps and into the street. I'll take the rest inside and string them along the hall on the second floor and down the stairs to the front door."

"No."

He lifted his head. "What?"

"I said no. This is my responsibility. I'll be the one to set the firecrackers inside the house and light them. You're clearly trying to spare me the risk of being discovered."

"What I'm trying to do is spare you a sight that might shock the bejiggers out of you." He hadn't given a thought to her being inside Rina's place to witness the chaos that would result from the firecrackers going off. "I think you'd better wait outside until I call you."

"No." She took the larger stack of firecrackers from him. "Do I light each one as I put it in place?"

He sighed with resignation. "All you have to do is to light the long fuse on the first packet. Place that one at the end of the corridor on the second floor. The fuse will allow you enough time to trail the firecrackers down the stairs to the front hall."

"A very efficient plan." Elspeth shook her head reprovingly, trying not to smile. "I do believe you've handled fireworks in this manner before."

"Well, the boys and I did stage a little surprise at the Nugget last year." He stood up and helped her to her feet. "But this promises to be even more interesting."

His enthusiasm was contagious. A tiny flare of excitement began to smolder beneath Elspeth's apprehension. "Is the front door left unlocked?"

Patrick nodded. "Rina wouldn't think of discouraging business, be it day or night."

"Then I guess I won't have any problem." She hesitated, then squared her shoulders and started across the street.

"You might have one problem," Patrick called out.

Elspeth stopped and turned to face him with swift alarm. "What?"

"Matches." He took a box from his pocket and grinned. "Catch." He tossed the box across the few feet separating them. "It's hard to light a fuse without them."

She caught the box and smiled lightheartedly back at him. She had never experienced this feeling of comaraderie before. "I'll remember that in the future." She turned and picked her way across the hard-packed wheel ruts of the street.

Ten minutes later she was standing in the foyer laying the last of the strings of firecrackers on the bottom step. The house was still in half darkness. Only the first gray rays of morning light that streamed through the bay windows of the parlor to her right served to pierce the duskiness. It was warm and close in the foyer, and the house smelled exotically of a mixture of perfume and cigar smoke.

She wished there were more light. She would have liked to have seen if the furnishings of a bordello were as interesting as she had imagined. Perhaps when the firecrackers went off she would be able to see more.

The front door opened quietly to reveal Patrick's thick red hair outlined against a pearl-gray wedge of sky. "All set?"

"Yes," she whispered. "I lit the first fuse just as you told me. Shouldn't it have gone off by now?"

"Any second." He closed the door behind him.

"What do we do now?"

"We get out of the line of fire." He drew her to the corner of the foyer farthest from the staircase. "And then we wait."

They didn't have to wait long. Patrick had scarcely gotten the words out when there was an explosion!

Elspeth jumped. She hadn't expected the noise to be quite so loud. The explosion had echoed like a cannon shot in the still house. The first explosion was followed immediately by another and another until the house was reverbrating with sound: Women's screams, hoarse masculine shouts, Patrick laughing softly beside her. Doors were opening upstairs and Elspeth could smell the acrid smoke of the fire-crackers.

"Here we go," Patrick murmured over the barrage of explosions. "How's this for a statement, Elspeth?"

The first explosion jerked Dominic from sleep. Gunfire. In the hall outside. He moved with the sure instinct that had guided him for the last ten years. By the time of the second explosion, he was on his feet reaching for his gunbelt. When the third explosion rocked the hall, he was at the door.

"Dominic," Rina said sleepily. She sat up and brushed a shining brown lock of hair from her cheek. "What the hell—" She broke off as another explosion jarred her fully awake. "No, Dom, don't go out there." She jumped out of bed, reaching hurriedly for her lacy peignoir.

Dominic wasn't listening. All his senses were strained toward the danger in the hall. God, he was tired of this. Tired of never going to sleep without

worrying if he'd face gunfire when he woke. He
yanked open the door, stepping quickly to the side to
avoid a possible spate of gunshots. The explosions
continued, but there were no bullets sailing through
the air, impacting floors and woodwork. He cautiously looked around the doorframe. The hall was
filled with smoke and the explosions weren't coming
from a gun. He stared blankly at the string of
explosives on the floor going off one after the other.
"Firecrackers!"

"What?" Rina was beside him. "Who would do a
thing like this?"

He didn't have to consider the possibilities for more
than a minute. He had been in the Nugget when
Patrick and his friends had ridden through the doors
on horseback throwing firecrackers right and left.
"For Patrick, every day is a day for celebration," he
said dryly. "I imagine this was his way of bidding us a
fond good-bye until next week. But, if I know my
nephew, he wouldn't be able to resist staying and
watching the fun." He was striding down the hall
following the exploding string of firecrackers. "And
when I catch up with him, I'm going to tie a string of
firecrackers to *his* tail." The explosions had reached
the head of the stairs and so had he. He called down
into the dimness at the foot of the stairwell. "Patrick,
I'm about to lift your scalp."

He thought he heard a shout of laughter amid the
explosions sparking down the stairs. It didn't improve
his temper. He started down but was forced to move
slowly to keep behind the exploding firecrackers. "Did
you consider the possibility you might have set the
house on fire? Or that someone could have started
shooting before they realized it was a tom-fool trick?"

"It wasn't Patrick's fault, Mr. Delaney." Elspeth
moved out of the shadowed hallway to the foot of the
stairs. She stood very straight, her eyes fixed on him
as if mesmerized. "This was entirely my idea."

She could barely get the words past her dry throat.
She had never seen a real live man naked, and
Dominic Delaney was boldly and unashamedly

naked. When he had appeared at the top of the stairs with only the smoke wreathing his nudity, she had experienced shock, and then, almost immediately, her usual curiosity.

Michelangelo. He was like a statue she had seen by Michelangelo in that museum in Florence. Powerful shoulders and pectoral muscles, a tight stomach and heavily corded thighs and calves. Only the colors were different, warm bronze instead of cold white marble. Dark hair feathered Delaney's chest and lightly dusted his legs. There was also hair encircling his . . . Her eyes widened as she stared in fascination. In all the statues she had seen, that portion of the male anatomy had either been covered with a fig leaf or else the sculptor had depicted it as minuscule and unimportant. Even Michelangelo. But Michelangelo was *wrong;* it was neither of those things. She jerked her eyes quickly back to his face. "I've come to ask you to reconsider."

The expression of stunned surprise on his face was superseded by ferocity. "The hell you have." He started down the steps toward her, each word punctuated by the explosion of the firecrackers. "I don't like women who use their sex as a shield to invade a man's privacy and put him at a disadvantage. I don't like it one bit."

"You said you wouldn't see me. I had to do something to change the state of things."

"In case you didn't hear me the first time, the answer is *no.*" His blue-gray eyes glinted fiercely through the smoke. "But you knew it would be no, didn't you, Miss Elspeth MacGregor?"

"Yes, but it appeared to be the only way to get you to take my offer seriously."

"Dom, what's going on?" asked a lovely brown-haired woman clad in a blue lace peignoir from the top of the steps. Her gaze fell on Espeth's prim, black-gowned figure at the bottom of the stairs. "Jesus, what's happened?"

"Nothing to concern you, Rina. Go on back to bed." Dominic Delaney's gaze never wavered from Elspeth. "I'll take care of this."

There were other faces peering over the banisters now, but Elspeth was scarcely aware of them. All her attention was focused on the naked man coming down the stairs toward her. She was exquisitely conscious of everything about him. The sleek ripple of the muscles of his thighs, the way his chest moved in and out with each breath. His strange blue-gray eyes gazing at her with insolence and anger and something else . . .

He stopped at the bottom step and stood there just looking at her in the duskiness of the hall. She couldn't breathe. She dimly heard the firecrackers going off on the porch but they seemed far away. Everything seemed far away except the man standing before her effortlessly holding her gaze with his own.

"Do you know that you're in a whorehouse, Miss MacGregor?" His voice was silky soft, almost a murmur. "Women have only one reason for being in a whorehouse. They're here to perform certain acts of pleasure, to entertain men."

His index finger reached out and slowly touched her cheek. She inhaled sharply. The skin seemed to burn under his touch. Ridiculous. It had to be her imagination.

"Since you're a woman, I have to assume you must be here for that purpose." His hand wandered down to caress her throat, his thumb delicately testing the wild beating of her heart. "And I suddenly feel a need to be . . . entertained."

Elspeth found her breasts were heaving with every breath. He couldn't mean . . . "No, you don't understand. I truly meant to—"

"Cut it out, Dom." Patrick stepped out of the shadows. "Can't you see you're scaring the hell out of her?"

"Am I?" Dominic's hand was gently stroking Elspeth's throat. He could feel it flutter beneath his palm. Her breath was coming in shallow little bursts. Her pink lips were slightly parted, and he could see the faintest glimpse of her tongue. He wondered what she would do if he leaned forward and parted those lips with his own tongue. "I thought you'd be around somewhere, Patrick. I'm sure you enjoyed the hell out of the show, but you really should have persuaded her not to do it. You might say I'm a little annoyed."

"More than a little." Patrick eyed him warily. "But you've frightened her enough. She doesn't know you're only fooling."

Was he only trying to frighten her? Dominic wondered. That had been his intention when he had started, but now he wasn't sure. His hand tightened on her slender neck. Touching Elspeth MacGregor was proving very unsettling. The flesh of his palm was tingling and he could feel a throbbing sensation begin in his groin. "Why don't you leave the matter to be decided between the two of us? It's time you got on your way to Killara."

"Let her go, Dom." Patrick's tone was hard. "I'm responsible for her being here. I can't let you do it."

"Since when have you had any say about what I do?" Dominic's hard gaze moved from Elspeth to Patrick's face. What he saw there surprised him. Christ, the boy was serious. Next, he'd be pulling a gun on him to protect his little owl. A fresh surge of anger provoked by sheer frustration tore through him. It was a frustration that could be easily satisfied, he assured himself. Rina or one of the girls would give him more pleasure than this skinny little bespectacled gnome. But he didn't want Rina or her girls, he realized in amazement. He wanted Elspeth MacGregor with a lust that was beginning to tear at his gut. It would go away, he told himself impatiently. As soon as she was out of his sight it would vanish as if it had never been. And the sooner that circumstance occurred, the better.

His hand dropped from Elspeth's throat. "You're right, it's time this stupidity ended. Here, hold this." He threw Patrick the gunbelt he still carried in his hand. "And open the door."

With a relieved grin Patrick moved swiftly to obey. For a moment he hadn't been sure Dominic would give Elspeth up without a struggle. Who the hell would have dreamed Dominic would become aroused by the little Scottish girl? And the fact that he had become aroused couldn't have been more obvious since Dominic was naked as a jaybird. Patrick flung the door open with a flourish. "Yes, *sir*."

"Brat." Dominic picked Elspeth up and slung her facedown over his shoulder.

"Put me down!" Elspeth shouted. She could feel the play of muscles in his shoulders as they braced beneath her struggling weight. He was walking quickly, and with each step her lips touched the middle of his naked back. His arm was around her knees and she could feel the heat from his body even through the layers of her petticoats. Fear. It must be fear that was making her heart pound so frantically, she thought. They were on the porch and then going down the steps. She could see the people who'd been peering over the banisters now streaming down the stairs. "Let me go!"

"I'm about to let you go." She was sliding down the front of his body to land in a heap of black silk and a flurry of petticoats in the dirt of the street. She fought simply to gain a sitting position.

Dominic Delaney was standing before her, legs astride, glaring down at her. "Now, let's go over it once more, Miss MacGregor. You don't exist for me. There are certain lines women don't cross without suffering the consequences. You crossed one today and didn't pay with more than a little indignity and dirt on your face. Next time you cross that line you won't be so lucky."

He turned and walked toward the laughing crowd of people gawking at them from the front porch.

She struggled to her knees and called after him, "I'm not giving up, you know. I'll keep on until you listen to me."

He didn't look back, and in a moment he had disappeared into the house.

Patrick was suddenly beside her, leaning down to lift her to her feet. He took off his red bandanna and gently rubbed a smudge of dirt from her cheek. "He was right, you know. You got off lucky. In this country a lady is treated as a lady only as long as she obeys the rules. We don't have as many rules as they do in other parts of the world, but the line he was talking about does exist."

"I'm not giving up." There was a touch of desperation in her voice. "I'll just have to think of something else."

"I didn't think you'd give up." Patrick sighed. "But do me a favor and stay out of Rina's place while I'm gone. You owe me that much for calling down Dom's wrath on my hapless head."

"Very well." It was an easy promise to make. She had never felt more frightened and vulnerable in her life than the moment she stood there in that warm, scented dimness with Dominic Delaney's fingers around her neck. "I won't go back there again."

Patrick stuffed the bandanna in the back pocket of his pants. "Well, that's something anyway. Come on, I'll take you back to the hotel."

"You're leaving town now?"

"Pretty soon." He'd have to stick around long enough to drop a few words into the right ears about Elspeth's virginal purity and her peculiar ideas of female independence. Those explanations, along with threats of murder or immediate emasculation if any man bothered her while he was at Killara, should offset the effect of any scandal Elspeth's visit to Rina's might bring down on her head. It probably would take him until noon to get the word around. That meant it would be late when he got to Killara tonight. Jesus, Gran-da was going to be wild. He took Elspeth's elbow and quickened his steps toward the hotel. "On second thought, I'd better leave town pretty *damn* soon."

4

❧❧❧

She was there again.

Dominic muttered a low and sincere curse. Rina glanced at him in surprise. Her gaze followed his and she chuckled at Elspeth's black-clad feature across the street. "Do you think I should invite her in for a glass of lemonade? She looks hot standing out in that blazing sun."

"Very funny." There was no amusement in Dominic's voice. His hand clenched on the starched lace curtain of the parlor window. She did look hot. She was covered from the tips of her shiny black shoes to her chin in a black gown similar to the one she had worn when he'd first met her. There was a small-brimmed bonnet perched on her head, its ribbons tied in a neat bow beneath her chin. One gloved hand clutched the handle of a black parasol which may have afforded some relief from the direct rays of the sun but not from the afternoon heat. "How long has she been there this time?"

"Since about ten o'clock this morning. Li Tong said she was standing across the street when he went down to the general store." Rina was observing the small black-garbed woman with critical eyes. "God, that's a terrible gown. She looks like a scarecrow. I'm glad she gives up when the sun goes down or she'd scare off some of my customers." She cast a speculative glance at Dominic. "Lord, though, you do have to admire her persistence, don't you?"

"The hell I do." Her persistence had been driving him insane for the last three days. His threat on the day Elspeth had invaded Rina's place had not even dented her determination. The tone of her pursuit had merely changed from active aggression to passive inevitability. Everywhere he looked he saw Elspeth MacGregor. He had kept to his word not to speak to her, but it was becoming increasingly impossible to ignore her. Every day she had been standing in that very same spot across the street waiting patiently for him to appear. When he left Rina's she trailed along behind him at a discreet distance. If he stopped at the barber shop, he could see her waiting outside. If he went to the livery stable to get his horse to go and check on one of his claims, she would smile politely as he rode out and settle herself on a bundle of hay to wait his return. When he went to the hotel for a meal, he could count on her being at the next table. She even trotted at his heels when he went to the Nugget every evening and stationed herself across the street.

As Rina had remarked, her vigil ended when the sun went down but it might as well have lasted through the nights for all it cut down on the talk. Hell, he thought angrily, he was the object of amusement for the entire population of this damned little town. She was now slyly called Delaney's "shadow." The snickers behind his back were no less stinging than they would have been to his face. And the most maddening aspect of Elspeth MacGregor's dogged pursuit was its passivity. He could take no action because she took no action. She was merely *there*.

"She'll give up soon and go away." Rina slipped her arm through Dominic's and leaned her head on his shoulder. "No woman can stand being ignored for very long."

Dominic wasn't so sure. Elspeth MacGregor had displayed a strength of determination that surprised him. It had been a bold and unconventional move to place him in this position and, if he read her correctly, boldness and a disregard of the conventions were foreign to her. He knew very well he had frightened her that morning in the hall. Yet she persevered and, in spite of his annoyance and exasperation, he found himself reluctantly admiring her courage.

Good God, if he continued in this vein, in another minute he would be feeling sorry for her, and that he refused to do. She was not only making him a laughingstock, but trying to force him into doing something he had no intention of doing. He'd be damned if he'd permit her to succeed in either. If she wanted a battle of wills, he would give it to her. He could hold out a hell of a lot longer than his so-called "shadow."

He would *not* feel sorry for her. She deserved her plight dammit, she'd brought it on herself. "One way or the other I'll make sure she gets out of my hair—and soon." He gave one last glance at Elspeth's forlorn figure through the lacy veil of the curtains. She was standing very stiff, her back straight as a rod. Too stiff. He knew what that ironlike rigidity indicated. There had been times when he had been on the dodge he'd had to ride days without rest, periods when his physical strength had been stretched to the limit. It was during those times that he had ridden with a back as straight as Elspeth MacGregor's was now. For he had known that to relax even a little would have been to collapse entirely.

The heat was stiflingly hot here in the parlor. He could feel the sweat trickling down his spine. The rays of the burning sun must make the outside heat a hundred times worse, he reasoned. Elspeth looked infinitely fragile standing there with no protection but that blasted parasol. The shadow case by the parasol made the soft, fair skin of her neck appear terribly delicate. Her neck *was* delicate. He could suddenly feel again its silky yet vulnerable skin beneath his palm.

"Christ," he muttered through clenched teeth. What an idiot the woman was. It was a wonder she hadn't collapsed already. "Goddammit, tell Li Tong to take one of the kitchen chairs and some water out to her."

He pulled away from Rina and strode swiftly out of the parlor.

"Miss MacGregor."

Elspeth turned as she was about to go out the door to look back inquiringly. Mr. Judkins, the proprietor of the hotel, was gazing at her with a troubled expression. "Yes?" she inquired softly.

"You shouldn't ought to go out this time of night, ma'am." He nibbled worriedly at his almost nonexistent lower lip. "Not alone. I'd be glad to get one of my boys to go with you."

She smiled gratefully at the small gray-haired man. Mr. Judkins had been very kind to her in the past few days. "I don't think that will be necessary. I have no intention of being gone long." Her smile widened. "Besides, I've been treated with the greatest courtesy by everyone in Hell's Bluff since the moment I stepped off the stage. I'm beginning to believe the stories about wild western towns have been exaggerated. I felt more frightened in Edinburgh in broad daylight than I do going out after dark here."

"There's more womenfolk in those big cities. I guess people get used to having them around and forget what it's like to be without them," Mr. Judkins said. "Ladies are precious as gold out here, and that's how we treat them."

"Then there's nothing at all to be concerned about, is there, Mr. Judkins?"

He hesitated. "Ma'am, I'm not worried about anybody in his right senses bothering you. A man in these parts would know we'd string him up quick as a jackrabbit if he offered a lady like you any insult, but rotgut whiskey has a way of addling a man's brain."

Elspeth felt a cold chill run through her, not at the implied danger but at the casual coldness of the man's words. Hang a man for merely offering a drunken insult? No, he must be exaggerating to make her feel more secure. "I'll be back soon," she assured him once more. "I'm certain that if I have any trouble, there will be someone nearby who will be as kind as you are, Mr. Judkins." She gave him another smile and closed the mahogany door behind her.

Her footsteps sounded firm and confident on the rough wooden boards that formed the sidewalk. Her words to Mr. Judkins had rung with confidence too. How she wished she felt as confident as the sounds of her words and steps. Her palms were moist with nervousness beneath her cotton gloves, and she had a sudden urge to turn around and run back into the hotel and up the stairs to the safety of her room. She didn't want to be out here alone.

She had become very accustomed to the tiny town of Hell's Bluff in the past few days, yet tonight this street appeared strange and unfamiliar in the darkness. The store and the bank on her side of the street were dark and she presumed deserted. The only establishment ablaze with lights and noise was the saloon on the corner across the street. The Nugget had a sign in huge red letters above its swinging oak doors, and no one could be more familiar than she with that sign. She had stood staring at it for three days in a row until dusk had fallen on the town. It had been a very important part of her plan for Dominic Delaney to know she was there and that he couldn't escape her presence no matter where he chose to spend his time.

But standing safely outside on the opposite side of the street and entering the rowdy brightly lit Nugget were two entirely different things. She knew Dominic might regard her appearance there as deliberate defiance of the warning he had given her. And there was no question in her mind that she must go into the Nugget tonight.

She was growing desperate. No matter how chary she was with her small hoard of funds, they wouldn't last for very much longer. She must at least persuade Dominic to talk to her. Surely he was softening just a little in his attitude. He had sent the Chinese boy with the chair and the water this afternoon. She was aware the small courtesy was far from a capitulation; it might represent a tiny yet significant break in the wall of his resistance, however.

But tonight she would be launching a further assault, invading another forbidden territory he regarded as his own. After tonight he would realize she would dare to go anywhere necessary to pursue him. Oh, merciful heavens, she was frightened, but it was a risk she simply had to take.

She picked her way carefully across the hard-packed dirt of the street. Several horses were tied at the hitching rail in front of the Nugget, and she caught a pungent whiff of liniment and manure as she passed. She was closer now, and the laughter and conversation pouring from beyond those swinging doors was much louder. Suddenly she heard a cascade of words that caused her eyes to widen in surprised recognition. It had to be Ben Travis. No one but the stage driver had both that volume and that raucous a vocabulary.

She paused outside the swinging doors. Panic was rising within her. If saloons were forbidden to ladies, surely there must be a good reason.

She took a deep breath and drew up to her full height. She mustn't be such a coward. This was old thinking in a new world. She pushed open the swinging doors and stepped inside. The sights and the sounds of the room instantly struck her with such force, it momentarily banished her nervousness.

Smoke. Eddies of smoke curled around her and infiltrated her lungs. Scent. The sour odor of beer and whiskey and sweat mixed with the kerosene of the lamps in the circular chandelier hanging from a chain in the center of the room. Sound. The tinkle of a Chickering upright piano in the corner of the room and the roar of voices that had overflowed into the street. Men. So many men. The majority appeared to be unshaven miners in shirt-sleeves and coarse rough trousers crowding up to the long bar at the opposite side of the room and sitting at crudely crafted tables scattered around the room. She could see an occasional cowboy who was dressed in the same tight denim pants and boots as Patrick Delaney had worn. A very few men wore the elegant longer coats and sported silk ties and high-necked fine linen shirts she could have seen on any street in Edinburgh.

She felt a swift surge of relief as she glimpsed one or two women sitting at the tables. In that first glance she had thought she would be the only woman in the room. The women had painted faces and lowcut satin gowns that revealed a shocking expanse of flesh. Hetaeras? she wondered with sudden interest.

Perhaps she could get closer to one of them and ask them a few tactful questions regarding their profession. It was seldom that a scholar of her sex was offered such an opportunity. A golden-haired young woman at the bar who was laughing with a man who looked as though he might be a prospector appeared to be approachable. Elspeth took an impulsive step forward and then skidded to an abrupt stop. Her eyes widened and she inhaled sharply. The prospector had plunged his big hand into the woman's gaping bodice and was fondling her breast. She didn't appear offended. If anything, she laughed harder. Still it might be better to wait until the saloon girl was less . . . busy, Elspeth decided.

"Miss MacGregor, what the hell are you doing here?"

She turned to see the square, ugly face of Ben Travis. It looked beautiful to her at that moment in spite of his scowl. "Oh, Mr. Travis, I'm so glad to see you."

"Well, I'm not glad to see you. You just sashay out of here before you get into trouble."

"I don't mean to make trouble. If you would just find me somewhere to sit down, I'll be very quiet and no bother to anyone."

He made a sound halfway between a grunt and a growl. "The hell you say. There'll be trouble aplenty without you even lifting a finger. Now, you go back where you belong."

"I can't do that." She met his gaze with determination. "I have to stay here for a short time. Will you help me?"

"Goddammit, you can't—" Travis broke off, his eyes narrowing shrewdly on her face. "Dominic Delaney? I've heard you've been trailing around after him like a calf does its mama. Is that why you're here?"

"He *is* here tonight, isn't he?" she asked, a touch of apprehension in her voice. It would be awful if she had suffered this situation for no reason.

Travis nodded toward a table in the corner of the saloon. "Over there. He hasn't seen you yet. He ain't going to be happy when he does, you know. You've been making things pretty uncomfortable for him."

"I know." She moistened her lips with her tongue. "It's not as if I'm a difficult woman, Mr. Travis. What I'm doing is necessary."

"Why?" he asked bluntly.

"I'm afraid that's a private matter between Mr. Delaney and myself."

He was silent a moment, glaring at her. "That uproar you caused at Rina's place wasn't so damn private. Come to your senses and get out of here."

She slowly shook her head.

He turned on his heel and strode to a table a few feet away occupied by two men. "Sam, you and Hiram belly up to the bar and let the lady sit down."

"Let her sit on my lap," the man named Sam said with a grin. "I'm not selfish about—" He broke off as his gaze traveled past Travis's brawny shoulder to Elspeth standing by the door. "Christ, it's the shadow!" He shot a look to the corner of the room and his grin became slyly malicious. "Sure, Ben, we'll be glad to let the lady have our table. Come on, Hiram." The two men rose, grabbed their foam-crested glasses, and strolled toward the crowded bar.

Ben held out a chair, motioning for Elspeth to sit down. "Well, if you want Dominic to know you're here, you won't have long to wait. Sam and Hiram will be sharing the joke with everyone at the bar."

"Thank you, Mr. Travis." Elspeth sat down and clasped her gloved hands together on the scarred surface of the table. She smiled tremulously. "I told Mr. Judkins, at the hotel, he had no reason to worry about me. I knew I'd find someone as kind as you to help me."

Travis glanced again at the smoke-wreathed table in the corner and his lips tightened grimly. "You may need more than kindness if you keep on pestering Dominic. He's not a man who'll stand for being made a fool of."

"I have no intention of making a fool of him."

"Then what do you . . ." He trailed off. "Never mind, I can see you're not about to tell me." He pulled out the chair opposite her. "I'll just sit here and make sure none of the boys bother you."

She shook her head. "No, I want him to see me alone. I have to let him know I'm not relying on anyone else." She paused. "If you want to hurry events along, you might call his attention to the fact that I'm here."

"From the sound of those snickers coming from the bar, I may not be able to get across the room in time to break the news first," he said dryly. "Can I get you a glass of water or a sarsaparilla before I mosey on over there?"

"No, thank you." She looked down at her clasped hands. "I'm quite comfortable."

Dominic played the ten of hearts and leaned back in his chair, his eyes studying the face of the Russian. It required little effort to read Marzonoff. The man was as transparent as the empty whiskey glass in front of him, altogether a terrible poker player. It was a puzzle why he insisted on entering the game each night when he lost steadily and in no small amounts. Hell, why should he worry about the man, Dominic thought impatiently. If Marzonoff's boasts were true, he could afford to lose much higher stakes without hurting.

"Dominic."

Dominic glanced up and then smiled lazily. "You want to sit in on the game, Ben?"

Travis shook his iron-gray mane. "There's someone here you should know about."

Dominic tensed. One of Durbin's hired guns? Durbin himself? He kept his features expressionless. "Who?"

Travis nodded to a table near the door. "Her."

For a moment Dominic couldn't believe it. Elspeth MacGregor, prim and proper, black-clad as usual, sitting with meekly folded hands. Then, as if sensing his regard, she looked up and met his gaze across the room. There was nothing meek about that composed stare. It was direct and challenging behind those wire-rimmed spectacles.

Oh, he believed it then all right, and rage tingled through his veins. He looked around the room. The grin on each face disappeared as Dominic leveled his gaze at each man in turn. He knew the smiles and snickers would return as soon as his attention was engaged by a man down the line, and the knowledge chafed at him like barbed wire on unprotected flesh.

"She shouldn't be here," Ben said gruffly.

"You're right. She shouldn't be here." Dominic's murmur was velvet soft, as his gaze fastened on Elspeth. "It was a mistake for her to come to the Nugget." He threw his cards facedown on the table. "I fold." He pushed his chair back and stood up. "I believe I'll call it a night, gentlemen."

He didn't look to the right or the left as he crossed the room toward Elspeth MacGregor's table. He knew he would see only smiles of frank enjoyment at his discomfort on the faces of those he passed. They would think she had routed him. It didn't matter. Not any longer. The only thing that mattered was the gauntlet that black-gowned witch had tossed down before him. His anger was so hot it was close to pain, and yet he was experiencing, too, a fierce satisfaction. She had once more stepped across the line and he could now retaliate. He would give her a last chance, but he knew he would be disappointed if she backed down.

He stopped before her table. Conversation had halted in the room and the only sound was the hollow tinkle of the piano. He lowered his voice to a level that was inaudible to everyone but her. "Leave Hell's Bluff. I won't tell you again."

He had spoken to her! Elspeth experienced a wild throb of hope that immediately turned to apprehension. His blue-gray eyes were so strange. Blazing fiercely, yet ice cold. Her throat tightened and her breath seemed to stop. It was a moment before she could force herself to speak. "No," she whispered.

Then, incredibly, he smiled. It was a smile filled with joyous savagery, lighting his dark face with a wild, wicked beauty. "Good."

He turned and in another moment had disappeared through the swinging doors of the saloon.

5

"Y ou should not have come here."

Elspeth looked away from the swinging doors to see Andre Marzonoff standing before her table. His plump face was sober and his hazel eyes concerned. "You made him very angry. For a moment, when he first saw you, he reminded me of my cousin, Nicholas. It is not safe to make such men angry."

Elspeth tried to smile and found her lips were trembling. Her heart pounded jerkily with a queer sort of panic. Dominic's eyes had been so . . . strange.

"Well, it's done now." She rose to her feet. "I can't turn back the clock. We'll just have to see what comes of it." She glanced around the room and suddenly shivered with uneasiness. She couldn't locate the reassuring face of Ben Travis in the crowd, but the other men in the room were looking at her with curiosity, insolence, even anticipation. There was none of the amusement she had recently encountered on any of the faces surrounding her, and she had a sudden memory of Dominic Delaney's remark regarding the line no lady could venture to cross. She turned toward the swinging door. "I believe I'll go back to the hotel. Good night, Andre."

"I will accompany you. I have no further interest in this place at present, and you should not be on the streets alone."

She would feel safer outside on those streets than in

here, she thought nervously. The atmosphere as well
as the attitude of the men gazing at her held a vague
element of menace. "Thank you, that would be kind of
you." She knew it was no real sacrifice for Andre to
leave the saloon now that the object of his almost
boyish hero worship had left the premises, but she
appreciated the courtesy. She had no desire to be
unescorted at this moment.

The hot stillness of the night hit her with renewed
force as she went through the swinging doors. She
heard a sudden release of conversation and laughter
in the saloon behind her.

"He has been most patient with you," Andre Marzonoff continued as he helped her from the wooden
sidewalk to the dirt of the street. "You must realize a
lady has certain limitations she must observe. In St.
Petersburg a woman who acted as you have would be
ostracized, not only by society but by her own
family."

"Then it's fortunate that I am not in St. Petersburg,
isn't it?" Elspeth was beginning to be a trifle annoyed
by Andre. The incident in the Nugget had been
upsetting enough without having to contend with his
sermonizing. Over the past few days she had developed a half-impatient fondness for the young Russian.
He displayed an almost pathetic eagerness for acceptance from these rough westerners which touched
even as it bewildered her. Why didn't he go home to
Russia where he belonged, instead of attempting to be
accepted in a society that was so foreign to him? If he
stayed a dozen years, he would never be a man of
Dominic Delaney's ilk, no matter how much he strove
to emulate him. And it was more than obvious he was
trying to emulate him in every possible way. He had
discarded his elegant city apparel, and was dressed in
the close-fitting trousers, white shirt, and black string
tie that Dominic favored. Even his gray waist-length
suede jacket was similar to the one she had seen
Dominic wear when she first had been introduced to
him.

"Why do you not go home?" she asked gently.

"You're a man who is accustomed to a different way of life from the one they live here. Wouldn't you be more comfortable with people and places and customs that are familiar?"

He shook his head. "I was never . . . comfortable in St. Petersburg." He didn't look at her. "You don't understand. At home there was always Nicholas. He was everything I could never be. He is a dead shot, a magnificent horseman. He can drink any man under the table and lure any woman into his—" He altered the course of his words to finish lamely, "I mean, he gets along very well with the fair sex."

"I see."

"Nicholas was . . . everything. I thought if I could get away from him, I might have a chance of becoming—" He stopped again. "I heard a man has the opportunity to become whatever he likes out here."

But Andre could never hope to become the man this Nicholas seemed to be, or what Dominic Delaney was, she thought sadly. How strange that in escaping from one overpowering presence, he would encounter yet another. Indeed, it appeared he had not only encountered but actually sought out a man as formidable as his cousin. How bewildered and unhappy he must be to be attracted to the very qualities in Dominic he had run halfway across the world to escape in Nicholas. "I hope you find what you're seeking, Andre."

"Oh, I will," he assured her quickly. "In no time at all I will be perfectly acclimated. I practice with my pistol every day and listen and watch. I'm learning a great deal."

"I'm sure you are."

Why was she worrying about Andre when she had such monumental troubles enough herself? He was wealthy and fortunate enough to be a man, which placed him in a considerably better position than she was in. She had been so sure her venture into the Nugget would bring a positive response. Well, she had most certainly wrung a response from Dominic Delaney, but the nature of it had bewildered as well as frightened her.

The hotel was only a few yards away, and unconsciously her pace quickened. She would face the possible consequences of her actions tomorrow, but now she wanted to escape upstairs to her room and shut out the fear gnawing away at her confidence.

There was someone in her room!

She could see nothing in the darkness, but as soon as she shut the door she was aware of the light sound of breathing and assailed by the unmistakable aura of *presence*. Her heart gave a leap and then started pounding wildly. She whirled, her hand searching wildly for the china knob of the door.

There was a low laugh from the rocking chair in the corner of the room. "You mustn't run away now." Dominic Delaney's voice was mocking and slightly amused. "It wouldn't be polite. I'm merely returning your call. I decided you must have wanted to see me very badly to ignore the warning I gave you at Rina's."

She froze with her hand on the knob. Dear heaven, she was frightened. She mustn't let him terrify her like this. He was here and no longer ignoring her. She should boldly take advantage of the opportunity to speak to him, but she didn't feel in the least bold. She felt small, nervous, and completely inadequate to meet this sudden challenge. "I did want to see you, Mr. Delaney." She tried to keep the quaver from her voice. "You must know why I . . ." She trailed off. The darkness, the knowledge that he was sitting there looking at her, suddenly made it hard to breathe much less speak. "Perhaps we'd better light the candle."

"I like the darkness. It creates a certain intimacy." She heard the creak of the rocking chair as he rose to his feet. "Though candlelight has its advantages too. A woman's skin always has a lovely soft luster in candlelight." He moved so silently she wasn't aware he was beside her until he spoke again. "I remember your skin as being very soft, Elspeth. I remember how smooth and warm your throat was beneath my hand that morning. I remember how fast your heart was beating and I remember your eyes looking up at me. What do you remember?"

She could feel the heat emanating from his big body and caught the scent of whiskey and tobacco that surrounded him. She moistened her lips nervously. "Nothing. I don't remember anything."

"Then perhaps I'd better refresh your memory. I was naked, Elspeth, and you were fully clothed. You had me at a disadvantage, and I don't like to be at a disadvantage." His voice was only a level above a whisper, but every word was spoken with mocking clarity. "This time I think it's only fair we're on an even footing."

"What do you mean?"

"I think you know what I mean. We're merely going to conclude what you invited that day at Rina's. Hold out your hands."

"Why should I— What are you doing?" He hadn't waited for her to obey but gathered her wrists with a lightning-swift motion, slipped a loop of rope over them, and drew the loop taut. The panic rose as she felt the loops tighten, rendering her helpless. "Let me go!"

"That wouldn't be reasonable, and I'm usually a very reasonable man. It's only when I'm pushed that I have a tendency to become impulsive."

"I'll scream."

"I understand it's the accepted thing to do, but I really wouldn't if I were you. Then I'd have to knock you unconscious and I've been taught never to strike a woman." His tone became silky with menace. "However, I might learn to enjoy violence in your case, Elspeth. You seem to arouse that emotion in me without the slightest effort. I could gladly have strangled you in the Nugget tonight."

"Why are you doing this?" She wished she could see his face. Perhaps he was only trying to frighten her. If so, he was certainly succeeding. She was trembling and she couldn't think of anything but how helpless she felt bound and sightless in the darkness. "Please, untie me."

"Presently." He moved away for a brief moment, and when he returned he had her cloak. He draped it around her shoulders and fumbled in the darkness for the button that fastened it at the collar. His fingers brushed her throat and she inhaled sharply. He heard. She could sense him grow still. He paused for a moment, his knuckles pressed against the soft flesh of her neck, letting her feel the hard warmth of his fingers. "I think you lied to me, Elspeth. I think you remember a great deal about that morning." Then, just when the touch of his fingers was beginning to cause an odd hot sensation, his hands fell away. "This will be a little warm, but it will hide the rope if anyone should see us riding out of town." He drew the hood up over her head. "You're taking this very calmly. Are you accustomed to being abducted, Elspeth?"

"No." She could barely force the word through the tightness of her throat. "I'm not calm. I'm not a very brave person, and I'm frightened."

For an instant there was a silence, a hesitance. "Was that supposed to disarm me? You gave me your answer at the Nugget tonight. Are you asking for another chance?"

"It would be the same answer," she said haltingly. "There is no choice. I cannot leave here without you, and I must find Kantalan."

"I think you'll decide differently by the end of the week. I've left a note on your pillow supposedly signed by you saying that you've decided to run away with me. Since you've been trailing after me for the better part of a week, I don't think anyone will have trouble believing you find me irresistible." His tone was mocking. "And those that have any doubts will think twice about calling me a liar. When we come back to Hell's Bluff, you won't find your stay in this town quite so comfortable. You'll either have to go to Rina's or accept the hospitality of one of the men you saw in the bar tonight. This hotel accepts only respectable women."

"Come back? You're taking me away from Hell's Bluff?"

"I can hardly take you to Rina's, as she might object," he drawled. "And what I have in mind for you can't be accomplished with the little privacy this room affords. I'm taking you deeper in the mountains to a cabin owned by a friend. He's off prospecting at the moment, so we should have no one to interfere with—" He broke off and turned away impatiently. "Why am I making explanations? You'll find out soon enough. Let's get the hell out of here. I have the horses tied to the hitching rail out back." His hand was on her elbow, propelling her across the room toward the open window. "I believe we'll avoid the main stairs. If we happened to run into someone you know, you might be tempted to scream, and I'm not in the mood to shoot anyone this evening."

The words were said calmly, almost casually, but they sent a shiver to the base of Elspeth's spine. The idea of violence was anathema to her, and the knowledge that blood might be spilled for her sake made her feel ill. "I wouldn't scream. Not if I knew it would mean a man's death."

"That's very accommodating of you, but I don't think we'll take the chance. This is between the two of us."

"Yes." She wished she could stop shaking. He was right, this was between them and no one else. He was terribly angry with her and meant to punish her in some way; nothing could be clearer. Well, she had known that taunting him would be dangerous and she had done it anyway. She mustn't be a coward now that he temporarily had the upper hand. What could he do to her that would be so terrible? He obviously didn't want to hurt her physically. Perhaps he was only trying to intimidate her into giving up and leaving Hell's Bluff. Perhaps being alone with Dominic could be to her advantage. She would be able to talk to him without having to pursue him and—

His big hands were on her waist, lifting her through the window onto the landing of the second floor balcony. The arguments she had been giving herself flew away from her like birds in autumn. His hands were terribly strong as they spanned her slight waist, and his features in the moonlight appeared flint-hard. She was once again acutely conscious of both the helplessness of her position and her femininity. Her breath caught in her throat as she met his gaze.

His pale eyes were searching her face. "You *are* frightened." His lips curved in a smile of savage satisfaction. "Good. I want you to be frightened of me. I want your knees to shake and I want your eyes to look at me as if you're afraid I'm going to eat you. I want to touch you and feel you tremble."

She drew a deep, quivering breath. "Then you're certainly getting what you want, aren't you? But there's something you should know."

His lips twisted in a sardonic smile. "I suppose you're going to tell me you have four fierce brothers who will ride in pursuit and avenge this shocking infamy I'm heaping on their little sister?"

"No, I have no one to defend me."

Something flickered in the hardness of Dominic's face and then was gone. "How fortunate for me. Then may I ask what you think I should know?"

"I cannot ride a horse."

The cabin before which Dominic had finally stopped was located on a plateau that bordered the steep incline of a rockstrewn gorge. It was a good ten miles from Hell's Bluff, and by the time it had come into view Elspeth had doubted she had an unbruised bone in her body and was positive there was not an inch of her flesh left unscathed. "You didn't have to make the horse run," she said tartly as Dominic reined in his black stallion in front of the cabin. "I know you're a wee bit angry with me but—"

"I'm more than a 'wee' bit angry." Dominic slipped from his saddle and came around to lift her down from the chestnut mare on which she was mounted. "And if I'd wanted the horse to punish you instead of reserving that pleasure for myself, I would have had her trot, not gallop. It's far more painful."

"It couldn't be."

"It is." He was swiftly untying her wrists and he paused to smile down at her, his blue-gray eyes glittering coldly in the moonlight. "I'll make sure your next ride is more comfortable . . . even entertaining."

His hand encircled her left wrist and he pulled her toward the small log structure that looked to be more of a shack than a cabin. When she drew closer she could see the crude structure had obviously been hurriedly built of logs that were still green and mismatched.

Dominic threw open the door and drew her into the darkness of the cabin before releasing her wrist. "Stay here." She heard the click of the heels of his boots on the wooden floor as he crossed the room.

As Dominic lit the oil lamp on the table across the room, Elspeth saw the inside of the cabin was just as unattractive as its exterior and consisted of rough pine flooring with a multitude of unfilled knotholes and a flat roof fitted so poorly she could see the glitter of stars through slender spaces between the mismatched logs. The small room contained little furniture. A horsehair mat in the far corner which presumably served as a bed and the pine table beside which Dominic was standing had one leg shorter than the others and sloped drunkenly toward an equally clumsily built companion chair. Instead of glass in the one window beside the door, newspapers, yellowed and made brittle by exposure to the elements, were nailed across the opening.

"Someone *lives* in this place?" Elspeth asked incredulously.

"Jim isn't here much. He's away for weeks at a time prospecting in the hills. It serves his purpose." Dominic's white teeth gleamed in the lamplight as he smiled mirthlessly at her from across the small room. "As it will serve ours. Soon you won't even notice your surroundings." He turned away from the table and headed for the door. "I'm going to unsaddle and water the horses. I wouldn't try to run away if I were you. There's no possible help within five miles of this place and the hills are full of snakes and scorpions. If you don't fall off the mountain, you'll have them to contend with." He paused at the door to look back at her. "And I'd find you anyway. I've gone to a hell of a lot of trouble to bring you here, and I have no intention of letting you get away."

Snakes. Elspeth tried to repress the familiar panic the thought sent streaking through her. She smiled shakily as she pushed her spectacles up to the bridge of her small nose. "I'm not going to try to escape. It would be foolish. I know nothing about mountains and snakes and . . ." She waved a hand. "I forgot what else you said."

"Scorpions," he repeated. He stood there a moment, glowering at her. "Why the hell are you being so meek? Why aren't you fighting me?"

"Would it help me if I fought you? Would it make you change your mind?"

"No."

"I didn't think so." She crossed the room and sat down on the wooden chair. Her spine was very straight as she laced her fingers together on her lap. "You're a determined man, but I don't believe you're a cruel one. I'll wait for you here and we'll discuss this turn of events when you return."

He gazed at her, a variety of emotions flitting across his face. Then he muttered something violent beneath his breath that expressed both his frustration and exasperation, turned on his heel, and strode out of the cabin.

Elspeth released her breath in a rush and sagged back in the chair. While Dominic had been in the room she had felt as if she were caged with a wild animal. What a foolish comparison, she thought wearily. She had no idea what it would be like to be caged with a beast. She knew nothing about dangerous animals or dangerous men. So what in heaven's name was she doing *here*?

The answer came to her at once. Kantalan. She had to find Kantalan. She mustn't fall apart now. She was actually doing quite well. Except for that hideously jarring ride, she had suffered no real pain or discomfort, and as yet Dominic had done nothing more than threaten her. Perhaps that was all he intended to do. She straightened in the chair and carefully composed her features. There was no shame in admitting to being afraid, no matter what her father had told her. The shame would lie in not facing down her fear.

The door opened and then slammed shut behind Dominic.

She instinctively braced herself, but he ignored her as he strode over to the horsehair mat in the corner and spread a clean tan woolen blanket on the mat's dusty surface.

He turned to look at her, a crooked smile lifting the corner of his lips. "You see how considerate I am? I wouldn't want that soft white skin to get dirty."

"Thank you."

His smile faded and anger tightened his lips. "Goddammit, fight me!" He reached her in two strides and jerked her out of the chair. His hands cupped her shoulders as his eyes blazed down at her. "I'm *not* going to discuss this. I've brought you here for one purpose and nothing is going to sway me from that purpose. Don't you understand that, dammit?"

She nodded. "You want to punish me. You needn't yell at me. You're making yourself very clear."

"I'm not yelling!"

"It seemed to me you were, but perhaps I'm so frightened I no longer know the difference." Her eyes widened behind the thick lenses of her spectacles. "What are you doing?"

He had stepped back and was shrugging out of his suede coat. "I'm undressing. It's not always customary in these instances, but I hate quick tumbles. I'd undress you first, but I'm not sure I'd be able to wait once I started." He had removed his shirt and belt and now placed them both on the table beside him. His fingers went to the waistband of his black trousers, his gaze fixed intently on her face. "Because I've been wondering ever since that morning at Rina's if the skin beneath those black draperies is softer than the flesh I touched. Do you know what sort of fires are kindled in a man by that kind of wondering?" He undid the first button of the trousers. "Shall I show you?"

She shook her head. "You're trying to frighten me. I know you have no intention of ravishing me. Why should you? I'm not the sort of woman men desire. You cannot want me."

"I cannot?" He smiled faintly. "I must have very peculiar tastes, for I find I most certainly can and do, and you're most definitely about to be ravished, Elspeth. Why the hell do you think I brought you here?"

Her eyes widened in astonishment. "You *want* me?" She shook her head dazedly. "I didn't think you meant to ravish me. It seemed most unlikely. I thought perhaps you meant to shame me, perhaps beat me, but I—" She broke off. "I'll have to think about this."

"It's a little late," Dominic said dryly. "I suggest you think about it afterward. You're going to be very busy in a few minutes." His hands were at the front of her cloak, his fingers undoing the single button that fastened it. He pushed the cloak from her shoulers and it fell to the chair behind her. "I find I'm too impatient to finish undressing. I want to look at you."

Elspeth couldn't speak, she could scarcely breathe. She kept her eyes fixed straight ahead. He was only a few inches away and she could see the tight dark curls feathering his chest and his small nipples almost hidden in that springy thatch. Everything about his body seemed . . . familiar. She hadn't realized how vividly every detail of his naked body had been imprinted in her memory, but she could recall every line of the sleek golden musculature of his chest and shoulders.

"Look at me." His fingers were lifting her chin. "I want to watch your face while I undress you. I want to know what you're feeling."

She swallowed. "I could tell you."

"No, that's not good enough. I want you to realize how vulnerable you are to me now."

She closed her eyes. "I think I've changed my mind. I believe you can be cruel."

His fingers left her chin and she suddenly felt a light touch at her left ear. She kept her lids closed, she didn't want to meet those mocking blue-gray eyes. She felt another touch at her right ear and she suddenly realized what he was doing. He was taking off her spectacles! Her lids flew open. "No! I—"

"Christ!"

She hurriedly lowered her long lashes to veil her eyes. "I'd like my spectacles, please. It's very difficult for me to—"

"Look up. Do you hear me? Look *up*, dammit."

She reluctantly raised her gaze to meet his own.

Dominic once more experienced the same shock he had received before. Her eyes were not brown as he had surmised, but a deep green and were flecked around the pupil with tawny gold. Enormous eyes, tilted up at the corners and framed with long black lashes that both shadowed and enhanced their exotic brilliance.

"May I have my spectacles back now?"

He shook his head. "I've always liked green eyes. I think we'll dispense with these for the time being." He tossed her spectacles on top of his shirt on the table. "And don't keep sidling away from me."

"They're not green." Her voice was muffled and she stared straight ahead at a point in the exact center of his chest. "They're not any color. They're witch's eyes, cat's eyes."

"An interesting comparison, and judging by your behavior since I've made your acquaintance, I can vouch for the fact that you come by it rightly."

"They're ugly." A slight flush was touching her pale cheeks. "Different."

"Is that why you wear those spectacles?" His fingers were removing the pins that held her bun in place. "So no one can see how ugly they are?"

"Certainly not, I would never be so vain. I need them. I do a great deal of reading in scholarly studies and my eyes become quite strained. Poor vision runs in the MacGregor family. My father purchased my first pair of spectacles when I was seven."

"I haven't seen you without them since you arrived in Hell's Bluff," Dominic observed as he threw the pins on the table. He watched the heavy coils of light brown hair tumble to the middle of her back. Another surprise. The candlelight revealed threads of pale gold in the shining brown mass. "You've clearly been doing a formidable amount of scholarly work of late."

The flush on her cheeks deepened. "I've grown accustomed to wearing spectacles. I feel uncomfortable without . . . What are you doing now?"

"Just running my fingers through your hair." He brought two long silky strands forward to nestle against her breasts. God, he realized his fingers were tingling as if they had been frozen and were now being painfully brought to life. The thick silky strands flowed through his fingers like warm honey. He wondered how that silkiness would feel against his naked chest as she bent over to . . .

"Why? Is it untidy?" She frowned. "It's entirely your own fault. You shouldn't have taken it down."

"Perhaps." The tingling was spreading from his fingers to his wrists and arms. His loins were aching, the muscles of his belly knotting. He shouldn't have touched her but he'd had no idea she would ready him so quickly. He was usually in control of his responses, but he found he was trembling now like an inexperienced boy. "But I think we'll leave it down anyway. Sit down."

She stared at him in bewilderment, her strange eyes shining like two gold-flecked emeralds in her pale face. He suddenly wanted to touch her hair again, feel the silk wind around his fingers and cling to them. He impulsively reached out and came within an inch of contact before he stopped, and then let his hand drop to his side. There would be time for that later, when his first hunger for her was satisfied. He repeated, more sharply this time, "Sit down!"

She dropped onto the seat of the wooden chair

behind her and watched as he knelt before her. He picked up her left foot and pushed the skirt of her black gown, crinoline, and petticoats above her knees. She made a low protest and tried to jerk her skirt down again.

"No!" His hand immediately clamped onto her wrist and his gaze met her own. "Make one move, and I'll rip this gown off you and then tear it into a hundred pieces. If you don't want to ride back into Hell's Bluff in your birthday suit, you'll believe me, Elspeth."

She nibbled worriedly at her lower lip. He meant it, she decided. Her hand moved reluctantly from her knee to grip the rough wooden table beside her with nervous tension.

He smiled faintly. "Very sensible." His fingers went back to her polished black leather and silk ankle-high boot and began unfastening the buttons on the side. His hands were trembling, he noticed with annoyance, and he'd never get these damn buttons undone if he couldn't manage to keep his eyes on what he was doing. Her legs were slender and shapely in the black cotton stockings, and he could see a plain black garter above her knee. Rina's garters were usually blue satin, made in New Orleans, and always intriguingly feminine, yet he had never wanted to remove them with this degree of frantic impatience.

He pulled her left boot off and tossed it aside. He braced her right boot against his thigh and began to unbutton it. Lord, he was aching. His chest was so tight he had to open his mouth to force air into his lungs. He caught a glimpse of pale soft thighs above the black garters and a stab of desire twisted like a knife in his belly.

"Are you all right?" Elspeth was looking down at him, her gaze troubled. "You seem to be in pain. Is there something I can do?"

He froze, stunned. Merciful Christ, what kind of woman was she? "You're about to do it," he said harshly as he threw the right boot aside. "Hell yes, I'm in pain, and you're going to stop it. Do you know how?" He roughly pulled the black garter off and jerked the cotton stocking off her right leg in one motion. He did the same with the left stocking and lifted his head to look at her. His blue eyes were blazing as he took her naked left foot and brought it to his throbbing loins. "Like this." He rubbed the sole of her slender white foot against him in a slow, yearning motion. "You're going to touch me, and I'm going to touch you. Then I'm going to come into you and you're going to take me, every inch of me. I'm going to use you to stop this ache and then I'm going to teach you how to make me ache again."

The hard length of him was burning against the soft arch of her foot and Elspeth could feel the muscles in her calf knot beneath his palm. Intimacy. She had never experienced such shocking intimacy. Waves of heat were washing over her and she was sure even the roots of her hair were hot. Her breath was coming in gasps and she was trembling so badly she thought she would fall off the chair. "Let . . . let me go."

He was still. His eyes were blazing into her own and his hand on her ankle kept her foot pressed firmly against him. "Do you understand now? This is *not* a pleasant outing. You're going to belong to me tonight."

"You do mean it." She was looking at him in wonder. "I wasn't sure—"

"Well, be sure," he said. He dropped her foot to the rough floor and stood up. "I bluff only in poker, Elspeth."

"You're going to ravish me." It was said with the same wonder he had seen in her experience. "Will it hurt?"

"Not if you don't fight me." Would it hurt her? He had never had a virgin, and the subject had never come up. He had heard that sometimes . . . He firmly blocked the thought. "If you don't make it difficult, I'll be careful to—"

"That means I'll be a fallen woman, doesn't it?" Her brow was wrinkled in a pensive frown. "Perhaps even a hetaera."

"What the devil is a hetaera?" He pulled her to her feet and his fingers began working swiftly at the buttons at the front of her gown.

"They were ladies in ancient Greece who were trained to pleasure men and—" She inhaled sharply as he slipped the gown from her shoulders to her waist and then to the floor, leaving her in only her chemise, crinoline, and petticoats. She looked straight ahead. "They were very accomplished at—" Garments were falling from her like maple leaves after the first frost. She closed her eyes tightly. "The hetaeras became well known for—"

"My God!"

She was perfect. Small and infinitely delicate with the clean symmetry of a young Venus. High taut breasts crowned with pointed pink nipples flowed down to a flat stomach and an impossibly small waist, then widened to pertly rounded buttocks. His gaze moved down to exquisite thighs that invited the touch and then up again to center on the golden-brown curls that shadowed her womanhood. He felt the breath stop in his lungs and the blood pound painfully through his veins.

"Am I . . . completely unclothed?"

Her eyes were still tightly shut as if her nudity would cease to exist if she could not behold it. He could see the delicate color move beneath the fair skin of her throat and shoulders and, for a moment, he felt a wild surge of tenderness. She was so goddam vulnerable. Why did the blasted witch have to look vulnerable? She was the epitome of a desirable woman and he was one yearning ache just looking at her; and at the same time her exquisite vulnerability caused him pangs of guilt at the mere thought of touching her. Hell and damnation, he would *not* let her sway him. She had humiliated and tormented him until he had been driven to this end and he was not going to let her go unscathed. Not that he had any choice, he thought grimly, there was no possible way he could stop himself from taking her now. "You're as naked as the day you came into this wicked world."

She moistened her lips with her tongue and he felt a jolt of pure lust strike his groin. "This isn't too terrible so far. Does it get worse?"

Tenderness flooded him again and with it a desperation born of guilt and frustration. "No, it gets better. Much better." He picked her up and carried her toward the mat across the room. "As I'm about to demonstrate."

Flesh against naked flesh. Elspeth could feel the dark curly hair of his chest pressing against the side of her breast, his warm muscular arm across her naked back. Heat again. Why couldn't she think? She was going to become a hetaera, but would that be such a terrible fate? In ancient times hetaeras had apparently had a greater freedom and independence than their more respectable sisters. There must be some disadvantages, but she was having trouble thinking of them at the moment.

Still, she must think, for this was a very important step in her life. She was merely caught unprepared because she had never thought she would be placed in this position.

"Stop shaking," Dominic ordered as he placed her carefully on the mat and settled himself beside her. "I told you I'd be careful." If he could, he thought desperately. The soft pressure of her body against his thighs was driving him insane. Her hair was a fragrant mass of honey silk splayed across his arm, and she was trembling like a bird. "I won't hurt you." Tenderness again. The thought of hurting her was becoming intolerable. He had to prepare her, ease her into passion. Damn, she was so *tiny* and he didn't know how long he could keep himself from mounting her. Just the thought of sinking into her warm satin tightness caused him to flex with mindless hunger. He drew a deep breath. "I'll pleasure you, Elspeth. Yield to me." His lips brushed the delicate skin at her temple. "I'll find a way to ease you through it."

Her lids lifted slowly and she looked up at him. "You don't wish to punish me any longer?"

His throat tightened. "No, not any longer."

His voice was so strange, she thought hazily, but no stranger than his eyes looking down at her or the heat of his skin against her flesh . . . It was all strange, all foreign. She couldn't think.

His hands were golden against her pale skin as they delicately touched her belly.

She inhaled sharply. Heat, heaviness, dizziness.

His face above her was taut, the long planes of his cheeks hollow. His dark hair shone with midnight flickers of fire in the lamplight. Beautiful. She hadn't realized a man could be this beautiful. Michelangelo's statues were beautiful, of course, but they were cold. Dominic wasn't cold, he was blazing. She could feel his fire coiling and sparking, wreathing her in flames. Yet he was scarcely touching her, the tips of his fingers brushing her belly with a touch as light as butterfly wings on the petals of a flower.

Did butterfly wings leave this trail of fire on a blossom's petals? she wondered hazily. Was this ravishment?

His fingertips had left her stomach and were moving over her, touching lightly on her breasts, the sensitive skin beneath her collarbone, the hollow of her throat. "Elspeth."

She tensed. "Yes?"

His fingers moved to her lips, his index finger tracing the curve of her lower lip. "I don't want to frighten you. How much do you know about what I'm going to do to you?"

The hot color stung her cheeks. "I've seen . . . drawings that were made by my father's students of murals on the walls in Pompeii . . . women are not permitted to view them . . . the murals, I mean. And once I saw a statue in a temple in India . . ."

Dominic felt an enormous surge of relief. At least she wasn't completely ignorant.

"It looks . . . uncomfortable," she whispered.

A faint smile tugged at his lips. "It's not at all uncomfortable. You'll see, Elspeth. It feels very right." His voice was soft, coaxing, as his hand moved down to her belly once more. His fingertips began to stroke the tight golden-brown curls and she felt a sudden hot tingle between her thighs.

He said it would feel right, but how could that be, when everyone said this was a sin? It had to be wrong, didn't it? She wished she had been taught more about the consequences of being a woman. Her father had never told her anything except to say it was something a plain body like herself would never have to fret about. The housekeepers who had come and gone through the years in their small home in Edinburgh had been hired to tend to the cooking and the cleaning and discouraged from wasting their time with Elspeth.

Except Clara. Clara had been younger than the rest and had a small child of her own. She had been kind and even let Elspeth slip out into the garden to play with Bobby when her father had business at the university.

Bobby.

Elspeth suddenly stiffened as the memory of that day in the garden came back to her. The other children with their faces pressed against the black iron gate and their harsh cruel words. Bastard, they had called Bobby. Taunting words that had caused helpless agony in a small child.

"No!" She pushed against Dominic with all her strength and jumped to her feet.

Elspeth was across the small room before his bemused senses could fully comprehend what she was doing. One moment she had been lying quivering in his arms, letting him fondle her, permitting him to do whatever he wished, and the next she was standing across the room. Her pale, naked body was even more alluring as the candlelight played upon it like a loving, golden hand, her long tawny hair flying about her in a wild shimmering cloud. He frowned. "Come back here, Elspeth." His voice held a dangerous softness.

She shook her head. "No, you're a terrible man. How could you do this?" Her voice was shaking and her eyes glistened with unshed tears. "Ravishing me is wicked enough, but how could you be so cruel to a bairn?"

"Bairn?" he asked blankly.

"If you ravished me, we could have a bairn. Do you deny it?" She plucked her black cloak from the chair and flung it around her shoulders. "I'm not sure I'd mind so much being a hetaera, but what of the bairn? Children can be very cruel to a bairn born on the wrong side of the blanket. They'd taunt him and throw rocks and—" She broke off, the tears suddenly pouring down her cheeks. "You're a cruel, cruel man and I'll *not* be ravished by you." She whirled and ran toward the door. The next instant the door was thrown open and she was gone.

6

A bairn.

Dominic rose slowly from the mat and reached for his white shirt lying on the table. There was no question in his mind that Scottish witch was driving him to madness. She had accepted her fate with surprising meekness, almost as if she felt she was deserving of punishment. Yet at the thought of possible harm to their child, she had reacted like a wild woman. *Their* child? Christ, he was already mad. He had hardly touched the woman and already he was imagining his seed filling her womb, their child forming.

He finished fastening his shirt and unbuttoned his trousers to tuck in the tails. What kind of bastard did she think he was? He had never fathered a child to his knowledge, but he would never abandon a woman who was carrying his baby. He would see that Elspeth was well taken care of and the bairn free from— Dear God, he was doing it again!

He strode through the doorway, his gaze searching the narrow trail in the direction from which they had come. The moon was almost full and the winding path hanging over the gorge clearly illuminated. No Elspeth.

Well, she couldn't have gone far. She had been wearing only the cloak and no shoes on her feet. The trail was full of sharp rocks that would cut her feet to ribbons before she had gone a quarter of a mile.

Perhaps he should just wait here for her to return to him in defeat.

He dismissed the thought immediately. He knew very well how determined Elspeth could be. She had amply demonstrated her strength of will to the entire town of Hell's Bluff in the last week, and would probably crawl all the way back to town on her hands and knees before she returned to ask him for help. Well, by God, no matter how stubborn she was, he would have her back. The thought of Elspeth on her knees before him, his fingers tangled in her long fair hair, was very pleasurable at this moment, when his body was aching so intensely it was difficult to move.

He turned on his heel and strode around the cabin to where he had picketed the horses. On horseback he would be able to overtake Elspeth in a few minutes. There was no place to hide even if she left the trail. The rocky sides of the gorge were dangerously steep and bare of vegetation except for a tall saguaro cactus here and there. She would be forced to stay on the trail and should be easy to spot.

A pale gleam of slender limbs beneath the voluminous blackness of a cloak. A broken doll thrown into the rockstrewn darkness below him.

"Jesus . . . no!"

He wasn't even aware he had muttered the words as he ran toward the steep, sloping verge of the gorge. He half-ran, half-slipped down the fifty-odd feet to the shallow, trickling stream at the bottom of the gorge.

Elspeth was ominously still, her head half in the water and half on the uneven stones that banked the stream. She didn't stir as he carefully turned her over. In the moonlight her skin shimmered as whitely as the tombstones in the family graveyard at Killara. He shuddered as the thought came to him. She couldn't be dead. Only a few moments before she had been alive and trembling in his arms. Dammit, he wouldn't *let* her die.

He thrust aside the cloak and pressed his ear to her naked breast. He couldn't tell if it was her heart or his own that was throbbing so erratically. His hands ran quickly over her limbs. Nothing seemed to be broken, yet how the hell did he know? She needed a doctor, but it was too far to take her back to Hell's Bluff until he knew she could stand the trip. He didn't even know if he should move her, but he couldn't leave her lying here in this damn creek.

"Snakes . . ." Her voice was almost inaudible, but it caused relief to cascade over him with a force that made him light-headed. She was *alive*.

He gently brushed the hair back from her temple and came away with blood on his fingertips. Her scalp was bleeding steadily, the blood darkening the fairness of her hair. He made an effort to mask the sickness he felt, but it wasn't necessary. Her eyes were still closed, her long lashes lying like sooty smudges on her pale cheeks.

An anxious frown formed a wrinkle between her brows. "Snakes," she whispered. "Don't let them—"

He closed his eyes. Snakes. He had deliberately held them up to her as a threat and now, when she was lying here helpless and unable to defend herself, the memory was coming back to torment her. "Don't worry. I won't let them near you," he said thickly. He opened eyes that glittered in the moonlight. "I won't let anything hurt you. Trust me."

She didn't seem to hear him. "S-snake." Her voice rose with panic and terror. "Sna—" She broke off as her body went limp against him.

The door of the cabin was thrown open with an explosiveness that sent it crashing against the cabin wall!

Patrick stood in the doorway. "Dom, you're a goddam son of a bitch. Why the hell did you think you could—" He broke off as his gaze fell on Elspeth's slight body lying motionless on the mat on the floor. "My God, what did you do to her?"

"What does it look like?" Dominic's fingers adjusted the white linen bandage around Elspeth's head, and then pulled the tan blanket closer about her throat. He didn't bother to turn around from where he was kneeling by the mat. "I've damned near killed her." He rose to his feet and stood looking down at Elspeth. "She may still die. I've done everything I can but it's been two days and she's not much better."

"*You* did this?" Patrick moved slowly across the room to stand beside him and look down at Elspeth. He inhaled sharply as he saw the livid bruises marking Elspeth's pale cheeks and throat and the bloodstained bandage on her head. She looked like a small, helpless child who had been mercilessly beaten. Sudden rage flared in his brown eyes as he turned to look at Dominic. "I hope to hell you're proud of yourself. You had to be crazy to do this."

"Yes." Dominic wearily rubbed the back of his neck. "I guess I was crazy. It's hard to remember. Let's go outside. I've just managed to get her back to sleep, and I don't want to disturb her. She has . . . dreams."

"How considerate of you." Patrick's voice was caustic as he whirled and strode across the room. "You brutalize her, almost killing her, and then you worry about disturbing her." He didn't stop walking until he was several yards away from the cabin. It felt good to take action, any action, and the morning sunlight was strong and clean after the sick horror he had experienced in the cabin. Poor little owl. God, he had never been able to bear cruelty to the helpless and he would have sworn Dominic would never have . . . He whirled to face his uncle, his eyes blazing. "Was it fun? She's so damn little." He drew a harsh breath. "Why? For God's sake, *why*, Dom? I know she must have made you mad as hell. They told me in town what she did to you after I left for Killara, but did she deserve this?"

"No." Dominic was staring unseeingly into the gorge below them. "She didn't deserve it. I was angry and I wanted her. It seems like everything I've wanted in the last ten years has been snatched away from me. I guess I got used to grabbing and holding on tight when I saw something I wanted." His lips twisted.

"Hell, maybe the anger was just an excuse. Maybe I was just grabbing again."

Patrick's gaze followed Dominic's to the gorge below. "Did you rape her?"

"No, but not because I didn't try. If I'd caught up with her before she fell, I would probably have—"

"She *fell*?" Patrick felt a rush of profound relief and his gaze flew back to Dominic's face.

Dominic nodded toward the gorge. "She fell down there and hit her head on the rocks. It happened on the night I brought her here. She was running away from me." His gaze lifted to meet Patrick's. "So yes, I did do it. It's my fault she was hurt, and it will be my fault if she dies."

For the first time since he had stormed into the cabin, Patrick noticed the puffy black pouches forming half moons beneath Dominic's eyes and the stubble darkening his jaws. He was bare to the waist, and Patrick had a fleeting memory of the fine linen bandage binding Elspeth's head wound. "She's that bad?"

Dominic nodded. "She sleeps most of the time, and when she's awake she's out of her head. I've been waiting for you to show up." He smiled mirthlessly. "I knew you wouldn't believe that note I left in her room at the hotel and would be riding on out. I need you to bring Doc Bellings here from Hell's Bluff."

Patrick shook his head. "Doc Bellings is on one of his binges and drunk as a skunk. I ran into him at the Nugget last night when I first rode in. He won't be any good to you until he sobers up." He made a face. "Hell, I wouldn't want that old sawbones to doctor me if he was as sober as a judge."

"You just have to get him here," Dominic said grimly. "I'll see that he sobers up."

Patrick didn't doubt Bellings would descend from his alcoholic euphoria with an icy plunge if Dominic was looking as deadly when the doctor appeared as he did at this moment, but he still hesitated. "I could go get Silver. Her village is closer than Hell's Bluff and she's sure used to tending battle wounds."

Dominic flinched. The term *battle wound* was certainly apt in terms of Elspeth's injury. "Will she come?"

"I think so. Who knows what Silver will do? She's wild as a coyote." He shrugged. "It's worth a try."

"Then go get her. She can't do any worse than I've been doing."

A shrill scream shattered the stillness.

Patrick jumped. "Jesus, what was that?"

"Elspeth. She's dreaming again." Dominic turned and started back toward the cabin, his shoulders bowed as if he carried a great burden. "For God's sake, get Silver here soon."

Patrick nodded absently, his gaze on the cabin. "My God, she sounded scared to death. What in bejesus could she be dreaming?"

"Snakes." Dominic didn't turn around. "She always dreams of snakes." He disappeared into the cabin.

Elspeth wasn't asleep, she was huddled against the wall by the mat, her eyes shining wildly in her white face and her gaze fixed in terror on the rough pine floor. She screamed again, the harshness flaying Dominic's raw emotions like the lash of a bullwhip.

"No snakes," he said firmly, hurrying across the room. "Do you hear me, Elspeth? There are *no* snakes." He knelt beside her and pulled her into his arms, rocking her gently. God, she was no more substantial than a dandelion puff. She had lost weight in the past two days. He had managed to get a little water down her but not a bite of food. "You're safe here."

"No, I *saw* it." She was fighting him, pounding his chest with her fists. "I saw it. It came sliding out of that hole." She pointed a shaky finger at one of the unfilled knotholes on the pine planking of the floor. "A cobra. Puffing up and weaving back and forth. So ugly. I promise I'll drink my milk next time. I know I was a bad girl, but don't leave me. Just make it go away, Daddy." The tears were running down her cheeks. "Make it go *away*."

"No cobra." He framed her face with his palms and

looked straight into her eyes. "There are no cobras here. That was another time, another place. There's nothing here that will hurt you." He had certainly chosen well when he had threatened her with snakes, he thought bitterly. She had obviously been terrified by one as a child, for her ramblings had been full of cobras and ayahs and a father he was beginning to dislike even more than he had previously. The pompous little bastard had clearly been as cold and unfeeling as the cobra Elspeth feared so greatly. His palm gently stroked her thin cheek. "And I'll not leave you alone."

"You will. You will." Her breath was catching in her throat as sobs shook her slight body. "You always do and it comes back. It comes *back*."

"Shh, not this time." He had to swallow to ease the tightness of his throat. "I'll stay this time and chase it away." He eased her down on the mat and lay beside her, cradling her in his arms. "You see, nothing can hurt you. Now close your eyes and go to sleep. Don't be afraid."

Her lids slowly closed and she relaxed bonelessly against him. "I try not to be afraid. I know you don't like me to be a coward." Her voice was a mere breath of sound. "I try to be what you want me to be. . . . I do try to please you."

"I know you do." In the last two days he had formed a very clear picture of the child, Elspeth, who had striven so desperately to gain the approval of a father who would tolerate neither weakness nor mistakes. "You do please me. Always."

"Do I?" The question was drowsily slurred and infinitely wistful. "I didn't think I . . ."

Elspeth was asleep, her breath a light warm whisper against the flesh of his shoulder. His grip tightened about her. God, she felt breakable in his arms, as if the slightest pressure of his hands would cause her delicate bones to shatter. Why hadn't he realized how vulnerable she was during those days when his fury and irritation had blinded him to everything but lust and pride? Patrick had known. A little owl who thought she was an eagle, he had called her. A very fragile, uncertain little owl who had forced herself to confront him on every occasion with more courage than a fiercer eagle might have possessed.

His hand moved over her hair with exquisite gentleness and a possessiveness that felt supremely natural to him, as if he were stroking the feathers of the bird to which Patrick had compared her. He didn't know exactly when he had realized he was regarding her with a gentleness and he had never known for any woman. One moment she was Elspeth, and the next she was *his* Elspeth, his hurt, broken child, and God help him, his responsibility.

He closed his eyes. Lord, he was tired. He hadn't slept since the night before he had brought Elspeth to the cabin. He was tempted to nap until Elspeth roused again, but if she regained her senses and recognized him, she might be more afraid of him than the damn cobra of her dreams. He slowly opened his eyes and carefully released her. He sat up and adjusted his suede coat she was using for a pillow before tucking the tan blanket around her bare shoulders. She moved restlessly and he froze into stillness until her breathing deepened once again.

He gazed dully around the small room. He had to do something or he would fall asleep, but he had promised Elspeth he wouldn't leave her. His glance fell on the knothole through which Elspeth claimed her dream snake had slithered into the room. Damn Jim, why hadn't he filled those holes? It wouldn't have taken that long. Why was he asking himself a question to which he knew the answer? he wondered. Gold fever. No time must be wasted on mundane tasks when wealth beckoned from the hills like a shimmering siren.

Well, he didn't want Elspeth to wake and see those gaping holes in the pine boards again; it might trigger another nightmare memory. He stood up and wearily arched his back to rid it of stiffness. He would look around and see what he could use to plug the knotholes that riddled the floor of the cabin.

* * *

Silver eyes were gazing at her with passionate intensity.

Elspeth fought her way through the thick, dark blanket pressing down upon her. Silver eyes. There was something very familiar about them, something she should remember. Dominic Delaney? No, there was no hint of blue in the eyes looking at her so calmly. These eyes were a true pale gray, framed by thick black lashes and shadowed by slender winged brows. The brows were familiar, she realized hazily. Those slightly winged, dark brows were similar to those of both Dominic and Patrick Delaney.

"Who . . ." Elspeth found she had barely the strength to form the word.

"Silver Dove." It was a woman's voice, low and melodious. "You were injured. Do you remember?"

Elspeth's brow wrinkled in a frown as she strained to pierce the dark blanket that persisted in closing over her mind. "I was . . . running. The rocks were slippery and I lost my footing and rolled down." She stopped as she recalled pain, blinding pain, then darkness. "I think I hit my head."

"Good." Silver Dove's melodious voice expressed satisfaction. "Dominic will be pleased that you won't remain a crazy woman as he first feared."

"My God, Silver, what a thing to say." Patrick Delaney suddenly appeared in Elspeth's range of vision and was also looking down at her. "Here she's just come to her senses and you have her worrying about losing them again."

"What can you expect of an ignorant little squaw? I speak what is true, not like a white man."

"Oh, for Pete's sake, will you stop that? Who are you trying to fool? Rising Star has made sure you're not ignorant, and we both know you say whatever you damn well please," Patrick said dryly. "And your tongue can not only tattle the truth but run on with a story as crooked as a dog's hind leg. Stop fooling, Silver. Elspeth's not well enough to be a good audience for you."

"I nursed her until she regained her senses, that is enough. She can't expect me to be what I am not." The melodious voice turned suddenly fierce. "If you wanted gentleness, you should have sent for Rising Star. You'll have none of it from me."

The passion in Silver Dove's voice was so intense it cut through the hazy blanket surrounding Elspeth's senses like a tailor's sharp scissors. Her gaze focused on the woman kneeling beside her. Only Silver Dove wasn't a woman, Elspeth realized with surprise. She was hardly more than a child, fifteen or sixteen at most, but a very odd-looking child. Her dark straight hair fell to the middle of her back from a beaded turquoise band encircling her head. Her face was thin, her skin dusky, her fine features dominated by those flashing gray eyes. Her slight body was strangely garbed in a full red calico skirt and a cream-colored tunic fashioned from the tanned skins of animals. Soft beaded leather moccasins shod her slender feet and calves, ending just below her knee. Was she a savage? Her clothing resembled that of the Indians who had been pointed out to Elspeth when she first arrived in the West. She tried to remember what Patrick and Silver Dove had said since she had opened her eyes, but she could recapture only disjointed phrases.

"You were closer than Rising Star," Patrick said bluntly. "Do you think Dom and I wouldn't have rather had someone who didn't threaten to cut our hearts out when we happened to get in your way?"

"You brought me here. You know me. You shouldn't have expected anything else."

Elspeth's head ached. "Are you . . ." She trailed off. It was hardly polite to ask someone who had evidently been nursing her for some time if she was a savage.

Silver Dove glared down at her. "Apache. Squaw. Injun. Are you afraid, white woman? I carry a little knife always and I have used it three times."

Patrick sighed and placed his hand on the Indian girl's shoulder. "This is my cousin Silver, and she's not as fierce as she pretends."

"I am *not* your cousin. Not until the old man says the words." Silver Dove jumped to her feet. "And he will never say them. The Delaneys think one Indian in the family is more than enough." She restlessly moved her head and her straight dark hair shimmered in the lamplight. "I'm bored with caring for Dominic's woman. I'm not a slave the Delaneys can summon when they wish and send away as they will. You can take care of her yourself until Dominic returns. I'm going back where I belong." She turned and moved toward the door, her carriage as light and graceful as a young forest animal.

Elspeth couldn't let her go without at least trying to express her appreciation to this fierce child. "Silver."

The Indian girl whirled at the door to look at her.

"Thank you," Elspeth whispered. "I didn't mean to be a bother to anyone."

Something flickered in Silver's face and then was gone. She opened her lips to speak, then closed them again and turned and strode out of the cabin.

Patrick dropped to his knees beside the mat on which Elspeth lay. "Waking up to Silver has to be something of a surprise, but she's actually been very good to you. She's nursed you day and night for the last week, and she may have saved your life. Dom couldn't get you to eat anything and he was afraid you'd grow too weak to survive." He grinned. "Silver managed. She pinched your nostrils shut and when you opened your mouth to breathe, she popped in a spoonful of broth and stroked your throat until you swallowed it. Dom was sure she was going to cause you to choke and started yelling at her. She told him he had a choice of finding a gentler way of pouring the broth down you or to get out of the cabin and let her do her job. He let her have her way."

Dominic. There was something she should remember about Dominic and the night she had fallen down the slope into the gorge, but her memory kept shying away from both the man and the events of that night. She would have to think about it soon, but she was too weary to make the effort now. She was so terribly weak it seemed impossible she would ever fully recover her strength. "Am I going to be . . . entirely well?"

Patrick nodded. "Silver says it will probably take a few weeks, but you should be right as rain. You've been out of your head a bit, and we've been more worried about that than anything else."

She smiled faintly. "You thought I was daft?"

He smiled. "Dom was afraid of everything under the sun. Chills, inflammation of the lungs, madness. I could almost sympathize with Silver when she threw him out of the cabin." He frowned with sudden indignation. "But I was being quite reasonable, and there certainly was no reason for her to boot me out."

She was trying desperately to think. He had said it would be a few weeks before she was well, but that would be too long. She had only a little money and she must set out for Kantalan before it was gone entirely. "I cannot wait." There was a thread of anxiety in her voice. "I have to go to Kantalan."

Patrick's fingers gently smoothed away the frown lines creasing her forehead. "Stop worrying, it will only set you back. Just think about getting well. Dom will be back from Hell's Bluff in the morning and you can talk to him then." He tucked a strand of pale brown hair behind her ear. "He rode into town to get supplies and to see if he can fetch some medicine from Doc Bellings. He'll be very happy you're back with us."

"Will he?" She wished Patrick wouldn't keep talking about his uncle. She was having difficulty enough blanking him out of her consciousness. She kept seeing those translucent eyes that were both soft and hard; she kept hearing his deep, gentle voice soothing . . . No, there was something wrong. Dominic was not a man who was either gentle or soothing, certainly not in regard to her. "Should you be away from Killara this long? Won't your grandfather worry?"

"He's probably sent one of my uncles into town to ferret me out of Rina's. Someone will have told him I left to hunt for Dom."

Dominic again. She closed her eyes, shutting out

both the name and the image it recalled. "I think I'll sleep now. I'm very tired."

"You do that." She heard a rustle as Patrick rose to his feet. "I'll be here when you wake up, and, if you need anything, just call and I'll fetch it."

"Go Patrick, can't you see you've worn her out." It was Silver Dove's voice.

Elspeth's eyes opened to see the Indian girl standing in the doorway.

An amused smile touched Patrick's lips. "You came back. Now, I wonder why you decided to do that, Silver?"

Silver gave him a disdainful look. "I've spent valuable time healing this woman. Why should I let your white man's blindness destroy what I've created? You would have her dead or crazed within a week."

"You're probably right." Patrick's expression was solemn. "So I guess you'd better stay around and protect her from Dom and me. Right, Cousin?"

Silver started to frown, then a faint reluctant smile touched her lips. "That is my intention . . . Cousin." She glided forward and dropped to her knees beside Elspeth. "Leave us, I will care for her until she is able to defend herself."

Defend herself. What a curious phrase, Elspeth thought. Is that how Silver looked upon life, as a battle in which one must always be on guard? How terrible for a mere child to have learned so harsh a lesson. She smiled gently. "I'm glad you came back."

"It had nothing to do with you," Silver said. "I told you why I turned around and rode back." She avoided Elspeth's gaze. "Close your eyes and go to sleep. Do you wish to undo all my work?"

"No." Elspeth obediently closed her eyes. "I wouldn't want to do that. It's very important I recover quickly."

Elspeth felt Silver's hand on her hair, smoothing it with a tenderness that amazed her. "Then sleep, I will do the rest."

7

"**S**he's awake!" A broad grin creased Patrick's cheeks as he began to untie the rawhide thongs of the saddlebags on Dominic's stallion. "Came around late last night."

Dominic went still. "And?"

"She's going to be fine." Patrick lifted off the heavy leather bag and dropped it to the ground. "Kind of hazy, but what can you expect?"

A dizzying stream of relief poured through Dominic. "You're sure?"

"One of the first things she said was that she didn't have time to be sick, she had to get to Kantalan. I think our little owl is definitely on the mend."

"It sounds like it." Oh, God, she was going to be all right! "Is she awake now?"

Patrick shook his head. "Silver gave her a bath, washed her hair, and fed her a little broth. She was pretty tired after that and went right back to sleep. Did you get anything from Doc Bellings?"

"Just some laudanum to help deepen her sleep. I thought it might stop the dreams. Maybe she won't need it now."

"Probably not. I hope to God that's all over. Any news from Gran-da?"

Dominic slipped from the saddle. "The one you expected. Cort was in town two days ago and left a message with everyone he met for you to get your tail back to Killara."

"And no messages for you?"

"No messages."

"I imagine Gran-da will have quite a few things to say when Cort gets back to Killara and tells him what you've been up to."

"I doubt it." Dominic began to unsaddle the stallion. "When he was a young man Da would have considered it pretty tame to carry off a woman."

"Maybe." Patrick's expression was skeptical. "But he's become real respectable with the years."

"He likes to pretend he's respectable, but beneath that Sunday-go-to-meeting smile he's as big a rascal as he ever was." Dominic's lips twisted in a bittersweet smile. "Perhaps that's why he still manages to forgive me for all I've cost him through the years. Like to like. I'm a true son to the old devil."

Patrick frowned. "Everything you've done, you've been forced to do, Dom. We all know that."

"Do we? Tell that to the woman in the cabin." Dominic's voice was thick with disgust. "I swear to God, I was going to rape her, and, instead, I nearly killed her. Ten years ago I would have shot the balls off any bastard who so much as thought of doing that to a woman. What kind of man does that make me?"

"You went loco for a little while. You would have come to your senses—"

"The hell I would." Dominic whirled to face him with a movement alive with barely contained violence. "She does something wild to me and . . . I would have done it, and if I'm ever left alone with her, I might still do it. I'm not the same man I was when I left Killara. Why the hell don't you all realize that and stay away from me?"

"We love you," Patrick said simply. "You're family."

Dominic stared at him for a moment. He felt as if he'd been struck in the stomach. He finally pulled his gaze away. "Haven't you ever heard of black sheep? The smart thing to do is to cast them out and let them go their own way."

Patrick smiled. "I never claimed to be smart. I kind of like black sheep. At least they're not boring." He paused. "I think you should know I'm not going back to Killara."

Dominic's gaze flew back to his face. "Oh, yes, you are. We've had this discussion before."

"As I remember, we didn't discuss it at all. You just told me what I was going to do. I've thought it over and come to the conclusion that it's my duty to stay with you. You obviously need my help to keep you from wandering further down the path to hell and damnation. It should be a very interesting experience for both of us." Patrick smiled blandly. "I'm staying glued to your side until you decide to come back to Killara with me."

Dominic's expression darkened. "I told you . . ."

Patrick held up his hand. "No one tells me anything these days, Dom." There was a hint of steel in his lazy drawl. "Remember that, will you? If you want me to go back to Killara, you'll have to go with me."

"You damn fool, you're going to get yourself killed," Dominic said harshly. "It's only a matter of time before one of Durbin's hired guns shows up in Hell's Bluff."

"All the more reason to go back to Killara. We could make sure no one gets to you there."

"They can get to me anywhere. Durbin's price doesn't require a fair fight. He'd be just as happy to have me bushwhacked."

"Your being on Delaney land would make it more difficult. You're not going to change my mind, Dom."

Dominic abruptly realized he was not going to be able either to persuade or intimidate Patrick, and the knowledge filled him with fear. He suddenly could see young Sam Bergstrom's dead, staring eyes, the slow trickle of blood from the corner of his mouth. He felt the hot bile rush to his stomach. God, not again. Not Patrick. "You can bet that I'm going to change your mind. Who the hell wants to be saddled with a snot-nosed kid like you? You'll only get in my way." He injected a taunting note of scorn in his voice. "What's the matter, did someone finally take the blinders off Josh? Did he find out how you feel about Rising Star? Is that why you want to leave Killara for a spell?"

The color flooded Patrick's face and his hands suddenly clenched into fists at his sides. "Shut up, Dom."

Dominic smiled coldly. "I don't remember ever going to bed with an Indian. Are they any different? Tell me, do they give a warwhoop when—"

Patrick took a step forward. "Shut up or, so help me God, I'll kill you, Dom." His voice was shaking. "How can you talk like that about her? I thought you liked Rising Star. You know she would never be unfaithful to Josh."

"Do I? You've been nosing around her from the moment you found out what women were for. Everyone but Josh knows how you feel about her. She must be damn good to keep you coming back—" Dominic broke off as Patrick's fist smashed into his mouth, snapping his head back and causing him to stagger sideways. He shook his head to clear it of the black spots dancing before his eyes. Christ, the kid had a wicked right hook. "Do you still want me to come back to Killara?"

"I want you to burn in hell," Patrick said between his teeth. "Don't just stand there, *fight* me."

Dominic shook his head. "I don't fight children. Go home and grow up." He turned away. "Maybe I'll give you your chance in a few years."

"The hell you will." Patrick fastened his hand on Dominic's arm and whirled him around to face him. "Damn you, I'm going to—" He broke off and suddenly the fury was fading from his face. "You did it deliberately," he said slowly.

"And I'll do it again." Dominic met his gaze with a cool steadiness. "I'll hurt you where you're raw. I'll uncover all the wounds you've hidden for years and make you bleed. Do you think you can stand that?"

"You son of a bitch."

"Yes." Dominic's lips twisted in a crooked smile. "That's what I've been trying to tell you." He jerked his arm from Patrick's grasp. "I've learned to do what I have to do to get my own way. Go home, Patrick, you won't like what I'll do to you if you stay."

He turned and walked around the cabin without another glance.

He almost trampled over Silver, who was standing only a few yards away, leaning against the rough logs of the cabin. "I was coming to see if you had brought any medicine for the woman," she said as she slowly straightened. "And then I decided to listen. We heathen Indians have no scruples about things like that, you know."

Something flickered in Dominic's expression. "I didn't know. The Indians I've known have usually had a more highly developed snese of honor than most white men."

She met his eyes. "Yet you speak of my aunt, Rising Star, as if she were a whore, as if all Indian women are whores. What you believe has little meaning to me, but I found it . . . curious. My aunt regards you with affection."

"I regard Rising Star with affection also. You weren't meant to hear my words; they held no truth. Sometimes it's necessary to . . ." Dominic trailed off and then continued wearily. "I apologize if I hurt you."

"You didn't hurt me, I permit no one to hurt me. I knew what you were doing. You wanted to send Patrick home to safety and you used what weapons were at hand. I would do the same." She smiled sweetly. "If I had not known that, I would have plunged my knife into your back, or better yet used it to remove the part of the body with which white men make whores of virtuous Apache women."

For a moment Dominic felt the heaviness of spirit he was experiencing lighten and a faint smile tugged at the corners of his lips. "Then I'm extremely glad you're so perceptive. I'm very fond of that particular body part."

"Most men are," Silver said dryly. "They pale and tremble when it is threatened. Why is that? I wonder. You'd think they would value their limbs or their eyes more. Men are very foolish." She dismissed the subject of masculine unreasonableness with a shrug. "Do you wish me to go away for a little while? Your woman is awake again."

"How is she?"

"She gains strength slowly; it will take time." Her eyes narrowed. "You could take her to Killara. They would treat her very well if she brought you back to them."

"No!"

"You need not shout at me. I do not care whether you ever go back. It is nothing to me. It is your woman who needs a place to heal. Are you going to keep her lying on that dusty mat on the floor? She would be better off at my people's village. At least there I could give her soft furs to cushion her and not have to—"

"Stop stinging me with that scorpion tongue, dammit," Dominic said. "I'm taking her back to the hotel at Hell's Bluff as soon as she's able to travel. When will that be?"

"She will not be able to sit a horse by herself, but if you could make her comfortable, she could leave tomorrow. It would be better than keeping her here. She is not accustomed to roughness." Silver continued grudgingly, "Though I think she would suffer it without a complaint. Her spirit is stronger than her body."

So Silver had discovered that as well. "She won't have to suffer it. I'll give her whatever she needs to make her well. Will you come with me, Silver? I don't know what kind of reception she's going to receive in Hell's Bluff." He smiled bitterly. "I made sure I burned all her bridges when I took her away. The good people of the town may be very cruel to her if we don't protect her."

"You . . . need me?"

"I need you."

Silver quickly took pains to mask any sign of the pleasure she felt. "Of course you need me. How could you take care of her by yourself? You are only a man, and a white man at that. I will come and no one will be cruel to her." Her smile was fierce. "More than once." She turned away. "Now I will go for a walk and you will tell her she will not be alone when you take her back to town. Wipe the blood from your face. You must not frighten her."

Dominic lifted his fingers to his lips and it came away with drops of blood. "Yes, ma'am." He jerked the handkerchief out of his back pocket and dabbed at his split lip. "Anything else?"

"No, not at the moment." She glanced back over her shoulder and smiled. Dominic inhaled sharply. At that moment she looked so much like Boyd, there could be no question of her parentage. Why couldn't Da see the resemblance? Why did he deny the truth so stubbornly? "I'll let you know if I wish anything else later. After all, white men have made good slaves for Apaches before this."

He bowed slightly. "Yours to command."

To his surprise a slight flush darkened her golden skin. "You needn't mock me," she said, her eyes blazing. "I know how you all feel." She turned and walked away swiftly.

Dominic gazed after her, silently cursing Boyd and Da and himself. At that moment he had seen a glimpse of something hurt and vulnerable beneath the fierceness Silver wore about her like a cloak. In no logical way could he compare her to Elspeth, but for a fleeting instant she had reminded him of his little owl, struggling desperately to be brave against overwhelming odds.

His little owl, his Elspeth. How easily possessiveness crept into his thoughts when they concerned Elspeth. But he mustn't think of her as belonging to him. He couldn't let her become closer to him than she was already, any more than he could allow Patrick to come nearer. He had done enough to her without exposing her to more danger. Not that she would want to be close to him, he thought moodily. She would probably be on the stage and hightailing it out of Hell's Bluff as soon as she could totter out of bed.

He drew a deep breath and squared his shoulders. It was time to face her. He had been dreading the confrontation since Patrick had told him she had regained consciousness, but he would put it off no longer.

Elspeth's eyes were closed when he walked into the cabin, but they opened at once to gaze up at him with startled alertness. She had been expecting him, she had known he would come, and yet her breath seemed to stop when she saw him. He was unsmiling and his familiar grim expression made her suddenly remember what she had been trying to forget since the moment she had awakened to see Silver sitting beside her.

The hot color flew to her cheeks and she tried to sit up. The tan blanket slipped and she grabbed at it frantically, abruptly conscious that she was completely unclothed beneath it.

"Have you no sense?" Dominic was across the room in three strides and dropping to his knees at her side. "Lie down before you fall down. You can stop looking at me like I'm some sort of ogre. I'm not going to hurt you."

"No?" she whispered. "You've changed your mind then? About ravishing me, I mean."

A flicker of pain softened his expression. "I've changed my mind. I won't ask you to forgive me, I know there's no forgiveness possible. But for God's sake, don't be afraid of me. I won't hurt you. All you have to do is concentrate on getting well."

The tension flowed out of her and she relaxed slowly. She nestled her cheek on the suede of his jacket that still served as her pillow. "I thought you would change your mind once you had gotten over your anger with me. You didn't really want to bed me. I knew that."

"Did you? Clever of you." He was acutely conscious of the vibrant textures of her. Her long hair was flowing silk against the rough black suede of his coat, and the flesh of her shoulders gleamed with the luminous transparency he remembered as if it had been carved into his memory with the blade of a tomahawk. Dear God, he was wanting her again. He hadn't expected desire. He had felt nothing but aching regret and tenderness all the time he was caring for her, and yet now desire was upon him again, sharper and more alive than ever before. "I'm no threat to you. Patrick said I'd gone loco. I guess he was right."

"Loco?"

"Horses sometimes eat loco weed and go berserk out here," Dominic said. "He meant I went wild and started acting crazy."

"I see. It's a very colorful word, isn't it? You have many words that—" She broke off as her throat tightened and the breath left her body. He was looking at her with that same expression she had seen as he lay beside her on the mat that night. His lips held a heavy sensuality and the hollowed lines of his cheeks were taut with hunger. Then he looked away and she could breathe again.

She must have been mistaken. He had said he no longer wanted her and there was no reason to disbelieve him. She knew very well she was not a woman a man would want to bed. "I should like to study the origin of some of your American words sometime. Perhaps when we come back from Kantalan I—"

"Kantalan." His glance flew back to her face. "I would have thought you'd realize by now that I have no intention of taking you to Kantalan." He slowly shook his head in wonder. "I can't understand you. You were nearly raped, you fell into a gorge and almost split your head open. You've taken risks that no sane woman would take, and all because you want to find a lost city which probably no longer exists, if it ever did."

"But it does exist," she said softly. Her eyes grew misty and faraway. "I know it does. All my life I've dreamed of Kantalan and known that I would go there someday. From the first moment I heard my father speak of it, I knew I'd walk the streets of Kantalan and see the temples and—" She broke off as

he made a sharp exclamation. She frowned in puzzlement as she saw his expression held surprise and for a
flickering moment even a touch of fear. Then it was
quickly shuttered again and she thought she must
have been mistaken. "Is there something wrong?"

"Walk the streets of Kantalan," he repeated. "It's a
curious phrase. I suppose it just startled me. You act
as if you can really see yourself there."

"I can." She raised herself on one elbow, her eyes
bright with eagerness. "Sometimes I see it and know
that I belong there. I realize it's only my imagination,
but there's nothing wrong with dreaming, is there?
Sometimes reality is more bearable if one comes to it
from dreams. Haven't you ever had a dream that was
so strong, so clear, it was more real than the world
around you?"

"Yes." Killara. Many times he had dreamed he was
home at Killara and woke to find only bitterness,
ashes, and loneliness. "Yes, I've had dreams like that."

"Then surely you realize how I feel about Kantalan.
Won't you take me there?"

Walk the streets of Kantalan. The phrase echoed in
his memory and sent a chill rippling down his spine.
Coincidence. It had to be the merest coincidence, but
it still brought him the same sense of fear and dread
he had known the night White Buffalo had told him
the prophecy.

She was looking at him as if he could grant her the
gift she had yearned for all the days of her life. He felt
suddenly heady with power. He could give her this.
He had hurt and shamed her, but he could make
amends by giving her what she asked. He opened his
lips to answer her and then closed them again
without speaking. If White Buffalo's prophecy held
any truth, what she wanted could also bring her death
and he would not risk it. Perhaps he believed more in
that prophecy than he had thought, perhaps his
skepticism regarding Kantalan had actually cloaked
fear.

He stood up. "No, I won't take you to Kantalan."
Her eyes were suddenly blazing with excitement.

"But you *could* take me. You know where it is, don't you?"

They had gone beyond subterfuge. He wouldn't lie to her again. "I know where Kantalan is supposed to be. That doesn't mean it's actually there." His lips tightened. "And I won't take you. Sometimes it's better for everyone not to have a dream realized."

"But why—"

"No!" The word echoed on the air like a whistling lash of rawhide. "I'm taking you back to Hell's Bluff tomorrow. We'll start out at sunset, it will be cooler then so the trip will be easier for you. You'll stay at the hotel until you're fully recovered and then I'll put you on the stage for Tucson. Can't you see you don't belong here? You almost *died*, dammit."

"I may not belong here," she whispered. Her eyes were enormous in her pale face. "But I do belong in Kantalan. Take me there."

He muttered a curse beneath his breath. "Didn't you listen to a word I said? You're not going to Kantalan. You're going home." He turned on his heel and stomped toward the door. "Make up your mind to it. You're definitely going home."

As he uttered the last sentence the door opened to reveal Silver gazing at him with raised brows. "You're sending someone else home?" she asked. "There will soon be no one left. I came to tell you Patrick has gone. He rode out a few minutes ago."

Dominic experienced a sharp thrust of pain. It was what he had wanted, what was necessary, but that didn't help relieve his sudden sense of terrible aloneness. "No, there will be no one left," he repeated dully. He moved past Silver and stood in the doorway watching Patrick's quickly retreating figure as the chestnut negotiated the twists of the winding trail that bordered the gorge. Then, as Patrick was lost to view beyond a curve in the trail, Dominic pulled his gaze away. "I picked up some soap and bandages in town. I'll fetch them from my saddlebags."

He shut the door behind him.

Elspeth gazed at the door, a pensive frown wrinkling her brow. She had glimpsed pain and sadness and poignant regret at the moment Dominic had left the cabin. She had thought him hard, even ruthless, and never dreamed he could display softer emotions. Her gaze moved to Silver's face. "Why did he send Patrick away?"

"He loves him and he fears for him," Silver said matter-of-factly. "There are many men who would like to kill Dominic and he thinks they will also kill the ones he loves. The Delaneys are a very close family and they protect their own." She came to Elspeth's side. "I'm glad he brought fresh bandages. It was difficult to keep these clean." She began to untie the white linen binding Elspeth's head wound. "It will be easier once we're in Hell's Bluff."

"The Delaneys," Elspeth murmured. She was suddenly intensely curious about the family that had brought forth such wildly differing offspring as Dominic, Patrick, and Silver. "Tell me about them, Silver."

"What do you wish to know?"

"Everything. I'd like to know everything."

Silver began to bathe the cut on Elspeth's head. "The old man, Shamus, and his wife Malvina, came here from Ireland in 1842. They had nine sons and five are still living—Joshua, Falcon, Dominic, Cort, and Sean. He has three grandchildren; Patrick, Brianne, and William."

"And you," Elspeth said. "Patrick said you were his cousin."

Silver's eyes flickered. "The old man will not admit I am his kin. There is no proof. My mother was only an Indian who caught his son, Boyd's, eye. He bedded her, left his seed, and rode out of our village without another thought. When my mother grew big with child, Sun Eagle, the brave to whom she had been promised, decided to redeem his honor. He killed Boyd Delaney and took my mother away to a tribe far to the north of here. When I was born, I had these." Her hand gestured to indicate the startling crystal gray of her eyes. "Sun Eagle was willing to accept my mother, but not look upon me, her shame, with every passing day. One night he rode down from the north and left me wrapped in a blanket on the porch of the homestead at Killara." Her lips twisted. "And the next morning Shamus sent me to the village of my mother's father, Black Bear, with a message that I was no blood of his."

Elspeth felt a surge of poignant sympathy. "How terrible for you."

Silver's expression became suddenly fierce. "Why? Black Bear was very kind to me. There were others in the village who had no use for a white man's leavings, but I had no need of the old man's charity. I would have been just as happy not to have ever seen the Delaneys again. It was Rising Star who made me come back to Killara."

"Rising Star? I've heard that name mentioned before."

"She is my aunt and married to Joshua. It was at the feasting when they were joined that Joshua's brother met my mother. Joshua took my aunt to Killara and she lives there like a fine lady." A fleeting wistfulness touched Silver's expression. "When I was five she came to our camp and took me home with her. For four months of every year she kept me with her, giving me schooling and teaching me white men's ways. It was a very brave thing for her to do. She has always been frightened of the old man and he didn't want me there, even for just four months out of the year."

"She sounds like a very splendid lady."

Silver's lips curved in a bittersweet smile. "I said she lives 'like' a fine lady, but she is Indian and the whites never let us forget." Her expression softened. "But Rising Star truly is a wonderful woman. I am proud to call her my aunt. She bears her pain with the strength of a great warrior."

"Pain?"

Silver's lips thinned. "You have heard enough about the Delaneys. If you want to know more, you must ask your man to tell you."

Elspeth's eyes widened in bewilderment. "My man?"

Silver shrugged. "Dominic."

Wild rose color stained Elspeth's cheeks. "You misunderstood. He's not my—" She moistened her lips and started again. "I know our circumstances are not the most proper but . . ."

Silver was gazing at her in puzzlement. "Why do you lie to me? When you wept and screamed in fear, only he could comfort you, and when he thought you were going to die, he was as fierce and sorrowful as if you had been his squaw for many years. I know the signs of belonging." An ironic smile touched her lips. "One who does not belong anywhere can always read such signs very well."

"Well, you've read the signs wrong this time." Had Dominic genuinely felt concern for her? The idea was fascinating. She wondered if he had really looked at her with pain and sorrow as Silver claimed. It was clear he wasn't as hard a man as she had first thought. His love for his nephew, Patrick, was plain enough to see; there was no mistaking the remorse he felt for his part in her injury. She had even believed for a moment that he was going to give in to her plea to lead her to Kantalan. Still, Silver had to be mistaken.

"You are smiling," Silver said softly, her shrewd gaze fixed on Elspeth's face. "I think perhaps the idea of belonging to Dominic does not displease you." Then, as Elspeth opened her lips to protest, Silver placed two fingers on them to silence her. "Hush, be silent now and rest. Later you can think of man-woman things."

The next evening Elspeth found she could think of little else besides man-woman things. For the principal reason that she found all the curves and valleys of her woman's body were pressed against Dominic's equally obvious masculine attributes.

Silver had dressed her in a pair of her own knee-high moccasins and a clean blue shirt belonging to Dominic that came past her knees. Then she had wrapped Elspeth so tightly in the freshly washed tan blanket that she could scarcely move a muscle.

"There. Just like an Indian baby in a papoose," she had said with satisfaction. "I will tell Dominic he can take you now. I will clean up the cabin and follow you to Hell's Bluff when I finish."

"Take me?" Elspeth asked faintly.

"You are too weak to sit a saddle. He will have to take you up in front of him." Then, noticing Elspeth's suddenly apprehensive expression, she continued comfortingly, "Don't worry, Dominic is a fine rider, almost as good as an Apache. He won't let you fall."

"That's very reassuring."

There was nothing in the least reassuring, however, just an hour later as she lay across the saddle in the curve of Dominic's arm. She was pressed against Dominic's hard, muscular body with every swaying step the stallion took.

The layers of material separating them might have been nonexistent for all the difference they made. Intimacy. She was feeling that same blinding sense of intimacy she had experienced when Dominic had taken her naked foot and held it against the same rigidity that was pressing against her hip at this very moment. The side of her soft breast brushed against him with every movement and she was beginning to feel a strange painful tautness in and around her nipples.

Heat. Heat was surrounding her, touching her, overpowering her. It was the blanket, she thought hazily. She had to get rid of this blanket wrapped so tightly around her or she would suffocate. She began to fight her way out of the woolen folds.

"What are you doing?" Dominic's voice was oddly thick. "For God's sake, can't you be still?"

"I'm hot. The blanket . . ."

"You can't be any warmer than I am," he said dryly. "And I don't have the excuse of a blanket."

"Please." The heat was growing. She could feel the flush of it on her skin and the crests of her breasts were beginning to feel acutely sensitive and swollen. "I think I'm getting sick. I want to sit up."

"So that you can fall off the blasted horse?"

"Silver said you wouldn't let me fall. Please, just for a little while. I'm beginning to feel so peculiar."

He muttered something beneath his breath and suddenly his hands were on the blanket, holding her steady with one while with the other he unwound the blanket from around her. "This is a mistake."

"No, I'll feel much better once I'm no longer so warm." Then the blanket was gone, draped over the horn of the saddle, and she did feel cooler with the gentle evening breeze caressing her cheeks and pressing the soft blue shirt against her body. Though she was still feeling that strange tingling in her breasts and difficulty in breathing. "Now help me to sit up."

He moved back in the saddle and was lifting her so she was astride the horse, her back pressed against his chest. His breathing was labored and as his chest lifted and fell, it touched her back with every movement. She guessed that shifting her had been strenuous for him and said, "I'm sorry I troubled you. I'll be fine now. Just forget about me."

Forget about her? Dominic almost laughed aloud. How could he forget about her when that enticing bottom was pressed against his groin and every motion of the stallion resulted in a friction that caused him to gasp with desire. "I'll try." His throat was so tight, the words were barely audible.

"You told me once I wouldn't be able to return to Hell's Bluff."

"There's no place else for you to go. I promise no one will make you feel the least bit uncomfortable." He could see the pale gleam of her thighs beneath the tail of his shirt and the start of the leather moccasins. He wanted to run his hand slowly down her thigh and then push the shirt up to her waist. He wanted to put his palms on the tight golden-brown curls he had fondled once before and press *hard*. He wanted to unbutton the blue shirt that clothed her and watch her breasts as they bounced and shimmered in the moonlight. He wanted to sink his tongue into the ear so close to his lips and tease her until she was as hot and aching as he was.

"This is a very nice horse," Elspeth said. "He has a much smoother gait than that horrible horse I rode to the cabin. Does he have a name?"

"Blanco."

"But he's black as midnight. Why would you call him Blanco?"

"Because he wasn't. At the time I thought it was hilarously funny."

"Really?" she asked doubtfully. "I don't quite see—"

"I was drunk."

"Oh." She turned to look at him and a swath of her hair moved against his lips in a silken, sensual kiss. "I'm afraid I paid no attention when you brought me here. How far is it to Hell's Bluff?

"Too far," he muttered. "Will you just not *move*."

"I'm sorry I bothered you," she said with hurt dignity. "I only wondered."

He was wondering too. He was wondering what she would do if he turned her in the saddle, freed himself, and sunk deep within her. He wondered if she would be frightened if he wrapped her legs around his hips and buried his tongue in her mouth. He wondered what she would do if he lifted her breasts to his mouth and suckled his fill. He wondered all these painful, hungry thoughts while the heat built and the swelling in his groin increased and he prayed he'd make it to Hell's Bluff before wondering became reality.

Elspeth leaned back against his chest and sighed despondently. He was angry with her again. The softness she had sensed in him when he had returned yesterday morning was now completely gone. Her gaze fell on his hand on her stomach that was steadying her on the saddle. It was a beautiful hand, she thought dreamily. His long, tanned fingers were splayed across the blue cotton shirt and looked slim, capable, and strong. She could feel the imprint of each finger through the thin cotton and she suddenly remembered how gently his fingertips had moved over her naked body, touching, brushing and then moving on until . . .

She moved restlessly against Dominic and she

heard him inhale sharply. She tried to turn and look at him again, but his hand on her stomach suddenly tightened, crumpling the fabric. "No!"

His voice held a heaviness, a guttural deepness that sent a queer warm shiver through her. Heat again. The wind that touched her face and pushed the cotton of the shirt against her breasts was no longer cool but scorching. It hadn't been the blanket, she realized, but Dominic Delaney who had brought the heat. She had always thought fear was cold, and it must be fear that was causing the blood to tingle through every vein.

After all, fear was the natural reaction when a man had nearly ravished you. Yet should she not be experiencing the urge to escape instead of this melting acquiescence? No, it couldn't be fear, then. Her brow wrinkled thoughtfully as her usual curiosity came to the forefront at this startling realization. She would think about it, examine this new emotion, and determine why it so unsettled her. Elspeth settled her head more comfortably against Dominic's breast, her gaze on the moon rising above the purple-shadowed mountains, and began to wonder.

She wondered why her breasts were suddenly swollen, the nipples pressing against the soft cotton as if pleading for release. She wondered why the rhythmic pounding of the leather saddle against that most private part of her was causing an ache that held no pain. She wondered why his hand on the gently rounded flesh of her stomach seemed to become heavier and more possessive with each passing moment. She wondered why his warm breath against her ear was causing an odd languor to attack the muscles of her neck and shoulders.

They were silent for the remainder of the journey. Wondering.

Dominic took no physical action.

Elspeth came to no conclusions.

It seemed a long, long time to both of them before they saw the lights of Hell's Bluff.

8

"It's nothing personal, you understand." Will Judkins's gaze sidled away from Elspeth's stunned expression as he opened the door to the hall. "You're welcome to stay until tomorrow morning. That will give Dominic time enough to find you a place more . . . suitable."

She hadn't realized how cold and stern the hotel owner's face could be. He had always had a genial smile on his face when he had encountered him before, and he had never shown her anything but kindness. Yet now his manner was brisk to the point of rudeness. "I thought your hotel was a very suitable place for me," she said haltingly. "I know I've been a bother for the last week, but it shouldn't be much longer until I'm well, and Silver has been preparing all my meals—"

"I don't look upon that dirty breed's presence in my kitchen as a help." Judkins's lips thinned. "And neither does my wife. That young heathen nearly frightened her out of a year's growth. She pulled a knife on her and told her to stay out of her way when she came downstairs or she'd take her scalp and hang it on the sign out front. My wife has refused to leave our room ever since, and *I'm* having to do the cooking for our guests." His gaze returned to where Elspeth was lying on the bed, and his jaw squared belligerently. "Not that there are many guests left, what with a half-breed and a fancy lady sashaying all over my

117

respectable hotel. I run a place where men can bring
their wives and children not a whore—"

"Silver is *not* dirty." Elspeth's eyes were blazing as
she sat up straight in bed. "I'd wager she bathes far
more frequently than you do. I don't know about her
being a heathen, we've never discussed it, but she's
kind and generous and if she threatened Mrs. Judkins,
I'm sure your wife deserved it."

"She did." Silver pushed the half-ajar door open
wide and entered the room carrying a round tray
covered by a blue and white checked napkin. "The
woman is a screeching fool. She called me a savage."
Her white teeth gleamed as she smiled faintly. "And I
showed her I could behave truly as the savage she
named me." She turned her gaze on Will Judkins. "As
I will show you if you do not stop bothering us."

Judkins's Adam's apple bobbed as he swallowed
nervously. "You don't scare me. You're nothing but an
Apache squaw. Shamus was right to bundle you back
to those other heathens. I would have done the same."

Silver's eyes widened until they seemed to hold
winter sunlight in their depths. "Do you wish to see
my knife too, white man?" she asked softly. "An
Apache squaw knows well how to use one. Perhaps
you have heard stories? They give prisoners to us
women first so that we may teach them the meaning
of pain before they learn of death."

Judkins moistened his suddenly dry lips. "This is
my hotel and if I say you go—" He edged toward the
door, his gaze fixed warily on Silver. "You go! I have
friends in this town. If you're not out of this room by
tomorrow morning, we'll maybe form a little party
and see how you like being run out of town." He
glanced at Elspeth. "None of this is my fault and I
won't lose money because Dominic is afraid Rina will
be jealous if he sets you up over at her place, where
you belong." His lips pursed and his voice rose
righteously. "You can't expect to have it both ways,
the wages of sin are—"

"Get out." Silver took a step toward him. *"Now."*
He took one look at her face and bolted out the door.

"The wages of sin," Silver repeated in disgust. "Everyone in town knows he spends every Saturday night over at Rina's." Elspeth's bewildered expression caused Silver to frown. "Did his words hurt you?" She crossed the room and set the tray on the nightstand beside the bed before she turned to face Elspeth. "He's a fool and a coward. He dared to speak to you in that way because he knew Dominic would be at the Nugget all afternoon. He probably hopes you will not tell Dominic of his rudeness to you." She smiled with infinite pleasure as she plucked the napkin from the tray. "I will enjoy very much watching Dominic kill him."

"No!" Elspeth's eyes widened in horror. "He wouldn't!"

Silver gazed at her in surprise. "Of course he will. You are his woman." She tucked the napkin into the collar of Elspeth's white cotton nightgown and handed her the small bowl of stew and a spoon. "Now eat and forget about the stupid man."

"I feel shamed." Elspeth smiled shakily. "I didn't think I'd feel this way. It shouldn't matter what other people think of me. I thought I was strong enough to ignore . . ." She blinked rapidly to rid her eyes of tears that were welling helplessly. "I suppose this means I'm a fallen woman now, at least in the opinion of everyone in Hell's Bluff. I wish I were like you, Silver. It would be easier if I could just ignore this."

Silver shook her head. "You never learn to ignore it," she said softly. "You do learn to accept and to deal with it. In many ways you are luckier than I, because you can go away and no one will know what happened here. I am what I am, wherever I go." She lifted her head proudly. "And I would not change it. I am Silver Dove Delaney. I will show the world that a half-breed can be the best of both worlds. You will see."

"I see now," Elspeth said gently. "I admire you very much, Silver. I wish you could share a little of your bravery with me."

"You need none of my courage. You grow stronger and braver every day." She tapped the bowl with her index finger. "Now eat and forget that fool. Dominic will tend to him when he returns."

Elspeth obediently took a bite of the rabbit stew. "I don't want you to speak to Dominic about this. I'll not have blood spilled because of me."

Silver frowned. "But Dominic should—"

"No, Silver." Elspeth's voice rang with firmness. "I won't have it."

Silver stared at her determined face for a moment before lowering her eyes. "No blood will be spilled, I promise you. Now, eat your stew. Dominic shot the rabbit and I cooked it. Your duty is only to eat."

Elspeth smiled. "You've both been very good to me. I'm sorry I've been so slow in recovering. I'm usually very healthy."

"You will be well soon." A sudden grin lit Silver's face. "Your voice is already much stronger. I heard you shouting at that fool, Judkins, halfway down the stairs." She looked at the flower pattern of the patchwork guilt covering Elspeth's lap and murmured, "Thank you."

"For what?"

Silver didn't take her gaze from the blanket and her voice was low. "For defending me, for saying I am kind. I am not kind, you know."

Elspeth felt a quick rush of affection. "You've been very good to me. How can you say you're not kind?"

"I cared for you first because I wished to please Patrick and Dominic. In spite of what the old man says, they *are* my blood." Her index finger began tracing the pattern of the quilt. "And then it was pride. I wanted you well so that I could point at you and say 'I did that. Apache or Delaney, I am the one who healed her.'"

"And now?"

"I think we are friends," she said shyly. "I've never had a friend besides Rising Star. It feels very strange."

"Yes." It felt strange to Elspeth as well. She, too, had suffered an isolated and lonely childhood, and friendship was as foreign to her as to this wild child who was stubbornly refusing now to look at her. Yet this companionable warmth and affection must be friendship. "Yes, I believe you're right. I think we are friends, Silver."

Silver released her breath, and Elspeth only then realized the younger girl had been holding it. She glanced up and smiled with a brilliance that lit her dark face with warmth, and Elspeth received a small shock. Why, Silver was beautiful! She had always been aware of the vitality and intensity that swirled around the Indian girl like tempest-driven clouds, but she had never realized that Silver was also quite lovely.

"Now, I had better leave and let you eat." Silver stood up. "I must not have my friend fading away from lack of nourishment. Who knows when I will find another one?"

She didn't wait for an answer but glided from the room. The door closed softly behind her.

Elspeth slowly finished the stew and put the bowl and spoon back on the tray on the nightstand. Then she lay back wearily on the pillows and closed her eyes. How foolish that she should feel so weak when only this morning she had been sure she was almost well. Each of Judkins's words had been like separate blows, robbing her of strength. It made no difference if he thought she was a hetaera like the lovely brown-haired Rina, who had peered over the banisters the morning that now seemed so long ago. She was a scholar and explorer, and what the world thought had no meaning for her. When she was a little stronger, she would ask Silver to get Dominic to come and see her. They would talk. She would soon bring him around, and they would be on their way to Kantalan.

She hadn't seen him since the night he had brought her back to Hell's Bluff, but Silver had made a point of telling her he was staying at the hotel instead of at Rina's. For some reason that knowledge had given her an odd sense of relief. Not that it mattered to her where he slept, she assured herself quickly. Silver had said he had been the one to comfort her during the time when her mind had been clouded with feverish dreams and visions. So perhaps because of that she felt safer with him close at hand.

Yes, that must be it. She breathed a sigh of relief at being able to find such a satisfactory explanation. She settled down for her afternoon nap, being very careful not to recall that she had never once, since the moment she had met Dominic Delaney, felt either safe or secure in his presence.

"The hypocritical son of a bitch." Dominic's lips thinned grimly. "I should have known he would try to sneak up and worry her. He's been whining and caterwaulling since the night I brought Elspeth here." He started to turn away. "I'll take care of it."

"You will do nothing."

Dominic's gaze flashed back to Silver. "The hell I won't. I promised her she would be safe and comfortable here. I've already broken my promise by letting that bastard get to her with his mealy-mouthed preachings. I'm going to make damn certain it won't happen again."

"I promised her no blood would be spilled." She smiled faintly. "However, I did not promise not to tell you the man is becoming a problem. If you add your threats to mine, it should be enough to stop him from speaking to her again. In a few days she will be stronger and we can move her to a place where she will not have to face these insults."

"And where is that?" Dominic asked bitterly. "Nowhere in Hell's Bluff."

"We will worry about that when the time comes." Silver paused. "She asked to see you. She will no doubt tell you she wishes to leave."

"No doubt at all." Dominic could feel the tension stiffening the muscles of his shoulders and neck. He didn't want to see her. He had been in a fever for her since the night he had brought her here, and he had no desire to feed his madness. He had not touched her that night, but he might just as well have done so. His imagery had been so clear and detailed, he felt as if he had taken her in a hundred exotic and erotic ways, and, dammit, he wanted to do it again and again, until reality and imagination became one fiery entity of satiation. What the hell kind of satyr did that make him? It was his fault she was both wounded and helpless, and yet he wanted to take advantage of her weakness. He had tried desperately to revive the tenderness and pity he had known when she was lying ill, but all he could remember was the feel of her. She was no longer his child, she was a woman and he could think of her in no other guise.

"Well?" Silver was looking at him inquiringly. "Will you see her? She is very determined. I think she will come to you if you do not go to her."

"It would be better if I didn't."

Silver's brow arched. "You fear to blacken her reputation? She has none. You have seen to that."

Dominic flinched. "I can always count on you to wield the knife. This time you're quite right, of course. I've seen to it that she has no good name left to blacken more. And that's all the more reason not to rob her of anything else."

She studied him. "You are saying you haven't bedded her yet. I find that very strange. It is clear you have a great hunger for her, and you are white."

"Not all white men take everything they hunger for."

"My father did." Silver smiled bitterly. "And I think you intended to take Elspeth also, did you not?"

"Yes."

"Then do not tell me white men do not take what they want." She paused. "But there is something you should know. Elspeth is now my friend. I will not let you bed her unless she desires it also." Her smile was a mere baring of even white teeth. "Go to see her. The memory of my little knife and my threat to plunge it into your back will make certain you rob her of nothing more than a few moments of her day."

Dominic experienced a niggling resentment, mixed with relief and amusement. He had brought Silver here to act as guardian for Elspeth, but he had never thought she would be guarded from himself. Yet who in Hell's Bluff was a greater danger to her? he wondered grimly. "All right, you little cougar cub, I'll see her." He turned and began climbing the stairs. "Just keep your knife out of my hide until you see it's needed."

The moment he saw Elspeth standing by the window looking down at the street below, he knew he would have to keep the memory of Silver's little knife in the forefront of his mind. She was dressed in a prim dark blue flannel robe that completely enveloped her tiny figure. The garment was utilitarian and uninspiring and should not have evoked anything but boredom in any observer. Yet all he could think was how light and silky her hair appeared against the dark material, and that the very shaplessness of the garment reminded him of the delicacy of the curves it concealed.

She turned as he walked through the doorway and for a moment the faintest color touched her cheeks. She was wearing those damn spectacles again, he noticed. It was the first time she had put them on since he had removed them that night at the cabin; she wore them now, he was sure, as a mask to hide behind. Judkins, he thought with a swift flare of anger. The bastard had upset her and the glasses were a first line of defense.

She smiled tentatively. "Thank you for coming; I felt I had to see you."

He closed the door behind him and then immediately wished he had left it open. The air of intimacy in the small room was suddenly overpowering. He cleared his throat. "Should you be out of bed?"

"Oh, yes, I get up a little while each day now. I'm much stronger. Soon I'll be entirely well." She moistened her lower lip with her tongue and he watched her in helpless fascination, feeling the familiar swelling in his loins. That little pink tongue had been one of the objects of his imaginings on the long ride to

Hell's Bluff. Now he could almost feel its warm moistness on his body.

"That's what I wanted to discuss with you," she continued a little breathlessly. "There's really no reason for me to stay here any longer. It's costing me far too much money and I'd be just as happy to return to the cabin." She moistened her lips again. "Far happier really. I'm sure the fresh air will be much healthier for me than— What are you looking at?" She touched her cheek with uncertain fingertips. "Do I have a smudge on my face?"

With an effort he pulled his gaze away. Lord, he had to get out of here. "No, I was just thinking how much better you were looking than the last time I saw you." He tried to focus his thoughts on what she was saying. "The money doesn't matter. I can make enough at the Nugget to pay for our expenses. We'll stay here until you're well."

Her eyes widened in distress. "But I really think—"

"Then don't think," he interrupted with sudden harshness. "Look, Judkins won't trouble you anymore. I know I broke my promise, but you can rely on me to see that no one else will bother you again until you're ready to leave."

"Silver told you." Elspeth frowned. "She wasn't supposed to. What do you mean, he won't trouble me? You haven't—"

"Killed him?" Dominic asked. "No, and it won't come to that. Threats work as well as violence with some men." He smiled bitterly. "In spite of what you may have heard, I consider it very serious indeed to take a life."

"But I have no right to stay here. Mr. Judkins owns the hotel, and he's quite correct in saying he decides who stays here."

"And just where do you suggest I take you? Rina's? That would really put a proper icing on the cake."

"No, I told you, the cabin will do just fine."

His gaze swung back to her face. "We'd be too alone there," he said bluntly. "There would come a time when Silver would go for a walk or a ride, when there would be no threat of her little knife, when I'd forget how you looked when you were lying at the bottom of that gorge."

She was gazing at him in bewilderment. "I don't know what you mean."

"I think you're about to find out." He was walking toward her, his light eyes intent on her face. "Do you remember what I did to you before you fell that night?"

"Yes." Her voice was only a level above a whisper.

He was so close now her could catch the faint floral scent that clung to her hair and see the delicate shadows in the hollows at her throat above the collar of the cotton nightgown. "I would do it again."

"You would ravish me?"

"Oh, dear Lord, I hope not." He reached out to touch the rapid pulse throbbing just below her chin. He knew a wild excitement as he felt the leaping response beneath the pad of his fingertips. Such a little thing and yet he felt a whiplash of heat add dimension to his manhood. "But I most certainly would try to seduce you." His fingers moved to touch the wire rim of her spectacles. "Why are you wearing these again?"

The pink in her cheeks deepened. "I told you I needed them."

"Yes, I remember you said so." His thumb moved to the sensitive spot just behind her ear and began to slowly rub it.

"I *do* need them. Besides, they can take nothing away from my looks."

"By all means, wear the spectacles. I think I like the idea of being the only man who knows what's behind them."

Exasperation and pity fought for dominance within him. Why did she persist in thinking herself so plain that men didn't want her? Her blindness to her beauty was not only idiotic, but dangerous. Yet it was a blindness he could now partially understand. The bits and pieces of her childhood she had revealed while she was feverish had drawn for him a very clear picture of her father. He held her to impossible standards while denigrating her completely; it was astonishing she had emerged with any confidence in herself as either an individual or a female.

"Your spectacles are like the veils those harem ladies wear." He tugged gently on the lobe of her ear. "But you should remember that the primary pleasure of any barrier to a man is removing it." The nail of his thumb pressed into her ear lobe with just enough pressure to tease without hurting. He could see the sudden leap of her pulse beneath the delicate blue veins at her temple. "I'm very fond of removing barriers."

Elspeth had a fleeting, disjointed memory of her disrobing the night she had fallen into the gorge. She swallowed. "Are you trying to seduce me now?"

"You bet I am."

"Why?"

"It's the way of a man with a woman."

She tilted her head and her eyes lit with the curiosity he now recognized as one of her more salient qualities. "Any woman?"

"No, not—" He broke off as he realized suddenly the denial sprang from a knowledge he had refused to admit even to himself. Now he comprehended the full extent of the sway she held over his emotions. He wanted no one but Elspeth. The realization sent a ripple of shock through him, quickly followed by defensive anger. He couldn't have Elspeth. And, when she was gone, would he be able to want another woman? The witch was damn near emasculating him. This madness had to stop. His hand dropped from her ear and he said with deliberate coolness, "All cats are gray in the dark."

She flinched as waves of shock and hurt swept over her. Then she lifted her chin proudly. "Thank you for explaining that to me. I think you're right about staying here in Hell's Bluff. I don't believe I'm a person who would like being mistaken for someone else, even in the dark." The flush tinging her cheeks had become scarlet. "And I certainly have no wish to be alone with you."

He felt unreasonably irritated. "You've forgotten about Kantalan," he drawled. "You were willing enough to do anything for me, with me, if I would take you to your precious Kantalan. Perhaps I was too hasty in refusing you; perhaps we could come to an . . . arrangement. Have you changed your mind?"

She was gazing at him with a look of utter confusion. "You have no intention of taking me to Kantalan. I think you're trying to hurt me, to shame me. Why are you doing this?"

He *was* trying to hurt her. He was using her childhood dream to hit back at her for the rage and frustration he was experiencing at the discovery that had rocked him to his bootheels.

"Because I'm that kind of a man," he said wearily as he turned toward the door. "I strike out and I'm not always careful about who gets in the way. Maybe you should try to remember that. It shouldn't be hard to do since I seem to give you plenty of opportunity to refresh your memory."

He strode quickly from the room and shut the door.

He stopped in the hall and closed his eyes. No, dammit, he wouldn't have it! It wasn't fair that he had developed this crazy obsession. Only now did he realize how odd it was he hadn't gone to Rina's in the last two weeks to soothe the fever Elspeth had ignited. He clenched his fists. He would *not* be dependent on Elspeth MacGregor. He would *not* need her as well as lust after her. She would soon be gone and he had his own life to live. He must cut these sensual ties before they became too strong to sever.

He opened his eyes and strode swiftly down the hall and started down the stairs.

Silver met him on the landing. She took one look at his face and the smile faded from her lips. "She is content?"

"How do I know?" he asked roughly, not looking at her. "I can't spend my whole life wondering if Elspeth MacGregor is happy or not. She said she would stay here. Isn't that what you wanted?"

Silver slowly nodded. "I thought that was what we both wanted."

He didn't know what he wanted anymore, except to possess that cat-eyed temptress in the room he had just left. But he was damn well going to find out if something or someone could keep him from falling deeper under her spell.

He passed Silver on the landing as he continued down the stairs. He could feel her gaze on the middle of his spine.

"Where are you going?" she asked softly.

He didn't look back. "Rina's."

9

"**Y**ou did not eat your dinner." Silver looked at the untouched chicken on the flowered china plate and then frowned at Elspeth. "How do you expect to get stronger if you do not eat?"

"I wasn't hungry. I ate all the rabbit stew you gave me for lunch." Elspeth smiled with an effort. "It was very filling. I guess the heat has taken my appetite away. I'll eat breakfast tomorrow morning, I promise."

"It *is* hot." Silver glanced uneasily at the darkness beyond the open window. "I was hoping it would grow cooler once the sun went down.

"The room will cool down later. There's always a good breeze from the mountains."

"Yes." Silver was frowning, her gaze still on the window. "It will grow cooler later, but you will still have to have the window open for a few hours." She suddenly turned away, picked up the checked napkin from beside the plate on the tray, and tore it swiftly into two strips.

Elspeth blinked. "What are you doing?"

Silver divided one of the halves of the napkin into two more narrow strips. Then she turned to Elspeth and held out the cloth. "Wad these up and put them into your ears."

"But why?"

"There are things happening tonight you should not know about." Silver turned away from Elspeth's gaze.

"Things you would not want to know about. Put the cloth in your ears and try to sleep, and, no matter what you hear, do not go to the window."

Elspeth sat up straight in bed. "How can you say something like that and expect me not to be curious? You know very well I'm going to have to know what's going on."

A tiny smile tugged at Silver's lips. "Yes, I know you are very curious about everything going on around you. I was hoping not to have to satisfy your curiosity this time." Her smile faded. "I heard talk when I went out this afternoon. They will be using the hanging tree tonight."

"The hanging tree?"

Silver nodded at the window. "The big oak tree you can see from here, the one that stands a little apart from the others at the edge of town. It is where men are taken and hung. You will not want to look at this. It is not a good thing to see."

Elspeth's eyes widened in horror. "An execution? The law is going to hang someone tonight?"

"There is no law in Hell's Bluff."

"Then who—"

"Vigilantes. Men of the town who take it upon themselves to punish the guilty. It is how things are done when there is no law."

Silver's voice was perfectly matter-of-fact and her very calmness sent a shiver through Elspeth. She remembered that first afternoon when she had looked out the window and thought how stately and dignified the old oak tree was, how comfortingly permanent in a town that appeared raw in its youth. And all the time it was a hanging tree, a death tree. Horror cloaked in deceptive beauty. "When?"

"Soon. The man was caught this morning and the trial was to be held at the Nugget at sundown."

"Trial?" Elspeth felt a rush of hope. "Then perhaps he'll be found innocent. Maybe there won't be any hanging."

Silver shrugged. "He was captured riding the stolen

horse. He even bragged about stealing it. He is a very stupid man. There is no doubt they will hang him."

Elspeth held up her hand. "Wait. There's something I don't understand. They're going to hang a man for stealing a *horse*?"

Silver looked at her in surprise. "Of course, it is a very serious crime. Horse thieves are always hung."

"I thought he had killed someone." Elspeth felt sick. She had run across this kind of ruthless code in eastern countries she had visited as a child, but she had never expected to encounter it here. "To take a man's life for stealing an animal is barbaric."

"To rob a man of his horse can be the same as killing him, Elspeth. Besides, it's considered wise to make an example of horse thieves to discourage the practice." Silver tilted her head, listening. "I hear something. I think the trial is over and they will be coming soon. Put the cloth in your ears. Quickly."

Elspeth gazed at her in disbelief at the childlike simplicity of the order. Silver actually expected her to stuff her ears so she wouldn't hear the sounds of death, just close her eyes and pretend it wasn't there. Elspeth suddenly swung her legs to the floor and stood up.

"No, you've been up once today," Silver protested. "You'll get dizzy; you know you will."

Elspeth ignored her as she crossed to the window. She had expected the oak tree to appear different to her now that she knew its macabre purpose. But it was still stately, still beautiful to behold, and for some reason that made what was happening tonight all the more horrible.

The evening breeze was cool and pungently scented with pine and creosote. She took a deep breath, suddenly conscious of how many wonderful tactile pleasures there were in life. Was that poor man they were going to hang feeling this same breeze on his face, had he breathed in these lovely earth scents and felt a sense of desperation knowing he would soon feel neither its freshness nor its coolness?

She could hear something in the distance, the

sounds Silver must have had heard. A deep rumble of voices interspersed with shouts and, dear God in heaven—*laughter*. "Can't we stop it from happening?" she asked in a muffled voice.

"No, the Russian is guilty. He must be punished."

"But it's—" Elspeth stopped, froze, her fingers clenching on the material of the curtain. "Russian?"

"The man who stole the horse is a Russian. His name is Andre Marzo—something." Silver shrugged. "I forget the rest."

"Marzonoff. Andre Marzonoff," Elspeth said numbly. Plump, eager Andre, who had been so desperate to gain the acceptance of these people was now going to be murdered by them? "No!" The cry was torn from her and she whirled to face Silver. "No, he didn't understand. They *mustn't* hang him. We've got to stop it."

Silver was startled. "You know the Russian?"

"Of course I know him. He's no criminal. He wanted only to be like them. He wanted them to admire him. Don't you see? He probably thought that stealing a horse would make him some kind of a hero in their eyes. He couldn't *know*."

The voices were coming closer and Elspeth felt panic grip her. "We have to explain to them. We mustn't let them hang an innocent man."

"He is not innocent. He stole the horse."

"But I'd wager anything I have that he had no idea what it meant. He undoubtedly thought that taking a horse would make him dashing and brave and . . ." Tears were glittering in her eyes, and she could scarcely speak. "He came all the way from his own country to find something that he couldn't find at home and now he's to die?"

Silver was suddenly beside her, trying to draw her away from the window. "You must not get upset, it is not good for you. I would not have told you the man's name if I had known you were friends."

"So I could stuff my ears and close my eyes and not know a man was out there dying?" Elspeth shook off Silver's grip and stepped back. "We have to explain to them that they've made a mistake."

Silver shook her head. "You do not reason with a lynch mob. They are like wolves when the smell of blood is in the air."

"I've got to try."

"Go back to bed," Silver said soothingly. "I will find Dominic. He may be able to save him. At least, the men of the town fear him enough to listen."

"I won't go to bed." Elspeth suddenly saw the gleam of a torch as several men rounded the corner. The deep rumble of voices was closer. Much closer now. "Hurry," she whispered desperately. "Do you know where Dominic is?"

"He went to Rina's." Silver was already running for the door. "Stay away from that window until I get back. Do you hear me? Stay away from the window."

Then she was gone.

Stay away from the window. Silver's last warning had ominous overtones. Stay away because she might see something that would horrify her? Stay away because Dominic might not get there in time? Rina's place was on the other side of town, at least ten minutes fast walk from the hotel and that meant another ten minutes on the return even if Silver found Dominic right away. If she could find him at all. He had to be in one of those bedrooms on the second floor with Rina or one of her ladies. Why else would he go there tonight? *All cats are gray in the dark.* The phrase fragmented, then exploded in her mind as she caught sight of Andre Marzonoff in the middle of the crowd in the street below.

He was the only man mounted on a horse, his hands tied behind his back. She noticed with aching sympathy that he was dressed in the gray waist-length jacket and black string tie he had affected since he had met Dominic. The street was jammed with miners, cowboys, and merchants. There were even a few women dressed in the gaudy satins that identified them as barmaids at the Nugget. Several of the men were carrying torches and as they drew closer, the light played across their faces. Elspeth gasped. Their expressions reflected such laughter and excitement, you would have thought they were ushering a hero home from the wars rather than a man to a horrible and humiliating death.

Andre was almost directly below her now and she could see his expression, too, in the harsh flare of the torches.

Bewilderment. Not terror as she had expected. Just the bewilderment and disbelief of a confused child. It *couldn't* happen to him. She couldn't let it happen.

Elspeth whirled away from the window and ran to the armoire across from the bed. She jerked a gown from within its depths and shrugged out of her robe. She didn't bother to take off her nightgown, but pulled the black gown over it. She fastened the front of the bodice with fingers that trembled with haste.

There was no time to put on her shoes and button them. She would just have to go barefoot. Who would notice her feet anyway? she thought wildly. They were going to hang a man down there in the streets and she was worrying about shoes.

She ran to the window, swung her legs over the sill to the second floor balcony. She cast a quick glance below and the blood froze in her veins. The mob had reached the tree!

She ran down the steps and then was tearing along the dirt street. She stumbled and fell to her knees and then was up again, running.

Thank God, the crowd seemed in no hurry to accomplish its purpose. A rope was thrown over the lowest branch of the oak tree in a fashion that was almost leisurely. There was more laughter and several ribald remarks tossed back and forth. Then a noose was slipped over Andre's head and tightened around his neck.

She had reached the outer edges of the crowd and she started to push her way through the throng. Her breath was coming in gasps and she felt dizzy and sick. "Stop! You've got to stop." They couldn't hear her. Her voice was so weak it was scarcely audible. "Don't do this!" she cried as loudly as she could.

She was suddenly closer, almost to the forefront of the crowd. Then the mob shifted and she was suddenly thrust against the rough bole of the oak tree. A blinding pain flashed in her head and for an instant her dizziness became blackness. Then the darkness cleared and she could see the reason the crowd had shifted. They were watching a tall, bearded man with a small hatchet who was hacking at the branches of a bush a few yards away from the oak tree. Elspeth looked desperately around the circle of spectators, seeking help.

There were faces she recognized, she realized with despair, but there would be no help. Will Judkins, Charlie Bonwit, the blacksmith at the livery stable, the golden-haired woman she had seen that night at the Nugget. They were all staring at Andre with the same expression. Anticipation. They all *wanted* this to happen.

"What in God's name are you doing here?"

Ben Travis!

She turned to him eagerly. "Ben, tell them to stop it. Tell them it's a mistake."

"It's not a mistake. The man is guilty as hell," Ben said bluntly. "Now, you get out of here and go back to Dominic."

"Dominic's at Rina's," she said dully.

For an instant there was a flicker of pity in Ben's roughhewn face. "So soon?" He glanced away almost as if he were embarrassed. "Well, he's a man who likes variety. Someone should have warned you about that before you ran off with him." His hand closed on her arm. "Go back to the hotel anyway. Sometimes the boys get kind of excited when they see something like this. There's no telling what kind of trouble you could get into here."

The bearded man had finished cutting the switch from the bush and was sauntering toward Andre.

"No!" Elspeth screamed. "Don't do this to him." She stepped forward, trying to get to the man holding the switch.

"Are you loco?" Ben grabbed her by the arms, holding her helpless. "You interfere now and they'll tear you apart."

She struggled desperately, her breath coming in harsh sobs. "Let me go. I have to—" She broke off as her gaze suddenly met Andre's.

He was only a few yards away and looking directly at her. His face was chalk-pale and his eyes still held that look of helplessness and confusion. But now there was stark terror in them also. Then, as she watched, two tears rolled down his plump cheeks.

"Don't let Nicholas know I was frightened," he called softly to her. "Don't tell anyone I wept. Don't tell . . ." His last words were drowned in the sudden cry that went up from the crowd as the switch whistled through the air and came down on the horse's hindquarters. It leaped forward!

Elspeth's scream ripped through the night.

Silver ran up the front steps, threw open the door, and dashed into the parlor, where five women in various states of undress lounged on the tufted sofa and the several chairs that furnished the room. "Dominic," she said breathlessly. "Where is he?"

"Busy." The red-haired woman who answered had one shapely leg thrown over the arm of the plumply cushioned turkish chair on which she was sitting. She smiled lazily at Silver. "Very busy. Even for Dominic. You can leave a message, but I don't think he's going to want to be disturbed."

A small bonehandled knife appeared in Silver's hand. "Where?" she repeated.

The smile disappeared from the red-haired woman's lips. "Rina." Her gaze was fixed warily on the glittering blade of the knife. "Upstairs. Second door to the left."

Silver turned and took the steps to the second floor two at a time. She threw open the door to Rina's room and stood in the doorway, her breasts lifting and falling with the force of her breathing, gazing impatiently at the naked man sitting on the bed and the equally naked woman kneeling before him on the floor.

"You have no time for this. Get your clothes on and come with me. Elspeth needs you." Silver marched forward, grabbed a handful of Rina's gleaming brown hair, and pulled her face from between Dominic's thighs. "Hurry, Dominic, we have no time."

"The hell we don't," Dominic growled. "Silver, I believe I'm going to scalp you. Get the hell back to the hotel and—" He broke off. He shook his head to clear it of the brandy fumes that were misting his thinking. "Elspeth? What's the devil's wrong with Elspeth?"

Silver nodded as she quickly gathered Dominic's clothing from the floor and tossed them to him. "You have to stop the hanging. Elspeth is very worried about the man."

"What hanging?" Dominic began to dress automatically.

"I told you about the hanging." Rina stood up and reached for the yellow satin robe edged with sealskin that was draped over the bedpost. "The horse thief." She slipped the robe on and turned to face Silver, gazing at her icily. "I don't like to be interrupted, Indian."

Silver glared back. "I robbed you of nothing you cannot replace. Find another man to pleasure you. I have need of Dominic." She bent, picked up one of Dominic's boots, and threw it to the carpet at his feet. She turned away. "Find his other boot while I get his gunbelt."

Rina hesitated and then a grudging smile touched her lips. She turned away and began looking for the missing boot.

"For God's sake, what has Elspeth to do with a horse thief?" Dominic jammed his foot into the boot while he finished buttoning his shirt.

"She says she knows the Russian and the hanging is a mistake."

"Russian?" He knew of only one Russian in Hell's Bluff. Andre Marzonoff. He knew very little about the man other than that he was a godawful poker player, but he vaguely recalled hearing he had arrived in Hell's Bluff on the same stage as Elspeth. "Andre Marzonoff is the horse thief?"

Silver nodded as she handed him his gunbelt. "And I think if you do not stop the hanging, Elspeth will try to do it herself."

"Christ." He buckled his gunbelt on with swift hands. Knowing Elspeth, he had no doubt she would try to stop it. "Why the devil did you leave her alone?"

"If you had not been here, I would not have had to leave her alone," Silver said with sudden ferocity. "Why did you not return when you knew there was to be a hanging? Even if Elspeth did not know the man, it would not have been good for her to see this happen."

"I forgot the hanging tree could be seen from the hotel. I guess I didn't think—"

"You thought of nothing but liquor and fornicating," Silver said coldly.

She was right, Dominic thought wearily. If he hadn't been desperately seeking to erase the tormenting need for Elspeth from his mind and body, he would have been aware of how the hanging would affect her.

"Your boot." Rina offered him the second boot she had found behind the chair. She cast a half-mocking glance at Silver. "Anything else, Indian?"

Silver nodded curtly. "He will need a horse. We will not get there in time on foot."

Rina moved swiftly and gracefully toward the door. "I'll have Li Tong saddle my mare." The door closed behind her.

Dominic pulled on his other boot. "How much time do we have?"

"It depends on how eager they are to hang him." Silver's lips tightened. "But Elspeth will not wait long."

Dominic felt a cold finger of panic touch his spine and he went quickly to the door. "Let's go!" He ran out of the room, down the stairs, and out on the porch. Li Tong had just finished drawing the cinches of the saddle on the mare tied to the hitching rail in the street. Dominic hit the saddle with one spring and pulled Silver up behind him.

Rina stood by the hitching rail, a derisive smile on her lips. "Take care of my mare, Indian. If you don't bring her back, I'll take the price out of your hide." Her gaze ran over Silver in sudden speculation. "Which might not be a bad idea. I don't have any Indian women at my house. Interested?"

"No, she's not," Dominic said shortly. His heels prodded the mare into a run.

Silver's arms tightened around his waist, her cheek pressed against his shoulder blade. The mare was fast, her gait smooth and even, but would she be fast enough? she wondered. No more than fifteen minutes had gone by since she had left Elspeth and perhaps . . . A sudden roar of voices disturbed the stillness, and Silver's hopes plummeted.

A piercing scream shattered the darkness ahead.

Dominic's body tensed, his spine became rigid. "Elspeth," he whispered. How many times had he heard her scream just that way in the night when she was attacked by those terrifying nightmares? Now it wasn't dreams but reality that was threatening her and he might be too late to drive it away.

He turned the corner and saw the hanging tree directly in front of him at the end of the street. He heard a second shout go up and felt a cold sickness knot his belly. He didn't have to look at the man dangling at the end of the rope to know it was over. Too late.

The mob was melting away quietly, not looking at one another, almost subdued now. It was always like that at any lynching Dominic had ever witnessed. First the exhilaration, then the quiet, casual dispersal as if denying the act had even happened.

His gaze anxiously raked the crowd. "I don't see her. God, she has to be here. I heard her, dammit."

"There." Silver pointed. "By the tree."

Dominic caught a glimpse of tawny hair against the

rough brown bark of the oak and urged the mare forward, picking his way through the crowd.

Elspeth was standing by the tree, staring blindly up at the grotesque obscenity that was now Andre Marzonoff. Ben Travis was beside her, speaking low but vehemently into her ear. She didn't answer him. She didn't ignore him. It was as if she didn't realize he was there.

Dominic's heart skipped a beat when he saw her face. She was marble-pale in the moonlight, her thin body swaying slightly. He stopped the mare before them. He didn't know what to say. What the hell *could* he say to her? "Elspeth, I'm sorry. Lord, I'm so so sorry."

She wasn't listening. "He was terribly ashamed of being frightened," she whispered. "Even at the end. He so wanted to be like Nicholas, like you, Dominic. He even tried to dress like you. You gambled, he gambled. You stole a woman, he stole a horse." The tears were running slowly down her cheeks. "I'm sure he didn't understand the difference. He wanted only to be like you. Why couldn't they see that?"

Dominic felt as if he were being ripped to pieces. He swung off the mare, tossed the reins to Silver, and took a step closer to Elspeth. He wanted to touch her, comfort her, but all he could do was stand and stare at her. "I don't know," he said hoarsely. "I guess we sometimes do things in too much of a hurry."

"They wouldn't listen to him. He could have paid for the horse ten times over."

"That wasn't the point," Ben Travis said gruffly. "He stole it." He turned to Dominic. "Get her out of here. I can't talk her into leaving."

Elspeth's gaze was still on the hanging man. "He won't take Andre down. He's going to leave him there all night."

"You know the rule, Dom. The body is to be left swinging for a full twenty-four hours."

"Cut him down, Ben."

Ben shook his head. "Not me. We made a rule and we've got to stick to it. That's the only way law can work."

"Law," Elspeth repeated wonderingly. "What law?"

"Our law. Hell, it's not perfect, but it's all we've got," Ben said. "And it's better than no law at all. I've seen lawless towns, and so have you, Dom."

"Cut him down."

Ben shook his head. "I'm not going to—"

A shot shattered his words. The rope shredded and Andre's body dropped to the ground. Dominic slid his Colt back into his holster. "Now you don't have to cut him down. Just go get the undertaker and get him buried." He paused. "Tonight. Tell Jake I'll pay for it and that I don't want any window displays or I'll see that he joins Marzonoff."

"The boys ain't gonna like this." Ben looked at Dominic and hastily added, "All right, all right, you don't have to be so damn touchy."

"What do you mean 'window displays'?" Elspeth asked, staring at Andre's body sprawled on the ground.

"Jake sometimes sets the coffin upright in the funeral parlor window after a hanging," Ben said absently. "And then he—"

"*Shut up.*" Dominic's voice cut across his words like the switch that had whistled through the air to sting the rump of the horse bearing Andre. "My God, Ben, will you get the hell out of here?"

The older man looked a little startled. "I didn't mean nothing." He cast an apologetic glance back at Elspeth as he turned and started down the street. "Sorry. I guess it does sound kind of bad."

"Barbaric," Elspeth whispered. "Monstrous. I can't understand this. When I first came here I thought everyone was so kind, and yet tonight . . . Everything is changed . . . different."

"Take her back to the hotel," Silver said fiercely. "She can hardly stand up. I will stay with the Russian until Jake comes."

"Elspeth," Dominic said softly. "Silver is right. Come with me. You can't do anything more here."

"More? I couldn't do *anything*. I was helpless. Do you know how that made me feel? I wasn't strong enough to make them listen. A man died because I wasn't strong enough to prevent it." Elspeth's voice was shaking with intensity. "No one has a right to be that weak. Not when it means a man's life. *You* could have stopped them, Dominic. Silver could have stopped them."

"You can't blame yourself. You've been very ill," Dominic said quietly. "You did all you could."

"I should have been stronger." She closed her eyes. "I *will* be stronger. I couldn't stand for anything like this to ever happen again because I wasn't capable." She swayed, her lashes flicked open and her eyes held rising panic. "Dominic, I think . . ." She took a wavering step toward him and pitched forward into his arms.

Dominic heard a low cry from Silver. Then she was off the horse and beside him. "She has fainted?"

Dominic nodded, and he picked up Elspeth's slight weight in his arms. He was raw and hurting, he wanted the welcome release of anger but there was no one he could fight. He could exist only with this burning ache that was compounded of pity, regret, and sorrow. "It's probably for the best." He cleared his throat to rid it of huskiness. "My God, I wondered how she lasted this long. We have to get her away from here before she regains consciousness."

Silver nodded. "The hotel?"

Dominic shook his head. Elspeth would never be able to stay in Hell's Bluff without being constantly reminded of the horror of this night. "No, go back to the hotel and pack up. Meet me out front in fifteen minutes. I'll go to the livery stable and hire a buckboard."

Silver nodded. She swung back on the mare. "We are returning to the cabin?"

"No." He turned away and started in the direction of the livery stable, his arms unconsciously tightening around Elspeth. "We're going to Killara."

10

❦

Dawn thrust luminous fingers through the dark passes of the Dragoon Mountains; pale sunlight gleamed on the white walls of a large two-story adobe house in the valley far below and glinted off the tiles of the roof, enriching their color to a blazing red. His mother had never liked that red roof since the moment she had set eyes on it, Dominic remembered. She had always claimed the gaudy color was more suited to a bawdy house than a respectable home, but his father had only laughed and told her that any number of the noblemen in Spain had roofs of that color, so the Delaneys were in fine company. Gaudy roof be damned, Dominic had always loved that house. It was the heart of Killara. It was home.

Dominic experienced the same wrenching pang of bittersweet happiness he always did when he returned to Killara. He deliberately forced his gaze away and glanced over his shoulder at Silver sitting beside Elspeth's prone figure in the bed of the buckboard. "We're almost there. Has she regained consciousness?"

"Not yet, but she has stirred a few times." Silver adjusted the blanket covering Elspeth and then lifted her gaze once more to Dominic. "Perhaps she does not want to wake up. It was not a pretty sight she closed her eyes on."

A thrill of fear clutched at him. "Trust you to look

144

on the bright side. Are you trying to scare the hell out of me?"

"Why not? You deserve it. If you had not gone to Rina's, Elsepth would not have tried to stop the lynching."

"I know. But there were reasons."

"Good reasons?"

"No," he admitted, his voice heavy with weariness. "They seemed good at the time, but a man can usually find a reason for anything if he looks hard enough." He glanced back at the house in the valley below. "Hell, maybe that's what I'm doing now." He flicked the reins and the team started down the winding road leading to the foothills. "Tell me when she wakes up."

The silence of the next few minutes was broken only by the creak of the buckboard and the clop of horses' hooves on the hard rocky surface of the trail.

"Are you going to stay with her?" Silver asked.

Dominic's hands tightened on the reins. He didn't answer for a moment. "No, I'll stay a few days and then go back to Hell's Bluff. You can take care of her. She won't need me here at Killara."

"Yes, I can care for her." She paused. "But I will not be welcome, and I will not stay if the old man does not want me."

"Then Rising Star can care for her. For God's sake, there are women enough in the house to nurse her if she has need of it."

"What makes you think she will stay if you are not here? She is your woman and a woman's place is with her man."

His woman. The words caused in him the same bittersweet feeling he had experienced when he first caught sight of Killara. "You're being mighty persuasive all of a sudden. Only yesterday you were threatening me with your little knife and now you're—"

"I did not want you fornicating with her unless she wished it," Silver said calmly. "It does not mean that I do not know you are her man. It is clear. Why are you laughing?"

"I was just thinking that Rising Star is going to

have a hell of time keeping my mother from washing your mouth out with lye soap. Lord, you have a foul mouth."

"Because I speak the same words I have heard men use all my life? Why should a woman be considered foul when a man is not? I will pay no attention to such nonsense."

"Silver, a woman can't—"

"A woman can do anything if she is strong enough. A woman can be anything a man is and more." She paused. "Much more. You will see."

"If she is strong . . ." The words were a husky wisp of a sound. Elspeth's voice.

Dominic jerked around. Elspeth's eyes were open and staring straight ahead into the wavering half-light of the valley below. A rush of relief poured through him. "Good morning," he said. "We were wondering when you were going to wake up."

"Were you?" Elspeth's lids fluttered shut again. "I'm in a wagon, aren't I? Where are we going?"

"Killara. I thought you'd prefer it to Hell's Bluff."

"Yes," she whispered. "Oh, yes." Andre's plump body dangling limp at the end of a rope, his eyes open and staring blindly ahead. Anything would be better than being in that nightmare town, where kindness masked brutality and nothing was what it seemed to be. "It was hideous. They have to be monsters."

"No. They're people just like you and me," Dominic said quietly. "A few of the men in that mob were even my friends." He paused. "No, *are* my friends. They thought what they were doing was right and I respect them for it."

Her eyes flew open to stare at him in horror. "Respect them? How could you respect them? I saw their faces. They *enjoyed* it."

"Some of them, maybe. Some people like death because it makes them feel more alive. You probably noticed them more than the others, because they push closer to warm their hands at it. The people you don't notice are the quiet ones who just stand and watch. Men like Ben Travis, who were there because they believed what they were doing was necessary."

Elspeth sat bolt upright, every muscle of her body tense with rejection. "They were wrong!" Her tone was vibrant with intensity. "Andre was—"

"Guilty." Dominic's voice held both sadness and inflexibility. "We live in a black and white world out here, Elspeth. I'm afraid the reasons don't matter much if a crime is committed."

"You're defending them." She was staring at him incredulously. "I suppose you would have been out there by that tree with them if you hadn't been more pleasantly occupied."

He winced. "I hope not. I hope I would have listened to Marzonoff and tried to talk reason to that crowd." His jaw squared. "But I won't lie to you. I'm no stranger to lynch mobs. I've watched a few bastards swing with as much pleasure as anyone you saw there in that crowd."

Silver shook her head. "Lord, what a stupid thing to say to her right now. Maybe the old man is right and you are not my uncle. I don't believe I want to claim such a peabrain as a relation."

Dominic cast her a fierce glance. "Was I supposed to deny it? You know damn well—" He broke off and turned back to Elspeth to continue jerkily. "Ben Travis was right. Our way isn't perfect, but we try to do the best we can. So don't tell me about monsters. You couldn't recognize them if you saw them. Well, I can. I know how they look and how they sweat and whine when they're caught. I've hung quite a few of them."

"And shot them, too, I'd wager," Elspeth said, her eyes blazing. "You're supposed to be a gunman, aren't you? I guess you're very proud of all the men you've murdered."

Silver inhaled sharply, her muscles stiffening warily as her gaze flew to Dominic's face. Rage. Cold rage. She automatically drew a few inches closer to Elspeth.

Dominic spoke very slowly and distinctly. "I'm not a murderer. I've not even been tempted to commit murder until I made your acquaintance. However, I haven't the faintest doubt that you could cause a preacher to break all ten commandments."

"Pay attention to the trail, Dominic," Silver said hurriedly as she grasped Elspeth's shoulders, pushed her down, and pulled the blanket up to cover her to the nose. "And you be still, Elspeth, arguing is not good for you."

Elspeth's eyes were blazing above the edge of the blanket. "I'm *not* arguing."

Silver cast a hasty glance over her shoulder. Dominic had turned around and was no longer looking at them, but the muscles of his shoulders and his spine were still rigid with tension.

"Hush," she whispered as she quickly covered Elspeth's lips with her fingers. "Now is not the best time to strike at him. He is already hurting and he may do something he may regret later."

"I'm not strik—" She stopped, arrested by Silver's words. "Why is he hurting?

"He is coming home," Silver whispered. "And he knows he must leave again. When one has a great thirst, a sip of water is only a torment. I know you are angry with him, but it is time to be patient. He came here only because he wished you to be free from pain. You owe him gentleness."

How strange to hear Silver speak of gentleness, Elspeth thought. She more often displayed ferocity and passion than tenderness. Her gaze wandered to Dominic, lingering on his dark hair and the tense slide of muscles coiled beneath his blue cotton shirt. Silver's uncle displayed that same ferocity and passion and yet he, too, could be thoughtful and gentle if it suited him. It was difficult to remember Dominic possessed those qualities when they were constantly being overshadowed by this maddening cynicism and mockery. Oh, she just didn't understand him. She turned away from him and looked instead at the purple-hazed mountains in the distance, blinking rapidly to keep back the tears. She didn't understand any of the people of this strange, wild land. How could brutality and gentleness exist hand in hand?

According to Silver, Dominic was suffering for her sake. There was so much pain in the world and one could only bear it with as much courage as possible. No! The rejection of that meek homily came immediately and with violence, jarring her out of the tearful apathy and confusion into which she had fallen. She was *not* going to sit calmly and "bear" anything ever again. The words she had heard Silver speak when she had fought her way up from the depths of sleep came back to her. She had thought she had been behaving with boldness and aggressiveness since her father's death, but she realized now it had been a mere travesty of strength. She had not been strong, she had been pitifully weak. Instead of solving her problems herself, she had nagged and prodded Dominic for help. If she had possessed true strength of will, she could have somehow prevented Andre's death last night.

"Elspeth?" A tiny frown creased Silver's brow beneath the turquoise-beaded headband. "What is it? Don't you feel well?"

Elspeth nodded. "I was just thinking about Andre." She closed her eyes, shutting out Dominic and Silver and all the support and warmth they lent her by their presence. Loneliness. Aching loneliness and the beginning of panic rippled through her. She would feel better, she assured herself in swift desperation. She had really been alone all her life and this was no different. When she spoke again her voice was only a thin thread of sound. "I was thinking about Andre, and about strength."

"There she is." Silver's voice held a strange tension as the wagon rolled onto the flagstones of the courtyard. "I should have known she'd be up and about."

Elspeth struggled to a sitting position, her glance following Silver's to the front door of the imposing house. "Who?"

"The old woman. Dominic's mother, Malvina Delaney."

Malvina Delaney stood in the shadows of the alcove sheltering the carved double doors. As the wagon drew closer, she stepped onto the flagstones of the courtyard. Elspeth judged her to be about sixty years old, her hair was still more brick-red than gray and her broad-boned face more interesting than attractive. She was tall and full-figured and wore a simple yet fashionable violet gown.

"It's about time you came to your senses, Dominic." Malvina Delaney said bluntly. Her tone of voice was unsoftened by the faint Irish lilt that enriched the sound of her words. "You should have brought the girl to me when the accident happened instead of calling on Silver. I tried to send Patrick to fetch you both when he told me about this foolishness, but the boy refused to budge from Killara."

Silver stiffened. "There was no reason to bring her here. I took very good care of her. Better than you could have done." She lifted her chin. "Better than anyone could have done. We had no need of you."

"Then why are you here now?" The older woman asked dryly. "Just passing through?"

Dominic jumped down from the buckboard. "Be quiet, Silver." He faced his mother. "We had to leave Hell's Bluff. Something happened that make it difficult for Elspeth to stay."

Malvina's gaze flew swiftly to Elspeth, raking her in swift appraisal. "Is she with child?"

"No." Dominic's reply was as curt and blunt as the question.

Malvina's expression reflected first skepticism and then disappointment. "Patrick said you hadn't bedded her, but I thought . . ." She shrugged. "She must be sicker than Patrick believed."

"You think a woman has to be on her deathbed to escape me?" Dominic's lips twisted. "Well, I guess a mother should know her own son."

Malvina nodded slowly. Her eyes glittered in the sunlight. "I know you." She took a step closer and suddenly reached out, her arms enveloping him in a fierce embrace. "Welcome home," she said huskily.

"Don't expect us to kill the fatted calf for you. As it is, we've had trouble rounding up enough cattle for a trail drive this year."

Dominic's arms came around her and gave her an equally fierce hug. "Patrick told me Da sold the south herd and the White Sulphur land to get the money to buy my pardon. It's a wonder you even let me set foot on the place."

"Patrick talks too much." Malvina took a step back, her arms falling to her sides. "It was Shamus's decision to sell. He wanted you free to come home." Her gaze turned to Elspeth. "She's a little pale and puny-looking, but if she's what you want, I guess we can work her into some kind of—"

"There seems to be a misunderstanding," Elspeth interrupted quickly. She instinctively straightened her spine and braced herself as if to withstand a gale-force wind. Indeed, she had felt she had been buffeted by those winds since Malvina Delaney ahd stepped out of the shadows to meet them. The woman exuded the same forceful presence as her son and Elspeth hadn't a doubt about her passionate devotion to him or her willingness to permit him to have whatever took his fancy. "I thank you for your hospitality, but I'll be staying only a few days, Mrs. Delaney."

Malvina Delaney studied her coolly, her hazel eyes narrowed. "We don't hold with formality here. My name is Malvina, and I seldom misunderstand my boys. Dominic has gone to a parcel of trouble for you, and he's not a man to put himself out unless he has a reason. You could do worse than to take Dominic as your man."

"That's enough." Dominic shook his head resignedly as he turned away from his mother. "I know better than try to change your mind when it's set, but if you make Elspeth uncomfortable, I'll have to take her away again."

Malvina's eyes widened in surprise. "I have no intention of making the girl uncomfortable. Fact is, I'm going to make sure she's given every consideration; I'll even move Brianne out of the best bedroom and let Elsepth have it." She beamed at Dominic. "Why don't you carry her upstairs while I go get Rosa to air out the clean linens?"

Dominic gazed at her suspiciously. "We'll have to find a place for Silver to sleep. She'll stay with Elspeth until she's well again."

Something flickered in Malvina's eyes and then was gone as her glance touched on Silver and then slid away. "She can sleep with Rising Star. Joshua and Patrick are over at Shamrock helping Cort and Sean build the new barn."

"What happened to the old one?" Dominic asked.

Malvina smiled grimly. "Anne's boy, William. He was sneaking a smoke in the hayloft and managed to set the place on fire. At least he got the horses out before the barn went up."

Dominic gave a low whistle. "I'll bet Da skinned him alive."

"He was tanned good and proper." Malvina nodded. "Brianne felt sorry for him and begged Shamus to let him off with nothing more than a good hiding. She's been over at Shamrock every day trying to keep William out of mischief while the men are raising the barn."

Silver noticed the bewildered expression on Elspeth's face and took pity on her. "Anne is the wife of Desmond Delaney, Dominic's older brother. Desmond wanted a place of his own and Shamus built them a cabin across the San Pedro river and gave them enough cattle to start the Shamrock spread. Then when Desmond was killed in the war, Shamus sent Cort and Sean to run Shamrock and help Anne raise William." She smiled grimly. "God knows she needs all the help she can get to tame that young hellion."

"Then William is your cousin?" Elspeth's brow wrinkled thoughtfully, trying to set the branches of the large family in place in her mind.

Silver hesitated as her gaze locked with Malvina Delaney's. Then she smiled slowly, her defiant eyes never leaving the older woman. "Yes, William is my cousin. You should have sent me to Shamrock to help with William, old woman. Who should know better how to handle a hellion than a savage?"

Malvina's face betrayed no reaction to Silver's challenge. She merely said, "Sean and Cort manage pretty well on their own." She turned to Dominic. "Shamus is in the library. He'll want to see you when you finish settling in."

Dominic nodded as he walked to the back of the wagon. "I want to see him too." He wrapped the blanket around Elspeth and picked her up in his arms.

"I can walk," she protested even as her arms slid around his shoulders and her eyes met his. Her breath was suddenly shallow and she experienced the same melting heat she had known yesterday afternoon when he had told her wanted her. No, that was not what he had said. He had told her he wanted a woman. *All cats are gray in the dark.* Then he had left her for Rina's place and a woman to satisfy his lust. Still knowing that, she felt every muscle and bone in her body reacting to his touch. "I *want* to walk."

His arms tightened around her. God, she mustn't fight him now. Not now, when there were too many raw emotions tearing at his control, hovering just below the surface and waiting to break free. He turned toward the front door his mother had left ajar. "Just because you want to walk doesn't mean it's best for you to do so. Since I've met you, you haven't shown many signs of having a well-developed sense of self-preservation. Don't worry, you won't have to put up with me handling you for much longer." Her eyes were wide and glistening with a breathless expectancy. Or was it fear? The answer seemed inconsequential to his body which responded as if she were stroking him. With an effort he pulled his gaze away from her, pushed open the door with his foot, then strode into the foyer.

Malvina gazed after them, her expression a mixture of triumph and satisfaction. "Patrick was right," she murmured. "He wants her."

"So?" Silver jumped down from the wagon, her

eyes narrowed on Malvina's face. "There is an entire whorehouse of women back in Hell's Bluff who Dominic has wanted at one time or another."

"Not like this." Malvina didn't take her gaze from the entrance through which Dominic had disappeared. "This one is different." She added absently, "And, Silver, a good woman isn't supposed to know about whorehouses, much less speak of them."

Silver stared down at her in disbelief. She should have been accustomed to Malvina after all these years, but the old lady's dual nature still managed to surprise her. The ruthless drive and practicality that made her a fitting match for Shamus should have been at odds with her facade of respectability. However, Malvina had managed to harness both her natural instincts and her ambitions so that they rode in tolerable, if not always comfortable, tandem. "But I am not a lady," Silver said, softly taunting. "We all now what I am, don't we, Malvina?"

Malvina's gaze shifted to Silver's face. For an instant Silver thought she saw a glimmer of compassion and the faintest trace of regret. Then her grandmother's face was once again impassive. "Just because you're a savage is no reason why you have to act like one. You've had a decent upbringing and Rising Star would be very displeased to hear you talking like a common guttersnipe." Her lips tightened. "If you want to stay at Killara to take care of the girl, you're going to have to watch your tongue. Brianne picks up enough bad language from her menfolks without you adding to it."

Silver kept her expression totally free from any hint of pain. Why did she let the old lady's words hurt her? She didn't need the old man or his wife or any of the Delaneys. "I'll say what I like. Do you think I care what you think of me? I wouldn't be here if Elspeth didn't need me, and the minute she is well, I will be gone."

"Perhaps that would be wise. You've never been comfortable here."

No, comfortable was certainly not the word for

Silver's feelings during her stays at Killara. Hunger, eagerness, resentfullness were far closer to the mark, but never had there been either security or comfort for her here. She raised her chin, her gray eyes glittering with defiance. "I did not choose to be here. I did not want you any more than you wanted me." She started for the door, moving with grace and majestic pride. "And I do not want you now. I may say the word, but I am not a whore nor do I make others into whores to suit my ends as you do."

"What do you mean?" Malvina's brow was furrowed in a frown.

Silver looked over her shoulder. "You know what I mean. I saw your face when you realized Dominic wished to bed Elspeth. You think she may be used as a weapon to keep him here."

"You're speaking foolishness. I would do no—" She broke off as she met Silver's contemptuous eyes and glared back at her with equal intensity. "Why not? He *belongs* here. Dominic hasn't been back to Killara more than five times in the last ten years. Shamus and I have done without him long enough. If the girl can hold him, why shouldn't he have her? He's a fine man and there's no reason why she should refuse him. She wants him between her legs as much as he wants to be there. You saw that as clearly as I did."

Silver nodded. "I saw it. But she does not know that she wants him. Her head is full of clouds and dreams of lost cities." She smiled icily. "And, until she does know she wants him, you are not going to push Dominic into bed with her, old woman. I'll be here to see to that."

"Will you?" Malvina smiled with a confidence that was not without a touch of pity. "Dominic has to be made to realize he has to stay here on Killara. It's the only place he'll be safe from Durbin, so don't get in my way, Silver. I can't afford to be kind."

"Kind?" Silver laughed shakily. "I do not remember you ever being kind to me."

"Don't you?" Malvina's smile faded and she suddenly looked old and terribly weary. "Perhaps you're right. I think I tried to be kind at one time, but you were always a difficult child and the situation was . . . complicated."

"Yes, I can see how 'complicated' it would be for you." Silver turned away. "It was lucky I never needed your kindness. I did not care, you know." She walked swiftly toward the door, carefully keeping her voice from betraying anything but scorn. "I never cared for any of you or your precious family. Not for a minute."

The door slammed shut behind her.

"Your home is very grand," Elspeth said breathlessly. She looked up at a black wrought-iron chandelier gracing the ceiling of the foyer. "I don't see how you can bear to live away from this house. It looks very Latin."

"Mexican." Dominic was climbing the curving staircase, the heels of his boots clipping loudly on the polished mahogany steps. "It would be strange if it didn't look Mexican. It was built by the vaqueros on the ranch, and their idea of a palace was their *patron's* rancho back home in San Felipe. When Da told them he wanted a palace fit for a queen, this is what they built for him.

"A palace," Elspeth repeated with an uncertain laugh. "Your father was obviously a very ambitious man. Did he want a kingdom to match his palace?"

He looked down at her in surprise. "Of course; he never intended anything else. That's why he left Ireland and came to America. There he could remain only what he was, a reiver and a smuggler and my mother only a housemaid in a lord's house. When Da married her, he promised he would give her a palace someday and that they would rule a land as wide and rich as all Ireland."

"And she believed him?"

"You haven't met Da yet. He's not a man who makes a promise lightly. Killara isn't quite as large as Ireland yet." His lips tightened. "The first thing we have to do is get back the land Da sold last year and then branch out. I've been thinking that maybe we should start acquiring land in Texas. There's not a hell of a lot of land in this territory that can support the herds we're going to be running once the railroad comes in. Our herds are smaller than they could be, and the cattle lose too much of their fat on the trail drives to market." His brow furrowed thoughtfully. "Maybe when one of my claims hits, I'll be able to—" He broke off and looked down at her. "Why are you laughing?"

"I was just thinking that your father isn't the only one with dreams of vast kingdoms," she said. "I think you have a few aspirations in that direction yourself."

The eagerness faded from Dominic's expression. "Perhaps you're right. I guess I like the idea of running a kingdom as much as he does. My father and I are cut from the same cloth. The only difference is that he's a builder and I'm a destroyer."

"What do you mean?" She had never seen him like this. They had reached a certain level of intimacy in these last few weeks, yet she realized now she didn't really know him at all. She had never seen the eagerness or excitement that had illuminated him when he had spoken of his plans for Killara, nor had she seen the pain and bitterness that was on his face now.

He shrugged. "Never mind. It doesn't matter." He was walking swiftly down the corridor, passing a number of polished wood doors. "I think you'll be comfortable in Brianne's room. She was the first girl born in the family and we all kind of spoil her. If Killara is a kingdom, then Brianne is our princess."

"She's very lucky. It must be wonderful to be a member of such a large and close-knit family." Elspeth tried to keep the wistfulness from her voice. "I hope she won't mind me ousting her from her bed-chamber."

"Not Brianne. She doesn't mind anything but being bored. To her, any change has to be for the better. It wouldn't surprise me if she talks Da into letting her spend the night with some of her friends in the Mexican village."

There was warm affection in his tone. It appeared Dominic was as fond of the Delaney "princess" as he was of her twin brother, Patrick. "Village? I didn't see a village on the way here."

Dominic paused in front of a door at the end of the hall and shifted his hold on her to open it. "It's over the hill, beyond the family cemetery. Da wanted it close enough so that a shot could bring the vaqueros running when they were needed but far enough away to give us privacy." He was striding toward a canopy bed whose rosewood headboard towered a startling nine feet and was crowned in the center with the carved head of a deer. The canopy and coverlet gracing the large bed were a rich bottle-green velvet. Plump, cozy pink roses patterned the thick beige carpet on the floor, and graceful green vines curved in feathery trails on cream-colored wallpaper. A black lacquer vanity and full-length oval mirror were luxuries a true princess would have envied, Elspeth mused. It was difficult not to compare this magnificent chamber with her own starkly ascetic room in her home in Edinburgh.

Dominic placed her on the bed and stepped back. "Silver should be here in a moment. Is there anything I can get you before I leave?" His words were impeccably polite.

She experienced a throb of disappointment, bewildering in its intensity. For a few moments she had thought she had come closer to understanding him than ever before, and now he had once more shut the door on revelation. The room that had seemed so welcoming was suddenly chill and foreign and the man before her was a stranger too. How else could she expect to feel in a place where young men could be taken out and hung like fowl in a butcher shop? She swallowed to ease the sudden nausea that assaulted her along with the memory of the hanging. She sat up hurriedly and smiled with an effort. "No, thank you." She smoothed a strand of pale brown hair neatly behind her ear with nervous fingers. "I'll be quite all right. Your mother said your father wished to see you, and I wouldn't want you to keep him waiting."

He hesitated, his eyes narrowed on her face. Then he sat down beside her on the bed. "A few more minutes won't hurt."

"No, really I—"

"I'm staying," he said flatly. "My mother was right, you're pale as death. I thought once you were away from Hell's Bluff it would be better. It's not, is it?"

She shook her head. "I keep remembering," she whispered. "I keep seeing. . . . You were there. You know what I see."

He nodded. "And I can't promise you it will go away, but it will lessen. In the meantime, you'll just have to try to think of something else." He smiled with surprising gentleness. "Would you like me to tell you about how my father managed to give my mother her palace?"

"You said your vaqueros had built it. 'Vaquero' is Spanish for cowboy, isn't it?"

He nodded. "It was little more involved than that actually. Sixteen years ago Da couldn't have afforded to build anything grander than a teepee. We'd been burned out three times by the Apaches and every time we gathered a decent herd together, the Indians raided us again, putting us right back where we started. Da finally managed to get one herd to market and decided he had to do something." He paused, a reminiscent smile touching his lips. "We crossed the Rio Grande and rode deep into Mexico to a village called San Felipe. Da had heard the whole country was suffering from a terrible drought at the time and the herds down there were skin and bones. But Lord, they were cheap." His grin deepened. "Very, very cheap. None of us spoke more than a few words of Spanish but Da managed to make himself understood. He bought any animal on four feet down to the last heifer and made a deal with every able-bodied man in the village to come back to Killara and work for us. He promised them wages, a place to build their own homes on the property, schooling for their children. They didn't have anything to lose and everything to gain. It was the kind of arrangement they understood on the ranchos down there. They accepted Da as their *patrón* and helped us drive the cattle home to Killara. Then we turned around and went back and moved the entire village of San Felipe to Killara." He made a face. "Hell, it was harder than shifting those longhorns. They brought everything with them, wheelbarrows carrying everything from furniture to pots and pans, and wagons filled with babies, grandmothers, chickens, and geese." He shook his head. "And mules. My God, how I hated those mules. There aren't any more devilish creatures on the face of the earth than those sons of Satan. I was only fourteen, but I felt as if I were ninety and climbing fast by the time we reached Killara."

A tiny smile tugged at her lips. She could almost see the young boy, Dominic, trying to deal with that motley collection of humanity and animals. "You carry your years very well. You don't look a day over thirty," she teased.

"Because I make sure I don't come within a mile of those long-eared fiends these days." He looked down at her hand on the velvet coverlet. Such a small hand, fine-boned, graceful, and fragile. Without thinking, he started to reach out and touch her. He stopped, letting his hand fall to the coverlet a few inches from her own. "Well, Da got his herd and my mother got her fine house. Da told the vaqueros if they'd build him a great house, he'd see that they would never have to worry about a place to live or work again. My brother Donal even found a bride down there, which was a damn good thing. We might not have gotten this place built for another ten years without Manuela to interpret for us." He grinned. "Come to think of it, the reason this place looks like one of those fancy hidalgo's haciendas is probably Manuela's doing. She was the daughter of a Spanish nobleman visiting in San Felipe when Donal met her, and she never did like the idea of living with a bunch of wild gringos. It's entirely possible she told the vaqueros we wanted a house like the ones she was used to in Spain. After Donal died she sure hightailed it back to Spain in a

hurry to live with her more 'respectable' relations."
His smile faded. "But she took her son, Lion, with her.
She had no right to do that. He was a Delaney and
Donal's son. He belonged to Killara."

She was gazing at him in wonder. "You love them
all, don't you? Every single Delaney who walks the
earth."

"They're my family," he said simply. "My blood. We
don't always agree, but the bond is there. We're a part
of each other and a part of Killara."

Elspeth felt again a piercing envy born out of her
loneliness. She looked down at Dominic's big, tanned
hand on the bed beside her. Why had he stopped
before he touched her? She would have liked to have
had the comfort of his hand on hers. But would it have
been comfort? There was an odd tingling in the center
of her palms as she thought about Dominic's fingers
moving on her flesh. His fingers were long and hard
and yet there had been no hardness as they had
moved down to curl in. . . . Her cheeks suddenly
flushed and she tried to remember what Dominic had
been saying. "You're very fortunate." Her words came
haltingly and she swallowed to ease the tightness of
her throat. "Sometimes families aren't quite so amia-
ble."

The velvet coverlet was soft beneath his fingers, and
he began to rub his palm lazily back and forth,
enjoying its texture. His index finger began to thrust
absently, rhythmically, into its soft pile. There
weren't many textures as sensually pleasing to the
touch as velvet. At the moment he couldn't remember
anything that equaled it except Elspeth's silky white
thighs, her tight springy curls clinging seductively to
his fingers. The muscles of his stomach began to knot
painfully and the air left his lungs. His hand slowly
closed on the fabric of the coverlet, his nails rending
its delicacy with unconscious force. He cleared his
throat but his voice was still a hoarse rasp. "So I
understand. You're right, I've been lucky."

"You can leave us now, Dominic." Silver stood in
the doorway. "You heard your mother, the old man
wants to see you."

For a moment Dominic was tempted to order Silver out of the room. He was hurting. He wanted to lock the door and lie down on this big soft bed beside Elspeth and take off— Christ, he couldn't stand much more of this. He forced his hand to unclench and release the velvet captured in his clasp and then stood up. "See that she has breakfast and then a good rest."

"I don't need you to tell me what to do," Silver said harshly. "I don't need anyone—" She stopped. "Get out!"

Dominic frowned, his gaze on her flushed cheeks and overbright eyes. "Silver, what the devil is wrong with you?"

"Get out! The patron wants his prodigal son. No fatted calf but . . ." She bit her lip and came forward to stand beside the bed. "Elspeth and I don't need you now."

"And I don't need either of you," Elspeth said quietly. "It's time I began to take care of myself. I'll stay here and rest for a few days and then I'll start for Kantalan."

Dominic slowly shook his head. "Why the hell won't you give up?"

"Because what I feel for Kantalan is very close to what you feel for Killara." She raised her hand to stop him as he started to speak. "You needn't be afraid that I'll badger you any longer to go with me. I realize now how unfair I was being to assume I had a right to demand that of you." Her lips were trembling as she tried to smile at him. "You were quite right to be annoyed with me. I'll just have to find Kantalan on my own."

"And how do you intend to do that?" Dominic's voice was harsh with barely concealed violence.

"I'll find the other person White Buffalo spoke to about Kantalan and question him about how to get there. Perhaps Silver could take me to her village and persuade White Buffalo to speak to me." Elspeth's gaze shifted to Silver's face. "If it wouldn't be too much trouble? I know I've already asked a great deal of you."

"White Buffalo is dead," Silver said. "Quiet Thunder is the medicine man now."

"Oh!" Elspeth was momentarily disconcerted and then brightened. "Then perhaps I could speak to him. The legend is supposed to be handed down from medicine man to medicine man."

Dominic frowned. "For God's sake, you can't go riding into an Apache camp and start asking questions. Geronimo . . ."

"I've never done anything to hurt them," Elspeth said. "Why should they hurt me when I want only to ask a few questions? Will you take me, Silver?"

Silver's golden face lit with a reckless smile. "Why not? I have no desire to stay in this house."

Dominic was torn between the desire to turn Silver over his knee and whale the tar out of her and an aching sympathy for the hurt he knew she was feeling. He had known as soon as he had seen Silver's face that his mother had said something that stung. They couldn't be together for five minutes without a quarrel erupting. He supposed it was natural for two strong women to be in conflict, but it was damnably inconvenient that Silver had been goaded to defiance at the same time Elspeth decided to exert her independence.

"Good, then it's decided," Elspeth said. "Thank you, Silver. I'll try—"

"No!" Dominic's low voice was explosive. "If you think I'm going to let you leave here and wander all over hell and back on some wild goose chase, you're dead wrong."

Elspeth frowned. "I don't know why you should be upset. I should think you'd be grateful. Perhaps you didn't understand me. I'm no longer asking you to do anything to assist me. Thank you for your concern, but you needn't trouble yourself about me at all from now on."

"Oh, needn't I?" Grateful? He wanted to put his hands around her slender white throat and strangle her. How dare she try to calmly dismiss him from her life. Didn't she realize she belonged . . . He blocked

the thought before it could take full form. Didn't she
realize how idiotic she was being? She would get
herself scalped or raped, possibly both, and all because she wouldn't give up a damned childish dream.
He rose and turned on his heel. "That's a great relief
to me. I certainly don't have the time to worry about a
crazy woman." He strode quickly toward the door,
every step radiating impatience and anger. "You can
do what you please."

"Thank you." Elspeth's voice was low and clear
behind him. "I shall."

Dominic closed the door behind him with a force
that was only a shade away from a slam. He stood
beside the door, his hands clenched into fists at his
sides. Jesus, she was going to do it. She meant what
she said and wouldn't ask him again to take her to
Kantalan.

The knowledge should have relieved him, but not
when he realized what Elspeth's next step would be.
He started down the hall toward the door at the far
end of the corridor. He should go down to the library
to Da, but it would have to wait. At the moment it was
urgent he speak to Rising Star.

11

A white mist, enormous dark eyes, and clear, gentle serenity.

Elspeth drifted softly up from the darker mists of slumber to look at the strange woman sitting in the tufted green velvet chair beside the bed. She felt no sense of unease or surprise, just the same tranquility that had flooded her when she had opened her eyes. "Hello," she whispered.

"Hello." The woman's voice was mellow as dark honey and a lovely smile lit her dusky face. "I hope you will forgive my intruding on your privacy. I asked my niece to permit me to sit with you until you awakened from your nap. I am Rising Star. I am married to Dominic's brother, Joshua."

Elspeth sat up quickly. "I'm very happy to meet you."

The woman before her was in her late twenties or early thirties and was as different from Silver as the sun was from the moon. The burning vitality that fueled every movement and action of her niece was missing in Rising Star. She sat in the chair as straight and graceful as a young queen, her loose white gown unable to disguise the fact that her slim body was heavy with child. Her thin high-cheekboned face was dominated by huge dark eyes that shone with humor and warmth, and her smile was truly beautiful. Glossy dark hair was pulled away from her face in a neat bun, every tendril carefully trained to smooth order.

165

"Dominic came to see me." Rising Star's lips curved in amusement. "He was most upset. I would be interested to know how you accomplished that feat. Dominic prides himself on his control. I haven't seen him lose his his composure since he was a young boy." The smile faded. "He had reason to develop control; his life has not been easy."

"You've known him for a long time? I understood he had returned to Killara only infrequently during the last ten years."

Rising Star nodded. "Yes, but I grew to know him well the year after I married Joshua. We became very close." She paused. "We shared . . . something. It became a bond." Her lashes lowered to veil her eyes as she looked away from Elspeth's face. "This morning he came to ask me to send a message to Quiet Thunder and tell him not to help you."

A swift flame of anger sprang to life within Elspeth. "That wasn't fair. He may not want to help, but he has no right to try to hinder me."

"No, he doesn't," Rising Star said. "Dominic hasn't learned that there are some patterns that can't be altered no matter how we try. He thinks if he denies that Kantalan exists, the prophecy will not come true."

"You *know* about Kantalan?" Elspeth's face was alive with excitement and eagerness. "What prophecy?"

Rising Star leaned her head on the high back of the chair, her gaze on the green velvet of the canopy. "Dominic does not want you to know. He is wrong. I told him that I would not put barriers in your way, and that I might decide to tell you everything. We must make our own choices." She shook her head wearily. "Though in the end there may be no choice for any of us. White Buffalo said the pattern was very clear."

"The prophecy," Elspeth said, scarcely breathing. She was so close after all these years. "Do you know where Kantalan is located? Did White Buffalo tell you?"

"Yes." Rising Star was silent a moment. "I've

known about Kantalan since my fourteenth year. After my rites of womanhood White Buffalo took me to his lodge and told me of the prophecy."

Elspeth held her breath, her heart pounding, afraid to say anything, afraid to do anything that might stop Rising Star from speaking.

Rising Star's gaze left the canopy to return to Elspeth. "What do you know of Kantalan?"

Elspeth moistened her lips with her tongue. "It's a city as architecturally beautiful as Babylon, whose people were peace-loving and more civilized than the ancient Greeks. They had acquired knowledge that was truly astounding. They worshiped the sun god, Ra, as the Egyptians did, and they loved beauty and art and music and—" She stopped. How could she put it into words? She finished simply. "It was paradise."

Rising Star shook her head. "No, not paradise. Kantalan was flawed."

"No!" The denial was as instinctive as it was violent. Elspeth drew a shaky breath. "I'm sorry. I didn't mean to raise my voice, but I think you must be wrong. The legends say it was a perfect city."

"A city is only as perfect as its people, and people are never perfect." Rising Star's lips tightened. "We work, we try, but our perfection, or lack of it, is always in the eye of the beholder."

There was a thread of pain in Rising Star's voice and Elspeth realized suddenly that the Indian woman was no longer speaking of either the poeple or the city of Kantalan, but something intensely personal.

Rising Star shook her head and tried to smile. "Centuries ago a young man named Cadra came to our village. He was very oddly and richly dressed and he wore around his throat a necklace of silver and turquoise. The young man knew many strange and wonderful things. Our wise men were like children compared to him. He could have become a god in their eyes, but he did not wish it. He said he had been sent by his mistress to live among them and tell the tale of Kantalan and prepare the way for the four who were to come after. Cadra became the medicine man of our tribe and lived with my people until he

died. He never took a wife and there were some who
said that his love was so great for the *clairana* he had
left in Kantalan that there was no room in his heart
for anyone else."

"*Clairana?*" Elspeth repeated. The word was unknown to her and yet oddly familiar. "That was the
name of his mistress?"

"No, *clairana* was her title. Sayan was the high
priestess of Kantalan, the keeper of the flames. She
saw visions of what was to come and many times
predicted disasters that enabled her people to keep
themselves from harm. She was the most honored
woman in Kantalan, and the priests of Ra were very
pleased with her." Rising Star smiled crookedly.
"Why shouldn't they be? They shone in her reflected
glory and soon came to think of it as their own. Then
their docile Sayan made a mistake. She fell in love
with a young soldier and they lay together. It was
forbidden for the high priestess to give herself, for
according to the traditions dictated by the priests, the
clairana must remain untouched. The priests declared
her no longer the *clairana* of Kantalan and told the
people that Ra had taken away her powers."

"But it wasn't true." It was a statement not a
question. Elspeth had the strange feeling she knew
every word Rising Star was going to say.

"No, it wasn't true, but no one would listen to her."
Raising Star's brow wrinkled thoughtfully. "I've often
wondered how she could bear it. I don't know if I
could have borne it in her place."

"She had pride. She was the *clairana*."

Rising Star nodded. "Yes, that must have helped, I
suppose. But when she saw the last vision, the
disbelief of the priests must have driven her mad."

The last vision. The holy flames burning in the
temple. The scented incense pouring slowly from her
hand into the fire, causing blue sparks to fly, the flame
to reveal its truth. Slowly Elspeth's eyes closed and
Rising Star's words swept over her, painting pictures,
lighting corners long darkened by time. She felt as if
she could actually see the young *clairana*, her dark

hair straight and flowing to her waist, as she stared into the flames.

"Kantalan is situated in a valley surrounded by mountains. The highest mountain was known as the Sun Child, a volcano. The people of the city became accustomed to the rumbling of its voice and the quaking of the earth. The Sun Child was Ra's child and they looked upon it with affection. The vision the *clairana* saw concerned the volcano. The Sun Child was going to spew out great billows of black smoke, poisonous smoke that would cover the entire valley and kill every living thing. Sayan went to the priests and begged them to send everyone away, to vacate Kantalan until the danger was over."

"They laughed at her." Elspeth could almost see them, their expressions scornful, their shaved heads adding to the ascetic sternness of their appearance. "They thought she was just trying to regain her status in the city. They called her a whore and sent her away."

"Yes." Rising Star's voice held a note of surprise. "Yes, they did. She decided to stay and accept the same fate as her people, but she sent her servant, Cadra, away to the north."

"And she died when Kantalan died, when Dalkar died."

"Dalkar?" Rising Star's voice was puzzled.

"Her lover." Elspeth's lids lifted heavily, dreamily. It was a moment before she could bring herself back from the ancient world that had seemed so real. "You told me his name was Dalkar."

"Did I?" Rising Star was staring at her uneasily. "I suppose I had to have told you. It must have slipped my mind." She rose to her feet and, for a fraction of a moment, she seemed flustered. Then, quite suddenly her serenity returned. "I believe I've given you enough to think about for the present. We'll talk again later." She crossed the room swiftly. "It's only an hour until dinner. I'll send Silver to help you dress."

"Wait," Elspeth called desperately. "You didn't tell me about the prophecy."

Rising Star paused, her hand on the doorknob. The

muscles of her back were taut and at first Elspeth thought she wasn't going to answer. Then she slowly turned to face Elspeth and smiled with an effort. "I was running away. You'll find I'm not a very courageous person. After all these years you'd think I'd be accustomed to the idea of—" She moistened her lips. "Sayan saw something else in the flames. She told Cadra that for centuries Kantalan would remain deserted, as if frozen in time. Then four people would once again walk its streets. When that day came, the Sun Child would tremble once more, fire would rain down, and Kantalan would be destroyed, disappearing from the face of the earth as if it had never existed." She paused. "Four would come to Kantalan and four would return from whence they came. Yet two would die when Kantalan died."

"That doesn't make sense. Is it some kind of riddle?"

Rising Star shrugged. "If it is, I don't have the answer."

"Do you believe it?"

Rising Star hesitated and then smiled sadly. "Sometimes I believe it. I've been taught there is a destiny for each one of us. What else can you expect from a superstitious savage?"

Elspeth could hear the echo of Silver's bitterness in Rising Star's words and experienced a pang of sympathy. "You think there is danger in Kantalan?"

Rising Star rubbed her temple wearily. "Oh, I don't know. There is danger everywhere. You must make the decision for yourself. If you still wish to go, I will draw you a map from the one White Buffalo gave me."

"Thank you, I would appreciate that very much," Elspeth said haltingly. She should be wildly happy, but it was difficult to throw off the chill that had struck her when Rising Star had told her of the prophecy. "Was Dominic given a map also?"

Rising Star's brows rose in surprise. "Of course. White Buffalo was a spirit man. He knew Dominic was one of the four who would walk the streets of Kantalan."

Elspeth's eyes widened. "Does that mean you—?"

Rising Star's lips twisted. "Oh, yes, from the moment of my birth White Buffalo knew that my destiny was to be fulfilled in Kantalan." She turned and opened the door. "And now there are three of us and only one more to come. The pattern is beginning to form." She glanced back over her shoulder. "Dominic has never known whether to believe the prophecy or not, but he has enough of his mother's Celtic mysticism to make him wary and enough of his father's cynicism to make it easy to ignore Kantalan's existence. Until now. You're forcing him to think of it again. Are you sure you want to do that?"

Elspeth shook her head. "I told him I didn't want him to go. It would be terrible to be responsible for—" She ran shaking fingers through her hair. "It's too wild and terrible to be true, legends become distorted and twisted through time. The prophecy could be nothing more than superstitious nonsense. I have to think."

Rising Star nodded. "Yes, we all need to think. White men believe we do have choices. Perhaps White Buffalo was only a foolish old man. None of us *have* to go to Kantalan." She smiled. "Do we?"

"No," Elspeth whispered. But if she didn't go, she would never see streets of matchless beauty, temples and pyramids of faultless symmetry, the Sun Child ribboned with glistening snow. "None of us *have* to go."

Rising Star's eyes were both sad and understanding as she gazed at Elspeth's wistful expression. "I won't see you at dinner. I prefer to have my meals in my room when Joshua isn't here. If you decide you want the map, let me know. But it would be no sin to wait a few days and consider the possiblities, would it?"

She didn't wait for an answer. The door closed softly behind her.

"You are very silent." Silver ran the silver-backed brush through Elspeth's hair with long, slow strokes. "Did my aunt's words disturb you?"

"Yes." Disturb seemed too mild a word to describe

the turmoil she was experiencing. "Rising Star certainly gave me a few things to consider."

"I did not know she knew of Kantalan or I would have told you." Silver's gaze met Elspeth's in the mirror of the black lacquered vanity. "I will go with you if you like. There is nothing for me here." She smiled bitterly. "There is nothing for me anywhere that I do not take for myself. Who knows? Perhaps I will find something different in your lost city."

Elspeth felt a surge of warm affection. "Oh, Silver, I would like that very—" She stopped. Even if Sayan's prophecy were mere legend as she was trying to believe, the journey itself might be very dangerous. She had already taken too much from Silver without giving anything in return. Friendship was new to her, but surely this was not as it should be. Even now Silver was treating her as if she were her handmaiden. She had bathed her and was now brushing her hair. And Elspeth was sitting here in her petticoats, almost purring with contentment and behaving as if this cosseting were her due. She reached out and took the brush from Silver's hand. "We will see. In the meantime, there is no need for you to treat me as an invalid. I'm almost well."

Silver's eyes widened. "It is no bother." She stood watching uncertainly as Elspeth began to run the brush vigorously through her hair, her expression reflecting a flicker of disappointment. "You are still weak. I am not sure you should go down to dinner."

"You've spoiled me far too long." Elspeth wrinkled her nose at her image in the mirror. "And I've allowed it far too long. It's time I took charge of myself."

Silver frowned and started for the armoire across the groom. "I'll get your gown. I had Rosa press it while you slept." She took out the black silk gown with the grograin trim and carried it back to Elspeth. "Though there was little that could be done with it. It is ugly. Everything I found in your trunk was ugly, except for that fine red blanket."

"That's not a blanket. That's a MacGregor plaid, my family's tartan."

Silver shrugged. "Well, it is finer than anything else

you own. Why is everything you wear black? You always look like a baby vulture."

"It's the custom. I'm in mourning for my father." Elspeth turned to look at the gown over Silver's arm. "It's only proper that I wear black."

Silver shook her head in wonder. "I have heard you scream and weep dreaming of this man. You do not mourn him. Why do you lie?"

"Of course I mourn him. He was my father." Elspeth stopped. Lies. Silver was right. When her father had died she had felt only relief and a poignant regret for the love that might have existed between them. Dear God, surely such an attitude must make her a wicked and ungrateful daughter. One must love and honor one's father. Her hand holding the brush dropped to her side as she stared blindly into the mirror. But she had *not* honored him. She had respected him for his truly superior intelligence, but there had been no honor and no love. Had the guilt of that realization made her cling to the trappings of tradition since she could not mourn him in her heart? Had she been deceiving herself about her honesty as she had about her strength? "You're very wise, Silver. I do not mourn him."

Silver grinned and tossed the gown carelessly on the bed. "Then you do not need this ugly dress any longer. We will find you something bright to wear that will make you want to sing like a lark."

Elspeth chuckled. "I certainly would prefer to be a lark instead of a vulture, but I'm afraid I'll have to wait until I return to Edinburgh. I have nothing but black clothing with me."

"I will ask Rising Star to lend you something pretty to wear." Silver had already reached the door. "She cannot wear her fine gowns since she has grown big with child. Put up your hair. I will be back."

She was gone, leaving Elspeth gazing blankly after her. As usual, Silver had taken matters into her own hands and Elspeth was moving along in her wake. Perhaps she should go after her and insist upon wearing her own clothing, as she certainly didn't wish to impose on Rising Star. As Elspeth started to get up, she glimpsed the black silk gown on the bed and suddenly realized that she hated the idea of wearing that drab gown. Its ugliness was not only in its color and clumsy fashioning but also in its reminder of her lack of courage during these past months. She deliberately sat back down on the stool and began to put her hair in its usual neat bun on top of her head.

The gown Silver borrowed was of white gauze with lace trim, demure, modest, and the most beautiful garment Elspeth had ever seen. The long tight sleeves and bodice fit her to perfection after Silver had pinned it at the waist. The lace trimming at the high neckline required no other ornamentation and made her neck appear long and queenly. The belled skirt drifted about her gracefully as she whirled to see herself in the cheval mirror. "I look so different."

Silver nodded with satisfaction. "An upside-down lily."

Elspeth laughed. She couldn't ever remember feeling this amazingly young and lighthearted.

"It could be better. I forgot that Rising Star does not wear colors. She does not like to displease the old woman, who thinks bright colors are not ladylike."

Elspeth looked at her in surprise. The violet gown Malvina had worn this morning had not been in the least restrained. "But Malvina wore—"

"I know." Silver's lips curved in a sardonic smile. "But the old woman is not Indian. Rising Star must be more careful."

"Your grandmother insists Rising Star be more circumspect in her dress than she is herself?"

"No," Silver admitted grudgingly. "She never says a word of reproof to my aunt. Rising Star is a Delaney, and though the old woman has no love for her, she treats her with honor and fairness. Rising Star has a great thirst for learning and the old woman respects her for that too." She turned away. "It is time to go downstairs; the old man likes his meals on time."

"Aren't you going to change?"

Silver looked down at the calico skirt, elkskin tunic, and beaded moccasins she was wearing. "Why? I am clean and my hair is combed. If they are not happy with me, then the old man can send me to the kitchen to eat with Rosa and Ricardo." There was a glint of furtive excitement in her eyes and her golden cheeks were flushed with color. "Shall we go see if he will do it?"

Silver actually hoped Shamus would respond to her rebelliousness, Elspeth realized with trepidation. She was obviously aching, burning, to be challenged. "You always look lovely." Elspeth frowned. "I'm sure it will be all right."

"We will see." Silver took Elspeth's arm with a gesture that held both defiance and bravado. Then, as they started for the door, an object lying on the vanity caught Silver's notice. "You've forgotten your spectacles. Shall I get them for you?"

Elspeth glanced back over her shoulder. "No, I'll get them." She turned and took a step toward the vanity. She stopped, looking at the spectacles and remembering Dominic's mocking words regarding them. Another self-deception? She hesitated. In a way this decision was more difficult than the one to cast off her mourning. She was nervous of the intimidating strangers she must meet tonight and the spectacles would have formed a protective barrier against them. The gold wire frames of the spectacles glinted enticingly, temptingly, in the lamplight. She drew a deep breath and forced herself to turn again toward the door. "No, I don't believe I'll wear them tonight. I don't really need them."

Shamus Delaney met them at the bottom of the steps. His smile was bold, warm, and held an impish charm that reminded Elspeth of his grandson, Patrick. "Ah, welcome, Miss MacGregor." His deep brogue lilted pleasantly as he held out his hand. "It's a good thing you decided to put in an appearance. I admit I was so eager to meet you, I was about to run upstairs and escort you down myself. I'm Shamus Delaney, and it's a rare pleasure to have you here at Killara."

"It's very kind of you to let me stay." Her small hand was immediately enveloped in his massive clasp. His palm was calloused and his strong grip made no allowances for her femininity. "I'll try not to trouble you any longer than necessary."

"Nonsense. Malvina will be disappointed if you run off before she can really get to know you, and I'm determined you won't leave us until you've seen all of Killara." His piercing blue eyes twinkled. "I'm proud as a peacock of my ranch. We've got everything you could want here in the Arizona territory. Your Edinburgh can't hold a candle to some of the sights I can show you."

Elspeth found herself melting beneath the beaming warmth of the old man. Old? The term seemed wrong when applied to Shamus Delaney. Though he must have been in his seventies, he stood ramrod-straight, his thin, rangy body still as powerful as that of a man of forty. He was dressed in a black suit and vest, crisp white shirt and gray tie, and his full mane of stark white hair shone softly under the flickering light of the candles in the chandelier. That totally white hair should have made him look older, but instead the silky purity of color made his weathered brown face appear younger in contrast. "You have a right to be proud of Killara. Your home is lovely."

He released her hand. "Malvina's done a fine job of it, hasn't she?" His voice was soft with affection and pride. "She reads all those fancy books and journals; she's particularly fond of that Miss Beetle's book on home management. She says all the fine ladies read it."

"I'm afraid I haven't heard of it." Elspeth found it hard to imagine Malvina Delaney poring over books and periodicals on homemaking. "But I've been in America for only a short time."

"It probably hasn't crossed over to the old country yet," Shamus Delaney said cheerfully as he took her arm. "But you mark my words, it will soon. My Malvina swears by it. You should have seen the hair picture she made from the directions in Miss Beetle's book." He chuckled. "Brianne swore she was going to strip her bald before the dang thing was finished, but it turned out real pretty. Come along, Malvina is waiting in the parlor to give us a little music before dinner. It looks like we'll have you to ourselves this evening. Dominic rode over to Shamrock this afternoon to see his brothers, and that wild granddaughter of mine hasn't come home yet." Shamus's gaze suddenly narrowed on Elspeth's face. "I hope you're not disappointed that Dominic isn't here. You two must have become very close friends lately."

Elspeth felt a surge of relief at the knowledge that she would not have to confront Dominic tonight. Her emotions regarding him were so chaotic that she had no desire to face him immediately. Rising Star's revelations and her own response to them must be absorbed before she was ready to speak to him again. "He has been very kind," she said stiltedly. "But it's always pleasant to get to know new people."

He nodded slowly, his gaze still searching her own. "That's true enough. You'll enjoy the little concert Malvina is going to give us. She plays the piano very well; she taught herself." The pride was again shining in his face. "There's nothing Malvina can't do once she sets her mind to it." Then, as his glance fell on Silver watching in the shadows of the curve of the staircase, his smile faded. "You know Malvina doesn't like to see you dressed in that heathen garb at her table, Silver. Go change."

Elspeth's gaze flew to Silver. The girl was standing perfectly still, glaring at Shamus Delaney. "No!"

For an instant there was an expression of utter weariness on Shamus's face before it hardened in annoyance. "Then I'll have Rosa send up some dinner to you. Delaneys don't serve savages in the dining room at Killara."

"No, they prefer savages to serve them in the bedchamber." Silver's eyes blazed clear and hot. "As my father demanded of my mother. Only he never bothered taking her to a bedchamber. A blanket thrown on the ground was good enough for an—"

"Shut your foul mouth." Shamus's eyes were suddenly glittering with fury. "I'll not have your impudence here."

Elspeth couldn't bear it any longer. Anger and pain held the two Delaneys captive. "No!" She turned and ran back up the stairs, her arm sliding protectively around Silver's shoulders. "I don't think I feel very well, Mr. Delaney. I believe I'd better go back to my room and lie down. Come with me, Silver."

"What?" Shamus's face expressed first surprise, then anger, and finally, grudging admiration. His lips twisted sourly. "I don't suppose you might recover if Silver joined us in the dining room?"

Elspeth nodded gravely. "Being with Silver always makes me feel better, Mr. Delaney. You're very lucky to have her as a member of your family."

It was a deliberate goad, but he failed to rise to the bait. "Yes, I'm very lucky in all my family." His gaze carefully avoided Silver as he bowed mockingly. "Malvina's waiting."

Elspeth kept a firm clasp on Silver's hand as she half-pushed, half-pulled the girl down the steps. "We're coming. I've always loved piano music."

"You haven't heard the old woman play," Silver muttered half beneath her breath. "You will wish you had gone back upstairs and covered your ears."

Elspeth learned what she meant in the next three quarters of an hour. Malvina drew sounds from the upright Chickering piano that were unbelievably unharmonious. Elspeth listened in amazement as Malvina thumped the keys with blatant disregard of tempo, her hazel eyes shining with enjoyment. Elspeth cast a surreptitious sidewise glance at Shamus sitting on the elegant amber tufted couch beside her and received another shock. His face shone with the same pleasure and pride as when he had earlier spoken glowingly of his wife's accomplishments. Great heavens, the man must be deaf not to recognize that Malvina was an abominable pianist.

Then, as Malvina finished the tune she was playing with a little flourish and turned to face them, Elspeth changed her mind. The look Malvina and Shamus exchanged was one of perfect understanding . . . and love.

"A delightful performance, my darlin'," he said softly. "You get better every time I hear you play."

Malvina's cheeks flushed with pleasure as she rose from the piano stool, her emerald taffeta skirts rustling far more harmoniously than her recent effort at the keys. "I thought you'd like it, Shamus." Malvina was suddenly no longer the grim, forceful woman Elspeth had met this morning. She was as eager and glowing as a young girl, her gaze shifted to Elspeth as if for approval.

What could she say? Elspeth wondered wildly. She moistened her lips with her tongue. "It's a very pretty tune. I don't believe I've ever heard it played quite like that before."

She heard a small rude explosion of sound from the window alcove where Silver was sitting. Elspeth carefully avoided looking at Silver and kept her polite smile firmly in place.

Without so much as a glance at Silver, Malvina turned with a sweeping movement of royal disdain. "There are some people who have no ear for music." She glanced at the fine bogwood clock that graced the mantel across the room. "It's growing late. We won't wait any longer for Brianne. Shall we go in to dinner?"

Shamus gallantly offered Elspeth his arm. "I told you we were in for a treat. Malvina could have been even better if she'd taken lessons when she was younger. She's been trying to teach Brianne how to play, but the girl won't sit still long enough to practice." He shook his head. "My granddaughter would rather be down at the Mexican village or riding herd with the vaqueros. Do you know what she begged me to get her for her birthday? A new saddle! Malvina wanted to send her to St. Louis to buy some pretty gowns, but Brianne wouldn't have any part of it. She wouldn't leave Killara." Affection and pride flickered in his expression. "She's a Delaney through and through."

Elspeth was growing more curious about Brianne Delaney by the moment. She obviously held a very special spot in the hearts of her grandparents, judging by Shamus's remarks. A Delaney through and through. She inhaled sharply as the tactlessness, even cruelty of those words impacted upon her. How did Silver feel to have her cousin spoken of with such warmth and affection while she was denied even recognition as a member of the family? It was incomprehensible to her that Shamus could be so warm and callous at the same time.

She cast an anxious glance over her shoulder at Silver as Shamus escorted her through the archway that separated the parlor from the dining room. She sighed with relief as she realized she needn't have worried about Silver's reaction. She doubted if Silver had even heard Shamus's words.

The young girl was standing by the piano, her fingers caressing the black and white keys with a loving touch. On her absorbed face was an expression that was an odd mixture of wistfulness, wonder, and hunger.

Elspeth was able to satisfy her curiosity regarding the Delaney "princess" a short time later. Brianne Delaney appeared in the dining room just as they were finishing their meal.

Her appearance was foreshadowed by the sound of the heavy front door being thrown open, the light clatter of boots on the tiles of the foyer, and then a hurried, breathless voice. "I *know* I said I'd be home for dinner, but William wanted to show me a pond he had run across in the foothills. And then when we got back to Shamrock, Dominic was there and I had to talk to him, didn't I? You know I haven't seen Dom since he dropped by last year and I couldn't just ride off without saying a word." A slim, delicate girl dressed in a dark brown riding skirt and white cotton blouse suddenly appeared in the archway. She paused to catch her breath and Elspeth was allowed a moment to absorb an impression of rich auburn hair in a single thick braid, green eyes dancing with humor and spirit, exquisite classic features saved from any hint of coldness by the faintest golden dusting of freckles over a small aristocratic nose. Brianne Delaney might be the Delaney "princess," but she was certainly down-to-earth royalty. She was too warm, too vital, too alive to be considered anything but entirely approachable.

Brianne's eyes brightened with curiosity as they fell upon Elspeth. She hurried forward, her hand outstretched. "How do you do. I'm Brianne Delaney and you must be Elspeth MacGregor. Patrick has told me all kinds of interesting things about you." Her grip was as strong and cordial as her grandfather's had been as she eagerly shook Elspeth's hand. "I've wanted to see London and Edinburgh since Rising Star persuaded Patrick and me to study geography with her."

"We can't even get you to St. Louis," Malvina said dryly.

"Someday." Brianne laughed. "There's plenty of time." She turned to Silver seated at the place next to Elspeth and gave her an affectionate wink. "Isn't that right, Silver? There's no hurry about leaving Killara when there's always so much to see and do here."

Silver returned her smile and Elspeth could see no hint of resentment in her expression. It would have been impossible for Silver not to be stung my the favoritism shown Brianne by her grandparents, but she obviously did not blame her cousin for their discrimination.

"You're too late for dinner," Malvina said with an effort at gruffness. "You'll have to grab a bite in the kitchen."

Brianne nodded. "Rosa will fix me something."

"And probably a better meal than she served us." Shamus grimaced as he shook his head with mock ruefulness. "She wouldn't want her *pequiña* to go hungry." Then the amusement faded from Shamus's face. "Did Patrick ride back with you?"

Brianne shook her head. "Cort told me he rode out of Shamrock five minutes after Dominic arrived."

Shamus frowned. "I thought he'd gotten over the

foolishness that made him fly up at Dominic. I'll have
to have a talk with him. It's not like Patrick to hold a
grudge."

Brianne avoided her grandfather's eyes as she said
lightly, "Give him a little time. Patrick won't let Dom
leave Killara without settling their differences." She
turned back to Elspeth. "Why don't I have Rosa fix me
a tray and bring it up to Rising Star's room? Then we
can get comfortable and you can tell me all about
Edinburgh and the journey across the sea and—"

"Miss MacGregor hasn't been well," Shamus said.
He turned to Elspeth. "You mustn't let this wild gypsy
impose on you."

"I don't feel at all tired." Elspeth found to her
surprise that it was true. She had been so fascinated
by the myriad complexities of the Delaney clan that
she felt as if they had lent her a large quantity of their
own vitality. "I would like very much to have a chat."
She smiled. "Though I imagine your account of your
life here will be a great deal more colorful than what I
can tell you. It's true I've done a good deal of traveling
but I've actually lived a very quiet life."

Brianne grinned impishly. "Well, from what Patrick
says, you've recently been making up for any past
monotony." She turned away and started for the door.
"Just give me ten minutes to talk to Rosa and then get
the smell of horse off me and I'll join you in Rising
Star's room."

"Elspeth is occupying your room because it's the
best bedroom," Malvina called after her. "And Dominic is occupying his old room, and Silver's here, so
you'll have to sleep in one of the guest rooms."

Brianne smiled and said over her shoulder, "I'll
sleep on the couch in the library. I've always loved the
smell of that room. The scent of ink and the leather
binding of the books and Gran-da's pipe tobacco . . ."

Then she was gone, her words drifting behind her as
they had rushed before her, in a bright, shining trail.

12

The flames of the candles in the wrought-iron chandelier had been extinguished and the hall was in darkness when Dominic opened the front door. He paused a moment, looking at the stairs and silently cursing the time it had taken him to ride from Shamrock. He had wanted to see Elspeth before she retired to her room and it was almost midnight. He had been worried all day about whether Rising Star had told Elspeth she had a map to Kantalan, and now he would have to wait until morning to find out. He shut the door quietly behind him and moved swiftly toward the curving staircase.

A door opened down the hall, releasing an arrow of light into the darkness and silhouetting the man standing in the doorway of the smoking room. "Dominic?"

Dominic paused with his foot on the first step. "Yes, Da."

"Come in and have a drink with me before you go to bed. How's the barn coming along?"

Dominic turned and walked toward him. "It should be finished by tomorrow evening. Josh told me to tell you he was going to ride up and check on those strays in the foothills before he came home."

Shamus nodded with satisfaction as he turned away from the door. "That's good." He crossed the room and dropped into the big chair by the fireplace. No fire burned in the dark grate on this warm night

183

and his father had discarded his jacket, vest, and tie and rolled his shirt-sleeves to the elbow. "I can always count on Joshua. He's a good, steady man." He picked up his half-empty glass of bourbon. "Get yourself a drink and let's have a talk."

Dominic smiled as he crossed the room to the cellarette and poured a small quantity of bourbon into a glass. This summons from his father was expected. During every visit to Killara there came a time when Da took him aside and tried either to bully or persuade him to his way of thinking. He might as well get it over with now as later. "Sean and Cort are doing a fine job with Shamrock." He turned back to Shamus. "Are you going to leave them there much longer?"

His father stretched out his legs before him and gave a long, mournful sigh. "I don't know if I can afford to do without them here on Killara. Cort is crazy to try his hand at some fancy horsebreeding at Shamrock and I'd hate to take him away, but I may have to do it." His heavy lids veiled his eyes. "After all, Killara is the primary property and I'm getting old. I can't be expected to shoulder the burden much longer."

Dominic's lips twitched. His father would as soon give up the burden of running Killara as he would give up his life. The rascal was positioning himself well in his first foray tonight. Dominic strolled toward the fireplace and seated himself in the wing chair opposite Shamus. "You have Josh. As you said, he's a good, steady man who eats, sleeps, and drinks Killara. You couldn't hope to have anyone better at your side."

"Yes, I could." Shamus's lids lifted to reveal keen blue eyes glinting sharply in the lamplight. "I could have you."

Dominic instinctively braced himself and tried to keep his face expressionless. "No, you can't have me. You don't even need me with Josh around."

"I do need you," Shamus growled. "The other boys are fine, but they don't have the hunger. They could keep Shamrock and Killara prospering, but they'd never reach out for more. Ever since you were a lad I've known that you had the same taste for power that I have. Together we could own the whole blame territory." His voice was fierce with intensity. "Hell, we could own the world!"

Dominic laughed, his eyes dancing. "You mean I'm as greedy a son of a bitch as you?"

"A little honest greed never hurt anybody; that's how empires are built. I've given you a fine start here with Killara and Shamrock. Why don't you see what you can make of it all?"

The challenge was almost irresistible, the lure of home, the opportunity to take hold and build, the companionship of the people he loved. Jesus, he wanted it all so much he could taste it on his tongue like the bourbon he had just sipped. He gazed blindly down into the amber liquid in his glass. "There's Patrick."

There was a snort of impatience from Da. "Do you want me to go down the list? Patrick is too young, it will be years before he's ready to take over. Sean and Cort are more interested in horsebreeding than cattle. God only knows when or where Falcon will turn up. He loves Killara, but he hasn't spent more than a month here since the start of the war. Joshua is steady but—"

"I *can't*." The words were wrung from Dominic. "Do you think I don't want to come home? God, I'd give my soul to—" He broke off and drew a deep, harsh breath. "It's not possible."

"Why?" His father pounced. "I bought you your damn pardon. It bled me white, but you're a free man now."

"I'm not a free man," Dominic said. He took a hefty swallow of bourbon. He needed it. "You know why I can't come back here. I told Patrick."

"You told Patrick you were afraid that one of us would get hurt if Durbin sent his hired guns here." His father was glaring at him. "Do you think we can't protect our own? This country is *mine*, and, by God, anyone who comes here will learn it."

"I can't risk it."

"Why the hell not?"

"No!" Dominic's gaze met his father's, his eyes blazing. "I know what can happen. I've seen it, dammit! And I'm not going to watch it happen again."

Shamus went still, his eyes narrowed on Dominic's face. "Watch what happen?"

Dominic drew a deep breath and leaned back in his chair. He should have known Da would claw until he got to the root of his resistance. "Two years ago I was in Virginia City. I was doing a little gambling, a little prospecting, anything that would keep me fed. It wasn't a good time for me." He looked down at the glass in his hand, recalling just how bad a time it had been for him. "I'd been on the run for eight years and there were times I almost wished I'd get caught, just to have it over. I was tired of moving from town to town, tired of never being safe, tired of never being able to get close enough to anyone to call him a friend. I met a young farmer in a saloon in town. His name was Sam Bergstrom, and I think he was the only man in Virginia City who didn't want to strike it rich. All he wanted was enough money to buy a farm and bring his parents over from Sweden. He was a kid, not much older than Patrick. I liked him a lot and we became friends." His hand tightened on the glass. "For a while it made life . . . bearable."

"Only for a while?" Shamus asked quietly.

Dominic nodded jerkily. "I was stupid. I shouldn't have taken the chance, but I wasn't really thinking. Two bounty hunters showed up about a month later. They weren't good enough with a gun to face me, so they decided to bushwhack me." His lips twisted bitterly. "But not in Virginia City. The vigilantes were strong as hell there, and they didn't take kindly to outright murder. One morning I got a note telling me to show up at a line shack outside of town or they'd blow Sam's head off." He finished the remaining bourbon in the glass in one swallow. "They'd heard in town that Sam was my friend and decided to use him as bait. They ambushed me on the way to the shack, but I'd been expecting it and got away from them. As I said, they weren't very good. I went on to the shack and found Sam." His words quickened, he wanted to get it over with. "They'd shot him in the head. I suppose he was just in the way and they'd decided to get rid of him. He was probably dead before they even wrote that note." He closed his eyes. "God, he was only nineteen."

"You killed them?"

"I killed them." Dominic opened his eyes to reveal a chilling bleakness. "I left the shack and went after them, and I didn't make it easy. It was the only time I've ever enjoyed taking a life." He set his glass down on the table beside him. "Not that it did any good. Sam was dead and I couldn't bring him back."

Shamus was silent for a moment. "It's not the same situation. The boy was helpless, and he wasn't a Delaney. We can take care of ourselves." He smiled grimly. "I'd like to see anyone come here and try to take you."

Dominic shook his head. "Well, I wouldn't like it, and it's not going to happen." He stood up. "I think I'll go to bed. Good night, Da."

"I'm not giving up, you know."

"I know," Dominic said softly. Da never gave up. It was one of the characteristics he admired most about his father. "And neither am I."

Shamus smiled suddenly. "But I have all the aces, Dominic. You want to come home, and we want you here. I'll find a way to keep you at Killara, where you belong." His eyes were narrowed thoughtfully. "I already have a few ideas on how I'm going to do it."

Dominic shook his head in amusement as he strolled toward the door. "I'm leaving in three days and going back to Hell's Bluff. That doesn't give you much time."

"Time enough." Shamus's voice took on silkiness as he continued. "By the way, Patrick didn't tell you the complete price of that pardon I had to buy for you. I didn't choose to tell him or the rest of the family just how greedy those politicians in the governor's office turned out to be."

Dominic stopped as if he'd been struck by a bullet. He turned around and gazed silently at Shamus. Waiting.

"I had to take a mortgage out on Killara," Shamus said softly, not looking at Dominic. "A very large mortage."

"God," Dominic whispered.

Shamus's gaze rose to meet his son's. "We could lose Killara. It needs every one of us to keep it alive, to keep it growing." He smiled with catlike satisfaction as he saw how upset Dominic was. "You might keep that thought in mind during the next three days, son." He stood up. "I believe I'll go to bed too. An old man like me needs his rest. Are you planning on going back to Shamrock tomorrow?"

"Yes," Dominic said absently, his thoughts on the news with which his father had just bludgeoned him. A mortgage. Even the thought of some pompous banker's hands on Killara made him sick to his stomach.

"Why don't you stay here and show Miss MacGregor around Killara instead? They don't need your help over there." Shamus turned out the lamp and the room was suddenly plunged into darkness. "You know, I believe I like her. At first I thought she was a little too missish for a man like you, but I've changed my mind. She has more to her than you'd think from a first look."

Dominic couldn't see his father's face in the dark but his tone was entirely too casual. He agreed warily. "Yes, she does."

His father passed him, surefooted and certain as a cat, and opened the door to the hall. "A woman is a strange creature. Sometimes she thinks she wants one thing and she really wants another. Did you know that our firstborn, Rory, was three months on the way when Malvina and I went before the priest?"

The inference was clear. There would be no interference, only approval, if he chose to bed Elspeth in his father's house. The knowledge sent heat tingling through him. First the shock of the mortgage on Killara and then this tacit permission to soothe the lust that had been tormenting him since he had first set eyes on Elspeth. Da was charging ahead with his usual ruthlessness, striking at him where he was weakest. "No, I don't believe you ever mentioned that fact."

Shamus's chuckle drifted back to him as he began to climb the stairs. "I thought it time I did. Good night, Dominic."

Dominic stood in the dark hall, his hands clenched into fists at his sides. Da had no intention that he should sleep well this night. He wanted him to lie awake worrying about Killara and then think about Elspeth lying in the room next door, and he had accomplished his goals with his usual satanic skill. Dominic deliberately forced his hands to open and relax. He drew a deep breath and headed across the hall, then up the stairs.

He had reached the top step when Rising Star's door opened and a figure in white drifted out into the hall carrying a candle in a copper holder. At first he thought it was Rising Star, and then the woman closed the door and turned, the flickering light illuminating the pale brown of her hair. Elspeth.

She saw him at almost the same moment, and froze, her eyes wide and startled in the pool of golden light formed by the candle. "Hello." Her voice was breathless, the words hesitant. "I hope your brothers are well. Did you have a pleasant day?"

"Yes." His gaze wandered over her, lingering. It was the first time he had seen her in anything but black, and the sight of her in the white gauze gown came as a shock. He hadn't realized what a difference the absence of that black mourning gown would make. She was suddenly a vibrant woman, a part of life and the living. "You look different."

She smiled. "That's what I told Silver. It's a very pretty gown, isn't it? I decided it was time to put away mourning and Rising Star permitted me to borrow it."

"Very pretty." He tore his gaze away from the womanly curves defined by the gown and looked back at her face. "You've spoken to Rising Star?"

"Yes. Brianne, Silver, and I spent the evening with her. I enjoyed it enormously." A tiny frown marred her brow. "I like both Rising Star and Silver so much. I can't understand why your mother and father won't accept Silver."

"Their experiences with the Apaches haven't been happy ones," Dominic said. "I'm not saying they're right not to accept Silver, but I can understand how hard they would find it to do. From the day we came to Killara we had to fight to keep our land and cattle." His face became shadowed. "Burnings, deaths, raids. My brother Rory and his wife died in one of those raids. There were times when we didn't know if any of us would see the next day. My brothers and I grew up believing the Apaches were the enemy. It was only after we got back from San Felipe and Da decided the fighting had to stop or we'd lose everything we'd gained that we paid a visit to Rising Star's village to try to make peace."

"But Joshua married Rising Star," Elspeth protested. "*He* surely couldn't have felt any enmity toward her people."

Something flickered in Dominic's face. "You've met Rising Star. She's very beautiful and Josh went a little crazy when he saw her."

"Are you saying he doesn't love her?"

"No, he does love her, there are just some problems—" He stopped. "Look, Josh's marriage is none of my concern."

"Why did your father let Joshua marry Rising Star if the family felt that way?"

"She was the chief's daughter and he knew it would clinch the peace and protect Killara."

Elspeth stared at him. "To protect *Killara*. What about Rising Star? What about the way she felt at being used as a pawn?"

He frowned. "She wanted Josh. Nobody forced her into the marriage. Josh and Boyd were damn close, and it was too bad that Boyd was killed by Sun Eagle so soon after Rising Star and Josh married. It made things a bit uneasy for everyone here."

"It made things 'uneasy' for Silver too," Elspeth said sharply. "What about her? None of this was her fault and yet all of you have made her the victim. Why didn't you fight for her, Dominic?"

"I wasn't here, dammit," he said testily. "And I was busy fighting a few battles of my own. Hell, I felt the same way they did until I found out a white man could be just as big a bastard as any Indian on the face of the earth. It was a very enlightening discovery."

"Well, someone should have helped her."

"Rising Star did what she could."

"It wasn't enough. You should have made your family see that they had a duty toward her."

"If they won't even concede that she's Boyd's child, how do you expect them to admit they have any obligation?"

"Oh, I don't know, but it's not fair." Tears glistened in her eyes. "None of it is fair."

His annoyance disappeared as he felt an aching tenderness stir. "No, it's not fair, but what my mother and father suffered wasn't fair either. In their eyes they're being generous just tolerating Silver's presence." His lips twisted ruefully. "I guess you've noticed she doesn't make it easy for them."

Elspeth shook her head. "She's in so much pain. Don't you see it? Someone has to help her." She turned wearily away. "Oh, what's the use of talking about it? Why should I expect anyone to help Silver?"

His gaze searched her face, noting its paleness and the dark circles beneath her eyes. "You'd better get to bed. You shouldn't have stayed up this late. You're doing too much."

Elspeth's shoulders moved in an impatient half shrug. "I refuse to pamper myself any longer, I'm getting stronger all the time."

He hesitated. "Did Rising Star speak to you about Kantalan?"

"Yes." Anger flared in Elspeth's eyes. "It was very wrong of you to try to persuade her not to help me, but I have no intention of discussing your interference tonight. The only thing I want to do right now is go to bed, cover my head with the sheet, and forget about you and everyone in the territory of Arizona. I'll talk to you in the morning."

He watched her as she marched militantly down the hall, holding the candle before her as if it were a torch. He felt as if he'd been cracked over the knuckles with a ruler like a naughty schoolboy. First Da then Elspeth had attacked him, and he was sure in both cases it was only the opening barrage with the heavy artillery to follow. Hell, maybe he should cut short his stay and leave tomorrow. The tension within him was increasing with every moment that passed and an explosion could not be far distant. He would be wise to heed the warning signs before it was too late.

Elspeth, bathed in the soft candlelight that turned the white gauze gown to mellow cream and revealed the threads of gold in her pale brown hair, was turning the knob of Brianne's door. Life. She was beginning to come alive. She was changing, blossoming, not only in body but in spirit. He wanted to *see* that blossoming, dammit.

And Dominic realized he would not leave Killara in the morning.

Malvina was not asleep when Shamus opened the door, though the hour was after midnight. It didn't surprise him to see her sitting up in bed, Miss Beetle's book open on her lap. He had known she would not sleep tonight until he came to her.

She looked up and immediately closed the book and placed it on the bedside table. "You spoke to him?"

He nodded. "It's going to be more difficult than I thought. He's being protective as hell of the family."

A tiny smile flitted across her lips. "He's his father's son."

Fierce pride glinted in his eyes. "He is that." He began to empty his pockets on the squat, bowlegged table next to the door. "I sent a message down to the bunkhouse in the village for Patrick to get his backside up here tomorrow morning. Dominic's always had a soft spot for Patrick and it may help to have their quarrel settled." He frowned. "But we'll probably have to use the Scottish woman. She may not be easy to manipulate. She stood up to me when Silver and me were having at it tonight."

"Good. Dominic needs a strong woman." She smiled. "He'd be bored with anybody who didn't strike sparks off him. I'm not worried. You'll find a way, you always do."

He grinned as he stripped off his shirt. "No matter how bad things are, you're always sure I can make everything right." His smile faded. "But I haven't always been able to do that for you, Malvina." He finished undressing and walked toward the bed. "I've tried my damnedest, but I haven't given you the life you wanted."

"Who says you haven't given me everything I wanted?" Malvina's hazel eyes flashed in the lamplight. "How many other women have what I have? Five strong sons and three grandchildren, a fine house and a husband who still pleasures me after all these years. A woman would be foolish to expect more than that from life."

He slipped under the covers and drew her into his arms. "I brought you to a land that killed four of your sons. You've had to work and slave by my side to build Killara. It was a hard life for a long, long time, and it's not easy even now."

A look of pain fleetingly crossed Malvina's face. "I could have lost the boys even if we had never left Belfast. Life wouldn't have been easy for us there either." She leaned her head on his shoulder, hearing the solid thump of his heart beneath her ear. "I don't think life is meant to be easy for people like us, Shamus. We're meant to work and endure, to build and to love." Her lips brushed the hollow of his shoulder. "You gave me that, too, Shamus. Through everything, you gave me that."

"Yes." His hand moved to smooth the hair at her temple. He was silent a moment, gazing at the flickering flame of the kerosene lamp on the table by the bed. "I would have sent Silver upstairs if the Scottish woman hadn't gotten all upset about it. I know you don't like to see her dressed like that in your house, but I thought it important we not get the MacGregor girl set against us."

"You were right." Malvina had tried to overcome the raw pain she experienced whenever she saw Silver dressed in her heathen garb; it triggered so many agonizing memories. Killara burned to the ground, Rory and Boyd gone forever, killed by those murdering savages. Having Rising Star here at Killara wasn't so bad, she tried to act like a civilized woman, but Silver . . . the girl's angry defiance was a constant reminder to Malvina of her barbaric origins. When Rising Star had first brought Silver to Killara, she and Shamus had tried to be gentle with the child, but Silver had been so difficult that they'd soon stopped trying to get through to her. She had appeared to resent them even more than they resented her presence at Killara. Yet the pain she had sensed in Silver this morning in the courtyard had touched her in a strange way. Touched her and made her uneasy. "Shamus, we weren't wrong, were we? About Silver, I mean."

Shamus's clasp tightened. "We weren't wrong." God knows, he wasn't sure Silver wasn't his kin, but it was too late to admit that doubt, even to himself. He had made his choice fifteen years ago, when he had found the baby on the porch and saw the pain on Malvina's face when she had looked at the child. It was enough that she'd lost Boyd that year. No Indian baby was going to be thrust on her to raise and remind her of that loss. The decision had been made and there was no use looking back now. Silver could take care of herself. The young devil even managed to get the best of him on occasion. "Silver isn't Boyd's child."

"Her eyes—"

"We're not the only family with light eyes in the territory."

"No." But there had been moments when Malvina had thought she had seen flashes of Shamus's power in those pale gray eyes of Silver's. Imagination, she assured herself quickly. If Shamus said Silver was not their kin, then it must be true. Relief surged through her and she relaxed against him. "You're probably right. Turn out the lamp, it's time we were sleeping."

Shamus reached across her and turned down the wick of the lamp. "Sleeping?" Tender amusement threaded his words in the darkness. "And it was you who were telling me how lucky you were I could still pleasure you? Now, you can't expect to challenge a man of my temperament like that, and then roll over and go to sleep." He moved over her. "Love me, Malvina."

Her arms went around him, holding him with more tenderness than passion. Passion would come, it always did, but she wanted the tenderness first. Her hands slid over his shoulders, enjoying the play of muscles beneath her palms. He was almost as strong now as when she had first taken him into her body those many, many years ago. God in heaven, she was lucky to have a man like Shamus. "I do love you, Shamus," she whispered. "I always will."

The light in the old man's room blinked out.

Ramon Torres leaned back against the corral post and drew in deeply on the thin brown cigarette between his lips and then exhaled slowly, thoughtfully. He had watched the lights go out one by one, and now the big house was entirely dark and silent.

In an hour everyone would be asleep and he would find a way to get in. He had already inveigled the information from Rosa as to which room Dominic Delaney had been given. He could take off his boots and creep barefoot through the halls. No one would hear him, for he had taught himself to move with the stealth of his Navajo mother. Would he be able to surprise Delaney was the question. The old man's son was a very dangerous man; his instincts had been sharpened by many years of living as a hunted man.

Torres smiled in the darkness. Ah, he knew all about the hunt. He had been a hunter all his life. He had hunted for money, lust, revenge, and many other things, and he knew the ways of game. The secret was never to attack the prey on foreign ground, where he would be uneasy and on guard. If the hunter staked out and waited until the victim came back to his home watering hole, he had a much better chance of putting him down. This method took patience and perseverence, but then, Torres was a very patient man.

He drew again on the cigarette. Now Dominic had returned to his home watering hole. Should he take him tonight? If he did, he'd probably have to kill everyone in the house to be safe from pursuit. Five women and old Shamus, besides Dominic Delaney. The women would be easy. A knife, silent and quick between their ribs as they slept. It was a pity he would have to kill Rosa too. Besides information, the plump widow had furnished him with many enjoyable romps in the past three months.

Shamus and his son would not be so simple to dispatch. They both had the warrior instinct and might be more difficult to catch off guard. Torres was sure Durbin would not object to the additional deaths, but he doubted if he would pay any more for them. He might do better to wait until his prey was alone. It would be the wise and cautious way to proceed.

Torres felt a sharp pang of disappointment as he took the cigarette from his lips and flipped it away. He stood still, looking broodingly at the orange tip glowing in the dirt of the stableyard. He was tempted to forget about caution and go after Dominic now. The blood hunger was upon him, as it always was when the kill was at hand. It was a sign he recognized and was usually able to subdue, but it was more difficult this time. He had waited too long for his prey to come into view and the hunger had sharpened to an unbearable intensity. When that happened, he, the hunter, was almost as much a prisoner as the prey.

He took a step forward, extinguishing the cigarette with the toe of his boot, grinding the tobacco thoroughly into the dirt until there was not a spark left. He did everything with great thoroughness; it was a quality in which he took pride. If something was worth doing, it was worth doing well.

He mustn't be impatient, he told himself. According to Rosa, he had three days to accomplish his kill. Then he would be five thousand dollars richer and able to ride down to Mexico and have a fine spree. The money would not last long, but perhaps that was good. The end of the money meant the start of a new hunt and the dark excitement of the hunger it brought with it. Lately he had begun to realize that he looked forward more to the hunt than the weeks of debauchery it paid for. He laughed softly to himself as he turned and began to stroll toward his horse tethered a few yards away.

It wasn't every man who was lucky enough to enjoy his chosen labor as much as he did. Yes, he was one very fortunate man.

13

Patrick strode out of the smoking room and headed for the front door. His expression was stormy and the sharp click of his boots on the tiled foyer reflected the rebellion he had not allowed himself to express in the presence of his grandfather.

"Wait, Patrick!"

He stopped and glanced at the woman coming down the steps. "Elspeth." His frown disappeared as his gaze ran over her slim figure dressed in a dark blue riding skirt, brown calf-high boots, and a white cotton blouse. He grinned. "Where's our little blackbird? You look a lot like Brianne in that outfit."

Elspeth pulled a face. "I should. These are her clothes. Rising Star, Brianne, and Silver got together last night, and suddenly I had a new wardrobe." A tiny frown wrinkled her brow. "I don't know if I should have taken advantage of their kindness, but they insisted. Perhaps I can find a way of repaying them." The frown faded and she smiled at him. "It's good to see you, Patrick. Are you well?"

He nodded, his gaze on her face. "I don't have to ask if you're better. You're a little pale, but otherwise you look as fit as you did when you came to Hell's Bluff." He glanced down at her boots. "I gather you're going riding."

She nodded. "I'm going to make the attempt. I thought I'd better really learn to ride before I start for Kantalan." Her expression brightened. "Perhaps you'd be good enough to take me to the corral and show me how to saddle one of those horses. I promise not to bother you after that."

"No bother." He opened the door and let her precede him. "I was going to the corral anyway." He scowled. "Gran-da tells me Dominic is down there looking at the new mare Cort bought for Brianne."

Elspeth cast a sidewise glance at him. "You don't seem to be pleased about the prospect of seeing him. Silver told me he sent you away from the cabin."

"He didn't send me away," Patrick said, stung. "*I* decided to leave." He smiled. "Let's just say that he can be very persuasive when he makes his mind up." His expression darkened. "Like Gran-da, who sent for me this morning and told me to settle my differences with Dom and make him feel welcome here."

"Are you going to do it?"

"Yes," he said grudgingly. "As I said, Gran-da can be very persuasive. He has a tongue like a bullwhip and the stubbornness of a mule." He paused, and there was a short silence before he burst out, "I would have done it anyway, I just don't like to be pushed."

And he also didn't like the humiliation of knuckling under to his grandfather, Elspeth thought. It said much for the loyalty and respect Shamus commanded that Patrick had given in to his demand. But the boy was definitely chafing and her glance wandered around the courtyard, searching for a way to change the subject. "Is that a chapel?" She pointed to a small stucco structure slightly apart from the main house. "I wouldn't have thought the Delaneys—" She broke off, but it was too late.

Patrick's eyes were already dancing with amusement. "You didn't think a family as iniquitous as the Delaneys would have any use for a church?"

"I didn't mean to be rude."

"No offense taken." Patrick chuckled. "Gran-da probably wouldn't have had the chapel built if it hadn't been for Manuela. She raised all tarnation until he finally gave in. She even had her own priest brought up from San Felipe and wanted him to live at

Killara, but Gran-da wouldn't have it. He built Father Benedict a house in the village and lets him say mass in the chapel for the vaqueros and their families on Sunday, but that's as far as he would go."

"That seems very generous."

"Oh, Gran-da can be generous." He scowled. "When he's not being a son of—" He stopped and then substituted "difficult." He stiffened. "There's Dom."

Elspeth followed his gaze. Dominic straddled the top pole of the corral fence, watching a sorrel mare in the corral. He glanced down at the vaquero on the ground beside the fence and said something, then laughed as the man answered. The vaquero had to be an old and trusted member of the Killara household, Elspeth thought absently; his expression held far too much affection for Dominic for the situation to be otherwise.

Then Dominic's gaze rose and he saw her and Patrick walking toward him. The smile curving his lips faded and then was gone. "Hello, Elspeth." He inclined his head. "Patrick."

Patrick was equally formal. "Welcome home, Dom." He looked from his uncle to the sorrel on the far side of the corral. "What do you think of her?"

"She's fast, but I've heard the Kentucky horses don't have the stamina we need out here and their temperament causes them to do some pretty stupid things." His gaze met Patrick's. "You know Killara can be pretty unforgiving of mistakes."

Patrick stood looking at him and then a slow smile lit his face. "I haven't found that to be true. You're usually allowed one mistake as long as it's not repeated."

Apology tendered, apology accepted, Elspeth thought with amusement and the pride of both men remained intact.

"I've been trying to get Brianne to let me ride the mare, but she's being damn selfish." Patrick glanced at Elspeth. "Maybe you'll have better luck."

Elspeth cast an apprehensive glance at the spirited

horse. "I wouldn't want to ride a horse Brianne valued. Besides, it looks a little . . . large."

"You're going riding?" Dominic's tone was sharp. "You don't even know how to ride. Where the devil is Silver?"

"Silver is spending the morning with Rising Star. I decided it was time I learned and I'm sure it isn't as complicated as—"

"Is Rising Star sick?" Patrick asked, his gaze anxiously on the house.

"No, but I understand they get little opportunity to spend time together and I didn't wish to intrude." She turned to Patrick. "Will you choose a horse for me?"

Patrick hesitated. "I don't think we have any horses that are right for a tenderfoot."

"Maybe the gray," said the vaquero Dominic had been speaking to as they arrived. "Nina is very old and has not the energy to cause the señorita trouble." There was a gentle smile on his round moon face. "Shall I saddle her? I don't think she would hurt you."

"Yes, please." Elspeth smiled gratefully at the Mexican. He was of medium height and garbed in dark denim trousers and a bright blue cotton shirt. A blue bandanna banded his forehead and held back the shiny dark hair that fell to his shoulders. His large black eyes were gazing at her with eagerness and warmth. "That would be very kind of you, Señor . . . ?"

"Ramon Torres," Patrick supplied. "This is Señorita MacGregor, Ramon." He looked again at the gray mare Ramon had indicated. "I think she'll do for Elspeth. Cut her out, Ramon."

"*Sí.*" Ramon nodded quickly and grabbed his lariat from the corral post. "It will only be a minute." He opened the gate and slipped among the milling horses.

"I don't like this, Patrick." Dominic's voice was tight.

Patrick looked at him in surprise. "Ramon's right. The gray is the gentlest horse on the ranch. All she'll have to do is hold on."

"I don't like her going riding at all. For God's sake, she isn't strong yet. What if she gets tired and takes a fall?"

"Will you kindly stop speaking of me as if I weren't here?" Elspeth asked in exasperation. "If I get tired, I'll stop. If I fall off, I'll get back on. It's very simple."

Patrick's lips twitched. "Yes, Dom, what's wrong with you? You heard her, you're building mountains out of molehills."

"I was the one who had to pick her up when she fell off one of those mountains, and I don't want to have to do it again."

Elspeth felt a swift jab of pain at the hardness of Dominic's voice. "You needn't worry, I have no intention of asking that of you." She turned to watch Ramon Torres stalk the gray with surprising grace and swiftness for a man of his stolid, squat proportions. "He's very good at this, isn't he?"

Dominic's moody glance left her face and shifted to the Mexican in the corral. "Has he been at Killara very long, Patrick? The last time I was here, old Tomas was taking care of the horses."

"About three months. We didn't really need anyone, but he was a wonder with the animals, so we took him on. It was a good thing we did, because we found Tomas in the stable with his head split open two weeks later. We figured he must have fallen from the hayloft and hit his head on the anvil." His face became shadowed. "I liked old Tomas."

"You hadn't met Ramon before today?" Elspeth asked. How strange. She couldn't have mistaken the expression on the Mexican's face as he looked at Dominic. She had received such a vivid impression of the man's feeling for Dominic. "I thought he had been at Killara for a long time."

"Dominic and Patrick both looked at her in surprise.

"Why would you assume that?" Dominic asked.

Elspeth frowned. "I don't know. I guess it was because he was looking at you with such . . . affection."

Patrick burst into laughter. "It isn't men Dom usually inspires to instant affection. Perhaps we should inquire about Ramon's tastes."

"I don't understand," Elspeth said.

Dominic shot Patrick a lethal glance. "Of course you don't, but I'm sure our Patrick will be willing to explain."

Patrick looked a little sheepish. "Sorry, that kind of slipped out." His gaze went to Ramon Torres, who had managed to lasso the gray mare and was leading her out of the corral. "Come on, I'll get you Brianne's old saddle from the barn. It will be lighter and easier for you to handle."

The two men had evidently decided the subject was closed, Elspeth realized with frustration. They had both laughed at her and yet she *knew* she was right. Ramon had looked at Dominic with an almost loving gaze. "Thank you, that would be a great help. I certainly don't want to have to depend on any *man* for assistance."

Patrick pursed his lips in a silent whistle. "No, ma'am. You sure wouldn't want that."

Elspeth smiled reluctantly. Patrick might belong to the conspiracy of male supremacy, but he was trying to help her. "Which way should I ride so that I won't get lost?"

"You don't have to worry about that as long as you stay in the valley. You can see the house from practically everywhere." He frowned. "Just stay away from the Mexican village. Sometimes the vaqueros drink a little too much mescal."

"You're letting her go by herself?" Dominic snapped. "For God's sake, what are you thinking of?"

"Gran-da told me to go back to Shamrock today and help them finish up." Patrick smiled innocently. "You're the only one who's not doing anything. I think you're the one who should go with her."

"No one has to go with me. I told you—" She broke off as she met Dominic's gaze. He looked so strange. His gray-blue eyes were blazing, yet the curve of his lips was not tight but full and sensual. The tension emanating from him was nearly tangible.

"I've stopped listening to what you tell me," he said thickly. He stood as if a statue, staring at her with his light eyes brilliant, restless. He turned away. "I'll go saddle my horse. Be ready to leave in ten minutes." Before she could speak he was walking swiftly toward the barn.

Patrick laughed softly. "I think Uncle Dom is a tad upset this morning. We'd better humor him and be sure we're ready when he is. I'll saddle the gray this time and tell you how to do it as I go along, okay?"

She nodded. "Splendid." She cast a glance at the entrance to the barn through which Dominic had disappeared. She didn't want Dominic with her, but no one seemed to care what her preferences were in the matter. She turned to Patrick. "Why don't you go and say hello to Silver and Rising Star before you leave? I know they want to see you."

Patrick's smile disappeared. "I don't have much time. I have to get over to Shamrock."

Elspeth frowned. He hadn't seemed in the least hurry to depart before this. "Don't you want to see them? I know you like Silver and I thought you and Rising Star were old friends. Brianne told me that you all had lessons together when Rising Star first came to Killara."

"That's right." Patrick kept his eyes fixed on the gray horse that Ramon was leading through the corral gate. "Rising Star didn't know how to read or write English, of course, so Gran-da hired a schoolteacher from back east to live at the house and give the three of us lessons." He suddenly smiled. "But in three years Rising Star knew more than the teacher, so Gran-da let the schoolmarm go and Rising Star taught us. I've never seen anything like the way she worked to learn. She couldn't seem to get enough. You should have seen the way her eyes would light up when she caught on to something. Lord, she was beautiful. Not like she is now. She's different now. Just as beautiful, but different. When she first came to Killara, Brianne and I were four and she was sixteen but she seemed as much a child as we were. She was always laughing and joking and making up games."

Elspeth's gaze rested on his face and she experienced a flicker of anxiety she didn't fully understand. It had something to do with the glow of tenderness illuminating Patrick's eyes. "Then why don't you go to the house and see them?"

He turned and looked across the courtyard at the house. He didn't speak for a moment and Elspeth had the feeling he had forgotten she was there. "Maybe I will," he murmured. "Just for a minute." He tugged his hat down over his eyes and turned away abruptly, starting across the stableyard toward the barn. "First I'll go fetch Brianne's saddle for you."

Elspeth stared after him, surprised at the suddenness of his departure, and then turned to look at Ramon, standing a few yards away holding the gray mare. His dark lustrous eyes watched her with bland good humor, and, as his gaze met her own, he smiled at her.

A sweet smile, but not the tender, loving one he had given Dominic.

"You were right, it is far more painful to trot," Elspeth said.

"What?" Dominic looked over his shoulder, his expression abstracted. Elspeth experienced a surge of annoyance. It was the first word he had uttered since they set out an hour ago and exactly reflected the moody remoteness he had exhibited the entire time. There had been no need for her to be apprehensive about Dominic's coming with her. She might as well have been alone. "You told me once it was more painful to trot than to gallop. I'm ready to attest to it."

"I do recall saying that." He remembered saying more than those words. He had told her that their next ride would be more enjoyable, but that hadn't proved true. Not for him. The ride back to Hell's Bluff from the cabin had been sheer torture, and this trip today had been little better. The tension coiled within him like barbed wire. No matter which way he turned to try to free himself, it only drove the barbs deeper.

He had tried not to look at her, not to speak to her, but it had done little good. She was *there*. He had never been so excruciatingly conscious of the physical presence of anyone before. Last night he had lain sleepless for hours, his body rigid and aroused and as aware of Elspeth lying in the bed in the chamber next door as if there were no walls separating them. His nerves had been tuned to such a pitch that he felt if she turned over in her sleep or her breathing changed tempo, he would know. "Do you want to stop and rest?" he asked.

Elspeth cast a glance at the red tiled roof on the house in the valley below. From here, on this summit in the foothills, it looked small and far away. Too far to attempt until she eased the nagging ache in the hollow of her spine and the numbness of her bottom. "Just for a little while." She added politely, "If you don't mind. I know I've taken a great deal of your time and—"

"For God's sake, I don't *mind*." He cut her off harshly. "Why didn't you tell me you wanted to stop." He got off his horse and came around to stand by the mare. "I told you this wasn't a good idea."

"It was a good idea," she said indignantly. "In spite of your forebodings, I didn't fall off and it's perfectly natural for me to become a little tired. There was no need for you to come with me, and I don't need you to stay with me now. Why don't you go back and—"

"Be quiet." He jerked her from the saddle with more swiftness than gentleness. "You wanted to rest." He set her on her feet, took the mare's reins, and turned away. "Rest."

She watched him lead his own horse and the gray mare down the trail and tether them to a pine tree several yards distant. Then he was turning and coming back to her, a brown saddle blanket over his arm, his expression as hard and closed as it had become from the moment he had seen her walking toward him across the stableyard this morning.

He spread the blanket beneath a pine tree a few yards away. "Sit down."

She was becoming very tired of both his churlishness and his orders, but it would have been ridiculous to refuse a much needed rest out of sheer contrariness. She crossed to the blanket and sat down. The ground was hard but far better than the saddle which had reminded her of an instrument of torture before she had been on it more than fifteen minutes. She stretched her legs out in front of her, supporting herself on her arms. The sky was a brilliant blue between the spiky fronds of the evergreen branches above her, and it was blessedly cool here among the trees. A bird was singing somewhere above her and the air was full of the scent of crushed grass and pine. The surroundings were inexpressibly soothing, and, in a world so lovely, she found it difficult to remain annoyed with Dominic.

Perhaps he had a good reason for his shortness with her; he had probably wanted to spend these precious hours at Killara with his family yet felt it his duty to come with her. Heaven only knew, she had been burden enough of late to annoy a saint. Her dreamy gaze shifted from the peaceful blue sky to Dominic, who sat leaning against the gray-brown bole of a pine tree a few feet away. His arms were linked loosely around his drawn-up knees and his black stetson was pulled low to shadow his features. It was a relaxed position, but he was radiating a tension that seemed to reach out and touch her with its leashed power. He disturbed her, and she didn't wish to be disturbed in this tranquil spot. She moistened her lips nervously with her tongue, trying to think of something to say that would rid the atmosphere between them of that disquieting emotional charge.

"Don't do that!"

Her gaze flew to his face. "I beg your pardon?"

He drew a harsh breath, his fingers clenching together so tightly his knuckles turned white. "Never mind." He closed his eyes. "Talk to me."

She stared at him in bewilderment. "What do you want me to say?"

"I don't care." Anything to keep him thinking and not feeling. Anything to keep him from going over the edge.

She was silent, looking at him. What did he want from her? He was in need—she could feel it—but she didn't know how to fill that need. Yet she desperately wanted to help him, she realized suddenly. "Shall I tell you about Kantalan?"

"Why not? Dreams are as good as anything else."

"It's not a dream." For some reason she experienced no resentment from the impatient comment. "Oh, I suppose dreams were a part of it, but if I hadn't had more than that to hold on to, they wouldn't have been enough to sustain me through all those arguments with my father."

"I thought he believed Kantalan existed."

"He did." She looked down and began absently to smooth the creases in her riding skirt. "That wasn't what the arguments were about. It was the city's origin that my father wouldn't . . ." She drew a shaky breath. "He said I was a fool, that I was an ignorant child who would never approach either his knowledge or his insight." Her nails dug into the heavy garbadine of the skirt. "Maybe he was right about me, but he was wrong in this. I *know* he was wrong. Kantalan wasn't built by the Toltecs, it was a separate colony. All the clues were there but he refused even to try to put them together."

"Colony?" Dominic's lids had opened and his light eyes were gleaming in the shadowy darkness of his face.

She wished she could see his expression, those translucent, burning eyes watching her were making her a little nervous. "Have you ever heard of a place called Atlantis?"

He didn't answer her for a moment. "If I have, I don't remember it."

"Atlantis was an island, the birthplace of civilization. It was destroyed by a great earthquake that sent it to the bottom of the sea. Everyone thinks it's a fable made up by Plato, but I believe it existed." She paused. "And I believe Kantalan was one of its colonies." She waited, as if expecting him to refute her words. When he didn't speak, she rushed on. "Oh, I know Atlantis was supposed to have been in the Mediterranean and Kantalan half a world away, but there are too many similiarities for them not to be tied together somehow. No argument can convince me that Kantalan didn't spring from Atlantis."

"I'm not arguing, Elspeth. I'm listening."

And watching her with an intentness that made her heart pound and her mouth grow dry. She looked down again, her finger nervously resuming its tracing of the crease in the fabric of her skirt. "I'm sorry, I guess I've become accustomed to defending my theory from attack." She moistened her lips again with her tongue. She heard a low sound, as if Dominic had suddenly shifted, but when she looked up she realized she must have been mistaken; he was sitting in the same place. Watching her. "It seemed so clear to me. There are so many similiarities."

"What similiarities?"

"The legend of Kantalan speaks of its great pyramids, and Atlantis had pyramids. Both civilizations worshiped Ra, the sun god. Atlantis had four rivers intersecting the city and Kantalan is said also to have had four rivers forming a cross in the middle of the city. The legend speaks of a great lodestone in the temple of Ra that had magical properties. What other civilization could have given birth to such a wonder? Oh, there are so many things. I believe that the Egyptians, Toltecs, Mayans, and the Incas were also colonies, but that they somehow evolved differently. Perhaps because of Kantalan's isolation it was able to retain its similarities to the mother country. Dear heaven, I hope that's true. Can you imagine actually being there, studying a city that's a mirror of Atlantis?"

"No, I can't imagine it."

"Well, I can." Her eyes glowed softly with excitement and her breasts were rising and falling with each breath. "I can imagine strolling through the streets and seeing the statues of the ten kings, of walking into the palaces and finding the ceilings of ivory and walls of gold. I can imagine seeing the four rivers that form a cross and the—"

"Stop!" He was suddenly beside her, pushing her back on the blanket. He had tossed his hat aside and she could see what had been hidden in its shadow. Her breath left her body and heat turned her bones soft and melting. His chest labored with the harshness of his breathing and a pulse pounded wildly in the hollow of his throat. "I can't imagine any of those things. I don't know anything about Atlantis or Kantalan. I don't even want to know. All I want is you." His lips covered hers with a fervor that brought no pain. His arms closed around her with desperation, his hands tangling in her hair as he moved over her. His lips worked swiftly, feverishly, draining her of strength in a hundred kisses that robbed her of breath and made her head spin.

"No!" she murmured. "I don't want this."

"Yes, you do," he muttered. "We both do." His tongue plunged into her mouth, stroking her with warmth. Lowering his hips, he moved slowly, yearningly, against her.

She gasped, a shiver tingling through her. Maybe he was right. Maybe she did want this to happen, she thought dazedly. It was difficult to decide with this haze of heat enclosing her. Dominic's fingers were swiftly unbuttoning her blouse, pushing down the straps of her chemise. She should stop him.

Her breasts were swollen, hurting as they had the night they'd ridden back to Hell's Bluff. She gazed up at Dominic's face in helpless fascination. His sun-gilded skin was flushed, his lips drawn back from his teeth in a feral grimace. Slowly he pulled down the bodice of her chemise and looked at her. Something strange began to happen to her then. Her nipples were turning hard, rosy, tight, and she had a wild urge to lift herself, offer her breasts to the man looking at them with such hunger. But she didn't have to offer, his dark head was lowering slowly and his breath came out in a low groan.

"This is what I've wanted to do a thousand times in the last few weeks," he said hoarsely. "I wanted to get rid of these damn clothes and look at you." His hand closed on her left breast and his palm tightened around it, throwing the pink crest into pointed prominence. "I wanted to make you bloom for me." His mouth enveloped her, his lips sucking strongly as if to pull the nectar from a honey-sweet flower.

Fire. In her veins, in the soles of her feet, in the air flowing through her lungs. She cried out, her spine arching up to him.

He was murmuring thickly, feverishly, as his tongue gently teased the nipple he had brought to life and subjugation. "I want to know that all I have to do is reach out and touch you and this will happen." His hand wandered down her body. "Spread your legs, love. I want to feel how soft you are down there." His palm gently rubbed between her thighs. She tensed, inhaling sharply. The material separating them was a pitifully inadequate barrier against the warm hardness and fiery friction. "I dream about you, do you know that? I dream I'm looking at this pretty part of you and I remember how you felt against my hand."

She wasn't fighting him, perhaps this was what she had wanted to happen. Perhaps she was so lost to virtue that she wanted to give herself to Dominic Delaney as his other women had. *Cats in the dark* . . .

"No!" She rolled suddenly to the opposite side of the blanket. She had caught him by surprise. "You're wrong, I'm not like . . ." Tears were suddenly raining down her cheeks. "Why are you doing this?"

"Why?" He lifted his head, his eyes blazing. "Because I'm going insane." His face was taut with strain. "For God's sake, stop crying." His hands closed into fists as if fighting for control. "You're not hurt."

She wasn't sure that was true. There was a dull, empty ache between her thighs and a sharp pain somewhere near her heart. She sat up, adjusted her chemise, and quickly buttoned her blouse. She rubbed her eyes with the back of her hand. "I know that."

"Then stop wailing." He stood up, leaned down, and lifted her roughly to her feet. "You've 'rested' long enough. We're going back to the house." He picked up his hat, turned, and strode down the trail to where the horses were tethered.

"I don't know why you're angry with me," she called. She wrapped her arms around herself to stop the trembling. "It's not my fault you're having to do without your hetaerae."

He didn't answer. He untied the horses and led them up the trail.

"It's not sensible to be upset with me just because I resisted your advances. You're certainly no gentleman."

A flare of anger lit his pale eyes with icy fire. "No, you're right, I'm no gentleman, I'm a fool. I've been acting like a bloody sheepbrain, sighing and afraid to speak, lusting but afraid to touch." His hands closed on her waist and he tossed her onto the saddle. "No more, Elspeth. No more."

She looked down at him, her fair hair tumbled to her shoulders in a wild cloud of tawny gold, her eyes as green as the pine forest around her. "What are you saying?" she whispered.

"That you've made me into a milksop, a weakling." His lips parted in a reckless smile. "Somewhere in our acquaintance I stopped being Dominic Delaney and became Elspeth MacGregor's whipping boy. But it's come to an end, Elspeth."

"I never tried to change you." She lifted her chin. "Not that you couldn't have used a good deal of reformation."

"Perhaps you didn't have to try. Maybe guilt did the task for you. Whenever I thought I'd broken the chains that held me, you managed to forge new ones to hold me at your heels." His smile deepened and she was suddenly seeing the rakish devil-beauty she had encountered that first evening Dominic had walked into the parlor at the hotel. "Well, it's over. I once told

Patrick I was my father's son. You'd best remember that, sweetheart. Da and I take what we want and worry about the consequences later." He turned away and swung into the saddle. "I didn't have to let you go just now. I figure that makes us even. I don't owe you anything any longer." He turned his horse and started down the trail. "And I won't be fool enough to let you go again. Lock your door tonight. Don't be alone with me for a minute. Never believe a word I tell you." He glanced over his shoulder to direct a mocking smile at her. "And you might remain a virgin for another twenty-four hours." He turned around and kicked the black into a gallop. "But it's not likely. Not likely at all, Elspeth."

Ramon Torres sighed morosely as he slid the rifle back into its saddle holster. He remounted Chiquita, turned, and whipped the mare into a dead run. It was necessary he be back at Killara before Delaney, and the man was moving at a breakneck pace down the trail. Ah, well, he would make it. He had scouted these hills and knew every shortcut possible. It was a necessary precaution for a man in his profession to know the lay of the land.

He really should have taken the shot, but he had never dreamed Dominic would stop before he had entered the little *gringa*. Ramon still felt the disappointment eating at him. He had wanted desperately to watch his prey moving in and out of his woman, unknowing of the power that, he, Ramon, held over him. He could feel his loins harden at the thought of looking down the sight of his rifle and slowly, very slowly, pulling the trigger.

His lips curved in a smile of genuine enjoyment as he realized what a fine death that would be for any man. He wanted Dominic Delaney to have a death worthy of him. He had a fine bold name and possessed the dark, dangerous beauty of a great cat. It was going to be a rare pleasure to put Dominic down, and this little setback should not really bother Ramon. He had found that unexpected twists of fate often made the game only more exciting. He was glad he hadn't been hasty. Now he could savor the kill. Perhaps he would even pamper himself and get close enough to watch Dominic's eyes as he died.

Dominic wanted the *gringa*. God alone knew why the man had stopped when she had resisted him, but it might be to Ramon's advantage. There was no more potent bait under the sun than a bitch in heat and no more thrilling kill than the death of a man who was enjoying life to the fullest.

He suddenly laughed aloud as an amusing idea occurred to him. Why not make Dominic a present of the *gringa*? Then Ramon could lie in the loft tonight and look at the great house and imagine what Dominic was doing to the woman. It would bring him the most delicious pleasure to know he was controlling the prey unbeknownst to Dominic, and the possession of a woman always brought a feeling of joy and satisfaction to a man that made life infinitely sweeter.

His laughter faded but the smile of satisfaction remained as he leaned low over Chiquita's neck and murmured softly, urging her to go faster. Ah, yes, Dominic Delaney might yet get his chance for the fine death Ramon had planned for him.

14

❧❧

"**I** am tired of being white." Silver flung open the door to Rising Star's room without knocking. She made a face as she saw Rising Star sitting, quill pen in hand, at the small secretary by the window. "I cannot breathe in this house. How can you bear it?" She pulled her tunic over her head and tossed it on the bed before dropping to the floor and crossing her legs. She brought her loose dark hair over one shoulder and began to braid it. "Come down off your fine chair and be Indian with me."

Rising Star slowly shook her head. "I'm comfortable here." She put her pen back in the crystal inkwell. "Where is Elspeth?"

"She decided to go for a ride and sent me to you. She said she did not need me." Silver shrugged her bare shoulders. "I do not care. I am tired of being a nursemaid anyway."

"Are you?" Rising Star asked. "Then it is good that soon she will no longer need you. You can leave this house and go back to where you are happier."

Silver's eyes narrowed on her aunt's face. "Why do you not come with me? You are not happy here either. They do not like Indians in this house and you cannot change what you are."

"I have made a place for myself here," Rising Star said. "I am content." She smiled as her hand gently touched her abdomen. "And soon I will be more content."

"Do you think they will love you more because you give them a half-breed baby?" Silver asked bitterly. "You are blind. They will treat your child as they treat me."

"You're wrong. Joshua will not permit his baby to be treated as an outcast," Rising Star said quietly. "He wants our child very much."

"Did he tell you this?"

"No, but I know it to be true," Rising Star said. "It is natural for a man to want a child. If I had been able to give him a son before, there would have been less—" She paused. "Things will be better once the child is born."

"How do you know?" Silver tossed the thick braid back over her shoulder and turned to face her aunt. "What if the child does not help? Will you stay here and grow old with these people who think you are less than they?"

"Joshua does not treat me as they do. There is love between us."

Silver's eyes blazed. "I do not understand a love that makes you grow quieter and sadder with every year. Joshua should fight them and make them treat you as a member of the family."

Rising Star shook her head sadly. "I cannot expect to be treated as a Delaney until I'm truly one of them. The child will help. Joshua will—"

"He is cold to you," Silver said angrily. "When he is with you, there is no closeness. He will not change because—" She stopped as she saw the pain that tightened Rising Star's features. She muttered something beneath her breath and suddenly sprang to her feet and ran across the room. She dropped to her knees before Rising Star, her arms encircling her aunt's waist, her cheek pressed against her breasts. Her words were muffled. "I am sorry. I grow so angry and the words rise up and cannot be stopped. I did not mean to sting you."

"I know." Rising Star's hand tenderly stroked Silver's shining dark hair. "But you're wrong, Silver, Joshua does love me. It is not easy for him to be married to me."

"Why? You give everything and take nothing. You have become everything they want you to be. They wanted no ignorant savages in their house, so you studied and became more learned than any of them. You cast off your comfortable Indian garments and wear clothes that bind and stifle. You speak softly and are kind to everyone." She lifted her head to smile wryly. "Even to me, who causes you much pain." The smile faded. "You are a great lady and they do not see it. It would be better for you to come away with me. I will take such good care of you," she promised with touching, childlike earnestness.

Rising Star chuckled. "And what would two lone women do wandering around by ourselves?"

Silver grinned back at her. "We would see all the great cities of the world. We would sing and dance. I would learn to play the piano and you could use the French you taught yourself. We would be white when we wished, and Indian when it suited us. It would be a truly splendid life, Rising Star." She lowered her voice coaxingly. "Come with me, there is nothing for us here."

Rising Star shook her head. "There is something for me, I believe. And if there is not, there is nothing for me anywhere. I love my husband, Silver."

Silver opened her lips to protest but then closed them without speaking. There was a moment of silence in the room before she said softly, "Then God deliver me from man-woman love." She lifted her chin and her gray eyes were suddenly dancing. "No, I will deliver myself and I will deliver you too. I will wait until the child is born and then I will come back and whisk you both away. I will show you a woman doesn't need a man to clutter her life. Friendship is much better. You have been white too long. You need me to show you how—" She broke off at the knock on the door. "Don't move, I will answer it." She jumped to her feet and walked swiftly toward the door.

"Wait," Rising Star said in alarm. "Your tunic . . ."

Silver glanced down at her partial nudity, and a mischievous smile lit her face. She tossed her head. "I

don't feel like putting it back on. I am being Indian
now." She reached for the doorknob. "And I am sure,
if it is Malvina or Shamus, they will understand."

"Silver don't—"

Silver threw open the door.

Full, exquisite golden breasts crowned by dusky
pink nipples thrust forward in naked taunting splendor.

"My God, Silver, what the hell are you up to?"
Patrick forced his gaze away from that beautifully
blatant nudity and raised it to her face.

"Oh!" Her smile disappeared and her lips turned
down with disappointment. "I was hoping it was the
old woman or Shamus."

"I see." He stepped into the room, retrieved her
elkskin tunic from the bed, and handed it to her. "In
fact, I'm seeing entirely too much. Now that you know
you can't do any damage, will you save my blushes?"

She shrugged carelessly. "I suppose I must." She
pulled the tunic over her head. "Did you see Elspeth?"

He nodded. "Down at the corral." His gaze went to
Rising Star at the desk. "I thought I'd drop by and say
hello. I haven't seen you for a week or so."

Rising Star's smile lit up her face. "That is your
fault. If you had not moved out of the house into the
bunkhouse in the village, we would still see each
other every day." Her eyes glowed softly. "I miss you,
Patrick."

He flushed. "It was time I moved out. I'm no kid any
longer and . . ." He trailed off awkwardly. "How are
you? The baby?"

"The baby is well, and I am well." Rising Star made
a face. "Though I'll be glad to have the next two
months over with. I'm tired of being fat and ugly."

"You're not ugly," Patrick said quickly.

Rising Star's eyes twinkled. "You mean I'm only
fat?"

"I didn't say that. It's natural. . ."

"For me to be fat." Rising Star chuckled. "What's
wrong with you, Patrick? I never knew you to be at a
loss for words before." She arched a teasing brow.
"Did seeing Elspeth bring about this sudden fluster?"

He blinked. "Elspeth?"

"Well, it's time you became serious about a young woman. Why don't you see if you can—"

"I have to leave." He jammed his hat on his head and turned away. "I just thought I'd see how you were feeling." He opened the door. "And to say hello to Silver, of course."

"Of course," Silver murmured ironically.

"I'll see you soon." The door closed behind him.

Rising Star's smooth brow wrinkled in a puzzled frown. "What's wrong with him? He's behaving very strangely lately."

Silver turned to her in surprise. Her aunt was not often blind to pain in the people she cared about, but there was no doubt she was not aware of the malady that afflicted Patrick. Well, Silver would not be the one to tell her. Rising Star had enough to bear without burdening her with a love she could not return. "He is not a boy any longer. You are used to thinking of him as the child you loved and taught. It is natural for him to draw apart from you now."

"I suppose you're right," Rising Star said wistfully. "I'll miss him, Silver. He always seemed like my child, my little brother. . . ." She made a helpless gesture with one hand. "Oh, so many things." She drew a deep breath and then straightened. "I'm being foolish to take on like this when I have so much to be grateful for." She stood up. "Why don't we go for a walk? It's the only exercise I get since I gave up riding last month."

"Why not?" Silver turned and opened the door, then she glanced back over her shoulder with a resigned smile. "I guess you're going to make me keep on my tunic?"

"You're entirely correct," Rising Star said serenely.

"I was afraid you were. Oh, well, I can wait." Silver's eyes lit with a speculative gleam. "Shamus did not care for me wearing my 'heathen' clothes in Malvina's fine dining room. Perhaps he would prefer me without any clothes at all."

* * *

Dominic had already dismounted and thrown the reins of his horse to Ramon when Elspeth rode more slowly into the stableyard. Without a glance at her or a word to Ramon, he turned and strode across the courtyard and into the house.

Elspeth gazed after him, a multitude of emotions pouring through her—anger, fear, indignation, and something else she refused to examine closely. She was only half aware of Ramon helping her from the saddle until he spoke. "Did you have a pleasant ride, señorita?"

She looked up. "What?"

Ramon was smiling at her, his black eyes gleaming in his round olive face.

"Oh, yes, Nina behaved very well."

"That is good. I hoped she might please you. Perhaps the next time your ride will be even more interesting."

"I found this one interesting enough." She handed the Mexican the reins and turned jerkily away. "Thank you, Ramon."

"It was my pleasure, I assure you."

She walked across the courtyard toward the front door, the muscles in her thighs and lower back protesting with every step. She wondered if she would suffer this way every time she ventured onto a horse. Surely it must lessen, or people would find a more comfortable way to get around. Dominic had appeared to experience no pain on any occasion she had ridden with him.

However, that was not a valid argument, she thought crossly. Dominic was hard in body as well as character, and would let nothing bruise or pierce that hardness. On the contrary, he would do the bruising. She involuntarily looked down at her breasts and a shiver went through her. His touch may not have marked her, but she felt as if it had. She could still feel his hands on her, branding her, possessing her.

He had been wrong. She could not want him in that wicked, lustful fashion. She had been confused and taken by surprise or she would have fought him. Yes, that was the truth of the matter—she had merely been confused.

"You move like a crippled woman."

Elspeth turned to see Silver and Rising Star walking toward her across the courtyard. "I'm not surprised, Silver." She opened the front door and limped into the foyer. "I believe I've discovered why carriages were invented. Why anyone would willingly put themselves through this agony is beyond my comprehension."

Silver laughed. "You should have taken me with you. I would not have let you do too much. First, a soak in a hot bath, then I have some salve that will help. You will be free of pain in the morning."

"I have grave doubts, but I fervently wish to believe you." She glanced over her shoulder at Rising Star. "Because I've decided to leave day after tomorrow for Kantalan. Will you draw me the map you promised?"

Rising Star frowned. "You are sure?"

"Yes, there really wasn't any doubt about my decision." Elspeth smiled. "and since I am the only one going, even if the prophecy were true, it couldn't come to pass. There have to be four to walk the streets of Kantalan, remember?"

"I remember." Rising Star's expression remained troubled. "Perhaps you are right."

"I will need a guide." Elspeth turned to Silver. "My father told me that Indians are always the best guides. Do you suppose you could hire someone for me in your village?"

"Why do you need a guide with me along?" Silver asked. "Apache girl children are trained in the same skills as boy children until they reach the time for womanhood rites. I can lead you safely to your Kantalan."

"No, Silver, you can't go with me. I won't take the responsibility for placing you in any jeopardy."

"But I *want* to go."

"No!" Elspeth said with ringing determination. "Will you hire a guide for me or must I go back to Hell's Bluff and try to find someone there?"

"You will find no one better than me," Silver said.

"I know," Elspeth said gently. "And no one I'd rather have with me. I'll miss you, Silver."

"Then why not take me along and—"

"No."

"I will ride out this evening and find you the best guide in my village. But it is no short journey. I will not be back until tomorrow night." Silver glared at her. "I think you are a very stubborn woman."

Elspeth turned stiffly toward the stairs. "We'll see how stubborn I am in a few minutes. I'm not at all sure my fortitude is going to last to get me upstairs."

"Let me help you." Rising Star moved quickly forward.

"Is there something wrong?" Malvina appeared in the doorway of the parlor. "Have you had an accident, Elspeth?"

"No, I'm only a bit sore and weary from my ride."

Malvina smiled solicitously. "You must really not rush your recovery, Elspeth. It's not wise to push yourself beyond your strength. We'll be happy to have you here as long as you want to stay."

Elspeth hesitated. "Silver is leaving this evening for her village to secure a guide for me, and I hope to leave Killara day after tomorrow."

Malvina's smile faded. "I'm sorry to hear that. We've scarcely begun to get acquainted with each other."

The woman actually appeared disappointed, Elspeth thought in surprise. "Perhaps when I return from my journey you will be kind enough to let me visit," she said gently. "I thank you for your hospitality."

"You're sure you can't stay longer?" Malvina asked.

Elspeth shook her head. "It isn't possible."

"How unfortunate." Malvina's tone was abstracted as she turned away. "If you'll excuse me, I'll go tell Shamus of your decision. I'm sure Rising Star and Silver will see that you're comfortable." She turned and hurried down the hall.

"She's leaving day after tomorrow on that blasted wild goose chase Patrick told us about." Malvina closed the door behind her and gazed at Shamus sitting at the desk across the library.

"And Dominic was just in here telling me that he

was leaving at dawn tomorrow to go back to Hell's Bluff." Shamus leaned back in his cushioned leather chair. "Something must have happened between them."

"But not what we wanted to happen. What are we going to do?"

"We'll work it out." Shamus closed the account book on the desk. "Let me think about it for a while, darlin.'"

"I don't want Dominic to leave again, Shamus," she whispered. "I'm afraid every time he rides out of here that he won't come back. I don't want to lose another son."

Shamus smiled reassuringly. "He won't be leaving Killara, Malvina. Now, come over here and sit down and let's talk it through. There's nothing we can't bring about if we work together."

She slowly crossed the room and sat down on the chair next to the desk. He was right, she had been foolish to panic. They would solve this problem together as they had every one they'd ever confronted. Shamus would think of something.

The knock on Elspeth's door was light but firm, and the door opened before she was given a chance to answer.

A plump Mexican woman in her late thirties stood there, a broad smile on her face and a tray in her hands. "I am Rosa Gonzalez. Señora Delaney said you were very sore and must not come down to dinner. I brought you some of my soup and a glass of lemonade."

Elspeth sat up in bed, her eyes widening in surprise. "Why, thank you. How very kind." She reached for her dark blue robe and slipped it on over her flannel gown. "But you needn't have done this. I'm not ill."

Rosa stepped into the room and nudged the door shut with her shoulder. "It was no trouble. Are you less sore now?"

Elspeth nodded. "Silver rubbed me with something wonderfully soothing before she left to go back to her village." She smiled. "At first I thought it was horse liniment, but it doesn't smell at all terrible. Once you grow accustomed to the scent it's even rather pleasant."

Rosa came forward and set the tray on the table beside the bed. She sniffed. "Mint and maybe a touch of clover. That Silver is clever with her herbs. Once I had a very bad belly ache and she brewed me a drink that smelled like a dead *gato* but it stopped the pain."

"I've found Silver clever at most things."

Rosa turned to pluck the napkin from the tray. "I hope the soup won't be too hot for you. I put many chili peppers in it." She smiled tentatively. "I thought if you did not like it, the lemonade would cool you down."

"I enjoy a touch of spice. As a child I lived for many months in India and became accustomed to exotic dishes."

Rosa looked relieved. "That is good, I know the *patrón* and the señora want you to be very happy here at Killara. They would not be pleased with me if you did not like my cooking."

"I enjoyed my dinner last night very much indeed," Elspeth said gently. "And I'm sure this soup will be equally good."

Rosa smiled uncertainly again and moved toward the door. "Good night, Señorita MacGregor."

"Good night." Elspeth gazed at the panels of the door after it had closed behind Rosa. The servant was obviously completely devoted to Shamus and Malvina and terribly afraid of displeasing them. Were all the vaqueros and servants equally loyal to the Delaneys? It must be like belonging to a wild highland clan to live with that kind of power. It was no wonder Dominic acted as if he were a law unto himself.

Well, day after tomorrow she wouldn't have to worry about any of the Delaneys. She briskly swung her legs to the floor and reached for the white napkin on the tray and spread it on her lap. She picked up the spoon and dipped it into the fragrant soup.

15

The stairs stretched mountain-high before him, and Dominic knew he was going to have a head as big as a chamber pot in the morning. He shouldn't have had that last drink with Da. For that matter, he shouldn't have had that first drink with Da. His father had kept the bourbon flowing as freely as his arguments as to why Dominic should remain at Killara. If he wasn't drunk, he was damn close to it.

He reached the top of the steps and moved slowly down the corridor. His gaze went automatically to the door at the end of the hall. The door to Elspeth's room.

She would be lying in that big soft bed, her fair hair wild silk on the white pillow. He had warned her to lock her door. Had she done it? He paused outside his own room, feeling the familiar swelling of his manhood as he thought of how she had looked this afternoon with her breasts bare, cheeks rose-pink, eyes limpid. No matter what she said, she *had* wanted him. Heaven save him from pure, virtuous women. They were all liars whose greatest delight was the torment of men like him. From now on he would stay with the kind of women he knew something about.

Hell, maybe it was a good thing Da had kept filling his glass throughout the evening. He might be able to sleep tonight. If he wanted to sleep. He took an impulsive half step toward Elspeth's door. Why not? he thought recklessly. The bourbon was setting off tiny fires in his veins, and he needed a woman. He had warned her that she was not safe from him.

He came to a stop even as he reached for the knob of the door. He was a fool. Why was he hesitating? Tomorrow he would ride out and perhaps never see her again. Why not take what had been withheld so long? He stood there for a full moment, his muscles tense and his heart beginning to pound. His hand slowly fell away from the knob and he returned to his own door. Yes, there was no question about it. He was a fool.

He entered his room, not bothering to light the lamp on the table beside the door. He stripped off his shirt, poured water into the basin on the washstand, and splashed water on his face. The cold shock cleared his head a little but did nothing to alleviate the turmoil in his body. He reached out blindly for the towel on the rack beside the washstand.

A sigh, soft and deep, floated from the bed across the room.

Dominic's hand froze before he touched the towel. His hand moved smoothly, swiftly, to the gun at his hip, drawing it even as he dropped to the floor. His gaze searched the darkness.

The sigh came again and with it a soft murmur.

Dominic rose slowly to his knees. He knew that sound. He had heard Elspeth utter that half-audible moan many times when she had been dreaming. He felt as stunned as if the bullet he had expected had torn into him. My God, had he blundered into Elspeth's room by mistake? No, he wasn't that drunk. This was his room and the bed Elspeth was lying in was his own bed.

He slid the Colt back into its holster and rose to his feet. He made his way to the table, fumbled for matches, and lit the lamp. His hand was trembling as he picked up the lamp and crossed the room to stand beside the bed.

She was naked, lying on the coverlet, her hair an unbound glory of lustrous brown shot with gold. Her eyes were closed, her lashes arcing onto the softness of her cheeks. Her pink lips were crumpled and slightly parted.

He stood looking down at her, the muscles in his belly knotting and his manhood becoming rigid. The scent of mint and cloves radiated from her pale skin, shining in the lamplight as if burnished by a loving hand. His. She had come to him.

He set the lamp down on the bedside table, unfastened his gunbelt, and set it beside the lamp. The long wait was over. He began to strip quickly, never taking his gaze from the woman on the bed.

Heat surrounded her, invading her senses, piercing the heavy veil of sleep.

"Elspeth." Dominic's voice, rough velvet. "Open your eyes."

Her lids were so heavy that it was a difficult command to obey. She wanted desperately to go back to sleep, but Dominic kept calling her as he had called her so many times before to free her from a prison of nightmares. She hadn't realized she had been dreaming, but it must be so or Dominic wouldn't be calling her. Her lids fluttered, then slowly opened.

He was so near, scarcely a breath away, looking down at her. His light eyes were hot and his lips were heavy with sensuality. He had looked like this once before, she remembered hazily, right before she had fallen down the slope. But that was a long time ago, a hundred nightmares ago, and she couldn't quite recall . . .

"No, don't shut your eyes again. Wake up, Elspeth."

She hadn't known her lids had closed, but she obediently opened them again to look into his face. How very unusual and shimmering were those gray-blue eyes gazing into her own. Dominic had such beautiful eyes. "I'm awake."

"Good." His voice was jerky. "Because I sure as hell can't wait any longer. *Come here*." His lips were on her breasts, this tongue flicking at the sensitive nipples. Flame shot through her and she cried out, arching up to him.

"And you can't wait either, can you?" he muttered. "Crazy. I was crazy not to . . ." His hand moved down her stomach to nestle in the curls at the apex of her womanhood, tangling, pulling gently as he suckled at her nipple.

Her heart pounded painfully, she couldn't breathe, her flesh was on fire. Hunger. She was experiencing insatiable hunger. She wanted more. Her hands went around his shoulders and slowly slid to his neck to curl in the thickness of the hair at its nape. "Dominic, I want . . . more," she whispered.

He chuckled. "Don't worry, I'll give you more." His fingers moved down, searching. "I'll give you all you can take." He found what he had been seeking and began massaging, stroking.

She convulsed, the muscles of her stomach clenching. Sleep vanished, the world vanished. All that remained was Dominic's skillful fingers and that secret part of her slavishly responding to his bidding.

His gaze was narrowed on her face, hungrily catching every nuance of expression. "Hell, I'll give you more than you can take. I want to make you want it so bad you'll beg me for it." His fingers began a circular movement.

She gasped and her teeth clenched. A pulse throbbed in her temple, another throbbed against his fingers. "Dominic!"

"I've wanted you too long," he muttered as he moved over her. "I wanted time to touch you, play with you, dammit." He parted her thighs, one finger running down the flowing heart of her. "Lovely. I knew you'd be this lovely."

She should be fighting him, she thought vaguely. There was some reason why she should be fighting him.

Then his finger plunged deeply.

She cried out, arching helplessly up to him, her fingers tightening in his hair, and all thought of resistance left her.

"Tell me you want it." His brilliant eyes blazed down at her. "Tell me you want *me*."

His gaze was holding her own, his finger moving rhythmically within her. Her throat was too tight to speak.

The rhythm escalated. "Tell me."

"*Yes*. Oh, yes."

His thumb pressed hard on that sensitive button, his finger delved deeper. "All of it."

Elspeth's head was thrashing back and forth on the pillow, her teeth biting her lower lip to keep from crying out. "I want you, all of you."

"You're damn right you do." His hands gentled, but his eyes were smoky-hot boring down at her. "And I'm going to keep it that way. I'm going to take you every way there is, and then I'm going to start over. I'm going to keep you so hot, all you'll want is what I'm going to give you now." His chest was moving with his labored breathing, and she could see the pulse leap in his temple.

He raised up on his knees and his rampant manhood was there before her. "See? I'm like this whenever I look at you, whenever I think of you, whenever I'm in the same room with you." He took her hand and brought it to him.

Warmth, smooth hardness, pleasant to the touch. Her grasp unconsciously tightened around him.

His features convulsed, the cords of his neck stood out and he threw his head back. *"God!"*

His nostrils flared as the tried to force air into his lungs. "Let me go, Love. I can't take this right now. Later."

She reluctantly released him. Beautiful. That part of him was as beautiful as the rest of him.

His face was heavy, flushed, as he looked down at her disappointed face. "You like me?" His lids half-closed, veiling his eyes. "You want me again?"

She nodded, staring up at him helplessly.

His hands gently widened her legs. "Here?" His palm covered her. Heat, possession, emptiness.

He knew. Dominic knew what she did not. She could see it in his face, feel it in the warmth of his hand. He knew how to stop the hunger and the fever. "Yes," she whispered.

He was there, nudging gently, his hands once more performing that fiery magic. "I'll try not to hurt you," he said thickly. "I can't promise, but I'll try."

He had said that once before, she remembered dimly, and it had something to do with the reason why she should fight him. But it wasn't the prospect of pain that had frightened her. It was something else.

He was entering her body. Fullness. Fever. His hard length fighting the tightness resisting it. On Dominic's face was an expression of terrible pleasure. His eyes shut as his hands closed on her breasts. "You're *killing* me," he gasped. "Tight. You're so tight."

Was that bad? It didn't seem so, for he wasn't trying to withdraw. In fact, he was pushing harder, farther into her. Why had he said it would hurt? There was no pain, just this exquisite fullness to combat the hunger.

He stopped, his eyes opening slowly. They were glittering, wild, almost unseeing with the pleasure enfolding him. He trembled; a shudder rippled through him. "It's time." He lowered himself over her, resting his elbows on each side of her. "Open your mouth, love. Take me into you."

Her gaze clung to his face as it lowered slowly toward her. There was nothing else in the room, nothing else in the world but his dark face and his body joined to hers.

"Merge with . . ." She forgot what she had been about to say as her lips parted and she took his tongue deep within her. He groaned low in his throat, but the sound was lost as their tongues met, toyed, blended.

He plunged forward, ripping aside the last barrier that separated them.

Pain, hot pain. Her cry was muffled against his lips. Then completion, fullness, delicious containment. One.

He lifted his head and looked down at her. "It's over. Did I hurt you?"

"Yes. But it doesn't matter." She lay there, full of him, and pushed up on her elbows to look down at their joining. How smoothly he fit within her, just like the statue she had seen in that temple in India. Yet the fit was the only smoothness about this jagged, pulsating, hungry intruder. She fell back on the bed. Her breasts beneath his hands were full, swollen, jutting up to touch his palms. "Is it truly over? There seems to be something . . . missing."

He flexed slowly within her. "I only meant the pain was over." He moved again and smiled with savage pleasure as she inhaled sharply and then moaned deep in her throat. "This is what it's all about, Elspeth. This is why you came to me."

She hadn't come to him, he had come to her, but it didn't seem to be worth arguing about at the moment. Her hands tightened on his shoulders as he began to move, buck, plunge with a rhythm that felt as if it were tearing her apart. She panted, her nails digging into his flesh. Hot liquid heat. Hunger. She was expanding inside, bubbling like the Sun Child, molten, and building toward an explosion.

"Elspeth." Her name was a groan on his lips, spoken between clenched teeth. She could see the glow of perspiration on his throat and chest and the pungent scent of bourbon and musk surrounded him. "Mine. You belong to me." He drove deep within her and stopped. "Say it." His breathing was so labored he could scarcely get the words out.

She knew what he wanted with an instinct as ancient as time. Even though the haze of heat, the rhythm that was storming at her body, she knew what he needed. "Yours." Her voice was scarcely audible, a mere wisp of a sound.

"Always?"

"Always."

He began to move again, harder and hotter, cradling her buttocks to lift her up to receive each forceful thrust.

Tears were running down her cheeks. The world was trembling, the tension growing, his thrust deepening. Unbearable pleasure. Exquisite. Titanic. How could it go on without destroying them both? Was this magnificent destruction of the senses when she had feared? No, she would have been helplessly enthralled with it as she was now. Then what?

The bairn. The answer came to her suddenly. That was what had disturbed her, the possibility of hurt to the bairn.

"Dominic." Her tongue moistened her dry lips. It was difficult to speak, but she must. "The bairn."

At first she thought he hadn't heard her. The rhythm didn't lessen, nor did the intense pleasure on his face. Then he looked down at her and shook his head to clear it. "What?"

"The bairn. What if—"

His fingers moved to her lips. "Hush." A smile so beautiful it took her breath away lit his dark face. "Mine," he said softly. "Do you think I don't know how to care for what is mine?"

No, Dominic would love and care for his child as he did for Killara. He would give it all his devotion and protection. Dominic would not let his bairn suffer hurt or humiliation. "Yes." She closed her eyes and let the sorcery of emotion flow over her. "You would know, Dominic."

A pang of tenderness shot through him, tempering his passion. "You have my promise, Elspeth." He kissed her lips with a sweetness that shook her even more than his raging possession. "Content?"

When she nodded, he once more started the rhythm that brought not contentment but soaring hunger and desire. She gasped, her hands fluttering up to clasp him.

"Elspeth, I think . . ." His eyes were glazed, his voice a hoarse guttural growl. He moved faster, deeper, the world was spinning, devoid of air, enveloped in flame. "*Take* me."

What did he mean? She was already taking him, all of him. He was part of her. Then she realized what he meant as the spinning increased before becoming a dizzying blue, snapping the tension and throwing them into radiant, pulsating darkness.

"Jesus!" Dominic's chest was rising and falling as he tried to get his breath. He didn't want to leave her, he never wanted to leave her. Yet if he didn't, he wasn't sure he wouldn't collapse on top of her. "Damn that bourbon." He carefully moved off her and drew her into his arms.

His head fell to the pillow, still covered by the brown velvet coverlet. Why hadn't she removed the coverlet when she came to bed? he wondered dimly. Now they were too exhausted to bother. His lips brushed her temple. "Are you cold?"

"No." The word was slurred. He could tell she was almost asleep again.

He nestled closer, his hands closing possessively over her breasts. He still wanted her, he realized in surprise. Neither the bourbon nor his pleasure, nor exhaustion had altered that state. He couldn't remember ever wanting a woman again so soon.

God, he was tired. He would make love to her once more in a few minutes. He would watch her face as he moved and enjoy her incredible tightness. But now he would let her rest and perhaps rest a little himself. His heavy lids closed, he felt awareness edging away from him. No! He tried desperately to capture it once again, but it was gone.

Elspeth woke with Dominic's hands cupping her breasts and the feel of his long, muscular body against her back. She stiffened with shock as memory of the night returned, ripping aside the comfortable veil of sleep. She kept her eyes tightly shut. Maybe that memory had been a dream. Perhaps Dominic's presence in her bed was also a dream.

Dominic stirred against her, his breath warm on her ear, his big hands tightened on her breasts, his palms gentle and possessive even in sleep. If this was a dream, it certainly was a tactile one, she thought desperately.

Oh, dear, it *wasn't* a dream. Dominic had warned her, but she had believed the threat was an idle one born of anger. She was a fallen woman! Strange, it didn't feel any different. She could detect no dark burden of sin weighing upon her. Perhaps that would come later. True, there was a slight ache between her thighs that could be a punishment for the iniquity of the act she had committed.

A warm wet tongue suddenly darted into her ear. Her lashes flew open.

"Turn over." Dominic's voice was dark and drowsy. "You have a magnificent backside, but I have a fancy to—"

"Brown," she said dazedly as her gaze wandered to the tan brass-studded chair across the room, then to the amber drapes at the window, and finally to the dark brown of the canopy over her head. "Why is everything brown?"

"I have no idea," he murmured. His fingers tweaked lazily at the nipples beneath his hands. "And frankly, I don't care. I suppose my mother likes brown. Turn over, Elspeth."

She threw off his hands and rolled panic-stricken to the far side of the bed. "No, I didn't want—" She broke off as she sat up and a bolt of pain zagged through her head. She rubbed her temple. "Merciful heavens, my head hurts."

"So does mine, but that isn't my primary discomfort at the moment." His gaze was fastened on her breasts. "Come here and see if you can make both the aches go away."

She gazed at him indignantly. "Have you no compassion? First you ravish me, then you carry me to your room so everyone will know of my disgrace. And now you expect me to submit to you willingly. I'm not lost to all shame even if I am a fallen woman."

There was a flicker of anger in his translucent eyes. "Elspeth, I'm in no mood for coyness this morning. My head feels as if it's been kicked by a horse. I thought you were done with lies. Now, come here and give me what I need before I forget to be gentle with you."

"Gentle? You weren't—" She stopped. There had been pain, but she could not deny he had tried to be gentle. A tide of scarlet dyed her cheeks as the memory of their bodies joined, his face looking down at her as he moved within her. "Well, even if you were, it doesn't matter. You can't deny you ravished me."

"Ravished?" His voice lowered to menacing softness. "I don't recall ravishing you. However, that may come to pass if you don't stop this blasted whining. God, how I hate hypocrisy." His lips tightened. "You came to me because you wanted me to do exactly what I did to you last night. I thought you'd at last decided to forget the lies a 'good' woman tells herself."

"I did not come here. Do you think you can hide your debauchery by claiming I came to you?" She jumped off the bed and looked wildly for her nightgown and robe. She didn't remember him removing them, but they surely must be somewhere. She snatched a corner of the velvet coverlet from the bed and held it before her to hide her nakedness. "Why do you not admit you crept into my room and took advantage of my exhaustion to carry me in here and have your way with me?"

He sat up, his expression stunned. "Are you mad? Why should I do that? One bed is as good as another." He added with a sardonic smile, "To any experienced debaucher."

She ran trembling fingers through her hair. She wished her head would stop aching. She couldn't seem to think. "How do I know why you would do it? I have no knowledge of these matters. What did you do with my gown?" She could see no sign of either her gown or robe. Would he have put them into his bureau drawers? She discarded the idea immediately. Her memory of last night had been of a Dominic far too impatient to be tidy.

He leered at her. "I burned them. I intend to keep you locked in this room so I may vent my lust on your virtuous body again and again. What else would you expect of a wicked seducer?"

Her eyes widened. "You can't mean it."

"Of course I mean it. Why shouldn't I—" He stopped. She was standing there, unclothed, only the scrap of brown velvet and her long fair hair veiling her nudity, her expression vulnerable and uncertain. A sudden wave of tenderness lessened the frustration and disappointment he was feeling. "No, I didn't mean it. I don't know where you put your clothes. Don't you remember?"

"How could I remember? You're the one who disrobed me." Her lips were trembling as she said with touching dignity, "I wish you would not make sport of me. This is not an easy matter for me to deal with. If you will tell me where my clothes are, I will dress and return to my room."

His eyes narrowed on her face. There was no coyness there, only genuine distress. She honestly believed what she was saying. He'd had a hell of a lot of bourbon last night with Da and he had been in a wild fever for her. Maybe he could have done what she accused him of.

He rejected the idea immediately; his memory of every detail of last night was too vivid. He distinctly remembered looking down at Elspeth and thinking how lovely her pale skin was against the brown velvet coverlet. He remembered lying down beside her and the damnably hard time he'd had waking her. Still, once awake, she'd been everything that was pliant and docile, looking up at him with those huge dreamy eyes as he entered her.

Sleep. Docile. Headache.

My God, would his father have dared?

Dominic inhaled sharply as he remembered how Da had kept the liquor flowing last night. And when had Elspeth *ever* been as docile as she had been when he had taken her in his arms in this bed? "That interfering son of a bitch." He swung his legs off the bed, stood up, and quickly began to dress. "Did you have anything to drink last night?"

She stared at him in bewilderment. "A glass of lemonade with my soup."

"You weren't at dinner. My mother said she had sent up a tray." He pulled on his boots. "Who brought the tray?"

"Rosa. I thought it was very kind of her."

"Oh, yes, very kind. Don't just stand there. Put something on."

"What?"

"Try the bureau drawers. My mother is very fastidous about not leaving garments strewn about."

The pink flannel nightgown and dark blue robe were folded neatly in the top drawer. Elspeth stared at them dumbly for a moment before she took the nightgown out of the drawer and pulled it over her head. "Your mother helped you to undress me? I can't believe any respectable woman would be a party to such an act."

"My mother's ideas of respectability are sometimes guided by her love for my esteemed father. I don't know if she was involved or not, but there's a definite possibility." He added water to what was in the basin from the night before, splashed his face, and reached for the towel. "Bring me a shirt from the second drawer."

She obeyed him without thinking. A curious intimacy existed in the simple act, she thought as she handed him the white shirt. Intimacy. The color suddenly stained her cheeks as she remembered the degree of the intimacy that bound them after what had occurred in that bed last night. "I'm going to my room now. I'll stay there until you've left Killara."

"The hell you will." His eyes were glittering with cold fury as he slipped his arms into the shirt and began to button it. "Thanks to my loving father, there's been a major change of plans."

He tucked his shirt into his trousers, grabbed her wrist, and strode toward the door. "Come along." He pulled her down the hall, his expression tight and grim, his grip on her wrist unrelenting.

"Where are we going?" she gasped, stumbling to keep up with him.

"I have a few words to say to my father."

"Then say them, but let me go back to my room."

He didn't answer as he started down the stairs.

"I'm not dressed!"

"I assure you that condition won't bother my father."

"It's very early. They might not be up."

"He'll be up." He stared straight ahead as he descended the last steps. "My father is always up by six."

"Good morning, Dominic." Shamus smiled genially as he stepped out of the parlor into the foyer. "You look a bit out of sorts." His expression reflected a flicker of surprise as his glance shifted to Elspeth and he noticed her state of undress but he rallied swiftly. "While you look charming, Miss Elspeth. I always think a woman most enchanting with her hair floating around her and her face bedewed by sleep."

"Thank you," she said dazedly. "That's very kind."

"Kind!" Dominic laughed harshly. "My God, don't you realize yet what they've done to you? You're the bait in the trap, the cunning little amusement that's going to keep me chained here." He faced his father. "Isn't that right, Da?"

Shamus's face became wary. "I don't know what you're talking about."

"I'm talking about the fact that Elspeth was drugged last night and put in my bed." Dominic grated the words out through clenched teeth. "My God, how did you have the—I brought her here to protect her."

Shamus's eyes widened and then narrowed thoughtfully as his gaze moved slowly from Dominic to Elspeth and then back again. "Do I take it you've enjoyed this young lady's . . . favors? Ah, now this is a very serious matter, Dominic. Surely you're not going to cast her cruelly aside and just wander on your way?" His voice lowered silkily. "Why not stay here and do the honorable thing by the poor lass?"

"I'll be damned if I'll be stampeded into doing what you want."

"Won't you, indeed?" Shamus asked softly. "Are you going to let her go then? Perhaps to fall into some other lucky man's bed."

Dominic's hand on Elspeth's wrist tightened with

bruising force. "Damn you, Da. You've gone too far this time."

"Yes, he has," Elspeth said slowly. Her free hand went up to rub her temple. Her head was throbbing terribly and the bewildering exchange between the two Delaneys had swirled around her like a tempest. It had taken her a few minutes to realize what they were actually saying. "And so have you, Dominic." She jerked her wrist from Dominic's grip and continued with great deliberation. "I'm a little confused, so please be good enough to help me. You put something in my lemonade to make me sleep more soundly, Mr. Delaney?"

Shamus shook his head. "I didn't say that, my dear." He sighed mournfully. "It's truly a grievous pass when a son doubts the honor of his own father."

"And then someone took me to Dominic's room and undressed me?"

He nodded. "So Dominic claims. But all of this is really unimportant now, Elspeth. We must set about putting right this wrong done you."

Unimportant? Incredible. The man was incredible. "And you made sure that Dominic had a wee bit too much to drink so that he wouldn't notice I was not quite myself."

"Now, I will admit to blame for Dominic's condition last night. I do hope the liquor didn't make him incapable of pleasing you." He darted a sly glance at Dominic. "It takes a bull of a man to pleasure a woman when he's had a drop too much. Perhaps he's not the man his father is."

Elspeth felt the hot color stain her cheeks, but this time it was with rage not shame. She stepped back, her eyes blazing with fury. "You *used* me. How could you dare to do that to a stranger in your own home? You've disgraced me and treated me as no more than a pawn in your Delaney quarrels." She turned to Dominic. "And you're no better. Do you know how a woman with no reputation is treated? I received a sample of that treatment in Hell's Bluff. It . . . it hurts." She blinked the hot tears away. "And yet you thought of nothing more than your own pleasure last night. I was helpless and confused, but you could have stopped."

"Could I?" Dominic's lips curved in a lopsided smile. "You're wrong, Elspeth. After I saw you, there was no way on earth I could have turned away. Da knows me very well."

"Because you're both selfish and wicked and—" She whirled and ran up the stairs. Her muffled words floated back to them. "You both deserve horsewhipping. I'll not stay here at your precious Killara another hour."

The two men stood there in silence until they heard the door of her room slam behind her.

"I believe she's a little upset," Shamus said mildly. "You'd better go smooth her feathers."

"Presently." Dominic turned to face his father, his expression hard. "There's something I want to get straight with you first. She's right, Da, we both used her for our own purposes. You used her as a bond to keep me here and I wanted her enough to blind myself to what you were doing." He paused. "And you tried to use me, too. I don't like to be tricked, Da." His voice lowered to a silky murmur. "Oh, you're very clever, but you're not going to get everything you want. You'll have your bond, but it won't keep me at Killara. I'll tell you how it's going to be. I'm going treasure-hunting, and I'm going to find that treasure. I'm going to bring back a bonanza of gold to Killara, enough to make us into the landed royalty you always wanted to be. And when I do that, I'm going to pay off that damn mortgage and decide whether I want to let you stay on here. And you're not going to have a damn thing to say about it."

Shamus shook his head. "Patrick told us Elspeth had a bee in her bonnet about Kantalan. You're not fool enough to think it exists."

"I'm damn well going to find out." Dominic smiled coolly. "And if it doesn't exist, I'll find some other way to get what I want. I'll rob a train or join the bandidos down in Mexico or—"

"And you'll have me paying through the nose for another pardon," Shamus said grimly. "Don't talk crazy."

"I feel a little crazy. Crazy and trapped. I don't like that feeling one bit, Da."

Shamus glanced up the stairs. "You'll find there are compensations for giving up your freedom, if you choose to do it."

"Of course I choose to do it," Dominic said harshly. "Maybe I'm not as much your son as I thought. I won't make Elspeth into my whore and then send her away."

Shamus lifted a brow. "Really? I understood from Patrick that that was your original intention. Have you undergone a reformation, Dominic?"

Dominic flinched as he remembered Elspeth's words of yesterday regarding his need for reformation. He turned away. "I don't think Elspeth would think so. In her eyes I'm Satan's favorite offspring." He started up the stairs. "Hell, maybe she's right. Send down to the village for Father Benedict and tell him I want him in the chapel in two hours."

"You're going to marry her?"

"Yes. I'll probably have to hog-tie her and drag her before the priest kicking and screaming." His lips tightened as he looked over the banister at his father. "But I'm going to marry her. She thinks she's already experienced the fate of a whore in Hell's Bluff, but she had Silver and me to protect her. She doesn't realize how much more she could be hurt. She's very . . . innocent."

Shamus nodded, his expression sincerely regretful. "I like the girl and I'm truly sorry this was done to her in my house." He hesitated. "I didn't do it, Dominic. I won't deny I'm delighted with the result, but I've never had to victimize women or children to get my own way." He smiled crookedly. "However, I can see how you might have jumped to that conclusion. I'd go to great lengths to protect someone I love." He paused before adding gruffly. "As I love you, Dominic."

"I know that," Dominic said wearily. Now he didn't

know what to believe. Da would sack, burn, and pillage the entire territory if it meant protecting his family, and there was no one else who would have had anything to gain by encouraging Elspeth's seduction. Yet Shamus had never lied to him before and it was not like him to deal in anything as underhanded as this scheme. He met his father's gaze. "If you didn't drug Elspeth, who did?"

"I have no idea, but I'll find out." Shamus's lips tightened grimly. "No one does this to a guest at Killara. You can bet I'll have a few questions to put to Rosa after we get the wedding out of the way."

"You do that," Dominic said. "But right now making sure that Elspeth is protected is more important than asking questions. We'll leave after the ceremony. I don't think Elspeth will want to stay here any longer than necessary under the circumstances. We'll need two burros readied as pack animals. Tell Ramon to saddle my horse and the gray Elspeth rode yesterday."

"Anything else?" Shamus's tone was threaded with irony. "I'd advise you to wait until you come back with your saddlebags stuffed with gold before you start giving me orders, Dominic."

"Just one more thing." Dominic stopped at the head of the stairs to look down at Shamus. "I hope to God you're telling me the truth, because if I find out you did this to Elspeth, I swear I'll find a way of punishing you, Da. Do you understand?"

Shamus glared up at him fiercely, then a faint smile curved his lips. "Oh, yes, I understand, Dominic. Who could understand you better?" He turned back to the parlor. "Now, run along and try to pacify your sweet little Scottish bride-to-be." He frowned. "I have to tell Malvina we have a wedding in the offing. She'll probably want to check Miss Beetle's book on the proper etiquette involved."

Dominic gazed after him blankly. Etiquette? The entire world had gone mad. He turned and strode down the hall toward Elspeth's room.

16

Elspeth failed to answer when Dominic knocked on the door. He repeated the knock, waited a moment, then opened the door and stepped into the room.

"I don't wish to speak to you." She folded the black gown in her hands and put it into the open portmanteau on the bed. She didn't look at him as she turned, crossed the room to the armoire, took out her black cloak, and returned to the portmanteau. "I don't want to see you. I don't even want to think about you." Her hands were trembling as she tucked the folds of the voluminious garment into the bag. "I have no intention of having anything to do with you or any other Delaney for the remainder of my life."

"We have to talk." Dominic closed the door and leaned back against it, watching her as she moved across the room to the armoire again. She looked so damn fragile with that full pink nightgown billowing around her. Slender bare feet peeped from beneath the hem of the flannel gown at every step, and lashes, spiky with the tears she refused to shed, cast shadows on her thin cheeks and half-veiled eyes. His heart twisted with tenderness that served to lessen the rage he still felt at the situation. Poor little owl. He could scarcely blame her for wanting to forget the existence of the entire Delaney clan. "You have a right to be angry, but it doesn't alter the fact that what happened between us last night has to be faced and dealt with."

She didn't look at him as she jerked another gown

out of the armoire. "I have no wish to face it, I intend to forget it. There is no reason why I should remember you or anything that happened here at Killara." Her back was very straight as she turned toward the bed and began to fold the gown. "You will have no place in my life in the future, and I'll not let you or your fine parents make me feel shame or—" Her voice broke and she stopped to draw a deep breath. "Please. Leave me."

"I can't do that." Dominic cleared his throat to relieve its tightness. He didn't know if he could ever force himself to leave her again. He wanted to sit down and cradle her on his knees, he wanted to stroke her slender shoulders, to tell her she didn't have to be brave and struggle through this alone. He wanted to tell her that he would always be at her side when she needed him.

But he couldn't tell her that with any degree of certainty. His chances of survival were thin. She would be better off without him. "There are matters we must discuss. You're upset or you probably would have remembered that there could be consequences from last night." He paused. "What if you're with child?"

She whirled to face him, her eyes enormous in her pale face.

"I promised you I'd protect our child, Elspeth." He met her eyes gravely. "You've got to let me keep that promise."

She moistened her lips with her tongue. "Do you feel certain I really might be with child? It seems unreasonable that I should be punished for sinning only the once."

Tenderness touched him again, mixed with guilt and another emotion he didn't want to define. "It wasn't a sin," he said gently. "Or if it was, the sin was mine." He straightened and moved toward her. "And no, it's not certain. Often a man and woman must lie together many times to beget a child." He stopped in front of her. "But we can't take the chance, can we? You wouldn't want to bring a bastard into the world."

She flinched. "No, I wouldn't want—" She blinked rapidly to keep back the tears. "So much pain. I would never want to cause a helpless child that much pain. Oh, I should have stopped you. I *did* sin."

He touched her cheek with his index finger. "You couldn't have stopped me." His index finger moved to stroke her lower lip with gossamer lightness. "I ravished you, remember?"

He was ravishing her now, she thought hazily. Ravishing her senses, robbing her of resistance, taking away her anger with the exquisite tenderness in his words and his touch. "Yes. I do remember."

Once more his finger traced the outline of her lip. "Then you know I'm entirely at fault and must make atonement."

Atonement. She felt a sharp pain. Her lashes lowered to hide her eyes. "It would not be honest of me to let you shoulder the entire blame," she said haltingly. "I was not myself; I offered no resistance. I can see how you might have mistaken my acquiescence."

Her admission was clearly painful for her, but she had made it regardless of the price. The poignancy of that realization touched and shook him. "Then it's the duty of both of us to see that things are made right. You can see that, can't you?"

She nodded, still not looking at him.

"You'll have to marry me, Elspeth."

Her lashes flew up. "I will?"

He nodded. "I've sent for Father Benedict. We'll be married in the chapel right away. If we have a child, there will be no whispers of illegitimacy."

"Couldn't we wait? Perhaps there will be no child. You said—"

"I also said there was a chance." His lips tightened. "My future isn't exactly certain, and I'll not risk leaving you unwed if there's any possibility of your bearing my child."

She shivered. Death. He was saying he might die before his child was born. The thought brought a strange sense of panic and violent rejection. "Dominic, I don't want you . . ."

"I know you don't want to marry me. For God's sake, what woman would want to link her life to mine? But it will be only for a short time. Within a few weeks we'll know whether or not you're to bear my child. If you're not with child, I'll arrange for you to divorce me."

"Divorce," she repeated, shocked. First a fallen woman and now a divorced one, she thought distractedly. One was almost as bad as the other. "And if I am with child?"

His expression became shuttered and his finger dropped from her lips. "Then I make no promises. You've already remarked on how possessive we Delaneys can be." He stepped back. "It's a chance we'll both have to take."

Her face was troubled. "I don't know."

"Christ." His voice was suddenly harsh with impatience. "Are you afraid I'll hold you to our vows for no good reason? Do you think I want to marry you? You once said I was no gentleman, and Lord knows, you're right. But I'm also not a welcher who doesn't pay his debts. I took something from you that I can't give back, but I can give you my name and the protection it affords." His gaze slid away from her. "And I promise not to touch you again as I did last night. If we're lucky enough to escape with no consequences, I'd be a fool to endanger my freedom a second time."

Why did his words cause her such a wrenching pang? Of course he had no wish to marry her, she told herself sternly. Last night had been a mere moment of uncontrolled lust to him. Any woman would have served as well. He had been as angry with his father as she had been at the trap laid for them.

His gaze shifted to her face. "You can see we have no choice in this."

"Yes, I can see," she said dully. "I suppose there's nothing else we can do."

His shoulders made an almost imperceptible movement, as if throwing off a burden. "I'm glad you're being sensible. We'll be leaving for Kantalan right after the ceremony."

"Kantalan." Her eyes widened. "You're going with me?"

The corners of his lips twisted with a crooked smile. "How else can I be certain I have no offspring wandering the face of the earth? I don't think I could trust you to come to me for help if you needed it." He turned away. "We're taking two extra pack animals. If Kantalan exists, then maybe the treasure does too. Lord knows, Killara could use a barrel of gold in its coffers right now." He moved swiftly toward the door. "So we're not burdening the animals with anything but necessities. You can forget about that portmanteau. If your belongings won't fit into a saddlebag, then leave them here. You'd only have to discard them when we load the burros with gold." He opened the door. "If there is any gold."

"But you do believe there is a treasure, don't you?" Elspeth asked softly. "And you believe there is a Kantalan?"

He looked back at her. "I did once. I believed everything White Buffalo told me at the time."

"Even the prophecy?"

He shrugged. "I was a wild, loco kid. That was before I gave up believing in dreams and lost cities. I'm different now."

Elspeth felt a tug of tenderness. He was not as different as he pretended to be. There were still a few dreams he believed in. He believed in his vision for Killara and suddenly she realized that he believed in something else. "You didn't really answer me. Do you believe Kantalan exists?"

He was silent a moment. "Yes," he said quietly. "I believe in Kantalan. I suppose I always have." The door closed softly behind him.

Elspeth stared straight ahead at the ornate gold design on the ivory-colored altar cloth; she could see the brown-robed figure of Father Benedict as he left them and mounted the three steps to the high altar. Did that mean it was almost over? She had understood very little of the Latin the priest had murmured over them, and had answered only when prompted by Dominic. She cast a sidewise glance at Dominic, standing beside her. His expression was grave, almost stern, as his gaze, too, followed the priest.

Husband. He was going to be her husband in a few short minutes. How strange to think of this wild, hard man in such domestic terms. Yet she was surely an equally unlikely bride in her brown riding skirt and boots. Her only bridal touch was the white lace mantilla Rising Star had draped over her neat bun before she'd entered the chapel.

"Your head must be covered," Rising Star had said gently. "It is the custom." Then she had leaned forward and brushed Elspeth's cheek with her lips and whispered, "There is something wrong here. Malvina would not tell me why this was done in such haste. Are you content with this marriage? May I help you in any way?"

Content? Elspeth didn't know what she was feeling at this moment but she knew it was not contentment. She also knew there was nothing Rising Star could do to alter the circumstances of this marriage. "No, there is no way you can help me," she had said softly.

Rising Star had been silent for a moment, her dark eyes troubled. "I told Malvina I would not come and watch this marriage. I would share your joy, but I will not share your vows." She turned abruptly away. "God be with you." Then she was gone, hurrying back across the courtyard toward the house.

Elspeth glanced down at the fragile mantilla falling in graceful folds around her. "It is the custom." It was clear Rising Star tried very hard to follow the customs of her husband's people, and expected Elspeth to do likewise. It was the custom for a wife to respect and love her husband. It was the custom for her to bear his children and work at his side. It was the custom for her to occupy his bed and offer her body when he so desired. . . .

"Are you all right?" It was Dominic's low voice, his concerned gaze on her flushed cheeks. "It will be over in a minute."

She drew a shaky breath. "Yes," she whispered back. "It's only that this is so . . . so unusual for me."

His eyes twinkled. "It isn't exactly an everyday affair for me either." He slowly reached out and enfolded her small hand in his larger one. Support, comfort, serenity. How could one simple gesture tell her all those wonderful things? But his did.

Her clasp unconsciously tightened on his hand as she looked up to meet his eyes. She inhaled sharply and then forgot to breathe. There was something waiting there, something just out of reach, something beautiful.

He was gazing at her, his light eyes softly intent, his expression no longer amused, but holding the same breathless wonder. He impulsively moved closer. "Elspeth, I—"

The priest was returning, his plump face solemn, his voice still murmuring the words of the ritual.

With a painful effort Elspeth pulled her gaze away from Dominic's. For a moment she had felt they were joined in an intimacy more complete than the one they had known in the night. There had been a question asked and answered, a memory perceived and accepted, a closeness once known reborn. She hadn't wanted to abandon that closeness. It was a part of the beauty, a part of the merging, part of what had been and always would be.

"Kneel."

Elspeth's gaze flew back to Dominic. "What?"

"We have to kneel for the blessing." His hand still held her own and she saw in his taut pale face the same poignant regret she was experiencing, as if he, too, had been pulled back too soon from that other place.

"Very well." She didn't move, gazing up at him.

"Now." His smile lit his dark face with a rare masculine beauty. "Together."

Together. What a truly lovely word, she thought dreamily. It encompassed strength and companionship, a linking of minds and bodies through an eternity of belonging.

* * *

In the rear of the chapel the heavy black woolen draperies that formed the walls of the confessional box moved slowly to one side as if shifted by an unseen hand.

The afternoon sunlight streamed through the narrow windows of the chapel surrounding Dominic Delaney and Elspeth MacGregor in a nimbus of radiance as they stood before the altar. They were gazing at each other, their hands clasped and their faces illuminated by another radiance that came from within.

How beautiful they were, Ramon Torres thought, sentimental tears springing to his eyes. The man was so tall and dark and strong, the woman small and fair and fragile in her fine white lace mantilla. Could anything be more joyous and touching than two souls joined by a love as strong as the one mirrored on their faces now?

The ornate wrought-iron grillwork surrounding the confessional booth was very convenient, Ramon Torres thought absently as he rested the tip of the barrel of his pistol in the opening formed by the fretwork. He carefully shifted the hole he had made in the black woolen draperies that formed the walls of the confessional. The grillwork masked any glint of sunlight on the barrel and enabled him a clear view of Dominic and his bride as they took their vows.

He noticed regretfully that they had turned to the priest again and he could no longer see the emotion that lit their faces. It was a pity he would not be able to see their expressions as the bullet struck Dominic. He had been anticipating that pleasure since yesterday afternoon, and had even dreamed of it during the night. He had awakened in the hayloft in a sweat of pleasure, spilling his seed on the straw, his heart throbbing with the sweetness of his vision. It was seldom he dreamed of his prey, and it was an indication of how important Dominic Delaney had become to him, how dearly he held him in his affections.

He felt a momentary flash of sadness as he realized

that Dominic would never know in what esteem he was held. He would not even know that it was Ramon who had given him his last night of lust with the *gringa*. The drugging of the woman had been easy enough, but there had been a certain risk in creeping upstairs after most of the household had retired to move her to Dominic's bed and strip her. Yet he knew the danger had been well worth it when he looked at the two of them now.

The drawback in hunting the most dangerous prey was that the shot must almost always be in the back. He had hoped for something different for Dominic, but circumstances had proved unkind. When word had come to ready the horses and the burros for the couple's departure, he had known the prey would be leaving his home grounds. If he was to take Dominic off guard, this would be his last opportunity.

Ramon's muscles tautened as he leaned forward, his eyes narrowed on the two figures at the altar. It was suffocatingly hot in the booth, but he scarcely felt the heat. He was too full of the familiar excitement that always preceded the kill. Soon it would be time. He must be very, very still as he sat here in their midst, only he deliciously aware that the god holding power in this holy place was Ramon Torres.

Elspeth and Dominic fell to their knees on the cushion before the altar.

A pistol shot ripped through the silence.

The sound reverberated in the chapel, tearing through the misty veil that softened the moment to reveal the harsh ugliness of reality. The altar rail in front of Dominic splintered to reveal the paler fiber beneath the polished wood.

For a split-second Elspeth didn't realize what had happened. Then she saw the deep red stain blossoming like a hideous flower on the shoulder of Dominic's black suede jacket.

Her gaze flew to his face. She saw pain, weariness, and the most heartwrenching emotion of all, acceptance, as he slumped over the altar rail and then slowly slid to the floor.

Elspeth screamed!

The raw sound ripped painfully from her throat. With frantic swiftness she crawled the few feet to where Dominic lay, and lifted his head onto her lap. "No, dear heaven, no," she whispered. "Dominic!"

He didn't stir, his dark lashes still on his pale cheeks, his breathing shallow.

She was barely conscious of Shamus's muttered curses, the pounding of his boots on the tile floor as he ran toward the back of the chapel. Where was he going? she wondered wildly. Didn't he realize Dominic needed help?

Malvina was kneeling beside her. "Give him to me. I'll take care of him."

"What happened?" Elspeth didn't take her gaze from Dominic's face. "That sound—"

"He's been shot." Malvina's tone was impatient. "Even a tenderfoot should be able to see that. Now move out of the way and let me tend my boy."

Elspeth's arms unconsciously tightened around him. "No!"

Malvina stared at her. "No?"

"You have no right." Elspeth's expression was fierce. "He's mine now, and I'll be the one who cares for him." She carefully laid Dominic's head down on the floor and smoothed back the thick dark curls from his brow. "Fetch Rising Star, she may have the same knowledge of herbal remedies as Silver does." She turned to the priest. "I'll need a knife to cut away his jacket, and some bandages."

Father Benedict nodded and hurried away toward the door beside the altar.

"And do you intend to dig out the bullet?" Malvina asked caustically. "You think you'll have the stomach for it?"

Elspeth swallowed. "The altar rail has been splintered. I believe the bullet passed through his body." She looked down at Dominic, the pool of blood seemed to be spreading. Dear God, what if he died? Emptiness, darkness, pain. "Go away, I don't wish to be distracted."

"*You* go away." Malvina's eyes narrowed. "Do you think I'll let a whey-faced ninny kill my boy with her clumsiness?"

"When I traveled with my father, I had to do a good deal of nursing because many of those in our party would fall ill or have accidents."

"But have you tended to gunshot wounds?" Malvina demanded.

"No." Elspeth took the lace mantilla from her head, folded it, and held it on the wound. Please God, if I have sinned, don't punish me in this way, she prayed desperately. Don't punish Dominic. "But it will make no difference. I will not permit him to die." She lifted haunted eyes that held absolute purpose. "Dominic *will* live. Do you understand?"

"No, I don't. . . ." Malvina's gaze met Elspeth's. She nodded slowly, grudgingly. "I think I do understand." She hesitated and then asked gruffly, "Will you let me help you? I've tended many a gunshot wound. Together we can keep him with us."

Together. A swift jolt of agony shook Elspeth. Only a short time ago she had been thinking what a lovely bridge the word was forming over the gap that separated her from Dominic. Now it was being spoken with such a different meaning by his mother, whose expression revealed, that she, too, felt desperate about Dominic's condition.

"Very well," Elspeth said. She looked down beneath her fingers at the white lace that was now turning brilliant scarlet with Dominic's blood. "I will let you help . . . my husband."

"He's stirring." Malvina's said to Elspeth, who was crossing the threshold into Dominic's room. "I told you that little scratch wouldn't be nothing to him. Hardly worth putting him to bed." She stood up, looking down at Dominic with fierce pride. "It takes something a lot more powerful than one little bullet to kill a Delaney."

Elspeth shuddered as she closed the door, and then moved toward the bed. "If the bullet had been six inches lower, even a Delaney wouldn't have survived." She set the small bottle of salve on the nightstand. "Rising Star gave me this to—" She broke off as Dominic moved restlessly on the pillows. A sweet stream of relief poured through her. Dear heaven, Malvina was right, he was going to get well.

"He'll be waking up soon." Malvina walked briskly toward the door. "I'll be going down to tell Shamus before he leaves for Shamrock. You stay with Dominic."

Elspeth's smile was faintly ironical. "Thank you, that was my intention."

Malvina turned as she opened the door. "Give up this stupid idea of leaving Killara. I can see that you care for my boy. Stay here and keep him safe."

"You call this safe?" Elspeth gestured impatiently to Dominic. "I beg to disagree."

Malvina looked slightly disconcerted. "Safer than anywhere else. We weren't looking for any of our own to turn bushwhacker. It won't happen again. Shamus will see to that. You just do your part and keep the boy here."

Elspeth moved around the bed to the chair Malvina had vacated. Her gaze didn't leave Dominic's face as she sat down and leaned wearily against the brass-studded leather back of the chair. "I can't keep him anywhere he doesn't wish to be. He pays no mind to what I want and don't want."

Malvina smiled grimly. "Then find a way to make him pay attention. You were willing enough to face up to me and make me do what you wanted. Dominic shouldn't be any harder to manage. You just do what I told you and—"

"No," Elspeth said clearly, her gaze lifting to meet Malvina's. "I will *not* do what you tell me. I will make my own decisions and take the actions I see fit. I can't let a Delaney guide my path."

The expression on Malvina's face reflected annoyance, yet a flicker of grudging respect. "You don't have to get huffy. In the end it will probably come down to the same thing anyway." There was suddenly a glint of genuine amusement in the older woman's hazel eyes. "Because you've forgotten something. You're a Delaney now too." She punctuated the statement with an emphatic shutting of the door.

Elspeth stared blankly at the dark mahogany panels of the door. Only now did it sink in that she was a member of this proud clan. No longer Elspeth MacGregor, but Elspeth Delaney, wife of Dominic Delaney, who was perhaps the fiercest and most dangerous of them all. A feeling of overwhelming pride surged through her in a passionate, primitive flow that contained elements of both excitement and challenge.

What strange transformation had happened to her in that blinding moment of revelation when she had thought Dominic had been killed? How could fear tear away the teachings of a lifetime and permit her to see the world with such simplicity? Questions. So many questions. She had been asking questions all her life and had at last found the answer to the most important one.

Love. She loved Dominic Delaney with all her heart and soul and realized now that everything else must stem from that source. It made no difference that Dominic did not feel a similar passion for her. No, she was lying to herself. That knowledge hurt unbearably but could not change her feelings.

"Elspeth . . ."

Her gaze flew back to Dominic's face. His eyes were open, glittering in the dimness of the bedchamber. His face was tense and the wariness in those eyes made her ache with sympathy.

"Everything is fine. The bullet went through the fleshy part of your shoulder. Your mother said it was a clean wound and you should be up in a few days."

"Who . . . ?"

"One of the vaqueros saw Ramon Torres run out of the chapel and jump on a horse tethered in the back." She swallowed hard. "It seems Torres was the one who drugged me and carried me to your room. Your mother questioned Rosa a short time ago and she said he had been in the kitchen while she had prepared my tray." She shuddered as she felt again the chilling horror she had known when Malvina had told her it was Torres who had been responsible for her disgrace as well as the attempt to kill Dominic. How could loving smiles and murder exist hand in hand? "What reason could he possibly have for doing something like that?"

"I have no idea. Some men are . . . twisted. Did Da get him?"

Elspeth shook her head. "By the time your father and the vaqueros reached the foothills, Torres had vanished. But your father isn't giving up. He's leaving right away for Shamrock to fetch Patrick and your brothers. He says they'll track him down if it takes a lifetime."

A string of curses worthy of Ben Travis issued from Dominic's lips as he struggled to a sitting position.

"No!" Elspeth leaned forward, her hands outstretched to prevent him from moving. "What are you doing? Your wound—"

"Hurts like the devil," he finished between clenched teeth as he thrust the coverlet back. She caught a glimpse of naked thighs as he swung his feet to the floor. "Which is a damn good reason for you not to argue with me. I'm in no mood to take interference kindly. Go get my clothes."

"Get them yourself." She stood up and glared down at him. "I'll not be a party to this daftness. You were shot less than three hours ago, and now you're behaving as if nothing has happened. I thought you were dead, the blood—" Her hands clenched at her sides. "He was aiming at your heart, you stupid man. If you hadn't knelt at just that moment, you would have been killed and yet you . . ." She trailed off in a helpless sputter of fury. "You're *daft*, Dominic Delaney."

"I've suspected that for some time," Dominic said wearily. "But not daft enough to bring any more murderers down on my family, nor to stay at Killara and lure Ramon Torres back to try again."

"He won't come back. He would be as daft as you are to come back."

"He was loco enough to take a shot at me within fifty yards of the homestead." His gaze met hers unflinchingly. "A foot to the left and that shot could have blown your brains out. I'm not taking a risk like that again. I'm leaving Killara tonight for Hell's Bluff."

She stared angrily at him. "And what if he follows you?"

"I'll be ready for him."

She wanted to scream at him, shake him, dig her fingers into that dark hair and pull hard. If she had to love a man, why couldn't it have been one with less stubbornness and more sense? She was so frightened for him she was trembling and ill with it, and he sat there with his lips set and his jaw squared and she knew she could not sway him.

"Very well." She whirled and stormed over to the bureau and pulled open the drawer. She grabbed an indiscriminate armload of garments, carried them back to him, and hurled them on the bed. "There are your clothes. Don't expect me to help you dress. Your mother said that a wound like that was nothing to a Delaney. I have other tasks to keep me busy if we're to ride out of here tonight. I have no time for tending obstinate, bad-tempered—"

"We?" Dominic frowned. "*We* aren't riding anywhere. You're staying here, where you'll be safe."

She planted her hands on her hips. "Oh, no, if you're determined to leave your sickbed, then we might just as well continue with our plans. Why should I let you go back to Hell's Bluff when you promised to take me to Kantalan?"

"Because the circumstances are different now, dammit. I'm being hunted."

"What's different about that? According to what Patrick and Silver have told me, you've been hunted by these killers for—" She stopped and tried to steady her voice. "I'll not let you break your promise to me. I'm going with you to Kantalan, Dominic. Or do you want me to go alone?"

"You can't go alone. Torres knows you're my wife. He'd follow you, use you to get at me." Dominic's stomach turned over as he had a sudden memory of young Sam Bergstrom's eyes, open and staring, the round bullet hole in his temple. "He'll *kill* you, dammit."

Elspeth smiled sweetly. "Then you'd better go with me, hadn't you, Dominic?" She turned and strode toward the door. "I'll tell your mother we're leaving. She's not going to be pleased. For some reason, she has a great fondness for you. At the moment I cannot imagine why."

"Elspeth!" His tone was somewhere between a growl and a shout.

"You don't need to raise your voice just because you're not going to get your own way in this." She glanced back over her shoulder. "I told you I had to go to Kantalan."

"And you can think of nothing else," he said between his teeth. "Nothing else is important to you."

"I'm glad you finally realize that." She slammed the door and immediately wilted against its smooth panels, her throat tight with tears. She hadn't thought she'd be able to hold on to her anger until she had gotten out of the room. She had been so frightened that he would ride out alone.

Boldness had been her only weapon against that terrible fear. She could not offer him a love he did not want and would not value. There had probably been many beautiful women who had loved and wanted Dominic Delaney. If he had not stayed with any of them, a plain woman like herself could not expect to hold him by her side. And, if she could not hold him, then she must go with him and find a way of protecting him. To Hell's Bluff or to Kantalan it did not matter, except that in the male-dominated world of the boomtown there would be many places she would not be permitted to accompany him.

A sad smile touched her lips as she remembered Dominic's last words to her regarding her obsession for Kantalan. It was just as well he didn't realize that the dream of a lifetime was now dimming in comparison with the passionate obsession embodied in one man.

She straightened slowly and then set off down the corridor, her footsteps firm and decisive as she went in search of Malvina.

Ramon Torres carefully fastened the long, bushy branch to his saddlebags and remounted his horse. As he rode, the branch would drag behind him and erase all signs of his passing, a trick he had learned from his comanchero father. He had learned very little else from that mongrel son of a bitch, he thought bitterly, except to dodge blows when the bastard had imbibed too much tequila. He should not be so uncharitable, he chided himself. After all, it had been the bounty on his father's head that had started him off on this most pleasant of occupations.

He could feel the excitement tighten his chest as he kicked Chiquita into a gallop. He didn't like this end of the game overmuch, but it would not last long, and then he would once more be the hunter again. Once he had lost Shamus and the men who rode with him, he would double back and begin to trail Dominic and his little bride.

If he knew his prey, Dominic would not let a minor wound stop him for long. Torres felt a glow of almost paternal pride touch him with gentle fingers. He should be angry that fortune had again robbed him of his kill, but that was not the case. Now Dominic knew that he was hunted, so every one of the last moments of his life would take on the brilliance of a facet of a fine jewel. When Dominic finally realized the end had come, it would be with a dazzling explosion of sorrow and panic.

It was a thought that soothed Ramon's impatience and frustration and caused him to smile in pure joy.

17

Elspeth cast a quick glance at Malvina saying farewell to Dominic a few yards away by the fence of the corral; she reached into the pocket of her riding skirt. "I've written a note to Silver." Elspeth thrust the folded paper into Rising Star's hand. "Please give it to her when she returns this evening. I wanted to explain and thank her for everything she's done for me."

Rising Star nodded. "I'm glad you thought of her." She smiled sadly. "It is important that Silver feels she has value to those she cares about. There are too many of us who love her and yet are afraid to show that love."

Elspeth's eyes widened. "But you can't be speaking of yourself. Silver told me how you saw that she was educated and insisted she stay here at Killara for a portion of each year."

"It wasn't enough." Rising Star reached up to pat the nose of the gray mare, her gaze avoiding Elspeth's. "I was afraid I'd lose what I had gained here. I'm not as brave and bold as Silver. I was afraid to take more than the tiniest step toward her. I will try to do better in the future. Perhaps when my child is born . . ." She trailed off and smiled. "Everything will be different then."

"I hope you're right," Elspeth said gently. "Goodbye Rising Star."

"Go with God." Rising Star took a step back. "Good

luck finding your Kantalan." The faintest shadow seemed to pass through her eyes. "I feel I should be going with you."

Elspeth shook her head. "You're with child and there's nothing for you in Kantalan."

"No, there's nothing for me there," Rising Star whispered. "Except, perhaps, my destiny." She moved her shoulders as if shrugging off a burden. "But that is the Indian talking. I must think like a white woman now. Whites believe they can write their own destinies. You are right, my place is here with my husband and my child." She turned away. "Now I must say good-bye to Dominic. Be sure to use the salve I gave you."

"If he will let me. He is very displeased with me at present."

"It will pass. I think he's worried you may be harmed if he takes you with him. I'm surprised that he consented to continue with his plans to go to Kantalan."

"He had no choice. Do you think I'd let the man ride out alone with a hole in his shoulder? His mother may think he's as invulnerable as Achilles and as immortal as Zeus because he bears the Delaney name, but I'm not so foolish."

A tiny smile tugged at Rising Star's lips. "I see. No wonder Dominic is displeased. He does not like having his decisions challenged. Your trip to Kantalan may be more interesting than I had thought possible."

The sun was going down when Dominic and Elspeth rode out of the stableyard leading the two pack animals. Rising Star and Malvina gazed after them in silence until they were lost from view. Then Malvina turned briskly back to the house. "No use standing around here with long faces. They'll be back. Dominic won't let anyone keep him from getting what he goes after; he's too much like Shamus." She started across the stableyard. "I've got things to do. Shamus and the boys will be riding in from Shamrock soon and they'll be wanting a meal as well as some food prepared for the trail. Rosa is weeping and wailing like a sick puppy over the way Torres used her." Her expression turned grim. "She's lucky I don't knock her silly head off for letting that murdering bastard crawl into her bed, instead of putting up with her foolishness."

"I could help you," Rising Star offered hesitantly.

Malvina paused and for a moment Rising Star thought she was going to agree. "That won't be necessary." Her tone was stilted. "I can manage fine by myself."

Loneliness. Just once why wouldn't Malvina let her do something? Rising Star wondered. Why couldn't she share in the running of Killara? She was so terribly lonely . . . and weary of being treated with the forced politeness of a guest who had overstayed her welcome.

Rising Star's hands clenched slowly at her sides as she watched Malvina disappear into the house. Patience. She must have patience. It would be different when the child was born. In spite of what Silver claimed, the birth of the child had to be the key that would open all doors. Joshua would be home tonight, and she would no longer be alone. Even though Malvina refused to allow her to help in the kitchen, there were many things she could do while she waited. She could practice her French or compose a poem. There were always books, the wonderful world of books that had once been her challenge and were now her solace. She squared her shoulders as she started across the stableyard. She was a very fortunate woman and she would be stupid to permit herself to be depressed by Malvina's coldness.

Joshua was here!

Even in the darkness Rising Star knew unerringly which of the riders in the stableyard was Joshua. He was not as tall as his father, his brothers, or Patrick; yet had his silhouette been identical to theirs she still would have been able to identify him instantly.

She let the lace curtain she had held to one side swing back into place and ran over to the oval mirror on the wall. She quickly tidied her hair, straightened the folds of her white cotton robe, and pinched color into her cheeks. Then she drew a deep breath and sat down on the edge of the bed, clasping her hands on her lap. It seemed a long time before she heard Joshua at the door.

He looked tired. His dark curly hair was frosted with fine motes of dust, and his green shirt, darkened by perspiration, clung to him like a second skin. Tenderness tightened her throat and moved through her in a soft, glowing tide. "You've been working hard at Shamrock?" She jumped to her feet and crossed the room toward him. "Are Anne and William well? Would you like me to tell Rosa to heat water for your bath?"

He shook his head and answered the last question first. "I only have time to wash some of the sweat off me and grab a couple clean shirts. Da doesn't want to let Torres's trail get cold." He crossed to the washstand against the wall and poured water from the pitcher into the basin. "Anne and William are fine."

"I was hoping you could stay until tomorrow morning," she whispered as she stepped behind him. Her arms slid around his waist and she pressed her cheek to his back. "I have missed you. Have you missed me?"

"Yes." She could feel the muscles of his spine tense against her cheek. "Yes, I've missed you." He dipped his palms into the basin and splashed water onto his face. "Hand me that towel, will you?"

She stepped back and handed him a white towel from the rack. Loneliness. Yet he had said he had missed her. She mustn't demand too much. She knew he didn't like to be crowded, but it was so hard not to— "You're tired. Perhaps you could join them later."

He shook his head as he dabbed the water from his face. "I want my chance at Torres." His voice was harsh. "He shot my brother, dammit."

"It was not a serious wound."

"That's not the point. He *shot* him. No one is going to hurt one of my family and ride away. You should know by now that Delaneys don't forgive harm to one of our own."

She flinched. "I do know that, Joshua."

"I guess you do," he said wearily, staring into her strained face. He threw the towel onto the washstand. "I've got to get downstairs. Da wanted us ready to leave by the time fresh horses are saddled and the provisions packed." He took a step closer and kissed her gently on the forehead. "Are you all right?" he asked awkwardly.

"Yes."

He hesitated, looking down at her with a curiously tormented expression. "And the child?"

"Well. I think it must be a boy. He kicks with the strength of a warrior."

A shadow crossed his face. "You're not in any pain?" His palm gently cradled the curve of her cheek. "He doesn't hurt you?"

Her hand covered his on her cheek, holding it there, desperately savoring the tenderness of the action. "There is no pain, and if there were, it would be pleasure-pain. We are going to have a fine son, Joshua."

He stared down at her softly glowing eyes and for an instant she again saw the torment before his hand dropped from her cheek and he turned away. "Take care of yourself while I'm away."

"When will you be back?"

"I don't know. We'll be gone as long as it takes to find that bastard." The hardness was once again in his voice. "We don't want him on Dom's trail." He opened the door. "Good-bye, Star."

"Joshua—"

He looked back over his shoulder inquiringly.

"Nothing." Her teeth pressed into her lower lip. "Good journey. I will miss you until you return."

He smiled. For a moment there was no torment, no harshness, no veil of guilt or memory between them. He was the young Joshua who had come to her village and captured her heart with his boyish smile and loving passion.

He closed the door behind him, leaving her with loneliness . . . and hope.

Silver threw open the door and burst into the room. Her clothes were as dusty and her skin as dirty as Joshua's had been. Her gray eyes were flashing. "Is it true?" she demanded. "I saw Patrick downstairs. He told me of the wedding, the shooting, Torres . . . Elspeth has really left without me?"

A tiny smiled appeared on Rising Star's face. "I believe that was always her plan. That's why you went back to the village to hire a fine guide for her." Her gaze searched Silver's face. "But I think you had no intention of fetching a guide to lead her to Kantalan."

"I did not lie," Silver said hotly. "I went to the village as I told her I would. Can I help it if I am the best guide in the village? She is far better off with me."

"Elspeth has Dominic now. He will see that she comes to no harm. You trust Dominic, Silver."

"Yes, but I wanted . . ." Silver nibbled at her lower lip. "This is all very strange. Did the old woman force her into the marriage?"

Rising Star shook her head. There was no use arousing Silver's fervent protectiveness by revealing Torres's schemes. "It was not Malvina's doing. Elspeth wed Dominic of her own will."

Disappointment clouded Silver's expression. "I thought perhaps . . ."

"I know." Rising Star picked up the folded slip of paper from the desk and handed it to Silver. "She left this note for you."

Silver unfolded the paper and scanned it quickly. Disappointment showed plainly in her expression. "I am not to follow her. She will see me when she returns. She holds me in the greatest affection." She suddenly crushed the paper in the palm of her hand. "But I want to be *with* them."

"She would only send you back," Rising Star said gently. "She feels she has taken too much from you."

"She does not understand. I want to help," Silver said. "Why does she not understand?"

Rising Star understood, if Elspeth did not. To be permitted to give service was to belong, to be denied the giving of gifts was to be shut out in the cold outer darkness. Oh, yes, she understood very well. "She wants to keep you out of harm's way. She does not mean to close you off from her or to hurt you."

Silver's head lifted, her light eyes glittering proudly. "She did not hurt me. I did not really want to go chasing after a dream city. It is probably better that I stay here. It is more important for me to help find Torres." She walked swiftly to the door. "Yes, I am needed more here."

"Silver, no!"

But Silver was gone, the bedroom door left ajar, and the soft thud of her moccasinned feet sounding on the stairs.

Rising Star moved slowly across the room to close the door, sympathy for Silver engulfing her. Would the girl never learn she could not force them to yield a place for her? She had received a thousand cuts to her soul, and yet she still rushed forward with reckless passion.

No, her own way was best, Rising Star thought. Patience and conformity to the rules of the white world were the best attributes for an Indian who wished to survive and live with them. Silver would just have to learn that lesson as she had.

Lanterns hung on the posts of the corral so the men could see to cut out and saddle the horses cast a soft glow over the scene. About twenty vaqueros were mounted and waiting to ride out. Cort, Sean, and young William were strolling toward the corral from the direction of the barn and Silver could see Patrick, Joshua, and Shamus just ahead, their destination the same as hers.

"Wait!" Silver ran across the flagstones. "I'm coming with you."

"The hell you are." Shamus whirled to face her. The

gray stetson on his head threw his face into shadow, and the lantern light behind him made his body look ominously large and dark. "This is Delaney business."

"That's why I'm going with you. You need me to help you find that son of a bitch who shot Dominic."

"Watch your language," Shamus said sharply. "You may not believe you're a female, but I won't have Malvina's ears sullied by your filthy mouth."

Silver made a gesture of impatience. "Malvina's still in the house. Besides, that is not important. Do you want to find Torres or not?"

"We'll find him," Shamus said. "Patrick is a damn good tracker. We don't need you."

"I *taught* Patrick," Silver snapped. "When we were children I took him out into the woods and taught him what I had learned from my grandfather, Black Bear."

"That's right, she did, Gran-da," Patrick interjected quickly. "There's no one better on the trail than Silver."

Silver shot him a glance of passionate gratitude that was immediately hidden beneath a facade of nonchalance. "You were not as clumsy as I thought you would be," she conceded. "But you were never as good as me."

"Thank you." Patrick's voice held a note of dry humor. "I'm glad you think I'm not completely beyond help."

"Patrick's good enough," Shamus said. "You get along back to the house."

"Why?" Silver's hands clenched into fists at her sides. "I can help you. Only a very stupid man would refuse help when it is offered."

"Or one who doubts the quality of the help," Shamus said. "I told you the Delaneys have no—"

"You *do* need me." Silver took a step closer. "I can track and live off the land. I can read the turn of a stone or the way a blade of grass is crushed. I can do anything I want to do. Hell, if I wanted to, I could build a fine rancho like this one. No, a much finer rancho. And I'm a Delaney too. There's no shame in accepting help from me. Let me find this man for you."

Shamus's eyes narrowed on her face. "You think you can do anything in the whole damn world."

She stared back at him unflinchingly. "Why not? Don't you, old man?"

Shamus started to turn away.

"Stop!" Silver's voice vibrated with emotion. "I want to hear you say it, Shamus. Just this once, tell the truth. You know I am a Delaney. Say it!"

He glared at her over his shoulder. "Why should I change my mind? There's no proof you're Boyd's daughter."

"You know it, old man." Silver's eyes blazed. "And I know it! I want nothing else from you. You can keep your rancho, your fine horses, and your cattle. I want only one thing from you. *Name me your kin.*"

Shamus gazed back at her, anger, defiance, and an odd element of pride illuminating his harsh features. He turned away. "We've got no time for this nonsense. Go back to the house and tell your aunt I told her to teach you some manners."

"*Tell* me."

He stopped and was silent for a long moment, his expression hidden from her. Then he looked back over his shoulder. "You're no Delaney. I said it fifteen years ago and I say it now."

Silver's lids fluttered for the tenth of a second, her body tensing as if it had received a blow. Her eyes shimmered in the lanternlight like crystal under clear water. "Then you lie," she said slowly. "And I am done with your lies." She turned and strode majestically toward her mare tethered at the corral. "And I am done with the Delaneys. I will not return here."

She ignored the silent vaqueros as she mounted then walked the horse up to where Shamus, Patrick, and Joshua stood watching her. She looked down at Shamus. "What a fool you are, Shamus Delaney," she said clearly. "Can you not see what you have lost in me?" She turned and kicked the mare into a gallop, her straight dark hair streaming behind her in a wild silken pennant as the mare stretched out in a dead run.

Patrick muttered a curse beneath his breath and took a step toward his horse.

"Where do you think you're going?" Shamus asked sharply.

"After her," Patrick said as he swung into the saddle. "She meant it, dammit."

"No." Shamus mounted his own horse.

Patrick frowned. "Gran-da, Silver shouldn't—"

"I said no! I still run Killara and this family, don't I?"

Patrick didn't answer, gazing mutinously in the direction Silver had taken.

"Don't I?" Shamus asked again with dangerous softness.

Patrick nodded jerkily. "But you've made a mistake."

"And now children are teaching their elders," Shamus drawled. "Next, young William will be telling me how to run my family."

"I'm no youngster," Patrick said, stung.

"Then concentrate on tracking Torres and on keeping him from killing your uncle." Shamus kicked his horse, and the animal bounded forward. The vaqueros fell in behind him and the stableyard was suddenly filled with clouds of dust and churning earth.

"You'd better catch up with him." It was Josh's quiet voice beside Patrick. "It will be daybreak soon and he'll need you when we reach the foothills."

"He was wrong, Josh."

Joshua's hand grasped Patrick's shoulder in silent support. Then the reassuring touch was gone and Joshua was gone, too, moving through the column of vaqueros to ride beside his brothers and Shamus.

Patrick could feel a little of the tension drain from him. Joshua always had that effect on him. Since he was a kid younger than William, Joshua's quiet strength had always seemed to spread a tranquil

balm when he was at his rawest. It had been Joshua
who had taken the time to teach him to throw a lariat,
to mend a fence, to ride the wild range ponies. Joshua
who had been neither father nor brother but something in between. How many cattle drives, how many
nights in the hills had they spent together in quiet
companionship? Nights that Rising Star must have
spent alone, Patrick realized suddenly.

His gaze flew to Joshua, riding now beside Shamus.
Joshua's eyes were fixed straight ahead, a faint smile
lifting his lips at the corners at something Cort had
said. He didn't look back at the house where Rising
Star waited for him. Why didn't he just look over his
shoulder and lift his hand in farewell? Rising Star
would be standing at the window watching Joshua
leave; Patrick had seen her there a hundred times
since she had come to Killara. And Joshua must know
she'd be there tonight.

It wasn't any of his business why Joshua didn't
acknowledge her presence, Patrick told himself desperately. Perhaps she wasn't at the window, maybe
Joshua knew she was tired and had gone to bed. There
wouldn't be any sense in Joshua looking back if he
knew she wasn't there.

But she *would* be there, Patrick thought, prepared
for bed, her hair brushed to hang straight and
shimmering around her. She would be dressed in
something loose and soft and white and the light
behind her would reveal the grace and strength of her
body. Joshua should know, no matter what she said,
that she would be at the window watching them
leave.

They would be out of the stableyard soon and it
would be too late. She would turn away, her shoulders would slump with disappointment. She would
turn out the lamp and go to bed. Alone. Hell, why
didn't Joshua— Joshua wasn't going to turn around.

Patrick's hands tightened on the reins until his
knuckles were white. And Patrick certainly wasn't
going to turn to look up at the window either. It was
loco for him to get upset like this over such a little

thing. Joshua's wife. She was Joshua's wife. Could she distinguish which rider was Joshua in the darkness? She had been married to his uncle for fourteen years. Surely she knew him well enough to recognize him at a distance. But perhaps not, perhaps he could make her feel a little less lonely if he— Patrick dropped back a few yards behind the last rider and looked back over his shoulder.

Rising Star was standing at the window.

He slowly lifted his arm and waved it in an arc. He could see her stiffen. Did she think he was Joshua? Oh, God, did he *want* her to think he was Joshua?

Her hand lifted in a gesture of farewell. Sweetness flooded Patrick's being, followed immediately by hot guilt.

What the hell was he doing? He spurred desperately and his horse leapt forward until he was riding beside Joshua at the head of the column.

Joshua looked at him and smiled. "You in a hurry?"

"No." Patrick swallowed. It had not been a betrayal. He had taken nothing from Joshua that his uncle had wanted. "You said Gran-da might need me up here." He kept his eyes on the foothills, away from that lighted window framing the glowing beauty of Rising Star. "So I thought I'd better come up and show you tenderfoots how to tell the difference between a horse's tracks and a jackrabbit's."

18

"**W**ill you stop being foolish and let me help you?" Elspeth's voice was tart with exasperation. "You've demonstrated how strong and stoic a Delaney can be. I think it's time you exhibited a little intelligence as well. You've made camp, cooked our meal, watered the horses, and treated me as if I were incapable of buttoning my own shoes. I may not be experienced on the trail, but I am not entirely stupid. Tell me what to do and I'll do it."

"There's nothing left to do. It's late. Crawl into your blankets and get to sleep. I'll just scout around on our back trail and make sure—"

"No," she said clearly. "Torres couldn't be after you yet, and I won't let you exhaust yourself. Sit down and let me take a look at your wound. With all this moving about you'll be lucky if it hasn't started bleeding again."

"It's not bleeding." He started to turn away.

"Let me see." Her fingers were quickly unbuttoning his white shirt. "Any man who would jump out of a sickbed and carry on as you've done is hardly to be trusted," she muttered. "Daft. Positively daft. Sit down."

"I'm not blee—" He inhaled sharply as her fingers slipped beneath the bandage, exploring the tender flesh around the wound. "Ouch! What the hell are you trying to do to me?"

"Reminding you that you were shot only this

afternoon. I thought it time someone did." She deliberately pressed again on the sore flesh. *"Sit down."*

He sat down.

She immediately knelt beside him on the blanket and quickly loosened the bandage. "That's better."

"In your opinion," Dominic said dryly. "It feels like someone stabbed me with red-hot splinters."

"I didn't really hurt the wound." She unscrewed the lid from the small jar of salve Rising Star had given her. "You weren't listening to me again. It was necessary I get your attention."

"I think you succeeded." He gritted his teeth as she carefully applied the salve. "You must have been taking lessons from Silver. The women of her tribe are very good at this kind of torture."

Her gaze lifted. "Am I hurting you?"

"Hell, yes."

"Good." She swiftly replaced the bandage and fastened it in place. "Then you'll have to take care that it will heal swiftly so you'll no longer need my clumsy nursing, won't you?" She sat back on her heels and met his gaze. "We'll start by avoiding putting unneeded strain on it. There are many things I can do to help. Patrick showed me how to saddle a horse. From now on I will do that. I can gather wood and I'll learn how to build a fire."

"It seems you're taking charge of everything," he said sardonically. "Am I allowed to do anything?"

"Yes." She swallowed. "I don't think I could kill or skin a rabbit as you did. I would appreciate it if you would continue to provide for our meals."

He studied her. "Yet you ate with good appetite."

"I realize it's foolish to be squeamish." She buttoned his shirt. "We must eat. If you think it unfair that I don't share in the preparation, then of course I will do so."

He shook his head slowly. "No, I think I can handle it by myself."

"And you will let me do the other tasks until your shoulder is less sore?"

A curious smile tugged at his lips. "What will you do if I don't?"

She smiled back at him with angelic sweetness. "Then I'll find it necessary to dress your wound five times a day instead of two, and we've already established how clumsy I can be."

He suddenly threw back his head and laughed. "My God, I've changed my mind. I think you could give Silver lessons. When I remember what a meek little miss you were when you first came to Hell's Bluff—"

"I was never meek. Unsure, perhaps, and frightened."

The grin faded from Dominic's face. "You didn't show it. You always stood up to me."

"I didn't want to be a coward." She gazed into the blue-orange heart of the flames. "My father always told me a MacGregor must never be afraid." She tried to smile. "Besides, it wasn't only you I feared. Everything was so new and strange to me and I felt very much alone."

"Did you?" Dominic didn't look at her. "I guess we all feel like that sometimes."

"And then so many things happened. I was injured, Andre—" She closed her eyes as that memory came back to her. "Poor Andre," she whispered. "We were alike, you know. Two strangers who couldn't understand this wild country."

"You're not like Marzonoff. Not any longer."

She opened her eyes. "What do you mean?"

"I mean you're beginning to understand us now." He smiled faintly. She looked surprised, he thought. Perhaps she didn't realize how much she had changed in these last weeks. Determination, courage, and dogged endurance had probably always been a part of her character, but now those qualities had been refined and sharpened. "Aren't you, Elspeth?"

She thought about it. Then she nodded slowly. "I guess I do understand you better than when I first came." Her lips tightened. "That's not to say I approve of the barbaric way in which you westerners accomplish your ends. I believe you need a great deal of civilizing."

"Uhmmm . . ." His lips twitched. "Like the civilized way you accomplished your purpose tonight? As I remember, you used both pain and intimidation."

"I didn't—" She stopped. "Well, perhaps I did, but it was the only way I could deal with a stubborn man who insisted on—"

He held up his hands to stop the flow of words. "I'm not quarreling with your methods. I thoroughly approve of them." He grinned. "I'm used to them. That's the way we do things out here." He added softly, "The barbaric way."

"It's not the same. I didn't . . ." She trailed off as she noticed the amused smile on his lips was deepening by the second. It was definitely time to change the subject. "How long will it take us to get to Kantalan?"

"I'm not sure. Perhaps three or four weeks." He reached into his back pocket and drew out a piece of soft deerskin and unfolded it to reveal a crudely drawn map.

Elspeth felt a flicker of excitement. "This is the map White Buffalo gave you?"

He nodded. "I dug it out of my saddlebags before we left Killara." His index finger tapped a spot at the top of the map. "Here's where we are now." His finger traced a line down the smooth leather surface. "We cross the Mexican border here and then bear southeast until we get to the Sierra Madre range. Kantalan is encircled by high mountains which White Buffalo said were impassable." His finger tapped a small X on one of the inverted V's forming a circle around the largest X on the map. "Except for a pass right here on the third mountain to the east of the Sun Child. It's hidden by a waterfall and, according to what Cadra said, we'll have to swim the horses thirty yards or so before we get to the shallows."

"No wonder no one has discovered it in all these years," Elspeth said. She pointed to the tallest of the mountains indicated on the map. "The Sun Child?"

Dominic nodded.

A shiver went through her, but she didn't know

whether it was from excitement or fear. "In only a few weeks we'll see it. We'll see Kantalan."

Dominic folded the map and put it back into his pocket. "If there's anything to see." He picked up a stick and stoked the flames of the fire. "Lie down and go to sleep. I want to get an early start. I'd like to be halfway to the border by tomorrow night."

"Very well." She obediently stood up and moved the few yards to where Dominic had fashioned her blankets into a pallet. She settled her head on her saddle and found it made a fairly tolerable pillow. "Good night." She pulled the blanket up to her chin and closed her eyes.

He watched her with amusement mixed with irritation. He might as well have been a eunuch for all the self-consciousness she was displaying in his presence. "I'm glad you're being sensible. Some women would be nervous about being out here alone with me. Some women wouldn't believe I'd keep my promise."

"Then they'd be very stupid," she said calmly. "Good heavens, you were shot today. You're exhausted and in pain."

But he wasn't dead, he wanted to tell her. And he was beginning to think that he'd have to be dead not to want her. His shoulder wasn't the only part of his anatomy that was throbbing.

What was he thinking? He should be glad she wasn't afraid of him. He had made a promise that was going to be difficult enough to keep.

He lay down and drew the blanket over him, deliberately turning his back on the slim figure across the fire. He didn't bother to take off his gunbelt. He would stay until Elspeth was asleep and then he would creep out of camp to make sure they hadn't been followed.

Torres. Clever, bold, deadly. Dominic knew that breed of man well. There had been many like Torres stalking him in the last ten years. Yet perhaps Ramon Torres could be the most dangerous of all. He had displayed great patience and his twisted, dark whimsy in putting Elspeth into his bed last night struck a chill through him. The thought of Torres handling Elspeth while she was unconscious and helpless made him sick with terror and fury, but it was the patience of the man that frightened Dominic the most. The knowledge that there was someone out there waiting, someone who would wait forever, if need be, for him to become careless. Waiting for him to fall asleep when he should remain awake, to relax when he should have remained alert, to take that one drink too many that would slow his speed.

But that would not happen tonight. Tonight there would be no carelessness, and, if Torres was out there, the bastard would just have to bide his time.

"Move over, Star."

It was Joshua's voice and it brought Rising Star from the depths of sleep to joyous awakening. She turned over, her arms going out to him. Her hands ran lovingly over his face, her fingers reading the lines of weariness and exploring the rough stubble on his lean cheeks in the darkness of the bedchamber. "Joshua." She nestled closer.

His hands settled on her shoulders, holding her away from him. "Don't come any closer. I smell of dust and sweat and I'm too damn tired to wash up right now."

"I don't care." It had been four long days, and now he was home. She wanted to light the lamp and look at him, see him smile at her. "I want to hold you." She took his left hand from her shoulder and lifted it to her lips to press her lips to his palm. "Did you find Torres?"

"No, he was damn clever about hiding his tracks. We've been searching those blasted hills, running around in circles, ever since we left Killara." There was frustration as well as anger in Joshua's voice. "Patrick finally found signs where he might have doubled back toward Killara. Da thinks he may be on Dom's trail again."

"You have given up?"

Joshua jerked his hand away from her lips. "Don't be silly. Of course not, we're going to change horses and set out again in the morning. We'll get him."

"I only thought—"

"Go to sleep. We're both too tired for thinking right now." He was silent a moment before he said haltingly, "I'm sorry, I didn't mean to be sharp with you."

"It doesn't matter. You are tired. I should not have questioned you until you'd had a chance to rest."

"For God's sake, it does matter." His tone was ragged. "Will you stop being so damn kind? I hurt you, didn't I?"

"Yes."

He didn't speak again, but she could feel the tenseness and pain emanating from his rigid body next to her own. She wanted to reach out and try to stroke the pain away but he would not let her get close enough. The barrier between them was too high to scale. They had to find a way to overcome that barrier, she thought desperately. They had to find a way to end their pain. But there was a way, she realized with relief. The child. "The baby moved much today," she said softly. "I took a long walk this afternoon and thought about the child and how he will love it here at Killara. I could see you teaching him to ride, putting him on his first pony, just as you did Patrick. It will be such a fine time when—" She broke off. He hadn't moved, but she could feel his withdrawal like a cold wind howling between them. "What's wrong?"

"Nothing."

"No, there's something wrong." Her hand went to his cheek and hovered there, afraid to touch him. "Tell me."

"I was just wondering if the child wouldn't be happier spending some time each year with your people," he muttered. "Like Silver."

The wind was no longer cold but icy, freezing her with its scourging bitterness. "Like Silver?"

"Not all the time, naturally, but . . ." He trailed off. "I thought it might be easier."

Like Silver. The words reverberated within her like a gong that had been struck by a giant hammer, sending out waves of shimmering pain, "Easier for who?"

He didn't answer. He didn't have to answer.

She sat up in bed and swung her feet to the floor.

"What are you doing?"

"I want to see your face." She lit the lamp on the bedside table.

"For God's sake, it's the middle of the night. We don't have to talk about this now. It's just something to think about."

"Yes, it's something to think about." She stood up and turned to face him. "You do not want the child." It was a statement not a question.

His gaze slid away from her. "I didn't say that."

"A man does not send his child away from him if he desires it." She wrapped her arms around herself, trying to impart warmth to melt the ice surrounding her. "Why did you not tell me?"

"I do want the child. It's only that there are—"

"Do not lie to me." Her words flicked like a whiplash. "For once let there be truth between us."

"I've never lied to you."

"Only because there have been no words spoken." She could hear the harshness of her voice, as if it were someone else speaking. "Silver said there was no closeness between us, and I told her it was not the truth. I said you loved me."

"I do love you."

"And I told her you would love your child," she whispered. "How I wanted you to love our child. I thought if I could give you a child you could love, then you would forgive me."

He slowly raised himself on one elbow, the sheet falling to his waist. "I don't know what you're talking about. Forgive you for what?"

"For not being white." She pushed up the sleeve of her nightgown to reveal the golden olive of her forearm. "For being Indian. For having the same blood as the people who killed your brothers. I cannot help what I am."

"I never said I wanted you to change," he said hoarsely.

"But you do not want a half-breed baby."

"I'll get used to it."

Pain writhed within her. "As you got used to having an Indian wife?" Her enormous dark eyes were glittering with tears. "I think not, Joshua."

"Star . . ." The pain, raw and naked, showed in his face. "It's not that I want to hurt you. I keep remembering . . ."

"Do you think I don't know this?" She smiled bitterly. "I feel your guilt every time you touch me. It was not my hand that struck down Rory and Boyd. I will no longer bear the responsibility for their deaths." She went to the bureau and opened the bottom drawer. "I have tried to be white for you, Joshua, but I cannot promise you a proper white Delaney baby. What if he has brown skin and dark eyes like mine? Will you hold him guilty too?" She pulled out a pale fawn-colored leather tunic, calico skirt, and moccasins. She had not worn these garments in over ten years and many times she had considered giving them to Silver. She pulled the nightgown over her head, threw it aside, and began to dress. "I don't think I could bear that, Joshua."

"I'll try to do better." He was pale beneath his tan. "I don't want to hurt anyone, not you or the baby."

"Would you make sure Malvina and Shamus treated him like a true Delaney? Would you love him and teach him as a father should? Would you fight for him?" She shook her head. "Somehow I don't think so." She pulled on her moccasins and turned toward the door. "You do not fight for me."

"You never asked me to fight for you."

She whirled to face him. "I have pride. I should not have had to ask. Do you think I would not have fought for you if you'd been a stranger in my people's village? You were too full of your own guilt and hurt to feel mine." She drew a deep, quivering breath. "Why? I could feel your pain as my own. A thousand times I wanted to reach out and comfort you as if you were my child instead of my husband. Were you too much white man, too much Delaney, to want to do the same for me?"

He swallowed and she could see the glitter of his eyes in the lamplight. "I love you, Star."

"I know you love me but it is not enough. Once I thought it was, but now I know there must be something else. You cannot love my body or my soul and hate what created both." She opened the door. "You cannot hate the Indian in me without hating me."

He threw the sheet aside and sat up. "It's after midnight. Where the hell do you think you're going?"

"I am leaving here."

"Dammit, you're with child. You can't just ride out."

"Why not?" Her lips twisted bitterly. "I'm no fine elegant lady, remember? We primitive savages ride until the moment of birth and then go into the bushes to squat and have our child. Then we get back on our ponies and ride until the sun has set. We have no fancy sense of delicacy as your white women do."

"For God's sake, Star, we can work this out," he said thickly. "Don't go back to your village."

"I have given enough. I will not see my son live the life Silver does." She stood there looking at him. She wished she could hate him. It would be so much easier than loving him like this. Would she never be able to look at Joshua without remembering the happiness of those first sunlit months? "Good-bye, Joshua," she said softly. "I'm sorry you cannot give me what I give you." She turned and the door closed behind her.

She had made camp and was fixing her evening meal the next night, when she heard a horse approaching. Joshua? She couldn't smother the flame of hope that sprang into her being or extinguish the wrenching disappointment when she recognized the man who rode into the circle of the campfire.

"Hello, Patrick," she said quietly. "Would you like something to eat? I have beans and bacon."

He shook his head as he dismounted. "I'm not hungry. I'll have some coffee though." He led his horse down to the creek and quickly unsaddled and tethered him before toting his saddle and blanket back to the campfire. He took the tin cup she handed him and settled cross-legged before the fire beside her.

He said nothing for a long time, just stared into the fire. "This is crazy, you know. Come home, Rising Star."

She shook her head. "Killara is not home to me."

"Then what is, for heaven's sake?" he asked with barely leashed violence. "You've lived with us for fourteen years. You're part of the family."

"You aren't blind enough to believe that. I thought perhaps it might be different one day but . . ." She shrugged. "What did Joshua tell you?"

"That you were upset about something and had gone back to your village. He said he'd let you have some time to think and then go after you in a few weeks." His hand tightened on the cup. "I told him he was a fool to let you go."

"He had no choice."

There was another silence.

"Why?" Patrick asked.

She didn't look away from the fire. "Joshua doesn't want a half-breed baby."

Patrick began to curse. "Christ, he didn't tell you that?"

"Not until I forced the words." She smiled sadly.

Patrick reached out an impulsive hand to comfort her. He stopped and his hand fell to his side. "You must have misunderstood. Josh wouldn't say something that would hurt you like that."

"I didn't misunderstand. And you're right, Joshua didn't want to hurt me. He is not a cruel man. He could not help himself." She lifted the cup to her lips. "He cannot change the way he feels. I think he's been trying for a long time to give me what I need. He cannot do it." Her voice became husky. "Perhaps none of us can really change. I tried to become white, and instead I became nothing."

"Don't talk crazy," Patrick said roughly.

She shook her head. "No, it's true, there is an old saying among my people: If you run headlong toward the sun, the spirits will steal your soul's shadow. I rushed blindly toward what I wanted on the horizon and now I cast no shadow, neither as an Indian nor a white."

"Rising Star, I—" He didn't speak for a minute. "You're not going back to your village, are you?"

"I didn't tell Joshua I was returning to my village." Her lips twisted. "Though I suppose it was natural for him to assume I would. He thinks of me as an Indian and an Indian belongs with others of her kind."

"But you're not going back to your family?"

"There is nothing for me there either. I have gone too far and not far enough."

"Then where?"

She took a sip of her coffee. "Kantalan."

He had half-known that would be her answer. "Why?"

"I don't know. Many reasons, I guess. White Buffalo once told me that my life was already laid out for me and there was nothing I could do to change it. Perhaps I want to prove him wrong. Or perhaps I want to find the treasure so that my child will not have to depend on the Delaneys to have a good life." She looked down into the dark depths of her cup. "Or perhaps I want to see if I can find my shadow again."

He swallowed. God, he was hurting. "Dominic and Elspeth are four days ahead of you. You're not going to be able to catch up with them."

"It doesn't matter, I will see them in Kantalan."

"You're with child, the trip will be hard on you."

"I'm healthy." She took another sip of coffee. "And, if the trip is hard, then I will not be able to think. I don't want to think right now."

He gazed at her helplessly. She sat there, cool and remote as a sparkling fountain. And Rising Star was never cool, dammit.

He threw the rest of his coffee into the logs. The flames hissed, sputtered, and then leapt high. "So we go to Kantalan."

Her gaze flew to his face. "We?"

"I'm going too." He stood up and began spreading his blankets. "I want my share of that treasure. Yes, sir, I'm going to be as rich as bejeezus. I'll wear one of those silk vests and have a gold timepiece with an emerald watchfob. All the ladies will be trying to marry me for my money, but I'll take my time about picking and choosing. Maybe I'll find myself one of those fancy princesses or an Oriental dancing girl."

"Patrick, you're going because you don't want me to go alone."

He took off his gunbelt and laid it beside his saddle. "Why should you say that? I like money as well as the next man." He sat down and pulled off his boots. "And I think I could make quite a splash if I was rich as a nabob."

She smiled. "I don't doubt that you could."

"Then quit trying to cheat me out of my share of the treasure." He stretched out and nestled his head on the leather saddle. "There will be plenty to go around."

"What about Torres?" she asked quietly. "Won't Shamus need you to help track him?"

"Nope." He pulled the blanket over him. "Torres wasn't trying to hide his sign when he doubled back. He probably thinks he's lost us. A blind man could read his trail now."

"Your grandfather still won't like you doing this."

"Too damn bad."

"Joshua won't—"

"Let Josh find his own treasure," Patrick interrupted. "Now, hush and go to sleep." He closed his eyes. "I'm tired of talking. I want to go to sleep and dream of princesses and Oriental dancing girls."

Tenderness pierced the ice surrounding Rising Star as she gazed at him. The firelight had softened the hardness of his face and reminded her how very young he was. Patrick was emerald watchfobs, and

Oriental dancing girls, firecrackers, and practical jokes. He was also sensitivity, gallantry, and a loyalty that was as warm as the fire she was gazing into now. Perhaps she would have a son like Patrick. Patrick was a Delaney, too, and it would be wonderful to bring up a son with those qualities.

"Go to sleep." Patrick didn't open his eyes.

She set her cup down, and lay down, pulling her blanket over her. "Sleep well, Patrick."

He didn't answer. Perhaps he was already on the verge of sleep. She found herself relaxing, the tension gripping her gradually ebbing away. She was no longer alone. The knowledge spread warmth through the desolation enfolding her. Patrick was going to Kantalan with her.

Four.

The realization suddenly jarred her from drowsiness. *Four will walk the streets of Kantalan.* Dominic, Elspeth, herself, and now Patrick. One by one they had been pulled by the invisible threads of circumstance until they were set upon the path to Kantalan. Whites would call it coincidence, White Buffalo had called it destiny. Which was the true view?

The embers of warmth she had been feeling cooled and a shiver ran through her. "Patrick?"

"Yes." His voice was wide awake. "Do you need something?"

"What would you do if I told you I wasn't going to let you come with me?"

"I'd follow you."

The threads tightened, brightened, almost revealing themselves to the naked eye. Destiny.

Patrick spoke again. "Is that all you wanted to know?"

"Yes, that's all."

They lay there but did not speak again.

Patrick's thoughts were on Rising Star.

And Rising Star's thoughts were on . . . shadows.

Sleep did not come to either of them for many hours.

19

❧❧❧

The town of Rosario, Mexico, baked in the late afternoon heat. Actually, it was more village than town, consisting of several tiny stucco houses, a church, a cantina, and a blacksmith's lean-to with a corral in the rear. Three brown-skinned women scrubbing clothes in the large chipped fountain in the center of the square stopped their work to watch Elspeth and Dominic ride down the street.

Dominic stopped before the church. "Stay here." He swung down from his horse. "I'll go and see if I can arrange for a bath and a place for you to sleep tonight. Father Leon is the only man in Rosario I'd trust to house you in this town."

Elspeth looked at him in surprise. "You've been here before?"

"About four years ago." He climbed the steps and opened the tall brass-studded door. "Arizona was getting a little too hot for me so I came down here. There's no law in Rosario."

"Then why didn't you stay?"

He looked over his shoulder as he stepped into the dim coolness of the chapel. "I got tired of drinking tequila." Then he was gone, and she heard the soft jingle of his spurs as he walked down the aisle of the church.

He had been homesick for Killara, Elspeth thought. Who could blame him? Even to her, the green valleys of Killara seemed like paradise after the hot, burning desert country they'd been traveling across for the past two and a half weeks.

She reached for the linen handkerchief tucked into her belt and wiped the back of her neck, thinking longingly of the dimness of the chapel. The fine dust was entering her lungs with every breath and the heat-blurred horizon was wavering before her eyes.

The women at the fountain were still staring at her. Elspeth smiled tentatively, but they did not return her smile. Their round brown faces were stolid, their dark eyes expressing no warmth only curiosity at the foreigner in their midst. She was suddenly acutely conscious of the whiteness of her skin, the fairness of her hair, and the delicate slenderness of her body. She looked quickly away from the women. No wonder Dominic had not stayed here, even though it was safer for him.

"Elspeth." She looked up to see Dominic coming down the steps. "Father Leon will let you stay at his casa next door to the church. He begs you to forgive him for not coming to greet you, and asks that you come to him. It's painful for him to walk."

Elspeth got down from the mare. "Is he ill?"

Dominic shook his head. "Crippled. Before he moved to Rosario he had a brush with the soldiers at a village closer to the border. They thought he knew the hiding place of Indino, a bandit who raided the silver shipments of the great mine owners in the area. They tied the Father down spreadeagled and galloped their horses over him."

Her eyes widened in shock. "A priest?"

Dominic nodded. "Compared to the soldiers, the bandits are gentlemen born and bred."

Elspeth felt sick. "How terrible. They could have killed him."

"Six months later Indino found the colonel who ordered the torture." Dominic took the reins of the mare. "I'll take the animals over to the corral for the night. I promised Father Leon I'd join him for dinner, but I have something to do first."

Torres, thought Elspeth. Every evening before Dominic settled down for the night he would go back and assure himself there was no one following them. "Aren't you going to stay with Father Leon too?"

He shook his head. "I'll find a bed over at the cantina." His lips twisted sardonically. "I'll feel more comfortable there." He started to turn away.

"Dominic."

He paused to look at her.

"What did Indino do to that colonel?"

"I don't think you'd want to know." He walked away, leading their horses and burros toward the blacksmith's corral.

Elspeth watched him for a moment before walking up the steps to the chapel. He was right. Barbarism and hardship confronted her every day; she didn't need to expose herself to more. Every time she thought she had grown as hard and tough as Dominic, something happened to prove to her how soft and vulnerable she still was.

At least she was no longer physically soft. The first few days of the journey had been agonizing and she had thought she would collapse from sheer exhaustion. It had been a nightmare hiding her weariness from Dominic to prevent him from insisting on doing everything himself as he had that first night on the trail. But as the days had passed, Dominic's wound had healed and she had found she, too, was becoming stronger. Her muscles were getting more supple, her endurance was increasing. The sun burned her skin in spite of the sombrero Dominic insisted she never be without, but the painful burn went away and her skin turned brown. She thought she looked like a withered hag, but she felt good. The knowledge that she was strong enough to withstand the elements and long hours on the trail, yet still have enough energy to help Dominic filled her with a serene sense of self-worth she had never before experienced.

"*Señorita, por favor.*"

Elspeth turned to see a small boy of about nine years of age standing on the step below her. His dark hair was a wild tangle, his face dirty, his shirt and trousers ragged. He was barefoot and the steps must have been terribly hot on the soles of his feet.

"You spoke to me?"

He nodded, his dark gaze fixed desperately on her face. "*Sí.*"

"You wish money?" she asked gently. "I have very little but I'll be glad to give you a peso."

He shook his head so emphatically, flecks of dust flew from the wild black locks. "No, I wish nothing from you," he said in Spanish. She had difficult understanding him. The accent was different, harsher than the soft Castilian she had learned in Spain. However, there was no misunderstanding the smile he gave her. It was as innocently beguiling as that of a Botticelli cherub. "It is I who have a gift for you."

Father Leon smiled as she came into the room. "You look *muy bonita*, Señora. Maria gave you the help you needed?"

"She was very kind." Elspeth hurried forward to take from him the tray containing an earthenware pitcher and a bowl filled with a savory mixture of chicken, corn, and green peppers. She had already found that the priest attempted to do far more than he should, given his infirmities. He was bent and twisted, scarcely able to shuffle without flinching, and yet he was trying to wait on them. "Sit down, Father Leon. This looks delicious. Has my husband come back yet?" She tingled with pleasure when she referred to Dominic in that possessive manner.

She set the tray on the long trench table and turned to look anxiously out the window. The sun was setting in a burst of radiant gold, scarlet, and mauve. It had been nearly four hours since they had arrived in Rosario, and she had seen nothing of Dominic since he had left her at the steps of the church. After these last two weeks she wasn't accustomed to being separated from him for more than a few moments, and his absence made her uneasy.

"He will come soon." Father Leon seated himself at the head of the table. "Dominic enjoys Maria's chick-

en stew far too much to linger long at the cantina."
His smile faded. "You must encourage Dominic to
stay away from the cantina now that he is a married
man. There are many ungodly activities at Miguel's.
Gambling and . . ." He trailed off awkwardly.

Hetaeras. The unspoken word jumped immediately
to the forefront of her mind. Of course there would be
women for Dominic to enjoy here. Dark-eyed brown-
skinned women who would welcome him into their
beds. The thought brought such a wild thrill of pain,
she had to lower her lashes to veil her eyes from the
priest. "Did he stay at the cantina when he was here
before?"

Father Leon nodded. "When he wasn't in the hills
with Indino."

Her lashes flew up. "He was a bandit?"

The priest smiled reassuringly. "No, he merely grew
restless with us here and he and Indino became
friends. It was natural they should, I suppose. In
many ways they are much alike. Indino, too, is an
unusual man."

"Since I crossed the sea I've come to the conclusion
there are no 'usual' men here," Elspeth said dryly. "I
believe I must have left all commonplace individuals
in Edinburgh."

Father Leon chuckled. "When men live without
laws, their good qualities as well as their sins tend to
be magnified. Perhaps because their temptations are
so much greater."

Elspeth frowned as she poured the frothy milk from
the pitcher into polished wooden cups. He was again
obliquely warning her about the temptations that
would assault Dominic at the cantina. He didn't
understand that there was nothing she could do to
keep Dominic from going to those fallen women. He
had married her to protect her, probably considering
that the full discharge of his duty to her. He had not
made promises of fidelity, and there was nothing she
could do to prevent him from taking his pleasures
where and when he wished. Her hand tightened on

the handle of the pitcher as a wild thought occurred to her. Unless—

"You look very thoughtful." Father Leon's eyes were narrowed on her face. "You must not be concerned, it takes time for two people to become accustomed to each other. I'm sure you will be able to persuade Dominic to give up drink, gambling, and—" he paused as if for inspiration—"other iniquities when he settles down and realizes how fortunate he is in his marriage to you."

The priest's words brought little comfort. If she was not with child, these two months were all the time she would have with Dominic. The realization brought a sense of desperation and caused that wild thought to come to mind once again. "I'm sure you're right, Father." She lit the fat tallow candle on the table. "I believe I'll have to make Dominic realize he's a married man now. I'll consider what you've said." She changed the subject. "I met a small child as I came into the church. He was very appealing." She paused. "He wanted to give me a present."

Father Leon nodded. "Ah, you are speaking of Rafael. I thought he would approach you before you left Rosario. It is a sad situation."

"I don't know what to do. I don't believe Dominic would like me to accept Rafael's gift."

"Then you must not do it. A woman must obey her husband."

"Sorry I'm late." Dominic stood in the doorway, his hat in one hand and a bottle of wine in the other. "I took advantage of a hot bath to soak the dust out of my bones." He held up the bottle and smiled at the priest. "I brought a peace offering, Miguel's very best."

"Which is very fine indeed." Father Leon returned Dominic's smile. "A fitting beverage to toast your lovely bride. Does she not look beautiful tonight?"

"Very beautiful." Dominic didn't look at Elspeth as he tossed his hat on a chair. "Amazing what a little soap and water can do."

He meant that at least she was scrubbed clean of

trail dust, Elspeth thought gloomily. She knew she wasn't attractive to him, despite his polite agreement with the priest. He had seen her in Brianne's dark brown riding skirt and white cotton blouse many times in the past two weeks. Then, too, she was tanned almost as berry-brown as those women she had seen by the fountain this afternoon, and didn't a man want a woman like her to have a milky white complexion? She had a sudden memory of the beautiful white gown Rising Star had permitted her to borrow on that first evening at Killara. How she wished she had something lovely to wear tonight.

"Sit down," she said. "Father Leon says you're very fond of Maria's chicken stew. It looks quite wonderful."

"It is." Dominic took the seat she'd indicated. "I can remember one night Indino and I rode thirty miles down from the hills because he swore he could smell her cooking it." His white teeth flashed as he grinned. "It was three o'clock in the morning when we rode into Rosario, and Maria wasn't pleased when we banged on her door and woke her up."

"Nonsense. She may have scolded you but she was flattered." Father Leon's eyes twinkled. "She still boasts of that night to the other women in the village."

Elspeth sat down opposite Dominic, watching the expressions change and flicker on his face as one reminiscence led to another. The stew was as good as Dominic had claimed, but she found she had little appetite. She was too absorbed in turning over in her mind the astonishing and frightening idea Father Leon's words had inspired. Was it possible that she could find a way of tempting Dominic into wanting to stay with her? She was no practiced hetaera, but he had said all women were much the same and perhaps—

"You're not eating." Dominic's gaze was suddenly on her face. It was the first time he had looked at her since he had entered the house and a little quiver of excitement ran through her. "Are you sick?"

"What?" She moistened her lips. "Oh, no, I'm enjoying it very much. It's just . . ."—she searched wildly for an excuse—"hot."

His gaze held her own and she felt the wild color sting her cheeks. What if he had guessed what she had been thinking? She felt suddenly naked and vulnerable, and the words tumbled from her lips. "Don't you think it's hot?"

"Yes." His nostrils flared as he took a deep breath and then forced himself to look away from her. "Yes, very hot." He suddenly stood up, the legs of his chair screeching as he pushed it away from the table. "I think I'll take a walk before I go to bed."

Father Leon's face clouded in disappointment. "Are you not going to join me in a glass of wine?"

"Not tonight." Dominic tempered the shortness of the refusal with a smile. "I'll see you tomorrow morning before we leave, Father. Good night."

Father Leon's gaze moved from Dominic's face to Elspeth's and back again. "You are welcome to stay here with your wife tonight. I think you will find the bed I gave her far cleaner than the one at Miguel's."

Elspeth held her breath, her hand tightening on the wooden cup.

Dominic didn't answer for a moment, and she could feel his gaze return to her face. "I don't doubt it." His voice was thick. "But I must refuse. I have a few friends I want to see at Miguel's."

Women friends? Elspeth wondered, experiencing a wild primitive anger that was a totally new feeling. Jealousy. She wanted to do physical injury to those "friends." She got hurriedly to her feet. "I believe I'll get a breath of fresh air before I help Maria clean up." She passed Dominic without a glance as she headed for the front door. "I'll be back shortly, Father."

The evening air was cool on her hot cheeks and she inhaled deeply, breathing in the pungent scent of creosote and chili peppers drying on the rawhide awning of the house next door. Light was streaming through the windows and doors of the small stucco buildings surrounding the square, and she could hear

the sound of a guitar echoing through the empty
streets from the direction of the cantina. She heard
the door close behind her. "It's much cooler out here,
isn't it?" she asked quickly. "I like Father Leon. It
seems impossible that anyone would want to hurt
him. He has the—"

"What's wrong?" Dominic interrupted.

"What could be wrong?" she asked, moving away
from him. "It's quite pleasant here. I'm glad we had
the opportunity to stop and sleep in a room with four
walls around us."

"There's something wrong. I know you well enough
now to understand when you're upset about something." He hesitated. "Were you afraid I was going to
let the priest talk me into sharing your bed?"

Heat rained through her every vein. "No. You had
the opportunity to force yourself on me any number of
times in the last weeks. What difference would it
make if we did share a bed?"

The same difference as the straw that broke the
camel's back, he wanted to tell her. He should never
have stopped here, but he had wanted to let her rest.
She had been so damn brave and uncomplaining that
he had felt guilty as hell at pushing her as he had
these last two weeks. Yet how could he explain that if
he hadn't been too exhausted to crave nothing but
rest, he would have been within her, his promise
forgotten, everything forgotten but the tightness, the
heat of her.

He shuddered. Damn, he shouldn't have let himself
remember how sweet she had felt around him. "I'll
see you tomorrow morning. I'll be here to get you
right after dawn."

"No, I'll meet you at the corral." He was leaving
her. He would cross the square to that cantina, where
there would be music and hetaeras and all the
pleasures he knew so well. "I can find my way."

"Whatever you wish. You'd better go back inside
now and get to bed."

Back to Father Leon and the small ascetic room
where she would sleep alone tonight. Dominic would

not sleep alone. The anger and hurt she was feeling suddenly flared hotly. She had been debating whether to accept Rafael's gift, but now it was decided. Any man who had the insensitivity to indulge himself with hetaeras while his wife was just across the square did not deserve any consideration. "Good night, Dominic." The edge to the words was sharp enough to whittle wood.

Dominic hesitated. "Are you sure you're all right?"

"Oh, yes, I'm perfectly splendid. Go on to your cantina." Why had she thought she might appeal to him as those other women did? He couldn't wait to leave her and go rushing to the eager arms of some black-eyed señorita.

He stood stock-still for a moment, then he shrugged and started across the square.

She watched until Dominic disappeared into the cantina before returning to the house. She carefully banished the look of anger from her face, assuming a cheerful smile as she went in to join Father Leon.

"A mule?" There was a lethal softness to Dominic's tone. "You actually bought a mule?"

"No, I told you, he was a gift," Elspeth said. She swung into the saddle of the mare. "I don't know why you're upset. He's much bigger than those poor little burros and should be able to carry a great deal more."

"Give him back," Dominic said curtly. "No mules."

"I can't give him back. I promised Rafael I would take him with us."

"Give him back." Dominic had enunciated every word with deliberate precision.

"You're being most unreasonable," she said sweetly. "And behaving atrociously, but I'll forgive you. I know you must be feeling bad. You look quite ill."

"I have a headache."

She nodded solicitously. "You really shouldn't drink so much. Look at the trouble it's caused you. The last time you overindulged, you ended up with a bride." She patted the mare's neck. "Now, come along and stop arguing. It would be stupid to refuse a valuable gift like Azuquita."

"Azuquita," Dominic repeated blankly. "Someone named that monster Little Sugar?"

The mule he was looking at was a good seventeen hands high, black as the bottom of a well, with a face full of sin. A tiny gold loop earring pierced the top of his right ear. Azuquita stared back at Dominic with a blandness that caused the hair on Dominic's nape to bristle.

"Well, Rafael actually called him Sweetness," Elspeth said. "Isn't that a good sign he has a lovely nature? I put the saddlebags on him myself and I found him very gentle."

"He's trying to fool you into thinking that. Then when you least expect it, he'll pounce. I know mules."

"I'm sure every mule isn't the same. You've merely had an unfortunate experience."

"We're not taking that mule."

The smile on Elspeth's lips wavered. "Of course we are. Rafael was most upset. Indino gave the mule to Rafael and the child loves Azuquita. But it seems the boy's father drinks too much." She inclined her head at Dominic. "You should sympathize with that failing. Anyway, when he overindulges he develops a violent dislike for Azuquita and beats him. He even threatened to shoot the poor mule the next time it annoyed him."

Dominic smiled sardonically. "I don't suppose you inquired what Sweetness had done to annoy him?"

"I'm sure it was something trifling. What could the animal have possibly done to deserve slaughter?"

"What indeed." Dominic said, his gaze on the mule.

Azuquita's lips suddenly pulled back to reveal yellow-white teeth.

"My God, the damn mule is grinning at me," Dominic whispered.

"I told you he was good-tempered."

"If I remember my scriptures, Lucifer seemed that way too—before the fall." He shook his head. "No, Elspeth."

Her smile vanished. "I didn't ask your permission to bring him. I won't have that animal brutalized or Rafael frightened or upset. I will care for him myself and you need have nothing to do with him." She grabbed the lead reins of the mule. "Come along, Azuquita." Elspeth's mare trotted out of the corral with the mule ambling docilely at her heels.

"Elspeth, there's no way that you can have nothing to do with a mule on the trail," he called after her. "They haunt you; they do things that drive you insane."

"Nonsense." She didn't look back.

Dominic began to curse beneath his breath as he mounted his horse. The imprecations involved Elspeth's soft heart, the mare and the donkey that had begot the mule, and the black entity that was Azuquita itself.

The first day the mule behaved surprisingly well, clipping along at a brisk pace as they turned east and began to negotiate the foothills of the Sierra Madres.

The second day Dominic's watchful regard registered an imperceptible slowing as boredom began to fester. On the third day Little Sugar began to turn sour. Not toward Elspeth. He behaved with admirable obedience with her. It was with Dominic he attempted to lighten his boredom.

It began with a light, almost playful nip whenever Dominic came within reach, then he began crowding Dominic's horse into an occasional tree or the wall of a cliff. Dominic countered by moving the mule from behind Elspeth in the column and placing him with the burros bringing up the rear.

On the fourth day Azuquita gnawed at the girth of the burro next to him until the saddlebag fell off his back. Since Dominic didn't discover it for some time, it took two hours to backtrack and retrieve the saddlebag and another hour to mend the girth. Dominic moved the mule back to his former place behind Elspeth.

On the fifth night a raucous bray woke Dominic in the middle of the night and he opened his eyes to see Azuquita's hindquarters descending on his face!

"What the hell?" He had time to roll only a few inches before he received the mule's bushy tail in his face. "You ornery eunuch." He brushed the tail from his face. "You loco fiend from hell. You evil son of a—" He broke off as he heard Elspeth's choked laughter. She was sitting up in her blankets across the fire, laughing helplessly. "This is *not* funny."

"I know. It's very serious." She immediately began laughing again. "He could have smothered you with his tail."

Dominic sat up and moved gingerly away from the mule, now sitting placidly and ignoring them, warming his broad backside in front of the fire. "He also could have crushed my skull if I hadn't moved fast."

"I think he was just being playful." Elspeth wiped her eyes on the corner of the blanket. "He did warn you. That bray would have raised Lazarus."

"Playful! He's trying to murder me."

"How did he get free?"

Dominic motioned to the gnawed and shredded rope dangling around Azuquita's neck. "I don't mind him breaking loose, but why the hell couldn't he have run away?"

Elspeth grinned. "He likes you."

Dominic gazed at her as if she had gone mad.

"No, I believe he really does like you," she insisted. "He only tolerates me, but I think he regards you as a true challenge."

"He tried to knock me off a cliff yesterday, tonight he tried to smother me. I hate to think what he has in mind for me tomorrow."

Elspeth's smile faded. "I have a confession to make. One of the reasons I brought Sweetness along was that I was a little annoyed with you."

"Why?"

"It doesn't matter. I admit I found Azuquita's pranks very amusing, but I realize now it wasn't fair of me to burden you with him." She lowered her gaze to the fire. "Perhaps we could find someone to leave Azuquita with until we return."

"The only people in these hills are bandits and their

women. If we gave Sweetness to them, I don't know if we'd get out of the hills alive."

Elspeth's hand reached up to comb through her loosened hair, causing the material of her blouse to tauten over the soft swell of her breasts. Dominic was suddenly conscious of her grace, her supple litheness. He felt a stirring heat and tried to blot it out before it could become the painful desire he had lived with for so long.

Azuquita turned his head and looked at them as if he had understood every word they had spoken. The son of a bitch probably had, Dominic thought crossly, he wouldn't put it past the hybrid warlock.

The torment of lust had lessened, Dominic realized with a jolt of shock. It had not disappeared entirely, he was still conscious of a nagging ache within him, but his annoyance with Sweetness had at least made him think of something else beside Elspeth. Now that he thought about it, for the past five days the mule had kept his mind so occupied, he hadn't had the opportunity to think of anything else.

An ironic smile flitted across his lips at the thought of how disappointed Azuquita would be if he realized his downright ugliness was acting in Dominic's best interest.

"Why are you smiling?" Elspeth asked, puzzled.

"I was just thinking that bringing Azuquita wasn't such a bad idea."

She looked relieved. "You're not upset about it any longer? Sweetness *is* very strong. I surely hope his behavior will improve once he gets to know you."

The mule's lips pulled back from his yellow-white teeth.

Dominic smiled back at him, mirroring the same toothy menace. "We'll see if your hope pans out." He got to his feet and grabbed hold of the shredded rope. Sweetness immediately tried to bury his teeth in Dominic's hand. "I think I'll be the one to take care of him from now on. As you say, we have to get to know each other."

Elspeth blinked. "If you're sure that's what you wish."

Dominic tugged at the rope. Azuquita didn't move. "On your feet, my little sugar." His tone was almost affectionate. "It's back to the other animals with you. You've done enough damage for one night."

It took him thirty minutes to get Azuquita off his haunches and tethered with the other animals. By that time Dominic was annoyed and exhausted enough almost to forget the silken warmth of Elspeth waiting for him only a few yards across the fire, and he fell asleep in minutes.

It was two days later that the heat that had followed them from Killara into Mexico appeared to be on the verge of breaking. Blue-black clouds rolled across the western horizon and in the afternoon the wind carried with it the bite of cool moisture.

Elspeth took a deep breath, letting the pungent dampness flow through her. "Doesn't it feel like a blessing? It rains frequently in Edinburgh, but I don't think I've fully appreciated it. I feel as if my bones are made of sand. Do you think the storm will come this way?"

"Yes." Dominic swung off his horse, with practiced agility dodged Azuquita's attempt to step on his boot, and grabbed the mule's lead rope. "And we don't have much time to build a shelter."

"We're stopping now? We still have a few hours before sunset."

"The storm's close enough. I like my comfort and I don't have any intention of sleeping in the rain." He was leading the stallion and mule into a pine grove at the side of the trail.

"What are you going to do?"

"Build a lean-to. I saw some ocotillo shrubs about a quarter of a mile back."

Ocotillo. She hadn't the faintest idea which bush he was talking about, but the word had a lovely musical sound. "How can I help?"

"Unsaddle the animals and tether them to a tree

that has a lot of protective foliage." He reached into his saddlebags and drew out a pair of heavy leather gloves and a sheath containing a hunting knife. "I'll be right back."

He was back in twenty minutes carrying a huge armload of narrow greenish-brown sticks from three to four feet in length.

"Ocotillo?" she asked.

He nodded. "You lay them close together and they form a pretty good roof for a lean-to. Pine branches are better for the supports though."

"Can we have a fire?"

He didn't look up. "A small one."

By the time the shelter was built, the grove was beginning to be inundated with the eerie golden light that sometimes precedes the darkness of a storm. The two gnarled support branches were nearly five feet tall; once the blankets were spread and a fire built, the tiny enclosure was reasonably cozy.

The wind was swaying the tops of the tall pines and the golden light was disappearing. Now there was only a still purple gloom reflected from the storm clouds overhead. Elspeth's head lifted, and she experienced a tiny thrill of excitement as if she, too, were mirroring the tempest about to be unleashed. The cool breeze lifted her hair from her forehead and she could smell the heady scent of rain, grass, and rich earth.

"It's wonderful, isn't it?" she asked softly.

"It won't be wonderful for long." Dominic crawled under the lean-to. "In about a minute the sky is going to split wide open and you're going to be drowned if you stay out there."

She didn't seem to hear him. Her gaze was on the darkening sky and she gave a little shiver of anticipation. "It makes me feel strange. I don't know . . . powerful. Do you know what I mean?"

His expression softened as he looked at her glowing face, radiant in the dimness of the grove. "Yes, I know what you mean. Now, come in under the lean-to before you get wet."

She sighed and then reluctantly crawled under the shelter to sit beside him, settling back against the saddlebags Dominic had propped against the tree. "It would almost be worth it."

He shook his head. "You'd get chilled and we sure as the devil don't want you ill again."

"I won't become ill. I've never felt more healthy in my life." It was difficult to remember a time when she hadn't felt this strong and well, and yet it had been only a month ago that she had been bedridden at the hotel in Hell's Bluff.

The rain began to fall, at first sporadically, then in huge drops, and as Dominic had predicted, the heavens opened. Rain poured down with stunning force. She could hear it pounding the ocotillo roof, but surprisingly few drops managed to pierce the branches.

The fire Dominic had built was small, but they managed to prepare a meal of beans and hardtack. After they had finished, there seemed nothing to do but sit and watch the rain.

20

Surrounded by the falling rain, gazing into the ever-changing brilliance of the leaping flames, was rather like being enclosed in a silver box holding a glowing ruby, Elspeth thought dreamily. It was not as exciting as the wildness that had preceded the storm but was still very satisfying.

"I think it's time to go to sleep."

Elspeth lifted her gaze from the fire to look at Dominic in surprise. "It's not even dark yet. Why would—" She stopped. She suddenly became conscious of how very small was their silver box, only a few feet separated her from Dominic and she could sense every action of his body: The rise and fall of his chest as he breathed, the tension of his hand as it gripped the blanket, the slight hollow beneath the bones of his cheeks as his lips tightened. And his eyes . . .

Dominic jerked his gaze away. "What the hell else can we do?" He shifted restlessly. "The rain doesn't look like it's going to let up. We may be stuck in here until morning."

"I see." The scent of rain, earth, and burning pine surrounded them together with the warm, clean male fragrance that belonged to Dominic. She wanted to breathe in that aroma, have it in her nostrils, in her body. The pagan thought sent a ripple of shocked awareness through her.

And that wasn't all of him she wanted in her body,

she realized. She wanted to be joined to Dominic in that same searing fashion she had known once before. She wanted to look at him without all those cumbersome clothes. She wanted to touch him as he had asked her to touch him before. She moistened her lips with her tongue as she experienced a hot melting sensation between her thighs. Lust. Strangely, she felt no shame. She had an idea that with Dominic lust could be almost as beautiful as love.

"Well, then cover up and go to sleep." Dominic didn't look at her as he pulled off his boots and then took off his gunbelt.

"We could play cards," Elspeth offered tentatively. "You could teach me that game you played at the Nugget."

"Poker?" He crushed out the fire and pulled the blanket up around his shoulders. "I don't seem to have the concentraion tonight."

"I know piquet. Perhaps we could—"

"Elspeth, I do not want to play cards."

She sighed. She didn't want to play cards either, but she certainly didn't want to go to sleep. If they played cards, she could have watched Dominic's expressions, and perhaps he would smile his special smile that lit his face with warmth. She thought for a moment. "We can talk. Why does the ocotillo keep out the rain so well?"

He closed his eyes and turned his back to her. "I don't want to talk."

"You're not being very sociable."

"I don't feel sociable."

It was no use. She reluctantly scooted down and pulled the blanket around her. "You obviously don't feel like being polite either."

Polite? He would have laughed out loud if he hadn't been hurting so much. The good Lord knew what he was experiencing had no resemblance to anything as civilized as the desire to be polite. Just don't talk to me, he prayed silently. Don't let me hear you move, don't make me look at you.

Two hours later the rain was still falling and

Elspeth was still wide awake. Dominic's breathing was deep and even, and he hadn't moved for a good twenty minutes. At least one of them was able to sleep, she thought ruefully as she stared into the darkness. She turned over on her back and looked up at the ocotillo sticks overhead. Perhaps if she counted them, it would lull her.

One, two, three, four . . . When she reached twenty-five she turned onto her side, her gaze on the sticks above Dominic's head. She forgot to count. She even forgot to breathe. One of the sticks was moving!

It was the last stick on Dominic's side of the lean-to. She stared in helpless fascination as the stick slid forward and then wound itself around the support post.

A snake!

Dear God in heaven, a snake! Curling slowly around the post, bonelessly gliding around and down toward Dominic's feet.

She wanted to scream, but she couldn't utter a sound. No. Make it go away. Please make it go away. But the snake didn't go away, it kept coming, gliding closer and closer to Dominic's feet.

"*No!*" She wasn't aware of the scream that had torn from her lips. She reached for the stick with which Dominic had stoked the flames of their small fire. She rolled out onto the rain-soaked earth and jumped to her feet.

"No!" She swung the stick and struck the snake on the support.

"No!" She swung the stick again.

"Elspeth, what the devil?"

She struck the snake again. "No!"

The support gave way and the ocotillo roof collapsed, landing on top of Dominic. She heard him cursing but paid no attention. The snake had fallen to the ground and she was hitting it again and again and again.

"Elspeth, for God's sake . . ." Dominic had managed to crawl from the wreckage and was beside her, trying to take the stick away from her. "Elspeth, stop it."

"It's a snake." She jerked her arm away from him. "Don't you understand? It's a snake."

"It *was* a snake," Dominic said. "It's dead now. Stop hitting it, Elspeth."

"No, it will come back. I have to . . ."

"God!" He tore the stick away from her hand and threw it aside. He grabbed her by the shoulders and shook her. "Listen to me. It won't come back. It's dead, Elspeth, you killed it." Rain was running down his face, plastering his dark curls to his head. "Everything is all right now, Elspeth."

"No, the snake . . ."

Dominic stepped back, releasing her. "I'll get rid of the snake. Stay here, don't move."

He was bending and picking up something. He had that horror in his hands!

"Don't do it! You'll—"

"Hush, Elspeth." His voice was soothing. "It won't hurt me." Then he was striding off into the darkness. He was back almost immediately. "There. It's gone. There's nothing to be afraid of."

The snake couldn't hurt Dominic. A harsh sob broke from her throat. It hurt. She hurt. She fell to her knees on the muddy ground, hugging herself, barely conscious of the rain driving ceaselessly against her body.

"Elspeth, no . . ." Dominic was kneeling in front of her. He sounded as if he were hurting, too, she thought numbly. She wanted to help him, but she couldn't seem to move. "Elspeth, love, don't do this to me. God, don't *cry*."

She couldn't seem to stop. The sobs kept coming, hurting.

Dominic's hands were cradling her face and he was looking down into her eyes. "Why didn't you just call me? You didn't have to do it yourself."

She shook her head. "I had to do it myself. Daddy said I mustn't be afraid. I mustn't be a coward."

"You're not a coward, you're very brave." Dominic's voice was urgent. "You have to believe that." His fingers gently brushed back a damp strand of hair from her cheek. "Why did your father say you were a coward?"

"The cobra. I didn't drink my milk that night and a cobra crawled through the window of my room." The words were tumbling out. "I woke up and it was on the table beside my bed, where I'd left the milk. Milk attracts snakes, you know."

"No, I didn't know."

"I screamed and screamed. My father was working in another room and came in to see what was wrong. He sent one of the boys to kill it. He was very angry with me. He had warned me about leaving my milk, but I forgot. I forgot. I didn't *mean* to do it."

"I know you didn't." Her cheek was suddenly against his breast. She could feel the warmth of his skin through the damp material of his shirt. His fingers tangled in her wet hair as he rocked her. "It wasn't your fault."

"I didn't want him to leave me. I was so afraid. He said I was a coward to be so frightened. He said—"

"I don't want to hear what he said," Dominic interrupted harshly. "It was all lies spoken by a cruel little bastard who deserved to be drawn and quartered." His arms tightened around her. "Do you hear me? It doesn't matter what he said. None of it was true. You would have been stupid not to have been afraid. You're a very brave woman."

"Not as brave as Silver." Her words were muffled in his shirt.

"Yes." His chin was nuzzling back and forth across the top of her head. "Just as brave. It takes a different kind of courage to face up to what we fear the most. You did that tonight. You went after that snake like a little tiger."

"I'm not a coward?" she whispered.

"No." His voice was choked. "God, no."

Relief was sweeping over her. Dominic said she had no reason to be ashamed. She was not a coward. No matter how many times she had defended herself to her father, she knew now she had never really been sure he wasn't right. She had desperately needed someone to say these words. The sobs lessened and then faded into tiny hiccoughs. "Thank you."

"For telling the truth?"

"For making me believe it was the truth."

He pushed her away from him to look down into her face. "Are you all right now?"

She nodded and then promptly gave another hiccough to belie the affirmation. She gave a husky laugh. "You're wet. I'm sorry that I seem to have destroyed your splendid lean-to."

"I've been wet before." His hands cupped her cheeks caressingly. "And you're not only wet, you're muddy."

"I rolled out of the lean-to into the mud." She hoped he wouldn't take his hands away, they felt so warm and loving. She wanted to turn her lips to touch his palm. "What do we do now?"

"We get you clean and dry. Lord knows how." His hands dropped away from her cheeks. Emptiness. Loneliness.

She suddenly chuckled as she turned to see the destruction she had wrought. The lean-to was now only a large heap of sticks.

"You find our situation amusing?" Dominic asked.

"I'm sorry. I was just regretting that I was too busy killing that horrible reptile to see your expression when the lean-to fell around your ears. You must have looked like Samson after he had destroyed the temple."

"The comparison isn't quite accurate." Dominic began to shift the ocotillo into some semblance of an orderly pile. "Though in both cases it was a woman who caused the destruction."

"Should you be doing that? What if that snake had brothers or sisters?"

"After that crash and screaming, there won't be a snake within five miles of here."

"What can I do?"

"Find a way to get dry." He had finally uncovered the saddlebags from beneath the rubble. "Do you have anything in your saddlebags that might help?"

"I don't think so. You told me not to bring anything that wasn't necessary and—" She stopped. "There's my plaid."

"Your plaid?"

"My family tartan." She knelt beside her saddlebag and unfastened the thong. "The MacGregor plaid."

"And you regarded this tartan as necessary?"

She didn't look up as she rummaged in the saddlebag. "Surely you must see I couldn't leave my plaid?"

Dominic watched her kneeling in the rain, muddied, soaked to the skin, her expression solemn. The tenderness he felt was almost unbearable. "Yes, I can see that."

"Ah, here it is." She drew out the folded red and black plaid and stood up. "I'll go see if I can get rid of this mud."

"And I'll see if I can rebuild the lean-to. Will you need the lantern?"

She shivered as she had a vision of a multitude of writhing snakes waiting in the darkness. But Dominic had said there would be no snakes, and he needed the lantern more than she did. "No." She turned away and walked down the incline toward the trees where she had tethered the animals.

The simplest way to remove the mud was to shed her clothes, take down her hair, and stand in the rain, letting the water cleanse her. It was a strangely sensual experience, standing naked in the forest as some primitive ancestress might have done.

She was almost sorry to have to step back under the tree. She brought her damp hair over her shoulder and wrung it out as best she could. She wrapped the large red and black plaid around her, draping it over her head and then folding it at her breasts. She drew on her brown leather boots and found the ensemble reasonably modest. The plaid was large enough to meet the tops of her knee-high boots and, as long as she kept a firm hold on the material at her breast, it was like being enveloped in a blanket. The thick wool was soft, cozy, and blessedly dry.

The rain had lessened to a fine mist by the time Elspeth walked back up the hill to where Dominic was reconstructing the lean-to. She was pleasantly surprised to find the task completed and Dominic building a small fire within the lean-to. "You've been very quick."

"I had a goad. I don't like being wet." The kindling finally caught but the fire immediately went out. Dominic muttered a disgusted curse. "It's no use. The wood is damp. Everything is damp. The blankets are dry because they were buried beneath the wood when the roof collapsed but . . . ." He trailed off as he looked up and saw her. The red and black of the plaid tartan was a vivid patch of color in the lantern light, beautifully framing her face, lending color to her cheeks. Her eyes were a shimmering deep emerald and she looked as exotic as a brilliantly plumed parrot. "I like your family tartan." He cleared his throat and lowered his eyes to begin working on the fire again. "Come under here before you get soaked through again."

It was another ten minutes before a small if smoky blaze was started. Though the heat was not needed for warmth, it still felt wonderful to ward off the dampness that clung to their clothing, hair, and skin.

"That should do it," Dominic said as he reached into his saddlebag and pulled out a length of cotton cloth with which to wipe his face and neck.

"You're very wet. You'd best change."

"In a minute." He sat down near the fire and held out his hands to the flames. He closed his eyes as the heat began to soak into him, an expression of sensual pleasure tautening his features. "I must be half cat. Lord, I hate to be wet."

Her gaze was on his face and she trembled. He had the same expression she had seen when he looked down at her in the big bed at Killara.

"I remember once when I was a kid out on a trail drive, a big storm blew up and we had to ride herd for three solid days in a steady downpour. I got so tired of mud and boots that squished and—" He broke off as he looked directly at Elspeth. He inhaled sharply. "Oh, no, don't do this to me. Not now, Elspeth."

"I'm not doing anything," she whispered. On the contrary, something was being done to her, for her bones were surely melting and she was dizzy and disoriented. "I'm just listening to you."

"You're doing something all right." His gaze clung to her face. "And you've got to stop it. I can't do this by myself; you have to help me."

"Help you do what?" Her tone was soft, edged with dreams. The beauty of his lips held her spellbound. She wanted to reach out and touch his lower lip, trace it to the corners where the smile began. She couldn't remember ever wanting to touch anyone before. Perhaps years ago, when she was a child, before her father had taught her that touching others was to be discouraged and suppressed.

"Elspeth . . ." He reached out impulsively to touch her, and then stopped. His hand fell to his side and clenched into a fist. "Don't do this to me. I'm trying like hell to keep my promise." His light eyes were glittering. "I'm *trying*, dammit."

It was the time for them to be together. She knew it in some mystical fashion that sprang from within her like a seedling searching for the sun. But to make it happen she must be bold, she must have the bravery Dominic claimed she possessed. "I've been thinking quite a bit lately." She lowered her eyes to the fire. "I believe I would like to have a child. After all, the life of a scholar can sometimes be lonely, and I doubt if I shall ever marry again. Perhaps this will be my last chance to—"

He stiffened as if struck by a bullet. "What the hell are you saying to me?"

The soft color stole into her cheeks. "I think I'm making myself reasonably clear."

"Oh, you're clear enough, but there's nothing reasonable about it, neither in your words nor in your thinking." He was suddenly kneeling beside her. He was pale, a muscle jerking in his cheek, and his gaze held hers with an emotion close to anger. "For God's sake, be honest with me, you don't want my child.

Shall I tell you what you want? You want *me*. You want me touching you, moving in you. You want me to unwrap you from that MacGregor tartan you're so proud of and lay you down and move over you. That's what you want, isn't it?"

"Yes." She lifted her head and looked at him. "I do want everything you've mentioned, but I would also like your child."

"Why?" he asked blankly. "Why me?"

"I told you, I don't think I will have the opportunity—" She stopped. She would not lie to him. She drew a deep breath and said simply. "I love you. I believe I always will, Dominic Delaney."

"My God," Dominic said softly.

"Naturally, I wouldn't want you to feel obligated, but if it would please you to . . . You said all women were similar. I would try to—"

"Shut up!" The hoarse words were wrenched from him. "Lord, love, please shut up."

"I can't." She looked at him, her green eyes shimmering with tears. "It's too important to me. You didn't seem to find me distasteful before and I would try my best to please you. I learn quickly. Even a hetaera must begin at the beginning, and from the murals on the walls of the temples, it appears some of them weren't attractive either. One of the ladies had quite a monstrous hooked nose and—"

His fingers touched her lips. "Shhh, you're tearing me apart. I can't take any more of this. I don't know how I've held on to my sanity for as long as I have."

She swallowed. "Then you will . . . do it."

"I'm very much afraid I will," he said regretfully. His fingers moved to caress her cheekbone. "For a while I thought I was going to turn into a gentleman after all. I guess I should have known I'd never make it." He pushed the plaid from her head and let it fall to her shoulders. "Your hair is still damp." He buried his hands in her long tresses, slowly letting the locks flow between his fingers. "Cool," he said thickly, "and slick."

She found she was holding her breath. The slight

tugging was setting off tiny sparks in her scalp. "You like it?"

"I like all of you," he murmured. "Oh, Azuquita, where are you now that I need you?"

"What?"

"Never mind, it's too late anyway." One hand left her hair to cover her hand clutching the plaid at her breast. He carefully unclasped her fingers and slowly pushed aside the edges of the tartan to reveal the nakedness beneath the wool. He froze, looking at her, the pulse in his throat hammering. "Oh, yes, much too late."

She closed her eyes, her cheeks ablaze with color. Shyness. Excitement. And a passionate desire for reassurance. "Why?" she whispered. "Why are you doing this? It isn't pity?"

"Pity? How little you understand." He carefully pushed the tartan from her shoulders and it fell to the ground behind her.

"Then why?"

He bent his head and laid his lips on the pulse pounding in the hollow of her throat. "Any number of reasons."

"Give me one."

"You don't have a monstrous hooked nose." He pushed her back on the tartan and shifted back to take off her boots.

"Oh." She tried to think of something else to say, but she was finding it increasingly difficult to form either words or thoughts in a mind overflowing with the physical imagery of Dominic. The sight of bronze skin, translucent gray-blue eyes, and a smile brimming with tenderness was causing her to gaze up at him in wonder. Then he kissed her, and thought disappeared entirely. When he lifted his head and would have moved away from her, she reached up to stop him. "No," she whispered. "Stay."

"I'll be back." He sat back on his heels and his fingers went to the buttons of his shirt, his gaze on Elspeth lying naked before him, her hair spread like a glowing tawny escutcheon on the red plaid of the tartan. If he lived to be a hundred, he knew he would remember this moment and the gifts she was offering him. Beauty, love, and courage—precious gifts, every one. He stripped off his shirt, peeling the wet material from his skin and tossing it aside.

Her shyness was gone, she realized with surprise. She was experiencing desire, anticipation, uncertainty, but no shyness. There was something so inexplicably tender in his manner that prohibited any feeling of discomfort. Would he think her bold? But surely the women he was accustomed to weren't shy either and he . . . She lost her train of thought as her gaze wandered lovingly over him. How beautiful he was. The soft dark thatch of hair on his chest was irresistibly inviting, and she sat up on one elbow to reach out her hand to touch it. He glanced up from unfastening his belt to look at her.

She felt the color sting her cheeks, not so bold after all. "This feels different from the hair on your head. Rougher." Her fingers tangled in the springy thatch. "You don't mind my doing this?"

"I like you to touch me." He took her hand and placed her palm flat against his chest. He held her gaze as he slowly rubbed her hand up and down over his flesh, letting her feel the textures of him, the smooth, warm skin over supple muscles, the faint prickle of wiry hair, the hard pounding of his heart vibrating through his body and into her own through the sensitive flesh of her palm.

She was suddenly trembling, her heart beating as erratically as Dominic's. Her hand slipped down over his torso, tracing the line of dark hair to where it disappeared into the waistband of his trousers.

He shuddered. She could feel the muscles of his stomach bunch and tauten beneath her hand. "I like it too much. You'd better stop. I can't hurry this time."

"Why not?"

He took her hand from his stomach and smiled down at her with an expression she had never seen before on his face. A glowing tenderness, almost a sweetness, that set oddly on his usually cynical features. "I told you once I wasn't a welcher. Last time you gave me more than I gave you. I was so damn drunk, all I could think about was how much I needed you. I should have been gentler. I should have taken more time." He lifted her hand to his lips and kissed the palm. His lips were warm, teasing her flesh. "I was rough as hell. It's a wonder you don't hate me."

"I don't remember you being rough." She remembered nothing but heat and possession and Dominic within her body. "It seemed entirely . . . adequate."

He flinched. "Adequate. What a puling word." A sudden flicker of humor touched his lips. "I guess I'll just have to work on changing your opinion. Stay right where you are, love." He moved out of the lean-to and rapidly discarded the rest of his clothing. Then he was kneeling beside her, his face alight with the same smile that had shaken her before. His bronze flesh was burnished by the firelight and his voice was velvet soft as he gathered her close. "Now, let me see what I can do about banishing that word from your mind. Part your legs, love." His fingers ran down her body, delicate and loving as a sculptor creating a work of art. Everywhere he touched was blessed with fire—her breasts, her throat, her belly. His hands nudged her legs apart and he moved between them, stroking the nest of curls surrounding her womanhood, his fingers splaying out to tangle and play. "You're different here too. Not rough, just different." His head bent and he slowly rubbed his cheek back and forth on her belly. The faint abrasion of the stubble on his chin was wildly exciting. "Soft and yet strong . . ." His teeth nipped gently at that softness, and then his tongue followed to soothe and tease. She could feel his warm breath on her flesh, then his moist tongue moving lazily. The muscles of her belly tautened in response.

"No, not yet." His hand moved up to rub gently at the rigid muscles, trying to relax them. "It will be better for you if you don't get excited too soon. Relax, love."

Relax? How was she expected to relax when every muscle was vibrating at an excruciating pitch of anticipation? "Don't be daft," she said tartly. "What a truly stupid thing to say."

Her sudden shift from docility disconcerted him for a moment, and he went still, his cheek on her stomach, his expression hidden from her. Then his shoulders began to shake. He raised his head to look at her, his face alight with laughter. "I'll try to refrain from any further idiocy." He shook his head, his eyes still glowing with laughter and tenderness. "I don't know why I expected you to respond as any other woman would. You've never done anything else in the ordinary way."

This was how he should look, Elspeth thought suddenly. This was how he would have looked if the gentleness and humor had not been stolen from him by those grim years of hiding and pursuit. She wanted to give him back those years of laughter with a desire that sprang as much from protectiveness as from passion. Her hand reached out and moved over his crisp thick curls, tenderly pushing an unruly lock back from his forehead. "I didn't mean to discourage you."

"Oh, you didn't." His fingers were between her thighs, searching. She gave a low cry as the search ended. Her fingers clenched helplessly in his hair as he began to press, rotate, flick. His gaze was warm with pleasure as he watched her face. "You couldn't discourage me. Not in the next thousand years. Do you like this?"

"Yes." She could scarcely speak through the haze of pleasure. She was trembling, shivering. What was he doing to her?

"Good." Two fingers plunged suddenly and she opened her lips in a silent scream as the breath left her body. Her head thrashed back and forth on the tartan as he began a rhythm that sent her into convulsions of pleasure and hunger.

"Dominic!"

"Shhh . . ." His face above her was flushed and sensual. "I know. Just let me do this for a little while. It will make the rest better for you." He wanted to pleasure her with an intensity that surprised him. He had always tried to give his ladies satisfaction; it made his own enjoyment stronger. But this was different. He felt that Elspeth's every response was linked in some mysterious fashion with his own. Every tingle of pleasure he gave her was his pleasure. He bent impulsively and kissed her lips with a softness that wove a honeycomb of golden sweetness about them both. "But I don't think I can wait much longer," he said hoarsely as he lifted his head. "May I come in and show you more, Elspeth?"

Her smile was radiant as she nodded. "Please."

He slid within her very slowly, letting her become accustomed to him. Fullness. That wonderful primitive joining. He began to move, alternating short strokes with long ones; depth with shallowness, swiftness with leisurely slowness.

His chest was moving in and out with the harshness of his breathing as he struggled to maintain control. "Elspeth, I've missed you so." His teeth were clenched, his words almost guttural. "The tightness . . . I feel as if you're grabbing me every time I—" He stopped and looked down at her, his light eyes glittering and wild in the firelight. "Do you know what you're doing to me?"

She was beginning to learn and that knowledge filled her with pagan anticipation. She suddenly made an undulating movement with her lower body. He gasped, and a shudder ran through him. She could do it, too, she suddenly realized with delight. She could give him this wonder he was giving her. She experimented again, clenching around him.

He closed his eyes, the pulse leaping in his throat. "Lord, Elspeth, don't do that. You're making me lose control."

But her delight was too heady, her sense of power too new. She ran her hand over the tangle of hair on his chest as she began a rhythm of her own.

His breath was coming in rough gasps as he opened his eyes. "All right, love," he said thickly. "If you want it this way, heaven knows, it's what I want too."

He plunged deep, piercing her, filling her, each thrust lightning fast, lightning hot, searing her. His palms cupped her bottom, squeezing the cheeks with every bold invasion, lifting her to each thrust, forcing her to take more of him. She tried to offer him that response she had so recently learned, but she was being overwhelmed, deluged in just the taking of him. She was half-sobbing in a fever of heating pleasure. Her nails bit into his arms, released, and then bit in again. The world was expanding, a silver box with a ruby center, a red MacGregor tartan, Dominic's eyes looking down at her with laughter and hot delight. Beauty merged with passion, as she was merging with Dominic.

His fingers moved skillfully as he thrust, and she felt something building that she vaguely remembered from that other time.

"Elspeth—" Dominic's face was tautened with strain. His fingers moved more urgently. "I can't hold on."

Hold on to what? she wondered dimly. Then she knew as the tension that had been building released in a wonder of rapture that shook her to the depths of her soul. She heard Dominic's low cry above her as that same rapture claimed him.

"Thank God," Dominic breathed. "I was afraid for a moment I'd leave you behind." He leaned down and kissed her again. Sweetness, gratitude, warmth were all there, wrapping her in a cocoon to shelter her from any chill that might follow the storm. "I don't want ever to leave you behind, Elspeth."

There was no danger of her ever letting him leave her, Elspeth thought. Not now. If he left her, she would follow him. If he grew tired of her as a lover, she would find a way to make herself necessary to him in another way. He had told her tonight that she was strong. Well, she would use that strength to make him belong to her in all the ways a man could belong to a woman. "I pleased you?"

"Oh, yes." His hand gently stroked her hair back from her face. "You're a joy and a surprise. Not one of those hetaeras you're always talking about could have been better, Elspeth MacGregor."

"Elspeth Delaney," she corrected him. She smiled up at him. "And I thank you for the fine words. I'll try to improve with practice." He had not said he loved her but he had said she had given him pleasure. It would have to do for now. "Shall we continue?"

He threw back his head and laughed. "Not now, I think it best if we rest for a while." He lifted off her and to the side before bringing her into his arms. His lips brushed her temple as he settled her head on his shoulder. "We have time."

She settled her cheek on his shoulder, running the tips of her fingers down the muscles of his chest in a loving caress. Drowsiness was already tugging at her as she murmured, "I hope your wound did not get hurt. You were very . . . vigorous."

He chuckled and bent down to kiss each of her lids with a touch as light as the breath of a butterfly. "You didn't hurt me," he teasingly mimicked her Scottish brogue. "And I'd far rather be considered vigorous than adequate."

The corners of her lips turned up, and she went to sleep . . . smiling.

Dominic's arms tightened around her with yearning tenderness. He shouldn't have done this. He shouldn't have taken what she offered, but he couldn't have stopped himself. The discovery of what she meant to him had shattered his control and torn aside the veil he had used to mask the truth. And now that he had taken her, he knew that he was not going to let her go again. The love she offered was even more precious than the irresistible draw of her body.

Perhaps he could make it right. He couldn't promise her permanency or even stability, but if he tried to make her happy in the moments they had . . . No, he had to do more than that. He had to find a way to protect her if anything happened to him. He had to keep her secure, and security meant money.

The Kantalan treasure.

He stared unseeingly into the darkness, turning over in his mind the possibilities the legendary treasure offered. Not for Killara, but for the woman in his arms. The woman he loved.

21

"**E**lspeth. Come, love, wake up."

It was Dominic's voice, but somehow different, vibrating with eagerness and laughter. She drowsily opened her eyes. His face was different too. He was laughing down at her, his eyes alight with the joy of life, and in the moment between sleeping and waking she knew that something in him had come right; a gift taken away from him had been returned.

"Is it morning?" she asked.

"No. But it's time."

"Time for what?" Her gaze ran over him lovingly. The fire had burned low, bathing him in a shadowy glow that glinted in the darkness of his hair and turned the bronze of his skin to copper.

"Time to further your education as a hetaera." His eyes were dancing. "I believe you expressed a willingness to learn new skills." He pulled her to a sitting position. "Well, one of the first things you must learn is to adapt yourself to your lord and master's whims."

"Indeed?"

He nodded as he carefully wrapped her in her plaid. "Oh, yes, that's most important."

"And what whim is this?"

"One I've been thinking about since the night I brought you back to Hell's Bluff from Jim's cabin." He gathered her up in his arms, ducked from beneath the shelter of the lean-to, and stood up. "We're going for a little ride."

320

Her eyes widened. "In the middle of the night?"

"Why not?" He strode toward Blanco, standing saddled and waiting a few yards away. "The rain has stopped and there's moonlight."

"We're not dressed," she protested in bewilderment. She was wrapped only in the plaid and he was as gloriously naked as he had been when he had made love to her earlier in the evening.

He chuckled. "I'll have no problem and you have your fine MacGregor plaid to keep you warm." He stopped, leaned down, and kissed her with infinite sweetness. "And I promise I'll do everything possible to help. You're not going to refuse me?"

How could she refuse him when he looked so endearingly boyish? "No," she said softly. "It's daft, but if it's what you want—"

"It's definitely what I want." He kissed her again, quick and hard, and lifted her onto the saddle. "Among other things." With one spring he was behind her, kicking the horse into a trot.

The moon cast a silver half light on the hard rocky trail once they had left the shadowy grove, and Elspeth found herself in a strange, mystical world. A warm gray mist was rising from the earth to wreathe around them and veil the spiky tops of the tall pine trees on either side of the trail. She felt as if they were alone in a wild secret garden at the beginning of time, when anything was possible and nothing was forbidden.

Dominic's warm breath was brushing her ear and his arms formed a deliciously secure haven around her. The breeze touching her cheeks and tugging at her hair was cool but not chill, bringing with it the heady scent of pine and rich damp earth. She suddenly found herself filled with wild exhilaration. "Do these whims strike you often? This is completely mad, you know."

"Is it?" His teeth gently nibbled on the lobe of her ear.

A tingle of heat ran through her. "Yes."

"I admit this is the first time this particular whim

has occurred to me." His hands were parting the tartan, slipping beneath the wool to cup her bare breasts. "But I won't promise it will be the last." His thumb and forefinger plucked at the sensitive nipples. "Does this please you?"

Fire, an aching throbbing between her thighs. "Yes, I . . . think so."

He laughed softly as he enveloped her breasts in his hands and lifted them high. "Only think?"

"It makes me feel odd . . . almost hurting. I suppose that's natural though."

"Where do you hurt?" One hand left her breasts and moved down to her taut stomach to rub gently. "Here?"

The muscles went rigid beneath his fingertips. "Yes."

His hand shifted lower and tangled in her soft curls. "Here?"

"Yes."

He tilted her back against him and his fingers wandered down to delicately circle and rub, his thumb pressing skillfully. "Here?"

She couldn't breathe, she was throbbing, burning. She wanted him within her. What were they doing on this stupid horse when they could be wrapped in each other's arms as they had been only a few hours before? "Shouldn't we be getting back?"

"You didn't answer me." His thumb pressed harder.

"Yes, but we're on—"

"I don't like you to hurt, love. I feel it my husbandly duty to rid you of the pain." He shifted back on the saddle, rolled the tartan from her body, then grasped her beneath the arms, lifted her high into the air, and swung her around to face him.

She was wide-eyed with astonishment, and couldn't have spoken if her life depended on it.

His hands cupped her buttocks, lifted her, and he slowly slid into her, filling her. She forgot where they were, she forgot everything but the *feel* of him. She closed her eyes, her head thrown back, her breath coming in little pants.

"Wrap your legs around me," he muttered. "Hold me."

She promptly did so and could feel Dominic's heart pounding against her breasts; his chest, rising and falling with every breath, brushed hard against her aroused nipples.

He brought her closer still and she could feel the prickle of the pelt surrounding his manhood brush that most sensitive part of her. She moaned, clutching helplessly at his shoulders. "Dominic."

"Hold on, love." He kicked the horse into a gallop.

The pounding.

The supple leather of the saddle beat against their flesh, driving her deeper onto the warm sword of his manhood. Elspeth felt a wild scream building within her, wanting to be let out.

Dominic arched her against him, bending his mouth to envelope her breast, suckling, biting. She sobbed. The arousal was too intense, the brand within her too hot, too hard. The pressure on her bottom too rhythmic, too pounding. Her head felt as if it were exploding, each single hair on her head burning, streaming out behind her in lightning flames of sensation.

It went on forever. Timeless. The hunger built, the pounding built, the fever built. The horse ran faster. Her hair was going to be torn from her head by the wind. Dominic's breath was a half sob in her ear.

"Now!" The word was spoken between Dominic's clenched teeth. "Now!"

Yes, now, Elspeth thought wildly. It had to be now or she would be lost forever in this maelstrom of heat and hunger.

She screamed, a sound harsh with primeval satisfaction as *now* came into pagan, magnificent being.

She collapsed against Dominic, her head cradled on his chest, struggling to get her breath. He cupped the back of her head with one hand as he reined the stallion to a walk with the other. As soon as she thought she could speak without gasping, she lifted her head to look up at him. He was as breathless as she, but he was smiling down at her with tenderness and that same touch of boyish mischief she had noticed before. "Shouldn't I move?"

He looked down at their joining and flexed lazily within her. He turned the stallion. "Why? Don't you like where you are now?"

The color flooded her cheeks. "Yes, but I thought . . . isn't it finished now?"

He laughed softly. "Oh, no, it's only beginning. Blanco has a hell of a lot of paces for us to try. Now we have to ride *back* to camp. I think you may enjoy that every bit as much, my love." He kicked the stallion into a lope. She gasped as the jarring rhythm rocked through her. "Yes, every bit as much."

The fire beneath the lean-to was reduced to glowing embers when Dominic laid Elspeth down on the blanket. "I'll be right back."

She watched him dreamily as he knelt and put fresh wood on the fire. Then he was beside her, gathering her close, his hand tangling in her hair as he pulled her head back to kiss her gently. "Are you tired?"

She shook her head. "It was very . . ." She searched for the correct word. "Stimulating."

He chuckled. "I'm in complete agreement. You're a constant astonishment to me, my lovely hetaera."

The smile faded from her lips and she glanced away from him into the depths of the fire. "You don't have to say that."

"Say what?"

"I mean, you don't have to pay me compliments. I think it's better if we're honest with each other. I'm well aware that I'm a plain woman."

He stared at her with blank amazement. It seemed a century since those first days when he had actually believed Elspeth plain. He couldn't even remember why he had thought it to begin with. Even masked by her spectacles and shrouded in those hideous gowns, he should have been able to see the beauty that was Elspeth. He had a vague recollection of her making some such comment before and he realized now that she could not see her own beauty. Her father had been such a bastard that he'd stolen her pride in the person she was inside and out. "Did your father say you were plain?"

"Of course." She didn't look at him. "But I always knew it anyway. I have a mirror."

"I wonder what you see in it. Is it what your father saw? No, it couldn't be that, because then there would be no reflection." His thumb and forefinger were beneath her chin, turning her face so he could look into her eyes. "Because he was a blind man, Elspeth. Blinded by cruelty, selfishness, and his own ugliness of spirit. You didn't believe him when he told you there was no Kantalan, why should you believe him when he told you that you had no beauty?"

Her eyes widened. "I don't know. I never thought about it."

"Then think about it now. Do you know what I see when I look at you?" He tugged at a lock of her hair. "This glows and shimmers with light every time you turn your head." His fingertips brushed her cheekbones. "Your skin is so soft I want to reach out and touch it every time you're within ten feet of me." His index finger stroked the curve of her brow. "And your eyes as green as the shamrocks my mother used to tell me about. Lovely eyes."

"Not . . . ugly?"

"No. Beautiful." The words were spoken in a tone only a level above a whisper. "Every bit of you is beautiful. Believe me, Elspeth. Your father lied to you. All I see is strength and beauty."

Joy cascaded through her, rippling, forming circles of radiance. It was difficult to believe him, but there was nothing but honesty in the eyes looking into her own. "I think you may be a wee bit blind yourself," she said with a shaky smile. "But I like your mirror better than I do my own." She could feel the tears burning behind her eyes and she quickly closed her lids to hide them.

Gentleness, kindness, laughter. Every moment he revealed another quality to love, presented her with another gift to enrich her spirit. Oh, and she did love him. She brimmed, flowed, and floated with her love for him. But it was all too much to think about after what had gone before. "I think it's time we went to sleep. Unless you have any more whims you wish me to indulge."

She could feel his gaze on her face for a long moment before his lips brushed her closed lids with velvet tenderness. "I think I've run out of whims for the moment." But not out of love, he thought. He knew now he would never run out of love for her. His love for Elspeth was as much a part of him as his yearning for Killara. "Go to sleep, Elspeth." He settled down beside her and drew her into his arms. "Sweet dreams, love."

But they would not be dreams of Kantalan, she thought drowsily, they would be dreams of Dominic and the expression in his eyes when he had called her beautiful.

Rising Star threw back her head, and her throaty laughter rang out. "Patrick, you fool, why don't you come into the water? I may be huge, but I'm not taking quite all of this pond."

Patrick shook his head, his gaze on the tops of the trees on the opposite bank. "Maybe later," he muttered. "I'll go set up camp. Don't stay in the water too long." He turned on his heel and strode quickly off into the trees.

A faint frown crossed Rising Star's face. Patrick was embarrassed. It had not occurred to her that Patrick would act like this when they had discovered this tiny pond in the foothills. After traveling the harsh desert country for the past weeks, the little oasis had been too inviting for her to resist. She had stripped off her clothes and slipped into the cool water as matter-of-factly as if Patrick had been the child she had known when she first came to Killara. She had forgotten he was now eighteen and possessed a white man's shame of nudity.

Still, it was a reaction she would never have expected in the Patrick who had ridden beside her, joking and filling the hours with laughter for the last two weeks. Without Patrick she might have fallen into a darkness of spirit that would have had no dawn. He had not permitted her to step into that void. Every time he had detected any sign of sadness or weariness, he had been there with a comment or a droll expression, taking away the ache before it could sharpen and become pain. He had been so kind and she really should not have laughed at him when he had refused to come into the water with her.

She waded out of the water, picked up the white cotton cloth she had left on the bank, and dried herself as thoroughly as possible. If Patrick had not displayed that unusual shyness, she would have remained naked and let the breeze and the last rays of the setting sun complete the drying. Instead, she hurriedly put on her blue calico skirt and leather tunic and sat down on the grass to pull on her moccasins.

"Coffee's on," Patrick called loudly, making a good deal of noise as he walked through the underbrush. An expression of relief brightened his face as he appeared on the bank and saw her. "You're almost dressed. That's good. I was afraid you'd be—cool," he finished lamely.

Naked was the word he'd intended to use, she thought as she lowered her head to hide her smile of amusement. "Except for my moccasins." She made a face. "I can't see over my stomach to put them on."

"Let me help." He dropped to his knees and took the moccasins out of her hands. "You should have told me these were causing you trouble before. I'll put them on for you every morning." He picked up her foot and slipped the soft cream-colored leather onto it, then rolled it up her calf. He smoothed the leather with his hands and picked up the other moccasin. His cheeks were flushed and his words tumbled over each other. "I can see how you would have trouble. I don't know how you women manage to—"

"Patrick," she interrupted gently. "Look at me."

He kept his gaze fixed stubbornly on the moccasin as he pulled it over her ankle and then up her calf.

"I'm sorry I embarrassed you," she said softly. "I sometimes forget you are white and not Indian. You seemed so much like the child I used to know that I—"

"I'm not a child." His voice was hoarse as he pulled down her calico skirt. He sat back on his heels, still looking at the moccasins on her feet.

"I know that." What words could she choose that would not offend his pride? "I suppose I needed to go back to that other time when I was so happy and tried to fool myself that things were the same. Forgive me."

"It's all right. I wanted you to forget about—" He broke off. "Not about Josh. Just what had made you unhappy. I'd never want you to forget about Josh." He raised his head to look at her.

A ripple of shock robbed her of breath. Oh, no, please God, no, Rising Star prayed silently. Not Patrick. But she had seen that expression too many times in her own mirror not to recognize it when she saw it. The stunning surprise showed on her face, and she knew he could read the realization in her own expression.

He drew a deep breath. "Don't be afraid. It won't make any difference. I promise you I won't bother you."

"Patrick . . ."

"No, no," he said urgently. "I tell you we can go on just the way we were."

When she knew the pain he was going through? "How long have you felt this way?"

He shrugged. "I don't know. Always, I guess. At least it seems that way."

Oh, God, why couldn't there be any justice? It wasn't fair Patrick must suffer too. "You'll have to go away."

"No!" The answer was violent. "I won't leave you. I know you can't love me, but it won't hurt anything for you to let me take care of you. You need someone to help you, and you won't go back to Josh."

She smiled sadly. "It will hurt you. I know how much it can hurt, Patrick."

"Because you've been hurt?" He drew closer and took her left hand in both of his. "But this is different. I know there's no hope you could love anyone but Josh." He forced a smile. "Think of me as one of those knights in the books you used to read to us. They never expected anything from their ladies, just to carry their favors and fight a pesky dragon now and then. I think I'd be a rip-snorting wonder as a dragon fighter, don't you?"

She was unbearably moved. Kneeling before her, the last rays of sunlight setting his auburn hair aflame, his young face grave, he could well have been Galahad from that time of courtly love. "Oh, yes, a great dragon fighter."

He smiled again, this time with the beguiling mischief that was so much a part of him. "And every lady needs a knight when she goes journeying. Why not me?"

She hesitated. Would it be too selfish of her to let him stay with her until they reached Kantalan? He had filled the days with warmth and laughter, and she desperately needed that laughter. "Patrick, I don't know."

"I do." He gave her hand a brisk squeeze and released it. "I'm going with you. Maybe if I find enough treasure to buy myself one of those Oriental dancing girls, I'll forget all about you. Did you ever think about that?"

"No, I never did."

"Well, it's something you should consider." He stood up and lifted her to her feet with easy strength. "I'm not going to moon after you forever. It won't hurt you to put up with me for a little while longer. Just until I know you're safe and happy again. You'll probably think it over and go back to Josh once we get back from Kantalan."

She slowly shook her head. "I do love you, Patrick, but it will never be the same as what I feel for Joshua."

"I keep telling you, I don't expect you to give me anything." He smiled and his hard young face was suddenly lit with a gentle beauty. "I'll be satisfied if you just take. All right?"

"No, it is not all right," she said quietly. "But we'll continue to Kantalan together. After that we'll talk again."

He let his breath out in a sigh of relief. "Fair

enough." He picked up the cotton cloth she had used to dry herself. "Now we'd better get back to camp before that coffee boils away." He took her elbow and turned her in the direction from which he had come. His touch was light but protective.

The glow of pleasure she received from that touch gave her a fleeting moment of misgiving. Then she dismissed it. It was surely natural for her to find joy in Patrick's companionship after the loneliness she had known. She turned to smile at him. "Thank you for helping me with my moccasins."

"Putting them on you kind of reminded me of the trick I played on Cort when we were on that trail drive two years ago." He grinned. "When he was asleep I bored a hole in each of his boots and then strung a piece of rawhide through . . ." His words rambled on, his tone easy and humorous, but that protective clasp never left her arm until they reached the camp.

There were rain clouds on the horizon.

Ramon Torres frowned as he paused at the crest of the hill. Bad luck. The rain would wash away the signs of Dominic and his *gringa* and he would probably not be able to find them again for a day or so. He had hoped to catch up to them by the end of the week when he had stopped at Rosario and learned they were only two days ahead of him.

Oh, well, he had been fortunate that the weather had held as long as it had. He would try to make it as far as he could on Dominic's trail before the rain came. Then he would wait out the storm and have time to sit before the fire and dream the death dream. He had been pushing so hard, he had been too tired to give himself that pleasure of late. Perhaps the deity guiding all hunters had intervened to remind him that his thirst would be whetted only if he took time to anticipate.

After all, what were a few days when the kill was so near?

22

Dominic slipped under the blanket and gathered Elspeth into his arms. She tried to relax. He was back. Nothing had happened to him. She knew he would sense her tension—as he seemed to sense her every feeling and thought these days. Each time he left her now to check their back trail for signs of Torres, fear made every muscle of her body rigid until she heard the sound of Blanco's hoofs returning.

"Elspeth?"

"Why do you do it?" she whispered. "Surely Torres isn't following us. There's been no sign of him in all this time."

His fingers gently massaged her rigid shoulders. "It doesn't hurt to be careful. I don't like to be surprised."

She turned to face him. "But you do think he's still following us, don't you?"

"I didn't say that. I only want to—yes."

"Why?"

He shook his head. "I don't know. I can *feel* him out there. Waiting."

She shivered. "Have you ever felt like this before?"

He nodded.

"Have you been right?"

He hesitated. "Yes."

She felt sick as she realized how many nights of fear and tension it had taken to develop in him the instincts of a hunted animal. "Why do you let them do this to you? That Durbin man has no right to send his

horrible killers after you. Why don't you go after him
and—" She stopped, horrified at the savage thought
that had come to her.

"Kill him?" Dominic asked quietly.

"I don't know." She swallowed. "I know only that it
isn't right for him to do this to you. He has to be an
evil, evil man to send men like Torres to try to murder
you."

"Or a man who loved his son and believed that I
murdered him."

"Patrick said it was a fair fight. You didn't murder
anyone."

"Because I let him draw first?" His lips twisted. "I
knew I was faster than he was. Do you know how I felt
when I realized he was going to back me into a corner
and make me draw? I was glad. I could feel the blood
surging through my veins and I felt drunk with power.
I don't know if I murdered him or not, but when I saw
my bullet tear into him, I felt as if I had." He looked
down at her. "Maybe I lied to you when I told you I
wasn't a murderer."

"Oh, no. No." Her arms tightened around him,
feeling his guilt and pain as if it were her own. For a
moment she had wanted Durbin dead, and she didn't
have the excuse of being the unthinking boy Dominic
had been those long years ago. "It wasn't your fault.
None of it was your fault."

"Maybe, but I know how Durbin feels. I'd probably
feel the same way if it were my son."

So he would continue to let Durbin send men like
Torres after him until someday . . . She couldn't
bear to think about it. There must be some way to
stop this horror from happening again and again.

"But Torres isn't close tonight?" she whispered.

"There's no sign of him."

She drew his head down and kissed him with a
passion that held a tinge of desperation. When he
lifted his head they were both trembling. She began
unbuttoning his shirt. "Then don't you think we'd
better take advantage of our privacy while there's no
danger of being interrupted?"

* * *

The earth was trembling.

It was a movement so faint, she knew it hadn't jarred her out of sleep. What was it, then?

Azuquita brayed harshly.

The other animals moved restlessly.

A wild rustle of wings shivered through the air as birds suddenly left the trees for the sky.

Then the mists of sleep vanished and she remembered . . .

She jerked upright, fear catching in her throat. "Dalkar!"

"What are you doing?" Dominic asked sleepily.

"Did you feel something?"

"No." He raised himself on one elbow. "What?"

"I don't know." She made a helpless motion with one hand. "Something . . ."

The trembling had stopped.

Azuquita was quiet.

The birds had returned to their trees.

"A dream?" Dominic asked gently.

"Perhaps it was a dream." She lay down again and cuddled closer to Dominic. "It was so real. Sayan felt the Sun Child trembling but she wasn't afraid for herself. Only for Dalkar."

He laughed softly. "I believe you're still half asleep. Who are Sayan and Dalkar?"

"Sayan was the high priestess of Kantalan who saw the vision in the flames and handed down the prophecy. I thought you knew about her."

"I vaguely recall Rising Star telling me something about her a long time ago, but I'm afraid I was more interested in tales of the treasure." He slowly began to stroke the soft hair at Elspeth's temple. "Though I don't remember her speaking of any Dalkar."

"Dalkar was Sayan's lover. She loved him so much . . ."

"Do you often dream of Kantalan?"

She nodded. "Lovely dreams. Sometimes they're sad but they're always beautiful."

"But you were frightened tonight."

"This dream was different. Not like a dream at all."

Yet, she thought, it had to be a dream and the trembling of the earth she had felt must have been only an extension of that dream. Dominic hadn't felt the trembling nor did he seem to feel the uneasiness she was experiencing.

"Dominic."

"Uhmmm?"

"How close are we to Kantalan?"

"I'm not sure. Maybe a day's journey until we get through these foothills and then a half day's climb to get to the waterfall."

Close. So very close. "What if we can't find the waterfall?"

"Then there won't be a pass. There won't be a Sun Child and there won't be a Kantalan."

"Nothing," she whispered.

"There will still be you and me and Killara."

The earth trembled again. She could tell by Dominic's expression that he didn't feel it. Perhaps she had only imagined that most evanescent of movements of the earth. "Yes." She closed her eyes and snuggled still nearer to Dominic, trying to ignore the whoosh of wings as the birds once more took to the sky.

The waterfall was exactly where the map indicated, streaming from a height of over two hundred feet to crash on the boulders that bordered the large lake.

Dominic emerged from behind the mist of the waterfall almost as wet as if he had charged through it and urged Blanco forward, picking his way gingerly over the rough rocks toward the spot where Elspeth was waiting on the bank of the lake. "The pass is there. The lake extends back beyond the falls about thirty feet. Once we're out of the water there's a narrow trail that winds up between the walls of rock of the mountain. The path is pretty rough, but as far as I can tell, it's clear. Which is something of a miracle considering it's been over three hundred years since it's been used. There was every chance the pass could have been blocked by landslides." He took Azuquita's lead rope from her.

The mule promptly sat down on the bank.

"That's all we need," Dominic said, irritated. "He's been as cantankerous as the devil these past two days. I practically had to push him up the lower slopes."

Elspeth didn't answer, her gaze was fixed in compulsive fascination on the darkness beyond the silver spray.

"I don't know why I should be surprised." Dominic was tugging futilely on the lead rope. "If there's any way to make a situation worse, a mule will find it. We'll be lucky if we get him off his haunches by dark. I wanted to be through the pass by—" He broke off as he turned and caught a glimpse of Elspeth's face. "What's wrong?"

Her gaze didn't leave the dark entrance to the pass. She moistened her lips. "It's real, isn't it? It was all true."

Dominic let the lead rope go slack as his eyes narrowed in concern. "I thought there was no question in your mind that Kantalan existed. This is what you wanted. Why are you afraid?"

"I don't know," she whispered.

"I could go on alone."

She shook her head. "I'm being foolish. Of course I'm going." She urged the mare forward. "I suppose I've dreamed of Kantalan so long, I'm afraid of being disappointed. How do I get Nina to swim?"

"Just follow me and hold on tight. The mare will know what to do. We'll stop and change clothes once we're out of the lake." He dropped Azuquita's rope and grabbed the burro's lead. He turned Blanco toward the waterfall.

"What about Azuquita?"

"He can sit there until his tail rots off," Dominic said grimly as he disappeared behind the falls. "I've had more than enough of our 'little sugar.'"

Elspeth followed him, letting Nina have her head. She gasped as the mare entered the icy water.

A raucous bray broke the silence. Elspeth glanced

back over her shoulder to see Azuquita still sitting on his haunches, glaring at them with an expression Elspeth would swear was supreme indignation.

Then the mule was lumbering to his feet and a moment later was in the lake, swimming hurriedly after Dominic and emitting loud shrill brays.

Elspeth began to laugh helplessly, the lilting sound rising above the roar of the waterfall and echoing off the stone ridges of the pass. "I told you Azuquita liked you," she called to Dominic.

Dominic looked over his shoulder to see Azuquita swimming directly behind him. "What do you mean? He just thinks he's going to get a chance to drown me. Can't you tell he's cursing me?"

Elspeth laughed again. She couldn't deny that Azuquita's braying held a surly note. "Perhaps you're right. I think you'd best get out of the water quickly."

Her laughter faded, but she felt distinctly grateful to Azuquita for putting at rest her strange feeling of reluctance to enter the pass. Now eagerness and excitement were once more beginning to claim her. She watched Dominic's horse begin to clamber up out of the water onto the trail and her knees unconsciously tightened, urging the mare forward.

The Sun Child, powerful and majestic, came into view when they were still some distance down the trail. Towering two thousand feet above the mountains around it, the volcano's upper reaches were composed entirely of gleaming gray-black lava rock while its foothills were verdant with trees and shrubs.

Then they came to the crest of the trail and Elspeth forgot everything but the view before her.

Kantalan.

They stood on the summit, looking down at the city spread out before them. The strong rays of the afternoon sun streamed down, bathing the ancient buildings and pyramids in golden light.

Elspeth gazed spellbound, scarcely breathing.

"Are you disappointed?" Dominic asked gently.

"No. Oh, no," she whispered. "It's beautiful. It's everything I dreamed it would be."

Dominic's gaze was on Elspeth, and he knew if there was not one particle of treasure in the city below them, he would still be grateful they had come to Kantalan. He would remember that expression of glowing radiance on her face until the day he died.

"The four rivers aren't rivers at all." She pointed to a narrow ribbon of water seemingly emerging from the foot of the Sun Child itself. "They're manmade canals. Isn't that interesting?"

"It seems to be to you," he said with an indulgent smile. "Though I can't understand why."

"Because it's clear the people of Kantalan deliberately tried to recreate their home city. Atlantis had four rivers intersecting like a cross, so when the colonists came here they dug canals to mirror the landscape they had known. It's much more significant than if the rivers had been natural." She drew a deep breath and her words tumbled out eagerly. "You know, if Atlantis was the birthplace of civilization, then it probably also contained the Garden of Eden. All of the legends of the garden mention four rivers. The Hebrew scripture says, 'And a river went out of Eden to water the garden; and from thence it was parted, and became into four heads.' The Scandinavians claim their sacred Asgard was watered by four primeval rivers of milk. The Chinese Tien-Chan was irrigated by four perennial fountains and the Slavratta of the Hindus possessed 'four primeval rivers' that flowed north, south, east, and west." She paused. "Like Atlantis."

"And Kantalan," Dominic said. "But if these canals are manmade, you won't find Eden here."

"No." Her gaze hadn't left the splendid city in the valley below. "But if Kantalan is a mirror of Atlantis, perhaps it's also a mirror of Eden." Her heels nudged Nina forward. "Come on, Dominic. I can't wait to see more." She was already several yards down the trail as she called back to him. "Do you suppose that large square building is the temple?"

The grounds surrounding the imposing building she had indicated were tangled and overgrown and bore no resemblance to the lush glory of Eden. Yet even as they rode through, it was obvious this had once been a formal garden, a classical one, with pools and fountains, flower beds and paths. However, it became clear as soon as they opened a massive twelve-foot set of double doors that this was not a temple but a palace. They looked into a chamber that was unquestionably a throne room.

A heavy layer of dust coated the white marble floors and the columns decorated with gold frieze. A double row of statues on alabaster pedestals formed a walkway leading across the vast marble expanse and up the three steps to a splendid elevated throne.

"It's gold," she whispered. "That throne must be pure gold."

Dominic nodded. "And, if I'm not mistaken, those jewels inlaid in the back are rubies."

Her gaze wandered around the huge empty room. "How beautiful it must have been." She took a step closer to one of the statues lining the approach to the throne, an elephant so exquisitely crafted, it appeared ready to raise its trunk and sound a triumphant trumpet through the cobwebbed stillness of the room. Her finger gently touched the satin smoothness of that trunk. "Ivory. Where did they get large enough quantities of ivory in this country to carve statues of this size?" She turned to him, her eyes blazing with excitement. "And this is an *elephant*. Elephants are found in Africa and Asia, not here. How would they be able to carve an elephant in such detail if they'd never seen one? There have been a few others cases I know about of a discovery of statuary like this. There was a wooden elephant found in the mounds in Wisconsin and similar artifacts found in the Cahokia mound in Illinois. Don't you see? They must have brought these statues with them, though I can't see how that would have been possible. Or it could be that the people originated in a place where they could have seen elephants.

He nodded and started across the room toward an ornately carved door to the left of the throne. "And I'll bet they brought more with them than a bunch of statues."

"Where are you going?"

"If this is the palace, where else would the royal treasury be but here?"

"Oh!" She couldn't keep the disappointment from her tone. "Now?"

He stopped and turned to look at her in surprise before smiling understandingly. "You want to find your temple and see if there's any more evidence of similarity?"

She nodded. "The temple is the storehouse of learning in most societies. I thought perhaps I could find a tablet or—" She stopped. "But naturally you want to see if the treasure actually exists. I can wait."

He hesitated and then turned and walked back toward her. "So can the Kantalan treasure. What's a few more hours after three hundred years?" He took her hand. "Which building should we try next?"

"The pyramid in the center of the city," she said instantly. "The shape had a mystical significance to the Egyptians, perhaps it's the same here." She paused. "I wouldn't mind going alone."

He shook his head. The city appeared silent and deserted, but that didn't mean there were no dangers. He wanted to be within hailing distance if Elspeth ran across a snake or other wild creature. "We'll leave the pack animals here. These gardens seem as good a place as any to set up camp. Let's go. You'll want to be able to look through the temple before dark."

Dominic was sitting on the stone steps and stood up as Elspeth came out of the temple and hurried toward him. She was carrying two large but very thin stone tablets in her arms, and he could tell by the excitement on her face that the question he was going to ask was completely unnecessary. "You found what you were looking for?"

"I think so. The hieroglyphics on these tablets are

completely unfamiliar. It may take years to decipher them, but there's a chance the entire story may be here." She crossed the road to where Nina was tethered and unfastened the thong of her saddlebag and took out the MacGregor plaid. She wrapped the tablets carefully and put them into the saddlebag. "The lodestone is in the big room in the center of the temple. At least I think that's what it is. I wonder what they used it for." She whirled to face him. "Oh, Dominic, you should have gone in with me. There was so much to see, so many strange and wonderful things to discover."

He shook his head. "This was *your* treasure. You waited a long time for your dream to come true. It was right that you experienced it first by yourself."

Another gift. She gazed at him, loving him with all her being. "Thank you."

He inclined his head. "My pleasure, Madame Delaney." His gaze narrowed on the sky feathered pink and gold above the mountains to the west. "Do you want to go back inside? You have about fifteen minutes until sunset."

She shook her head. "I think I'd like to walk back to the palace. I want to see *everything*. I want to walk down some of the sides streets and try to imagine the people who lived in those beautiful stately houses. Could we do that?"

He took her hand. "Why not? I'll come back for the horses later."

Stillness. The only sound in the entire city seemed to be the click of their boots on the cobbled streets. The houses and public buildings were in amazingly good condition, Elspeth noticed. They could have been built yesterday and yet had an air of timelessness about them. She had noticed that same strange quality in the pyramids of Egypt.

"Where did everybody go?" she asked softly. "There should be bones or something, shouldn't there? Do you suppose they heeded Sayan's warning and left Kantalan after all?"

"Perhaps," Dominic answered. "Even after all this

time there should still be some remains. I took a good look around while you were in the temple and found a few skeletons on some of the back streets. Dogs and horses, I think. But nothing in any of the houses but dust and broken pottery."

"But if they did escape, why didn't they come back?"

Dominic shrugged. "Maybe they didn't want to chance the same thing happening again. If I came back and found all the livestock dead, I might have second thoughts about—" He broke off in mid-sentence."

Elspeth had stopped dead still in the middle of the street. She was pale, her gaze fixed on the upper story of a large house just ahead. It was an imposing stone house with an upper balcony overlooking the street.

"Elspeth?"

"They didn't leave." The words were so low that he had to bend his head to hear them. "The people climbed to the first plateau of the Sun Child to give sacrifices that night. They never left that plateau. They never came back to the city."

"How do you know?" His gaze slowly followed her own to the balcony. A heavy filigree curtain fashioned of a metal blackened by time and the elements veiled the interior of the house. "What are you looking at?"

"They're there. Dalkar and Sayan. They're there beyond that silver curtain."

A shiver ran down his spine. There was absolute certainty in her voice. "How do you know?"

"How do you know Torres is still following us? I tell you, they're *there*."

"Do you want to go inside?"

"No." She closed her eyes and two tears brimmed and then ran slowly down her cheeks. "Only their bodies are there. What they were and are and ever will be moved on when the Sun Child destroyed the people of Kantalan." Her eyes opened and she started to walk swiftly down the street, past the house of Sayan, keeping her eyes fixed straight ahead. "I don't want to talk about it anymore. Perhaps it's only my imagination. I want to make camp and eat something, and then . . ." She wanted to do all the mundane things that made up the ordinary routines of life. She didn't want to think about Sayan and the love that had tortured and destroyed her. She didn't want to think about death.

Dominic was beside her, taking her hand again. "Wait for me," he said. "I'm going with you, remember?"

She drew a tremulous breath. "But how far?"

"All the way," he said gravely. "I thought you knew that."

She experienced a showerburst of joy that took her breath away and banished the melancholy that had claimed her. It was immediately followed by intense exasperation. "How would I know?" she asked tartly. "When you never saw fit to tell me. For all I knew, you meant to leave me and go back to Hell's Bluff or to perdition or to—"

His fingers were on her lips. "Hush," he said softly. "How could I leave you when I can't trust you out of my sight? If I turn my back, you're likely to fall down a mountain or take off for El Dorado." His words were teasing but his eyes were saying something . . . beautiful.

Her breath caught in her throat. "That's not a very good reason for staying with a person. If you have something to say to me, I wish you'd speak out. I'm no mystic who can read your feelings in the flames. I'm not Sayan, for goodness' sake."

"Aren't you?" he asked with a curious smile. "If you want a declaration, love, I'll try to accommodate you. I love you. I love you more than my family, Killara, or my life. I think you are my life now. Is that enough for you, Elspeth?"

"Oh, yes." She blinked rapidly to keep back the tears. "Quite enough." She suddenly hurled herself at him, hugging him with all her strength. "But you certainly took your time about it."

He laughed helplessly. "Elspeth, you're like no one else." He kissed her with a tenderness that caused her throat to tighten. "And I'll thank God for that fact for the rest of my life." His smile faded. "I guess I was afraid it would be bad luck to tell you. Everything I've ever really wanted seems to have slipped away from me. I couldn't take a chance on losing you too."

She swallowed. "Then why tell me now?"

"I thought you needed to hear it," he said simply. "I didn't have the right to protect myself if it was going to keep you from having anything you need or want."

She gazed at him, something inside her melting helplessly. "Daft. Completely daft, Dominic Delaney."

"Oh, yes, more daft every day, love." He pushed her away. "Now, let's get back to the palace and set up camp. Declarations are all very well, but I never was very good with words." His eyes were twinkling as he slipped his arm around his waist and turned her toward the palace. "I'm much better with action."

23

$\sim$$\sim$$\sim$

Something cold and metallic was slipped over her head and then arranged carefully to encircle her naked breasts.

Elspeth opened her eyes to see Dominic smiling down at her. His light eyes were glittering with excitement and seemed to hold all the beauty in the world.

She smiled back at him drowsily. "Again?"

He laughed. "I'd be delighted, but not until you tell me how much you like your necklace. It's the first time I've ever given a lady jewels worth a king's ransom, and I expect at least a polite thank-you."

Her hand went to her chest and her gaze followed it. "Dominic!" She wore a long chain of diamonds interspersed with large square-cut emeralds. Facets of the diamonds caught the firelight and turned it into a dazzling array of brilliant hues that cascaded down her body. "Where did you get it?"

He nodded toward the palace across the garden. "The royal treasury. That necklace is only a small sample. The room is overflowing with chests of jewels and gold." His index finger tapped one of the emeralds. "Just one of those stones would buy another Killara. Do you know what I can do with such an enormous fortune?"

"Create the Delaney Kingdom." A tiny smile touched Elspeth's lips. "Long live the king."

"You can laugh, but that's what a treasure like this

can buy." He pulled the necklace taut, twisting the diamond chain beneath her breasts to lift them into prominence. "I thought the emeralds would match your eyes, but maybe rubies would be better." His head bent to nibble teasingly at her rosy-pink nipple. When he lifted his mouth, the nipple was no longer pink but cherry red and distended with arousal. "Do you fancy rubies, Queen Elspeth?"

"I fancy King Dominic." She took his hand and held it to her breast so that he could feel the erratic pounding of her heart. "See?"

His hand closed on her breast, his thumb gently flicking the nipple he had brought to fiery attention. "I don't think you'd be so unappreciative if I brought you another of those damn clay tablets with that hen-scratching on it."

"I didn't say I was unappreciative," she protested. "I merely appreciate you more." She lowered her eyes demurely. "As a proper wife should."

"There's nothing proper about you, my love." He gathered her up in his arms, blanket and all. "As I'm about to prove."

"Dominic!" She clutched at his shoulders as he began to stride across the garden toward the palace. "Where are we going?"

"The royal treasury. There's something I want you to see."

"Couldn't it wait until tomorrow?"

"Maybe. But I want you to see it tonight." His eyes twinkled down at her. "Call it a whim."

Heat tingled through her as she remembered Dominic's last "whim." "Indeed?" Her voice sounded breathless even to her own ears. "You could have waited and let me put some clothes on. It appears all your whims involve having me naked as Eve."

"I thought it fitting." Dominic was now crossing the moonlit throne room. "Eve should be right at home in the Garden of Eden. You know, I think I'd have liked the people of Kantalan. I went through several chambers before I found the treasury, and every room—no matter what appeared to be its primary purpose—

had some object of artistry or learning in it." His expression was thoughtful. "Even the treasury. You would have thought the idea of the acquisition of wealth would have been at odds with—" He stopped. "But you'll see for yourself."

"You could let me down. You're always carrying me around as if I were a child."

"The floors are dusty. I'll put you down when we reach the treasury. I lit the torches on the walls and tried to clean up the floor a little. At least you won't be ankle-deep in dust and cobwebs. It's just ahead." He was mounting the two steep steps leading to the tall brass-studded double doors he had left thrown open when he had hurried back for Elspeth. Then he was within the chamber, setting Elspeth carefully on her feet. He noticed with satisfaction that both the torches on the wall and the wood fire he had lit in the huge copper brazier in the center of the room were still burning brightly, the flames casting leaping shadows on white marble walls and shimmering on several gold and silver chests in the room.

Elspeth clutched the gray wool blanket together at her breast, her gaze wandering over statues in alabaster, silver, and gold, and over plates and vases bejeweled with precious and semiprecious stones. In one gold chest with the lid thrown open she caught a glimpse of long strands of lustrous black pearls, emeralds, rubies, and diamonds.

She shook her head dazedly. "So much. I can't believe it."

"Neither could I, but that wasn't what I wanted to show you." Dominic placed his hands on her shoulders and turned her so she was facing the south wall. He gestured to the intricate design carved on the white marble surface. "Look."

"The solar system," she whispered. "Good Lord. It's our solar system!" A huge round sun encircled by planets occupied the entire south wall and was executed with superb artistry on the white marble. The relative size and features of each planet were faithfully detailed even to the rings of Saturn. "What is it doing here? I would have thought this would have been in the temple."

"Perhaps the royal family was interested in astronomy." Dominic nodded to the long alabaster bench before the copper brazier. "Maybe the king liked to sit there among the treasures of the earth and look at the planets. It must have been very chastening for him to know that regardless of how rich he became, he could never fly from this planet to all the others."

"Da Vinci thought we could fly. I wonder . . ."

"No," Dominic said firmly. "I'm willing to accept the thought of you wandering off to find El Dorado or Atlantis as long as I can trail along beside you, but I at least insist you remain on earth." He arched a brow. "Do you notice anything strange about that rendering of the solar system?"

"Strange?" She frowned, her gaze returned to the wall. "No, everything seems to be in order. What—" She broke off and her gaze flew back to Dominic's face. "There are *ten* planets circling the sun."

He nodded.

"But there have only been eight planets discovered."

"Maybe they knew something we don't," he said softly. "Was there a telescope in the temple?"

"Yes, quite a large one in the same room that contains the lodestone." Her eyes were blazing with excitement. "Oh, Dominic, isn't it exciting? There's so much to see, so much to learn. Let's go there now." She stopped. Dominic was laughing softly and shaking his head. "No?"

"Tomorrow. There are a few other things I want to show you here tonight." His smile lingered. "Perhaps not as interesting to you, but I found them fascinating. They caused me to view the people of Kantalan in an entirely new light."

"What things?"

"Step this way, milady." He took her elbow and propelled her across the room, around the blazing fire in the copper brazier, to the open golden chest against the far wall. "Let's see if we can find something a little more elegant than that blanket for you to wear. If I remember, I saw something in here that will do nicely." He rummaged in the chest, tossing strands of pearls and rubies carelessly aside. "Here it is." He pulled out a garment that glittered gold in the firelight. "I think it's a cloak of some sort. It's not as heavy as it looks, and it's lined with silk." He shook out the folds. "It's a wonder the silk didn't rot. Perhaps being closed up in the chest protected it." He looked up when she didn't say anything. "Don't you like it?"

She touched the cloak with gentle, tentative fingers. The garment was a shimmering mesh of woven gold bordered in emeralds and pearls. "It's magnificent," she whispered. "It looks like something that should be worn by an empress."

"Then it may be good enough for you." He reached out and unclasped her fingers from the blanket. "Try it on." The wool blanket fell to the floor and something hot and intent flared in his eyes as they ran over her glowing nudity garbed only in the necklace. "And do hurry before I realize what an idiot I am to have you put on clothes."

She smiled shakily. "You once told me a man's chief pleasure was in removing barriers." She could feel her nipples tautening, her breasts swelling as his gaze touched them. "Have you changed your mind?"

"No." He stepped closer and threw the golden cloak around her shoulders. The silk lining was a cool, sensuous shock against her warm flesh. He fastened the round emerald and pearl brooch at her throat with trembling hands. "It just becomes more difficult to wait when you know what's beyond the barrier."

"You don't have to wait." The words were spoken in a tone a level above a whisper. "It's more difficult for me to wait now too."

His fingers tightened spasmodically on the brooch before he forced himself to release the jewel and take a step back. "Sometimes it's better to wait." The pulse beating wildly in his temple and the flush darkening his long jaws belied the words. "It makes the pleasure sharper. I'd wager that the people of Kantalan knew the value of anticipation."

"Why do you say that?"

He was searching in the chest again. "I'll tell you—or rather show you—later." He found the four objects he was looking for and drew them out. "Wear these."

"Bracelets?"

He nodded as he clasped a broad band of emeralds and pearls around her left wrist. "To match your necklace." He clasped an identical bracelet on her right wrist. He knelt before her, pushing the cloak aside. "And these are to match the bracelets." He fastened a jeweled band around first her left ankle and then her right. He sat back on his heels and looked at her pale bare feet flowing into delicate slender ankles and sweetly curved calves. The hard shimmering jewels shown in barbaric splendor against her soft flesh and a sudden wrench of sheer lust tore through him.

"I think you should wear those all the time." His palm cupped her left calf and squeezed gently. He heard the soft hiss of the intake of her breath, but he didn't lift his gaze from the delicate shapeliness of her limbs. His fingers moved up to rub the soft skin behind her knee. "Will you do that when we're alone like this?" He leaned forward and nibbled gently at the soft fullness of her thigh. "Will you let me put them on you then?" He parted her thighs gently. "You look so pretty. They match your eyes."

"You're not looking at my eyes."

"No." He blew gently on the secret heart of her womanhood. "But maybe I will later. Will you?"

She shivered and swayed toward him. "Yes . . . anything you want. Dominic, I—" She gasped as his warm tongue flicked out with expert precision.

He sat back on his heels again, his fingers gently massaging the flesh behind her knees. His gaze lifted slowly to her face. His skin was pulled taut over his cheekbones and his light eyes were burning as he searched her expression. "Now you're ready to learn something new about Kantalan." He rose lithely to his feet and took her hand. "Come with me." He led her toward the far corner of the room. "Astronomy wasn't the only interest the royal household had. Evidently Kantalan was a society composed of very sensual people." He stopped before a collection of statues on a long, low marble table against the wall. "Look at them," he said softly. "Have you ever seen anything like this in your temples in India?"

Elspeth's eyes widened as her cheeks grew warm. The statues were incredibly beautiful in both material and execution and more erotic than anything she had ever seen anywhere. Each foot-high statue portrayed a man and a woman in a different position in the act of love, some she had never dreamed possible. In every statue the woman was depicted in fragile mother-of-pearl and the man in a rich ebony wood; the materials were so smooth and polished they begged to be touched. The tactile artistry added to the subject matter brought a surge of arousal rippling through Elspeth. "Never. They're shocking."

He was standing behind her, his breath warm against her ear. "And are you shocked, love?"

"No." Her tongue moistened her lower lip, her gaze fixed in fascination on the statue directly in front of her. Did men and women actually do that? "I suppose I should be, but I think I'm more curious than shocked."

"My God, I'm lucky. Every man should be so fortunate as to have a curious woman in his bed." His teeth bit gently on the lobe of her ear. "Let's see what we can do to satisfy that curiosity, Elspeth."

"Have you made love in all these ways?"

"Most of them. The Kantalanians must have been pretty agile to have managed some of those positions." His tongue plunged into her ear. She shivered and melted back against him. "That one you're looking at now can be rather amusing."

"Amusing? I never felt amused when you . . ." Her words trailed off as the magnitude of his arousal became evident even through the garments that separated them.

"And I have never felt amused when loving you," he said hoarsely. "Never with you, Elspeth. Loving you is like nothing I've ever felt before."

"Then all cats aren't the same in the dark?"

"No." His hands closed on her shoulders. "God, no, love."

"Then it was very wicked of you to tell me such a falsehood. It . . . it worried me."

"I'll try to make amends." His hands splayed out and slid over her shoulders to cup her breasts through the gleaming gold of the cloak. "Will it help to know that I haven't wanted to touch any other woman since you invaded Rina's with those damn firecrackers." He stroked gently up and down, the silk lining of the cloak rubbing teasingly against her nipples.

"Yes." Her gaze was fixed in fascination on the lifelike eroticism of the statues. The male was on his knees, his shoulders hunched and strained. What beautiful shoulders he possessed, Elspeth thought. They were corded with supple muscle, and the taut bulging line of his brawny thighs reminded her of Dominic's in the last instant before he plunged forward and . . . Her chest was so tight she was having difficulty forcing air into her lungs. She swallowed and tried to remember what she had been saying. "But I think I'd be very fierce if you ever visited one of those hetaeras again."

His hands slipped beneath the cloak, plucking at the crests of her nipples. She made a low sound deep in her throat. "I find I'm only interested in one hetaera these days." He pinched her with just enough pressure to send a tingle of heat through her. "Elspeth MacGregor Delaney." His left hand slid down her body to the soft swell of her belly, and his palm began to rub, pet, and then, with sudden impatience, pressed her hard against him. "Touch them."

"What?" She couldn't think; her bones seemed to have no substance because of the heat of him against her.

"The statues. The texture is very pleasing to the touch. Rub your hand over one of them."

She reached out a hesitant finger and brushed it

against the rippling musculature of the shoulder of the male figure on the statue before her. The wood was warm, it felt almost as alive as it looked.

Dominic's hand suddenly closed over her own on the statue. "More," he whispered. "He likes it. Close your eyes and feel the tension of him and think about what he's doing to her."

She closed her eyes and arched her head back against his shoulder. Her lips parted and her breathing was shallow as she allowed Dominic to move her palm slowly over the figure. Here palm was tingling and the aching emptiness between her thighs was increasing with each passing second. Why could she still see the statue even though her eyes were closed? But now the ebony wood figure was no longer small but life-sized and alive. Moving. Sleek and hot. Dark rippling muscle and driving thighs.

"Do you feel it?"

She moistened her lips and nodded dreamily.

Dominic's hand on her breast cupped and squeezed gently. "Do you want it?"

She nodded again.

Dominic gently pried her hand from the smooth warmth of the statue. "Now?"

"Yes."

His hands cupped her shoulders and steadied her as he took a step back. "Not yet."

Her eyes flew open. "No?"

She heard him moving behind her and and she started to turn to face him. "Why?"

"Don't turn around. Keep your eyes on your friend in the statue there."

"Why?" she asked again.

"Anticipation. The oldest game in the world and probably more fun than any of those variations you're looking at now."

He was right. She could feel the tension increasing with every breath as she waited. Why wouldn't he let her turn around and face him? She wanted to reach out and touch him as she had touched the man in the statue.

His hands were on her shoulders again, shifting the

cloak to bare her body and form a shining cowl
around her throat and then trail down her back in a
golden train. He lifted her fair hair, threading it
through his fingers before letting it float down in a
wild tawny cloud around her. Then his hands were
gone and she heard him moving away from her.

"Dominic, where are you going?"

"Not very far. Come and join me."

She whirled to face him in a brilliant swirl of gold
and emerald and pearl.

He was sitting across the room on the wool blanket
he had spread over the marble bench before the
copper brazier. The leaping firelight played on the
bronzed slide of the muscles of his brawny shoulders.
He was beautifully nude and male and as aroused as
the man in the statue.

He held out his hand to her, his light eyes soft and
liquidly intent in the fireglow. "Come, love."

She walked slowly toward him. There was something wildly barbaric and exciting in coming to him
like this. She could see the jewels glitter on her ankles
with every step; she could feel the sensuous tug of the
golden cloak as it brushed the floor behind her. She
was beautiful to him; she could see it in his face. He
wanted her. His gaze clung and moved down her body
in an almost tactile caress. Anticipation.

She stopped before him, feeling bold and breathlessly shy at the same time. "Now?"

"If we wait any longer, I may die of frustration. You
look—" He stopped, groping for words. Elspeth was
pagan queen and sensual slave. Sorceress. Mistress.
He slowly shook his head. There were really no words
but one to describe her: *Beloved*.

She put her hand in his but stopped as he would
have drawn her into his arms. Her smile was suddenly mischievous as she unfastened the brooch at her
throat and let the cloak fall to the floor. "Not yet." She
pushed him down on his back. "Anticipation, remember?"

"Elspeth . . ." Dominic's voice was hoarse. "I
can't—" He gasped as she suddenly straddled him,
sheathing him with teasing slowness, allowing only

the shallowest entry. He grasped her hips, trying to draw her down upon him, but she would not permit it. "Dammit, Elspeth, you're *killing* me."

"I want you to love me in all those different ways." She clenched around him, her gaze narrowed on his face. His lips were parted, his nostrils flaring, and he was beautiful in his need. "Will you do that for me, Dominic?"

"Yes, anything," he said through clenched teeth. "Just let me come up in you and—"

"Like this?" She moved the slightest bit and he flexed yearningly within her. "Enough?"

"No." He groaned, his lips drawn away from his lips as if in pain. "More."

She clenched around him once again and he gasped, his fingers digging into the blanket beneath him.

"But what about anticipation?"

"*Damn* anticipation."

"That's my view on the subject." She smiled lovingly down at him. "We don't need anticipation, Dominic. We don't need anything but this." Then she released him, took him, let him enter as he willed. This time it was she who gasped. "Dominic!"

He wasn't listening, he drove upward in mindless, frantic hunger and then began a heated rhythm more urgent than they had ever known. The rhythm increased, the tension grew. Elspeth's head was whirling. Her fingers moved over Dominic's shoulders in feverish pleasure. Textures. Warmer than the wood of the statue, bronze not ebony. Yet the two had somehow blended and become one in her mind.

He plunged deeper and she moaned as the tension mounted. Fire flickering on white marble walls. Ten planets spinning around a burning sun. Jewels, pearls, overflowing a golden coffer. Dalkar. Merging. The flames burning in the temple. A silver filigree curtain holding back the indigo night. A promise . . . fulfilled. Dalkar-Dominic!

Joy!

Afterward they lay holding each other, their breathing gradually slowing, lost in a haze of warm pleasure.

Elspeth's lids lifted slowly. "Dominic?"

"Yes, love?"

"The flames didn't lie," she said dreamily. "It is forever. You and I." Her eyes fluttered shut. "Isn't that wonderful?"

He could tell she was on the drifting edge of slumber, scarcely aware of what she was saying. He kissed her gently. "Wonderful. *You're* wonderful, love." He sat up and began wrapping her in the wool blanket. "But now it's time to go back to camp." He rose from the bench, crossed the room to where he had discarded his clothes beside the chest, and began to dress.

"Why? I like it here, don't you?"

"Yes, I do like it here." He liked it too much. He felt the same mysterious sense of belonging that Elspeth was experiencing. Since the moment they had ridden into the city there had been some unusual hold on both of them. *Home.* The word suddenly popped into his mind from out of nowhere. But Kantalan wasn't home and Elspeth's blissful contentment might possibly pose a danger. "But we'll go back to camp anyway. That bench would be damn hard to sleep on."

"If you say so."

He crossed the room and gathered her up in his arms, brushing her closed lids with the lightest of kisses. "You're being amazingly docile."

"I'm sleepy."

He laughed as he turned and walked from the chamber and down the hall. "I knew there had to be some explanation."

She pressed her lips to his shoulder in a loving caress. "I do like my necklace and bracelets and I thank you exceedingly."

He chuckled. "You're exceedingly welcome."

There was something she had meant to ask him when he had first come back from the palace, but so much had happened since then that it had completely slipped her mind. What was it? Suddenly it came back to her. "Why did you go searching through the palace in the middle of the night? Couldn't it have waited until morning?"

"Probably." She was lying against him as sweetly relaxed as a small child, and he was reluctant to disturb her by discussing the uneasiness he was feeling. After all, there had been nothing to provoke that uneasiness. The Sun Child was as majestic and unmoving as the golden throne in the palace, and the city of Kantalan was also still and completely lifeless.

It was that complete absence of life that was bothering him. There should have been rats, reptiles, or birds inhabiting the city, but there was nothing. Once when he was a child a tornado had touched down at Killara, and he remembered that minutes before the funnel was sighted there had been a great flurry of activity as birds, horses, and cattle tried to run from a threat invisible to man. The prophecy? Hell, there was *something* strange happening here.

He tightened his arms around her as he quickened his steps across the garden. "I couldn't sleep and thought I might as well take a look. I'll load the treasure in the saddlebags tomorrow morning and then help you search the temple. We should be ready to go by tomorrow night."

"So soon? I thought we'd stay a few days."

He hesitated. "We'll see. We'll talk about it tomorrow." He laid her down on the blankets before their campfire and knelt down beside her. He tilted her chin up on the curve of his finger. Her eyes were cloudy with sleep as they looked into his own. "Tonight I'd rather discuss something else. Tell me that you love me, woman."

"I told you." Her eyes were almost closed. "I'm sure I told you."

"Then tell me again. It bears repeating."

Her voice was so low he could scarcely hear it, drifting like a phantom wisp of smoke from her lips: "I love you. I will love you until there is no sun, no moon, and no homeplace left on this earth."

The first sight to meet Elspeth's eyes when she woke the next morning was Patrick squatting beside her, a mischievous grin on his face. "Good morning. I thought I had better wake you first. Dom has a nasty habit of reaching for a gun when you surprise him." He lifted a brow as he sat back on his heels and appraised Dominic's relaxed form huddled beneath the blanket. "He usually sleeps lighter than this." His gaze moved back to Elspeth's bare shoulders and the lump beneath the blanket was clearly Dominic's hand on Elspeth's breast. "He must be . . . tired."

Elspeth could feel the color rush to her face as she hurriedly sat bolt upright, jerking the blanket up to her chin. "Yesterday was quite exhausting. Azuquita . . . the palace . . . the temple . . ."

"I see." Patrick nodded solemnly. "That seems clear."

"Leave her alone, Patrick." Dominic raised up on one elbow. "What the hell are you doing here?"

"I decided I wanted a little of that treasure for myself," Patrick said lightly. "And from the looks of the necklace around Elspeth's neck, I gather I'm not going to be disappointed."

"Patrick came with me." Rising Star was coming across the garden toward them. "He tells me he wants to buy an Oriental dancing girl."

"Rising Star!" Elspeth's eyes widened. "But why? The baby . . ."

Rising Star smiled. "I'm fine. My son must be more Indian than white. He likes being on a horse."

Elspeth frowned uneasily. "But there's still the journey back."

"I have almost a month more before giving birth. There's nothing to worry about."

"Does Josh know about this?" Dominic asked.

"He knows I have left Killara." Rising Star reached down and picked up the coffeepot from the stones encircling the fire. "I will get water for coffee. Patrick, you start breakfast."

"Yes, ma'am." Patrick sighed as he turned back to Dominic and Elspeth. "You can see why I want one of those Arab harem girls to bow and scrape for me. A man doesn't get any waiting on around here." He rose to his feet and bowed. "Anything else, ma'am?"

"No, I think not." Rising Star's gaze met Patrick's with intimate understanding. "Perhaps later." She turned and walked across the garden toward a small pool fed by a canal running through the tangled wilderness of shrubbery.

The humor immediately disappeared from Patrick's face as soon as she was out of hearing. "She's left Josh," he said curtly. "And I don't want either of you to be bothering her about it. Do you understand?"

Dominic's gaze followed Rising Star. "Why did she do it?"

"Josh told her he. didn't want the baby."

"My God," Dominic murmured. "Josh wouldn't—"

"He did," Patrick interrupted harshly. "She wouldn't lie."

"No, Rising Star wouldn't lie," Dominic said quietly. "So where does this leave you?"

Patrick's lips twisted. "Exactly where I was. She's Josh's wife." His gaze went to Rising Star. "She wants the treasure for the child; she thinks it will help keep him safe."

Dominic's gaze flitted briefly to Elspeth. "I can understand that. Well, one saddlebag filled with the jewels I saw in the palace should guarantee he'll be surrounded by a wall of gold for the rest of his life."

"Good." Patrick's gaze turned to Elspeth. "I wish you'd try to talk to her and find out what she's planning on doing. If she's not going back to Josh, I can't let her run off alone. She'll need someone."

Elspeth nodded. "I'll try." How terrible that this could happen to someone as beautiful and kind as Rising Star. And how unfair that Elspeth's own love was opening like a flower while the other woman's was blackening and shriveling. "If you'll let me put on my clothes. Turn your back, Patrick."

"If you insist." Patrick turned away. "But with profound regret."

A few minutes later Elspeth was dressed and walking across the garden toward Rising Star.

Patrick turned back to watch Dominic pull on his boots. "We didn't get Torres. It looks like he may still be after you."

Dominic nodded.

"Gran-da and the rest are probably still on his trail."

Dominic smiled mirthlessly. "Then after some three hundred years Kantalan may suddenly become very well populated."

Patrick shook his head. "I don't think anyone would ever find the entrance behind the waterfall without a map."

Dominic wasn't as confident. As time passed, Torres was beginning to take on supernatural qualities in his mind. "Maybe." He stood up. "After breakfast I'll show you where the treasury is. Rising Star can help Elspeth in the temple and we'll load up the horses and pack animals. You and Rising Star take the burros and mule through the pass and wait for us on the banks of the lake."

"What's the hurry?"

"I don't know." Dominic moved his shoulders impatiently. "Something's . . . something's very wrong here. I've got to stay and give Elspeth as much time as possible to look through the temple, but there's no reason you and Rising Star can't leave. I'll try to be out of Kantalan before dark."

"You believe the prophecy?"

Dominic's gaze shifted quickly to Patrick's face. "Rising Star told you?"

Patrick nodded. "She didn't think it was fair for me to go with her without knowing. There are four of us here now, just as the prophecy foretold." His gaze searched Dominic's face. "Well?"

"I don't know if I believe it or not." Dominic turned away. "But something's not right. You make breakfast and I'll go bring the pack animals to the front entrance of the palace."

"You too?" Patrick sighed. "Everybody in the whole blamed world is giving me orders. I sure need one of those dancing girls."

"You'll be able to buy an entire harem with your share of the treasure." Dominic said with a grin over his shoulder. "Not bad wages for cooking one breakfast."

* * *

By noon both the horses' and burros' saddlebags had been loaded with treasure and the last large pack put on Azuquita's protesting back. Dominic stepped back, avoided the mule's vengeful nip, and turned to Patrick. "Don't let him get too near the burros or he'll gnaw through their girths. We don't want to lose this load."

"I'll watch him." Patrick glanced at Dominic curiously. "Where did you get him? You always swore you'd never have a mule."

"It's a long, sad story." Dominic made a face. "I'll tell you about it someday when I need to arouse your sympathy. By the time we get back to Killara you'll understand how noble I've been."

"Hmmm." Patrick mounted his horse. "He doesn't look so bad. Maybe you didn't know how to handle him."

Azuquita's lips curled back in a toothy grin.

"You know, it could be you're right," Dominic murmured. "I never was any good with anything but horses. Why don't you take him over for me on the way home?"

Patrick frowned uncertainly. "Well, I don't know . . ."

"It's settled then." Dominic beamed. "You're probably right about old Sweetness, and you won't have any trouble at all." He mounted Blanco and tossed Azuquita's lead rope to Patrick. "May you be very happy together."

"We're not getting married," Patrick said dryly.

"Oh, but I assure you that you'll feel very close to Azuquita before this is over. He'll be like a brother to you." Dominic's horse trotted out of the garden onto the street. "Like Cain was to Abel."

24

Elspeth took a step closer to the mosaic on the wall of the temple, her eyes blazing with excitement. "It's a serpent gliding around the bole of a palm tree. Oh, Rising Star, I wish there were some way I could take it with me."

"Patrick told me you didn't like snakes." Rising Star smiled. "Why would you want an entire wall with the picture of one?"

"This is different." Elspeth's fingertip reached out to touch the smooth amber of the trunk of the palm tree. "It's a link, a symbol. Don't you see? The palm represents the tree of life, and the serpent, evil. It's the legend of the Garden of Eden. In Tyre they discovered ancient coins with this same design and in Guatamala copper coins with the identical serpent and tree. And now it's here in Kantalan too. A common symbol uniting cultures thousands of miles apart."

"Coincidence?"

Elspeth shook her head. "There are too many coincidences, too many stories about godlike white men from the east. Quetzalcoatl came from the 'distant east' to become patron god of the Toltecs. Samé, the great Brazilian leader, came across the ocean from the rising sun. The Mayans claim that the birthplace of Tulan was across the sea to the east. There's even one Mexican legend that says after the flood, Coxcox and his wife landed first at Antlan and then journeyed to Mexico. If they came from Atlantis,

361

it would be logical for them to name their first landing place Antlan. And according to folklore, all the races that settled in Mexico trace their origin back to a wonderous place called Aztlan." She stopped to draw a breath and smiled apologetically. "I'm sorry. I tend to get excited when I talk about anything that touches on Atlantis."

Rising Star shook her head. "I find it very interesting that you think we're all voyagers from this Atlantis. My people too?"

"In the beginning."

"Then we're all the same, just fellow voyagers from the same port of origin." Rising Star's eyes were wistful as she looked at the mosaic. "How sad that some stay on course and some are lost forever. Wouldn't it be wonderful if we could all travel together, respecting and helping each other."

Elspeth experienced a pang of compassion. "Perhaps someday we will."

"Someday." Rising Star turned away. "Now, what shall we gather to take with us—something smaller than that monstrous wall?"

"Rising Star." Elspeth hesitated. "Patrick is very worried about you."

Rising Star stopped but didn't look at her. "I know. He has a warm heart and he cares for me. I'm sorry he's in pain."

"Dominic and I care about you too. Let us help you."

Rising Star's voice was muffled. "What can you do? Can you fade my skin from brown to white? Can you turn the clock back and bring Boyd and Rory to life? Can you make Joshua love me as much as I love him?"

Elspeth could feel the tears sting behind her eyes. "No, I can't do those things, but I can offer you and your child a home with us and the affection of friends."

Rising Star turned to her, a misty smile lighting her face. "That's a beautiful gift, Elspeth. Thank you."

"Will you come with us?"

"I don't know. I must think about it. Right now I'm

trying not to think at all until I heal." She looked back at the mosaic. "Perhaps there is an Eden for me somewhere too. I hope so." She laughed shakily. "Maybe I'll take Silver and go in search of it. Living in Eden would be too tame for her but she'd enjoy the quest."

Elspeth nodded. "Yes, I believe she would enjoy it." Her eyes were troubled as she gazed at Rising Star. "We can't promise you Eden but—"

"You are kind." Rising Star's voice was suddenly brisk. "But it is I who must make the decision on this. In time I will rid myself of this sorrow and make a fine life for myself. You will see, I will be content again." She walked quickly across the chamber toward the table on which they'd placed a number of objects. "Dominic and Patrick will be here soon and you must choose which of these is most important to you so that I can put them in the knapsack."

Content but not happy, Elspeth thought as she gazed at Rising Star, wanting to give comfort and having none to give. She smiled with an effort. "The compass, I think." She pointed to a small wooden container. "And that box of white powder. I have an idea it might be gunpowder. Some scholars believe that Atlantis invented gunpowder even before their colony in China. And perhaps that strange amulet with the cross . . ."

Dominic and Elspeth stood on the top step of the temple watching Patrick and Rising Star lead all the pack animals up the winding trail to the pass. They had reached the halfway point when Dominic smothered a smile as he saw Patrick tugging at Azuquita's lead rope. The mule had stopped and plopped down stubbornly in the middle of the trail. It was too far to hear, but he'd bet Patrick was swearing a blue streak.

"Why did you send them away so soon, Dominic? They didn't even have a chance to look around the city."

"Kantalan doesn't have the same meaning for them

as it does for you." Dominic's gaze was still on Patrick and Azuquita. "Did you talk to Rising Star?"

She nodded. "She wouldn't discuss her future. Oh, Dominic, she's so unhappy. What will she do?"

"I wish I could say I knew. Maybe Patrick—"

"Patrick?" Then as she grasped his meaning her eyes widened in surprise. "But she thinks of him as a child. He's much younger than she is."

"That's not unusual in Rising Star's tribe, and he loves her. In time she might come to love him in the same way."

"And you could accept that? Joshua is your brother."

"And I love him," Dominic said wearily. "But I love Patrick and Rising Star too. Why should all three of them be miserable?"

"Patrick would have to leave Killara, and I think he loves it almost as much as you do, Dominic."

"Yes." His gaze left Patrick and shifted to Elspeth's face. "Sometimes we must choose to give up what we love." He turned back to the entrance of the temple. "Have you found anything else you want to take with us?"

"I tied a few artifacts in a knapsack and fastened it on Nina's saddlehorn," she said absently as her gaze returned to the figures on the trail. "How strange. Dominic, look at Azuquita."

Dominic turned to see Azuquita leap off his haunches, his long ears laid flat against his head. The mule lunged forward, tearing the lead rope from Patrick's hands. He shouldered Patrick's horse aside and passed Rising Star at a gallop.

"Damn, I've never seen him move that fast," Dominic said with a grin. "I wonder what's gotten into him? I bet Patrick—"

The stone steps suddenly jerked beneath Dominic's boots, throwing him to his knees! "What in—"

The steps were splitting, great jagged cracks gaping like hungry mouths in the stone.

"Dominic!" Elspeth screamed. "What's happening?"

Dominic's gaze flew to the Sun Child. A thin wisp of black smoke belched into the air. Poisonous smoke?

"Oh, my God!" He leapt to his feet and caught Elspeth's hand. "Come on." He pulled her down the steps, tossed her on Nina's back, and slapped the mare's rump. "Get going! Follow Rising Star and Patrick. Don't wait for me." He jumped on Blanco and turned the stallion to follow Elspeth.

"Of course I'm going to wait for you." Elspeth had reined in Nina a few yards away. The streets were shivering, undulating as if they were alive. It was like riding on the back of a giant serpent flexing in the sun. "It's the Sun Child, isn't it? Do we have time to get out of the city?"

"How do I know?" Dominic yelled as he grabbed Nina's reins and put both horses to a run. The balcony of the house they were passing suddenly shattered and fell to the street. Blanco reared, pawing the air. "Lord save me from an obstinate woman. Do you want to get yourself killed? My saddlebags are heavily loaded and Blanco may not be able to move as fast as your horse. Get *going*, dammit."

"I'll wait for you." Elspeth was pale, but her lips were firmly set. "But I think we'd best hurry."

Dominic cast her a glance that was a mixture of desperation and exasperation. "If we get out of this alive, remind me to tell you about the virtues of wifely obedience." He turned down the street leading to the trail to the pass.

They had to stop twice to avoid falling columns, but they were finally climbing, leaving the city behind.

The billows of smoke had increased but there was still no sound except the shattering cacophony that came from Kantalan itself as the earth quaked and shivered, bringing houses, palace, and temple alike crashing. The trail was also shaking, and Dominic could feel Blanco trembling with fear.

"Patrick and Rising Star have reached the pass," Elspeth called back to him. "Does that mean they're safe?"

Dominic shook his head. "With the mountain shaking like this, there are bound to be landslides. We just have to hope there's not too much loose rock. There's a chance the—"

The world exploded.

Elspeth's mare fell to her knees and Dominic had to jerk Blanco aside to keep him from stumbling over the fallen horse. Then Nina struggled to her feet and Elspeth had time to glance at the Sun Child.

"Merciful God," she whispered.

A third of the top of the mountain had blown away in the explosion and a thick stream of orange-red lava—like an obscene tongue of fire—poured down the mountain toward Kantalan.

"Not very merciful at the moment," Dominic muttered. "Let's hope for more leniency in the next ten minutes or so."

The sky was raining fireballs of lava, some as large as a man's torso. It was no longer early afternoon but night, the entire valley shrouded by black smoke. The only illumination was the fireballs being hurled into the air and the stream of lava rushing toward the city in an invincible tide of destruction.

"Cover your nose and mouth," he shouted, tying his bandanna over his lower face. "Even if the fumes aren't poisonous the smoke could still—" He broke off as a small fireball hit Blanco's left flank. The horse gave a shrill neigh of terror and then bolted. Elspeth's mare followed in a flight of panic, straight up the trail, ignoring the trembling earth and tumbling rocks, desperately fleeing from the fire falling from the sky.

Dominic managed to rein Blanco in as they reached the pass. The trail was straight down, and a misstep could cause the fragile bones of the horse's legs to snap. He cast a hasty glance down the trail as he waited for Elspeth to reach him. There had been no slide yet as far as he could see, but that didn't mean there wasn't a blockage farther on.

Elspeth was now beside him, her eyes streaming above the handkerchief tied over her nose and mouth. "Patrick and Rising Star—"

"They should be almost down to the waterfall by now if they . . ." He didn't complete the sentence, there was no use stating the obvious when Elspeth was frightened enough as it was. "Let me go first and keep a tight rein."

"Oh, Dominic." Elspeth was looking back at the city with shocked sorrow. "Kantalan."

Dominic's gaze followed hers. The lava that had entered the canal at the foot of the Sun Child had flowed into the other canals and there was now a flaming cross intersecting the smoke-shrouded darkness of the city. Elspeth and Dominic were breathless with wonder at the sight. Slowly the canals began to overflow and the lava spilled out to begin to cover the city.

"We have to go," Dominic said gently. "Now, Elspeth."

"I know." She closed her eyes. Good-bye Kantalan. Her eyes flicked open and she turned to face the trail leading through the pass. "I'm ready to follow you."

He nodded and began the downhill trek.

The way was clear for the first few hundred yards, then they ran into minor landslide but nothing the horses couldn't pick their way around. Three quarters of the way down there was a more serious blockage, and they were forced to get off the horses and climb over the four-foot-high pile of rubble, tugging the leads of the horses until they managed to clamber over the obstruction.

The ground was still shaking, but Dominic was allowing himself to be more hopeful. He caught sight of the lake a few hundred feet ahead of them and turned his head to call back to Elspeth. "Just a few minutes more."

She nodded silently.

He turned back to the trail.

Another explosion rocked the mountain.

"No!" Dammit, not when they were so close.

"The Sun Child." Elspeth's gasp behind him. "Another eruption."

Huge jagged cracks were appearing in the stone on

either side of them. A cool rush of air, pocketed for
perhaps a million years within the bowels of the
mountain, touched their faces. "Run for it!"

Huge chunks of rocks dislodged from the cliffs,
hurtling down behind them, in front of them, all
around them. They plunged into the cold water of the
lake at the same time. The horses swam frantically. A
boulder the size of a tree plunged into the lake behind
them. Crashing, roaring noises assaulted their ears;
shards of smaller stones were flying through the air.

Then they were climbing onto the rock-strewn bank
behind the waterfall, the mist bathing them in a
soothing balm. In another moment they had made
their way under the waterfall and around the rocky
ledge to the grassy bank.

Elspeth's breath was coming in little gasps, her
chest hurting, her eyes burning. "Are we safe?"

"I think so." Dominic was in little better condition
than Elspeth. He pulled the bandanna from his face.
"I don't know." He slipped out of the saddle, crossed
the short distance separating them, helped her off the
mare, and swiftly untied the handkerchief from her
face. "Are you all right?"

She nodded, her gaze returning to the waterfall.
"Kantalan's gone, but we saw it," she said softly. "And
it was as beautiful as I knew it would be. We were
there, Dominic. I'll remember that for the rest of my
life."

"Then maybe Kantalan won't be gone after all. Not
as long as it exists here." Dominic touched the center
of her forehead with a gentle fingertip. "And here."
His hand brushed her left breast lightly.

"Perhaps." Her lips were tremulous as she smiled at
him.

"I think we'd better find Patrick and Rising Star
and make camp. We need to build a fire and dry out."
He continued in a deliberate, matter-of-fact tone. "It
may turn cool when the sun goes down."

It didn't feel cool now, she thought. A suffocating
heat pervaded the air and there was a haze of smoke
even here on the other side of the mountain. Still, it

was important that they locate Patrick and Rising Star. Her boots were squishing uncomfortably as she shifted from foot to foot. "I'd imagine they would stay near until they knew we were safe. Shall we—"

Patrick burst through the underbrush at the side of the bank. "Come quick." His hair was water darkened to deep brown and formed a spiky helmet around his pale face. "Rising Star's horse fell in the pass. I think she's going to have the child right away."

Rising Star did not have the child right away.

She underwent nearly eighteen hours of agonizing labor before her son struggled from her tortured body. He was immediately followed by a tiny girl child.

"Twins." Rising Star laughed huskily as Elspeth put the second tiny blanket-swathed baby in the curve of her arm. "The Delaneys wouldn't do things in the ordinary way, of course." She looked at Patrick over Elspeth's shoulder. "I suppose I should have expected it. Twins run in the Delaney family. You and Brianne . . ." She trailed off, her eyes closing. "I did not do this well. Indian women are supposed to be much better at having babies. I may have become too much of a white woman."

"You've done splendidly." Elspeth brushed the sweat-dampened hair from Rising Star's forehead with a cool cloth. "You have a fine strong son and a beautiful little girl."

A faint smile touched Rising Star's lips. "I shall call the boy Kevin, a white man's name, but the girl I will keep for myself. I will call her Ko-Do, the firefly."

"They're both fine names," Dominic said gently.

"Yes." Rising Star was almost asleep. "Fine names . . ."

Dominic's hand clasped Elspeth's shoulder. "You need to rest too. Patrick and I will watch over her."

Elspeth shook her head. "You haven't had any sleep either. I'll go change my clothes and wash up. Perhaps she'll wake again and can take a little nourishment. She seems very weak."

Patrick was staring down at Rising Star, his features drawn with fear. "She's going to be fine now."

Elspeth stood up and turned to walk away.

"She's going to be fine," Patrick repeated sharply. "It wouldn't make any sense for her to suffer like this and not get well. No woman should have to go through what she has."

"None of us is a doctor," Dominic said wearily as he rubbed his stubbled cheek. "We can only do our best, then pray. She seems to be sleeping well now. After what she's gone through it's probably the best medicine for her. Why don't you make some coffee? We need it."

"You make it," Patrick said jerkily, falling to his knees beside Rising Star. "I'm staying here."

Dominic hesitated, his gaze on the boy's tense face. Then he nodded and turned away. "I'll make the coffee."

Two hours later the tiny girl child, Ko-Do, died peacefully in her sleep. First she was there, life burning brightly, then she was gone like the firefly after which she was named.

"What the hell are we going to do?" Patrick asked, looking down at the child. "We can't tell Rising Star it's all been for nothing. What if the boy dies too?" His hand clenched into a fist of impotent rage. "What can we tell her?"

"Nothing." Dominic took the baby girl gently away from Rising Star. "For now. If we have to lie to her, we will. The boy seems healthy enough."

"Seems," Patrick echoed. "He's *got* to be all right."

Rising Star began to hemorrhage an hour later. They all worked frantically to staunch the flow, but the bleeding would not stop. By nightfall even Patrick realized they couldn't save her. All he could do was hold her hand and stare desperately at her still face.

She woke only once. Her lids opened heavily and her great dark eyes searched Patrick's face above her. "So White Buffalo was right." Her voice was a mere breath of sound. "There is no choice." Her gaze wandered down to where the baby girl had slept within the curve of her arm. "Ko-Do?"

Patrick opened his lips to speak but couldn't force the words through the tightness of his throat.

He didn't have to speak. He could see by her expression that she knew. "Poor little Firefly." She shook her head. "And poor Patrick." Her lids shut again. "Don't be sad. Maybe I'll be able to find my shadow . . . and Ko-Do. It won't be so lonely with Ko-Do there." She was silent and at first he thought she was unconscious. "Silver . . . help her, Patrick."

"I will. I promise you."

"And my son. Don't let them steal his shadow. . . . Don't let them. . . ."

The words drifted away, and a few minutes later Patrick knew that Rising Star was no longer with them.

Dominic and Patrick built a coffin large enough to accommodate both Rising Star and Ko-Do. The two were wrapped securely in Elspeth's plaid and buried that night in a grassy glade several yards from the lake. There were no words spoken over the grave. None were needed. Their silence as they stood there was eloquent with sorrow.

Patrick turned away and stalked back to the campfire. Dominic and Elspeth followed more slowly.

Patrick was already saddling his horse when they came into the circle of the campfire. "The baby has to be fed," he said jerkily. "He'll die if he doesn't get milk. He's *not* going to die. Where's the nearest village?"

"No village. Probably Indino's camp is the closest thing to it. It's about a day's hard ride into the hills." Dominic knelt and drew a rough map in the dirt with a stick. "Tell him I sent you."

"I'll fill a canteen with broth." Elspeth ran her fingers wearily through her hair as she turned away. "I hope it won't make him sick. It's the only thing I can think to do. I only wish I knew more about babies."

Ten minutes later Patrick swung up into the saddle and Elspeth handed him the canteen and the small bundle containing Rising Star's son. Patrick scarcely looked at Elspeth and Dominic as he wheeled and rode out.

Elspeth shivered and drew a step nearer to Dominic, her gaze following Patrick's rapidly moving figure. "He looks ten years older."

"And probably feels over a hundred."

"What do we do now?" Elspeth felt empty.

"We try to sleep for a few hours and then we break camp and start for Killara." He rubbed the back of his neck to ease the tension knotting it.

"Rising Star . . ." She could feel the tears rise to her eyes. "Patrick is right. It's not *fair*."

"No." His arms went around her and he held her tight, pressing her cheek to his chest. "No, it's not fair."

"She was so beautiful and gentle." The tears were running down her cheeks, dampening his shirt. "She was—"

"Shh, I know." His voice was husky, and Elspeth suddenly felt a warm dampness on her temple. He stood there rocking her, sharing her pain and his own, until the fire burned low and the darkness began to be lightened by the first streaks of dawn.

25

After several hours' sleep, Dominic and Elspeth started their journey back to Killara. The pace was slower due to the heavily burdened pack animals, and the mood was subdued and dispirited. Dominic deliberately kept them on the trail until well after dark to make sure they would both be too weary to think of anything but sleep.

But sleep didn't come to either of them. They lay together watching the fire, wide awake, thinking.

"Do you suppose it was my fault?" Elspeth asked. "If I hadn't insisted on going to Kantalan, none of this would have happened. Rising Star wouldn't have died."

"How can you ask that? She could have taken a fall anywhere and she might have gone to Kantalan regardless. Patrick said she wanted the treasure for the child." Dominic's lips brushed her temple. "Rising Star blamed no one."

"Oh, I know." Elspeth was silent a long time, gazing into the fire. "Do you suppose she's happy now? Everyone is supposed to be happy in heaven, aren't they?"

"So the priests say. I guess I've never thought much about it."

"Neither have I." She was silent again. "I think Sayan and Dalkar must be happy, but they're together. Rising Star was so alone."

"Perhaps that was why she was given Ko-Do."

"Yes."

Elspeth was quiet so long that Dominic thought she had fallen asleep. "We're so lucky to be alive, Dominic. I don't want to be in heaven with you yet. There's so much I want to do on earth. I want to see you build your kingdom of Killara. I want to have your children and watch them grow up." Her cheek nestled in the hollow of his shoulder. "I won't let you die, Dominic. I couldn't bear it."

"I'd have a little trouble adjusting to it myself." For the first time since they had left Kantalan there was a note of dry humor in his voice. "Particularly since I'm not sure I'll qualify for pearly gates and streets of gold. Well, with the Kantalan treasure maybe we can pave our own streets with gold."

"I guess I haven't thought much about the treasure. I was so concerned with proving my theory about Atlantis and then when Rising Star died . . ."

Elspeth's voice was becoming husky and Dominic quickly sought a subject to distract her. "We could form an expedition and go back to Kantalan."

She shook her head. "It would take years to excavate the ruins."

"We could still try to do it." He paused. "If that's what you want. I've got what I came to Kantalan for. I'd like you to find your treasure too."

"I have found it," she said softly. "I saw it. I know it exists. I'd rather remember Kantalan as I first caught sight of it than as it is now."

"Then what about those mounds in Wisconsin or Illinois you told me about?" Dominic asked. "Maybe the mound where they found the statue of the elephant. We could go there and see if it has any link with Atlantis." He frowned thoughtfully. "We could drop off some of the treasure at the Wells Fargo office in Tucson and let Da take care of the rest. He could pay off the mortgage and start expanding our holdings."

"The Cahokia mound would be more likely. It's shaped like a truncated pyramid." Her eagerness faded and anxiety clouded her face. "Now? You're talking about going to Illinois immediately? What about Killara?"

"I've been away from Killara for a long time."

"But not because you wanted to be. Are you still trying to protect your family?"

"Nothing has changed to make my being there any safer for them. I guess you know I'm going to surround you with a small army of Pinkerton men while we're in Illinois." His arms tightened around her. "Nothing is going to happen to you."

"Pinkerton men?"

"A company that provides guards for hire among other services."

"But Killara—"

"Illinois will be safer for both of us." He hesitated before adding haltingly. "And I want our time together to be happy."

His words sounded frighteningly temporary, she thought. He wanted to make these moments as happy as possible because he feared they would not have a lifetime together. She started to protest, then thought better of it.

There had to be something they could do. She would not accept the fate of Sayan, Dalkar, and Rising Star. She would find a way. "Very well, we'll go to Illinois," she said as she relaxed against him and closed her eyes. "It would probably be better to go before I'm with child. A dig can be very strenuous, and besides, I think you'd like your son to be born at Killara."

His child, Elspeth, their life together. Dominic lay there thinking about them long after Elspeth had fallen asleep. God, how he wanted to be able to hope again. Yet how could he hope for anything when he knew men like Torres were constantly on his trail?

Torres. He was close. Dominic could feel it. They were probably moving toward Torres now that they were on their homeward journey. Torres could pounce tomorrow, or the next day, or the day after. He stiffened as he realized he was thinking like a goat staked out for a tiger. Hell, he might just as well meekly bare his chest for Torres's bullet. And if he waited for Torres's attack, Elspeth might be caught in the crossfire.

He carefully released Elspeth, rolled away from her, and quickly put on his boots. He bent swiftly and kissed her lightly on the temple before reaching for his guns. He hesitated, looking down at her. Dammit, he didn't want to leave her. Then he stood up and moved silently from the fire to where the animals were tethered.

It was time the prey turned hunter.

The flames were leaping high, and delicious visions danced before Ramon Torres's eyes. He always enjoyed this moment of meditation preceding slumber. It was almost as satisfying as dreaming of Dominic. It would be soon now. The death would come soon. He must be close and—

The flames of his campfire suddenly erupted in a series of explosions.

Torres rolled to the side, reaching for his rifle.

"Afraid, Torres?" The voice wafted out of the trees that surrounded him. "Pine nuts. A little trick my nephew, Patrick showed me. Almost as noisy as firecrackers, aren't they?"

"Dominic?"

"You wanted me. Now come and get me."

It wasn't supposed to be this way, Torres thought with indignation as he cautiously crawled out of the glare of the firelight. *He* was the hunter. Dominic had no right to turn on him in this fashion.

When he reached the cover of the shrubs behind him, he balanced the rifle against the bole of a tree, his gaze anxiously searching the darkness. Nothing. Not a whisper of sound, not a stir of movement. Where had Dominic's voice come from? Behind that big cluster of rocks? He would have to draw him out again.

"It was very stupid of you to warn me with your little joke," he called out. "A clever man would have cut me down before I could make a move. But then,

I've found honorable men are seldom clever, and you're an honorable man, Dominic."

"Am I?" The voice was mocking.

He *was* in the cluster of rocks. Yes, now he could see the gleam of the barrel of Dominic's rifle on the rock next to that beech tree. Torres felt a fierce rush of joy surge through him. He began to crawl carefully through the underbrush, but he couldn't resist the opportunity to speak to Dominic—it was so rare to talk with the prey. "Oh, yes, you have a code, my friend. It is very dangerous to have a code. It makes a man vulnerable."

"Why are you so determined to get me, Torres?"

Torres moved closer. A large boulder overlooked the cluster of rocks where Dominic had taken cover. He would circle around behind it and rush him from the rear. "Because I have a fondness for you." It was the truth. His powerful passion for Dominic was coursing through every vein as he thought of the pleasure his prey was going to give him. "Because you deserve to be killed by a great hunter, Dominic. You deserve to be killed by me."

"Torres, you aren't a great hunter."

Anger sparked through Ramon. It was unfair of Dominic to insult him when he had only kind thoughts for his prey. "I will show you soon, my friend." It was time to be silent as he circled the rocks. He mustn't give his position away because of vanity.

"Did you hear me, Torres? A great hunter wouldn't have missed that shot at the church."

Sorrow rushed through Torres. How sad that Dominic was fighting against the knowledge of the greatness of Ramon Torres. It would diminish the glory of Dominic's death.

It was time. He cocked the rifle. He couldn't see Dominic, but he knew he was there in front of the huge boulder. He drew a deep breath and then dashed from behind the boulder, his rifle pumping shots at Dominic in a deadly battery of bullets.

But it wasn't Dominic! It was only Dominic's rifle propped on the rocks.

"Torres."

He whirled to see Dominic sitting on the lowest branch of the beech tree smiling down at him. The colt forty five in his hand was leveled directly at Torres's chest.

A thrill of terror shot through Torres. Cornered. Helpless. Prey. He frantically lifted his rifle.

The bullet tore through Torres's chest, knocking him to the ground. He tried to lift his rifle but he couldn't move. Cold. Why was he so cold? He dimly saw Dominic climb down from the tree and come to stand over him. Dominic's expression was grim and his face pale in the moonlight. It was all wrong, Torres thought. He should be standing over Dominic, watching the life flutter from behind his eyes. That was the way it should be. Dominic was the prey. He, Torres, was the one who was the hunter. It was all wrong. . . .

Dawn was breaking and Elspeth was awake when Dominic returned to camp. She took one look at his face, and her worried frown faded to be replaced by understanding. "Torres?"

Dominic nodded as he unsaddled Blanco. "He won't bother us anymore."

Elspeth shivered. "I was so frightened when I woke and found you weren't here." Her eyes were suddenly blazing fiercely. "Don't you ever leave me alone that way again. I was sitting here imagining all kind of horrors."

"Then you imagined right." A little shock ran through her as he turned to face her, and she saw the desolation in his eyes. He took her in his arms. "It's always a horror."

Her arms went around him in fierce protectiveness and her voice was almost a maternal croon. "It's all right now. Everything will be all right."

"Yes." His arms tightened around her. "For now."

It must not happen again, she thought desperately. She could feel his pain and weariness. He mustn't ever have to go through this again. An iron-hard resolve formed within her, even as she held him and tenderly rocked him as if he were a beloved child.

This would not happen again, she vowed silently.

Patrick came upon Shamus and his band of men two days ride out of Rosario. He reined in and quickly motioned to Consuela that all was well. The woman's experience with bands as ragtaggle as the Killara riders did not inspire confidence.

The surprise that flickered across Shamus's face was immediately replaced by a sardonic smile. He inclined his head. "Patrick. Do you suppose I could be enlightened as to what the hell you're doing down here? The last I heard you'd taken off after Rising Star to try to bring her back to Killara." His glance shifted to the Mexican woman riding behind him, a papoose strapped to her back. The woman stared back at him without expression. "Who's your lady friend?"

"Consuela," Patrick said. "And she's the lady friend of a bandit named Indino. He sent her with me to wet-nurse Kevin."

"Kevin?" Shamus repeated.

Patrick's gaze turned to Joshua riding beside Shamus. "Rising Star's son."

Shock turned Joshua pale. "My son."

Patrick shook his head. "Rising Star's son," he repeated deliberately. "Not yours. You didn't want him, remember?"

"What are you talking about?" Joshua's voice was hoarse. "How can you have my son? What's Rising Star doing down here in Mexico? She was going back to her village."

"If you'd followed her when she left Killara, you'd have found out she never intended to go back to her people." Patrick smiled bitterly. "She had no people. We Delaneys took that away from her too."

Shamus's eyes narrowed. "She followed Dominic and Elspeth on that wild goose chase?"

"No wild goose chase. Kantalan was there, and so was the treasure. Dom and Elspeth are on their way back with enough gold and jewels in their saddlebags to buy everything west of the Mississippi."

"Well, I'll be damned," Shamus murmured.

"And Kevin's share will make him damn near rich enough to be considered a human being," Patrick said. "Maybe not worthy of being a Delaney, but close."

"Naturally Rising Star's and the boy's share will go to Joshua," Shamus said, his thoughts on the possibilities Patrick's news opened to him. "They're family and—"

"No way in hell," Patrick interrupted. "Rising Star's share goes to Kevin and he keeps control of his share."

"Patrick, this is none of your concern," Joshua said quietly. "Star and I will talk about it and decide—"

"Rising Star is dead."

Joshua made a low sound deep in his throat. His hands tightened on the reins. "No," he whispered.

Patrick gazed at him unflinchingly. "She died in childbirth. Kevin's twin sister died too."

"She should never have left Killara. The journey was too much for her."

"Killara was too much for her. We were too much for her. What the hell did you expect her to do? You told her you didn't want the child—" He broke off, trying to stifle the helpless rage burning within him, the rage that had possessed him since he stood over Rising Star's grave. "My God, how could you do that to her?"

"Patrick." Shamus's voice was stern. "Don't talk to your uncle like that. He's just suffered a grievous loss."

"So have I." Patrick's gaze was fixed implacably on Joshua. "So have we all. God, some of you don't even know that. She was . . . wonderful."

Joshua stared at him in helpless misery.

"Patrick, I won't have this," Shamus said. "You straighten up and keep a civil tongue in your head."

"I've said all I wanted to say to him." Patrick's gaze

shifted to Shamus. "Now I have a few words to say to you, Gran-da."

"They'd better be a hell of a lot more respectful than the ones you've just spoken to your uncle," Shamus said.

"Don't count on it. I don't feel very respectful at the moment. I feel mad as hell. There's going to be a few changes at Killara."

Shamus winged brow lifted. "Indeed?"

"Rising Star's son is going to be treated as a Delaney. I'm not saying you have to love him, but by God, you're going to accept him as one of us."

"I don't take orders, Patrick."

"Too bad," Patrick said. "Because you're going to take this one. If you don't, I'll find a way of taking Killara from you, Gran-da. I'm going to be rich as bejesus in my own right and I'll learn how to use that power." A flicker of pain crossed his face. "I figure the treasure may come in handy to buy more than emerald watchfobs and Oriental dancing girls."

Shamus gazed at him, his expression unrevealing. "You're upset, boy. We'll talk about this when we get back to Killara."

Patrick shook his head. "This is how it's going to be. Kevin is going to be treated like a crown prince in this kingdom the Kantalan treasure is going to buy because I'm going to be there to make sure he is. I'm moving back up to the house and I'll be watching you, Gran-da."

Shamus smiled genially. "Your grandmother will be glad to see you back under our roof. She never did like the idea of you down at the Mex village. There's too much mischief a boy can get into down there."

"I mean it, Gran-da."

The smile faded. "I know you do. I'm not an unreasonable man. Maybe we can come to an agreement."

"No maybe about it." Patrick turned his horse and began edging around the column of riders. He glanced over his shoulder. "There had been no sign of Torres when I left Dom and Elspeth."

"He was in Rosario. He's after Dom all right." Shamus frowned. "Where are you going?"

"I'm leaving Consuela and the baby at Rosario with Father Leon. Kevin's too young to make the trip home to Killara yet. I'll get them settled and then leave for the border right away. In a few months I'll come back and bring them home."

"Why don't you wait in Rosario until we come back through after we get Torres?" Shamus asked.

Patrick shook his head. "I have something to do." He met Shamus's gaze. "I'm going after Silver."

Shamus went still. "My, my," he said silkily. "And are we to make her a crown princess too?"

"We'll be lucky if she doesn't decide to take over the whole shooting match," Patrick said. "But if we treat her nicely, I figure she may let us keep an acre or two. And you *will* treat my cousin nicely, Gran-da."

"Cousin! She's no—" Shamus broke off. "You're asking too much, Patrick."

"I'm not asking." Patrick urged his horse forward. "Silver Delaney is coming home to stay, and you won't find her as easy to ignore as you did Rising Star."

"Patrick." Joshua's voice stopped him. "Where is Star buried?"

Patrick turned around again. "Beside a lake in the Sierra Madres. Why?"

Joshua moistened his lips with his tongue. "I want to bring her home to Killara."

Patrick stared at him in disbelief. Now he wanted to bring Rising Star home. Now, when it was too late. He opened his lips to blast Joshua with a scathing condemnation. Then he stopped, the words unspoken. Lines of suffering cut deeply into Joshua's face, and his eyes were brilliant with tears. He was in pain. In his way he had loved Rising Star. Not enough, dammit, but as much as he was able to.

Patrick's own eyes were dry as he looked at Joshua. He hadn't wept when Rising Star had died. He had been too full of anger and despair. Now he wished he had tears to shed for all of them. Joshua, Rising Star, Ko-Do, and himself. What a godawful waste of love.

But he had no tears, he had only a purpose, and it was time he set about accomplishing that purpose. "Dom and Elspeth will tell you the exact location of Rising Star's grave," he said wearily as he kicked his horse into a trot. "I'll see you back at Killara, Josh."

It was an evening two days later that Shamus and his men rode into Dominic and Elspeth's camp.

"Torres?" Was the first question Shamus asked.

"Dead," Dominic answered.

Shamus nodded curtly. "Good." His gaze turned to Elspeth. "We ran into Patrick. He tells me your journey wasn't as foolish as I thought."

"Is that all he told you?" Elspeth asked quietly.

"No." Shamus motioned to the man riding to his right. "This is my son, Joshua." He gestured carelessly to the other three men clustered about him. "Sean, Cort, and my grandson, William. This is Dominic's wife, Elspeth, boys."

There was a polite murmur from the young men, but Elspeth barely acknowledged it. Her gaze was focused on Joshua's pale, tragic face. She had been prepared to dislike him, yet how could she condemn a man who was already broken by grief? "I was just cooking supper. I'm afraid there's not enough for everyone."

"We'll cook our own." Shamus turned back to Dominic. "We have some talking to do."

Two hours later the glade looked like the campground of a small army. It was an army, Elspeth thought ruefully, a Delaney army, rushing to the rescue of one of their own. Her gaze turned to Shamus and Dominic across the campfire from her. They had been talking for nearly an hour, and by the expression on Shamus's face, she could tell he wasn't at all pleased by the conversation.

As she watched, Dominic got abruptly to his feet and strode over to where Sean and Cort were playing cards. Shamus stared after him for a moment and then stood up and marched over to Elspeth.

"You're sending him on another tomfool trip," he accused, glaring at her. "There's no sense to it."

She met his gaze steadily. "You have to admit our trip to Kantalan wasn't foolish. Perhaps the one we're about to make will be equally successful."

"But Dominic doesn't need any more money. The Kantalan treasure is enough for any sane man."

A faint smile touched Elspeth's lips. "I'm surprised to hear you say that. I gathered from Dominic that you didn't know the meaning of the word enough." She paused. "Besides, there are all kinds of treasures in this world."

"You're trying to keep him away from Killara."

"I would never do that." She looked down at the cup of coffee cradled in her hands. "He loves it too much. He even loves you, though heaven knows why."

"Then tell him you want to forget about running halfway across the country, and come home where you both belong."

She shook her head.

"Dammit, what's wrong with everyone?" Shamus exploded. "You, Patrick, Dominic. Can't you see I'm doing what's best for the family?"

He honestly believed what he was saying, Elspeth thought. And for the first time she caught the faintest glimpse of vulnerability beneath the old lion's roar. "No, *we're* doing what's best, and you'll have to accept it."

"The hell I will!" Shamus fought and eventually conquered his frustration and anger. He forced a smile. "Look, I know you're probably upset about Rising Star's death. Perhaps Malvina and I should have been friendlier to Joshua's wife, but we were never unkind to her. You don't have to be afraid we'll—"

"I'm not afraid of you," Elspeth said clearly. "I know you now. I know you're ruthless, stubborn, and sly. I also know you're loyal, protective, and love your family. In many ways I respect and admire you and in others . . ." She shrugged. "However, I do not fear you."

He blinked in surprise but rallied quickly. "Then there's no reason why we couldn't all get along very well together . . . eventually."

"Perhaps." She threw the remains of the coffee into the flames and set the cup down. "But not now." She stood up. "Don't worry, Mr. Delaney, your son will come home to Killara, but it will be when we wish it, not you." She turned away. "Now, if you'll excuse me, I think I'll go and try to further my acquaintance with Sean and Cort. I'm looking forward to getting to know them. The Delaneys are such an interesting family."

She turned and walked toward Dominic, Sean, and Cort, leaving the patriarch of that "interesting" Delaney family frustrated and perplexed.

Dominic stayed up late talking to his brothers. It was close to midnight when he finally slipped beneath the blanket with Elspeth, who immediately turned to face him and came into his arms. She didn't speak for a moment, content to be close to him with this army of strangers camped around them.

"I saw Da talking to you," Dominic said. "He didn't upset you, did he?"

"No." She was silent for a moment. "I believe I'm beginning to be a wee bit sorry for him. Everything around him is changing and he doesn't understand why or how to stop it." She paused. "Are we going back to Killara before we leave for Illinois?"

He shook his head. "There's no need now. Da can take the pack animals and treasure home and we can catch the stage in Tucson."

"I see." It was the answer she had hoped he would make. "How long will we be in Tucson?"

"The stage leaves twice a week. With any luck we won't have to be there more than overnight."

"Oh." She paused. "I thought perhaps we could stay a little longer than that. I have something to do in Tucson."

"What?"

She thought quickly. "Shopping. The only things I have with me are worn to rags."

"They have better stores and dressmakers in St. Louis. We'll have to stop there anyway."

"But what would I wear on the trip? No, I need a few days in Tucson. Besides, I'm very tired. I might need to rest a bit."

Dominic felt a pang of remorse mixed with tenderness. Of course she was tired. She had been through trials that would have tested the endurance of a strong man. "Why didn't you say so? We'll give you all the time you need. A month if you like."

Elspeth closed her eyes quickly to prevent him from seeing the flicker of guilt she was experiencing. She feigned a yawn. "A few days will be quite sufficient. "Good night, Dominic."

26

The name of the establishment was inscribed with discreet richness in gold letters on the plate glass window. *Charles Durbin and Sons, Bank of Tucson.* Elspeth paused to gaze at the inscription for a moment before she swept toward the front door. She closed her lacy parasol and opened the door.

Two women were standing in line at the teller's cage across the room, and a young man with sandy hair was bent over a ledger at a desk immediately to her right. She turned to face him. "I would like to speak to Mr. Durbin, please."

He looked up. Then he hastily rose to his feet with flattering alacrity. "I'm Mr. Durbin. George Durbin."

"No, the elder Mr. Durbin. Your father, I believe."

Disappointment flickered in his face. "Certainly. May I say who wishes to see him?"

"Elspeth . . . MacGregor."

He nodded and hurried toward the door of the glass-enclosed office to the right of the teller's cage. Elspeth's gaze followed him as he opened the door and spoke to a man at a large mahogany desk. Charles Durbin wasn't what Elspeth had expected. He was somewhere in his early fifties, with dark hair abundantly flecked with gray. He was slightly rotund. An indulgent smile creased his plump cheeks as his son spoke to him, and the sharp blue of his eyes softened for just an instant as he nodded and then leaned back in his big leather chair.

The younger Durbin came out of the office. "He'll see you now."

Elspeth bestowed a glowing smile on the young man as she moved toward the door. "Thank you, you've been very kind." She entered the office and closed the door behind her, smiling coolly at the man behind the desk. "It's good of you to see me. I've come on a rather important matter."

Charles Durbin rose to his feet, a genial smile on his face. His gaze ran over the lady before him with discreet admiration. No wonder George had run in here all flushed and calf-eyed. He found he was a bit dazzled himself. A gown of emerald green silk displayed the delicate curves of Elspeth MacGregor's exquisite figure and reflected the deep green of her eyes. A saucy lace bonnet with a green plume was perched on shining hair that might once have been light brown but was now sunstreaked to a shade nearer tawny gold.

"I'll be delighted to help you, of course. You wish to open an account?"

"No, I wish to close one." She moved to stand before his desk. "An account that has been open for too long."

He frowned in puzzlement.

"I'm afraid I didn't tell the entire truth to your son. I was afraid you wouldn't see me. My name is Elspeth MacGregor Delaney." She paused. "I'm Dominic Delaney's wife."

The smile on Durbin's face vanished. "You're right. I wouldn't have seen you. Please leave."

"Presently. After I've said what I wish to say." She placed the tips of her fingers on the desk and leaned forward. "It has to end. You have to stop sending killers like Torres after my husband."

"Get out of here!" Durbin's face was suddenly twisted with hatred. "Did he send you to beg for him?"

She shook her head. "He doesn't know I'm here and I have no intention of telling him about our discussion. This is between the two of us, Mr. Durbin. You see, Dominic is acting under a disadvantage with you. He bitterly regrets killing your son and so he won't confront you as you deserve to be confronted." Her eyes widened as she saw a flicker of expression cross Durbin's face. "Why, I think you must have realized how Dominic felt all along. You knew you were safe to do anything you liked because he was no threat to you personally." A glint of anger appeared in her eyes and a fierce smile curved her lips. "I'm afraid you'll find that's all changed now. *I'm* not at a disadvantage."

Durbin's plump face was turning beet red. "I'll have you thrown out into the street."

"I think not. It would reflect quite poorly on a respectable businessman like yourself to manhandle a woman. Be patient, I won't be here long." Her smile faded. "Just long enough to warn you."

"Warn me?"

"Oh, yes, I believe your code out here requires a warning." She paused. "Though the men you sent after Dominic often gave him none."

"Your husband is a murderer who should be shot down like a dog in the streets."

"My husband is a wonderful man who deserves to live, and I'm going to see that he does." She stared unblinkingly at Durbin. "Now, listen to me. If my husband is shot, stabbed, or run over by a coach, I shall make you pay. If he catches influenza or stumbles down the stairs, I shall still make you pay. It would be wise of you to surround Dominic with bodyguards as you did with murderers, if you wish to survive."

"And what harm do you think you can do to me?"

"Dominic and I have come into a great deal of money. More money than you can possibly imagine. You're a banker, Mr. Durbin. You know the power of money. I will ruin you." She paused. "And I will ruin your family. I've inquired, and I understand you have another son besides that handsome boy out there; you also have a very pleasant wife, I'm told. I'm sure you wouldn't want their lives made . . . uncomfortable." She took a deep breath. "And after I've ruined both you and your family, I will walk up to you and shoot you dead."

"You're bluffing."

"Am I?" She smiled mirthlessly. "Look at my face. What do you see there, Mr. Durbin."

He studied her. He inhaled sharply. "My God, you'd actually do it. Murder! They'd hang you."

"Not murder. Justice. And if I've learned one thing since I came to your Arizona territory, it's how much deference is paid to women here. I think your courts would be very sympathetic to a grieving widow." She straightened and stepped back from the desk. "Now I must leave. Dominic and I are catching a stage for the East in thirty minutes and I mustn't be late." She turned and walked toward the door, her silken skirts rustling. "Good day, Mr. Durbin."

"You bitch." The curse came with the snarling venom of an animal at bay. "You're a fit mate for that son of Satan, Dominic Delaney."

She glanced over her shoulder and smiled with dazzling sweetness. "I hope so. Oh, I *do* hope so, Mr. Durbin."

The door closed behind her.

Young George Durbin jumped to his feet and was holding the front door open by the time she reached it. "I hope we'll see you again soon, Miss MacGregor."

"Mrs. Delaney," she corrected him. "Mrs. Dominic Delaney. Thank you, but I don't think you will. I believe I've completed my transaction with your father." Only time would tell if Durbin would be frightened enough to cease his persecution of Dominic, but the shock and fear she'd seen on the man's face had made her wildly hopeful. She unfurled her ruffled lace parasol and stepped out onto the sidewalk. "Good-bye."

Dominic was waiting at the Wells Fargo office when she turned the corner. His frown disappeared and an indulgent smile lit his face as he caught sight of her. "It's about time you got here. I was just going to look for you. I don't see why you had to go shopping today anyway. I thought you had already bought out all the stores in Tucson."

"Not quite. Are we ready to go?"

"Almost. We're the only passengers, but Ben has to wait for a mail shipment."

She closed her parasol. "Ben Travis? He's going to be our driver?"

Dominic nodded as he opened the door of the coach. "I wasn't sure you'd be pleased. He was here when Marzonoff was lynched." ·

"He's your friend. I can never condone what happened to Andre but I'll try to understand."

He lifted her into the coach, brushing her nose with a light kiss. "Do you have everything?" He glanced down at the dainty lace recticule in her hand. "Where are your packages?"

"No packages." She smiled radiantly. "And yes, I have everything." A knowledge of her own worth, passion, love, and this man who had given them all to her. "Everything."

A rattle of shots broke the silence when the coach was only a few miles out of Tucson.

Elspeth's heart jerked crazily. Durbin? Had she been wrong to believe she had frightened the man enough to stop his pursuit of Dominic? Dear heaven, and she had been the one to tell him they were taking this stage! She could hear Ben Travis shouting a litany of curses as he brought the coach to a halt.

Dominic drew his gun swiftly. "Get down on the floor, Elspeth."

"Dad blast you, Patrick. I warned you I'd blow your head off if you pulled this foolishness again," Ben yelled.

Patrick!

"Easy, Ben. I missed Dom and Elspeth in Tucson and I just wanted to say good-bye."

"Then say it and let me get going. I have a schedule to keep."

A moment later Patrick climbed into the coach. He was dusty and travel-stained and Elspeth had a fleeting memory of the first time she'd seen the boy in circumstances almost identical to this.

But it wasn't a boy who faced her now. There was a new maturity looking out of Patrick's dark brown eyes, and Elspeth experienced a pang of poignant regret for the lovable, mischievous lad who had vanished when Rising Star had died.

"Gran-da told me when I rode into Killara with Silver that you were going east," Patrick said. He held out his hand to Dominic. "Don't stay away too long. We're going to need you."

Dominic shook his hand. "A year or two."

"I have a favor to ask. I've been thinking about sending Silver to school in St. Louis." His lips twisted. "Oh, not for a while. Not until Gran-da gives in and accepts her as a Delaney. I'm not about to remove the bit until he gets used to it. But afterward it may make it easier for Silver if she has some of the wildness tamed out of her."

"And you think a fancy school will do it?" Dominic asked dryly. "Heaven help them."

"It's worth a try. Will you and Elspeth keep an eye on her? St. Louis isn't far from where you'll be digging, is it?"

Elspeth shook her head. "Not far at all. Of course we'll take care of her."

Patrick breathed a sigh of relief. "Good. This isn't easy for me. I'm not used to looking after anyone but myself."

"You're doing very well, Patrick," Elspeth said gently.

He leaned forward and kissed her forehead. "Good-bye, Elspeth, and thank you."

"Good-bye, Patrick." She could feel the tears brimming in her eyes and determinedly blinked them away. "Take care of yourself."

He opened the door and jumped to the ground. Then he turned to face them, and for an instant Elspeth was sure she saw the glint of mischief she had thought gone forever. "Oh, I almost forgot to tell you, Dominic. I brought you a present from Killara. I'm sure it will prove to be just what you need when you're working around the dig." He slammed the door of the coach and disappeared from view.

Elspeth frowned. "What did he mean? I don't see any present. Do you—"

A blistering round of curses from Ben Travis turned the air blue. "Patrick, dammit, you come back here!"

"Can't, Ben. I'm in a hurry to get home to Killara." There was the sound of hoofbeats and the ghost of a breath of laughter.

"But you *can't* leave him tied to my coach. I have a schedule to meet," Ben shouted.

There was no answer from Patrick.

"Patrick, you bastard, he's sitting down in the middle of the road!"

"Oh, no." Dominic groaned softly. He pulled his hat over his eyes and slid down in the seat. "He wouldn't do this to me."

Elspeth began to laugh helplessly as she scooted over to poke her head out the window and take a look for herself. "I'm afraid he already has, Dominic."

Azuquita.

THIS FIERCE SPLENDOR by Iris Johansen sets the stage for more exciting love stories of those colorful men and women who founded the Delaney Dynasty. The next trilogy from the bestselling trio of authors Iris Johansen, Kay Hooper, and Fayrene Preston has the overall title *THE DELANEYS, THE UNTAMED YEARS*. All three of these thrilling novels go on sale April 20, 1988 and are excerpted in the following pages—

    COPPER FIRE by Fayrene Preston
    WILD SILVER by Iris Johansen
    GOLDEN FLAMES by Kay Hooper

COPPER FIRE

by Fayrene Preston

Minutes later Brianne closed the door to her room, then leaned back against it. Across the room, Sloan sat. He was so still he might have been dead—except for his eyes. They were blazing with a fiery, golden life. She should say something, she mused, but for the life of her, she couldn't think of anything. So she waited.

"Did you get your gentleman friend settled?" he asked in a voice that was very low and quite calm.

"I don't know him well enough to call him a friend. And yes, he's in his room."

"No doubt in one of Mrs. Potter's finest."

"He's on this floor," she admitted, thinking that she had never known anyone who could manage to convey so much displeasure without using a trace of emotion in his voice. "But he's at the other end of the hall."

"I must confess, I'm surprised."

"Oh?" She pushed away from the door and walked to the edge of the bed. "At what?"

"That you can still manage to stand upright with the problems of so many people weighing on your shoulders."

"Henrietta and Phineas are no burden."

He came up out of his chair and was standing in front of her before she had a chance to blink. "You little fool! Don't you know the jeopardy you put yourself in by stopping to help a strange man?"

"I couldn't just pass him by!"

Gripping her shoulders, he spoke from between clenched teeth. "Not only should you have passed him by, you should have ridden so wide a circle around him, he wouldn't have even known you were in the area!"

She wrenched out of his hold. "I wasn't going to leave someone alone out there who needed help!"

"No, of course you wouldn't! That would have been the sensible thing to do, wouldn't it?"

"Sloan! I was raised to take care of myself. I can put a bullet in the center of an ace of spades at a hundred paces."

"But can you put a bullet in a man's heart?"

"If I have to."

"I don't believe you."

Swiftly, Brianne moved to where her gear was piled and jerked up her rifle. Pointing it straight at his heart, she asked, "Do you want me to prove it?"

He smiled, and his voice softened. "You wouldn't even get that rifle cocked, redhead."

She believed him, and tossed the rifle down. "Get out, Sloan."

"When I'm good and ready."

Brianne exploded. "I don't understand you!"

Sloan didn't understand himself either. And he didn't understand her. She was standing within arm's reach of him, her hair streaming in wild glory down her back, her skin giving off the sweetly seducing fragrance he had first smelled when he had seen her rising from her bath. Only a thin sash held her robe around her, and delicate satin ribbons closed her gown over her breasts.

Angry at her for putting herself in danger, and angry at himself for being angry, he reached for her.

She didn't come to him easily. She pushed against him, fighting with all her might. But his strength was the greater, and so was his need.

His mouth crushed down on hers, his powerful arms pulled her tightly against him. Reason wasn't entirely lost, but what was left was fogged by a pounding desire. He stripped off her robe, then fell with her onto the bed.

Brianne felt the impact of the mattress against her back and was furious. She didn't want to feel the weight of his leg as it lay over hers. She didn't want to experience the rub of his tongue against her own. She didn't want to feel his hand covering her breast. She didn't! She didn't!

Sloan's fingers grasped a ribboned bow and pulled. So easy. He untied another, and another, until he could lay the edges of the gown back, baring her breasts. He tore his mouth away from her lips so that he could see her, and what he saw nearly took his breath away. No woman could be so perfectly formed, he thought. It had to be an illusion.

Brianne raised her fist and hit against Sloan's chest, but the blow had all the force of a puff of wind. When had she become so weak? she wondered. When had she become so hot?

"Stop," she said, in a voice that sounded more like an entreaty than an order. "Please . . ."

Gazing into her emerald-green eyes, Sloan saw that they had softened. He liked that look. "I don't want to stop, Brianne." A soft breath escaped her lips, and he tried to capture it with his mouth. "Say please again," he whispered against her lips.

Desire was a new sensation to Brianne. How easy it would be to give in to it; heat was exploding everywhere in her. Yet she couldn't surrender. It wasn't in her makeup.

She tried to twist away, but with one strong arm he brought her back. She rolled her head, trying to escape his mouth. "Stop it, Sloan. Now!" Her words were whispered, but he heard.

He raised his head again to look at her, but he kept his hand on her breast, as if he had no intention of letting her go. "I want you, Brianne."

"But I don't want you!"

He smiled. "I can make you want me, and I won't even have to work at it." To prove his point, he caressed her slowly, teasingly. She moaned. "See?" he murmured.

Brianne looked up at him and was immediately confused. How could Sloan's face remain so hard, even while he was seducing her, *even while he was smiling*?

Then, as if a flash of light had suddenly sought out and revealed the darkest place in her mind, she remembered why his smile seemed so familiar to her. She had seen that same smile on the only living thing that had ever hurt her—a wolf. He had looked at her with pale gold eyes and a teeth-baring smile right before he sank his teeth into her arm, tearing at her flesh.

The memory gave her back her strength. In the space of two heartbeats she rolled off the bed, lunged for the rifle, aimed it right at his heart, and thumbed back the hammer. "This is a Model 1873 Winchester .44/40," she said, "and it is now cocked, with a bullet in the chamber and fifteen more behind it." A forceful and cool assurance filled her voice.

With her face flushed with anger, her gown gaping open and exposing heaving breasts tipped by rigid nipples, Sloan thought he had never seen a more beautiful woman in his life. God, but he wanted her!

"Mrs. Porter is going to be awfully upset if she finds blood splattered all over this room," he said calmly.

"I'll buy this damn hotel if it comes to that! Now, get up, Sloan, and get out of here."

He sat up, slid to the edge of the bed, and stood up. Slowly, he walked toward her, stopping only when the barrel of the rifle was touching his chest. "You're an interesting lady, redhead. You're wealthy enough to buy a hotel, you have guts enough to shoot me, and you're beautiful enough to make me want you like I've never wanted another woman. I'll leave for now, but I'll be back. We're not through, you and I. Not nearly."

WILD SILVER

by *Iris Johansen*

Mikhail, Nicholas's servant and friend, threw open the door to the cabin and strode into the stateroom. Nicholas rose easily to his feet, his gaze on the bundle over the giant's shoulder. "Good Lord, Mikhail, did you have to use two blankets? She must be smothering."

"I should have used ten," Mikhail muttered as he strode across the room and dropped his burden on the bed. "And I should have let you come with me. I should have let an army come with me." He unwrapped the blankets with two quick jerks and Silver tumbled free, rolling over to the opposite side of the bed. Her wrists were tied behind her back and a handkerchief gagged her mouth, but her eyes blazed up at them as she continued to struggle to free herself. Mikhail tossed the blankets on the floor and reached over to pull the gag from Silver's mouth, quickly jerking his hand away as her strong, white teeth snapped at him. "She is a wild animal." There was a curious note of pride in his voice as he gazed down at Silver's face. "If I had not taken her by surprise, I do not think I would have been able to overpower her. She is a fine, strong warrior." He carefully brushed a strand of hair from Silver's eyes, his expression gentle. "It is all right now. No one is going to hurt you."

"But *I* will hurt you." Silver glared up at him fiercely,

still struggling desperately against her bonds. "You can't do this!"

"It appears that he can, because he has." Nicholas strode forward to stand over her. Her long hair was lying in wild, silken disarray against the peach-colored velvet of the spread, and he felt a sudden thrust of desire tighten his groin. He had been sitting there, imagining how she would look lying on his bed, and the reality was even more erotic than his vision. "Though not without some effort."

"You!" Her light eyes glittered with rage as she began to curse him with venom and amazing proficiency.

He lifted a brow. "My, my, she's quite talented, isn't she, Mikhail? The last time I heard a vocabulary so explicit was from my groom at the estate on Crystal Island. Should we release her, do you think?"

"Only if you wish to relieve yourself of a few fistfuls of excess hair," Mikhail said dryly, gingerly touching his own tousled red mop. "Before I got her hands tied I was sure she would strip me bald. Best wait until you have talked reason to her."

"Reason?" Silver struggled into a sitting position. "There is no reason connected with this outrage. It's madness, as I'll soon show you."

"I'm sure you'll try." Nicholas smiled. "And it will be fascinating to watch your attempts. I may even be sorry to see you depart after you tell me where your uncle has disappeared to."

"You'll be sorrier to see me stay," Silver hissed.

A flicker of anger crossed Nicholas's handsome face. "I believe you're beginning to annoy me. So far you've cursed me, threatened me, and insulted me."

"Let me loose and I'll do more than that to you. I'll stick my knife in you, as I did your friend."

Nicholas stiffened. "Knife?" His gaze flew to Mikhail. "She *stabbed* you?" His attention had been so absorbed with the girl he had scarcely glanced at Mikhail. Now he saw that the Cossack's tunic was torn, and a rivulet of blood stained the whiteness of the left sleeve.

"A pinprick." Mikhail bent down, pulled a small dagger out of his boot, and tossed it to Nicholas. "Yet it might be wise to remember she is not without fangs."

"Like all vipers." Nicholas looked down at the dagger, his beautifully molded features hard as the marble of a tombstone. "She could have killed you. I should have gone myself, my friend."

A touch of anxiety clouded Mikhail's features. "A pinprick," he repeated. "She was only defending herself. The wound will be gone by tomorrow."

Bewilderment pierced Silver's seething fury. It was clear the big Russian was defending her from Nicholas Savron's anger. Why would he help the prince abduct her and then rush to her defense?

"Do you need a doctor?" Nicholas asked gently. "I'll have Robert dock again and send someone for help."

"The woman—"

"The woman is not worth one drop of your blood." Nicholas gave Silver a glance as cold as winter sleet. "I will deal with her later."

Mikhail shook his head. "I have no need for a doctor. She did not hurt me."

"Only because you—" Silver broke off as Mikhail shook his head warningly at her. "I *will* speak. Do you think I'm afraid of either of you?"

"You obviously have no need to fear Mikhail. It seems he's been foolish enough to take a liking to you," Nicholas said softly. "But you'd do well to be afraid of me. I value Mikhail, and I don't think I've ever been quite so angry with anyone in my entire life."

"Liking? He *abducted* me."

"On my orders. And he insisted on going alone, because he felt it would be safer for you."

"Or because you were too cowardly to go with him," Silver said contemptuously.

Mikhail inhaled sharply and took an impulsive step forward, as if to place himself between Silver and Nicholas. "Nicholas, she is only a woman. She did not—"

"Only a woman," Silver repeated indignantly. "A woman can do anything a man can do! She can do more! Why do—"

"*Shut up!*" Nicholas shouted, enunciating with great precision.

"I should not have taken the gag off her." Mikhail sighed morosely. "I should have known her tongue would be as sharp as her dagger."

"Go take care of your wound." Nicholas's gaze was narrowed on Silver's face. "I have a fancy to prove myself to the lady."

Mikhail gazed at him helplessly. Nicholas was dangerously infuriated, and it was evident that Silver Delaney was not about to try to placate him. "You gave your word."

Nicholas glanced at him incredulously. "Good Lord— she stabbed you and you're still defending her?"

Mikhail's jaw squared stubbornly. "You promised me."

Nicholas muttered something fierce and obscene beneath his breath. "And I'll keep my word, dammit."

Mikhail turned toward the door, and then glanced over his shoulder at Silver, a gentle smile lighting his craggy features. "I will be back soon. Do not be afraid."

Silver gazed at him. "I'm not afraid and I need no protection."

Mikhail slowly shook his head and shut the door quietly behind him.

Silver immediately turned to Nicholas and opened her mouth to speak.

Nicholas raised his hand. "Not one word, or I'll put the gag back on you."

She hesitated, and then pressed her lips together.

"Very wise. I'm holding on to my temper by a very precarious thread, Silver."

He sat down on the bed beside her, not touching her, but close enough so that she could feel the heat emanating from his body. The faint scent of musk, brandy, and tobacco drifted to her nostrils.

"I'm about to give you the rules that will govern your stay while you're on the *Rose*. Are you listening?"

She gazed up at him mutinously.

"I see you are." He smiled faintly. "First, let's discuss why you're here."

"You want Dominic."

"Exactly. I suppose I should give you the option of telling me where he is."

"Would you let me go if I did?"

"I'm afraid I'd be forced to do so. Do you wish to oblige?"

Silver drew a deep breath. Lord, she hated lies. Still, if

it would give Dominic a little more time . . . "He and Elspeth went back to Killara, in the Arizona Territory."

Nicholas's expression hardened. "I see you're as prone to falsehood as the rest of your sex. Randall's investigators ascertained that your uncle was most definitely not at Killara. It's obvious that asking you for the truth will accomplish nothing, and I admit I'm a trifle disappointed. I thought you more honest than most."

A flush stung Silver's cheeks. "I'm honest with those I respect. You deserve only lies from me. I'll tell you nothing about Dominic."

"But when he finds you're gone from Mrs. Alford's nunnery, I'd say there's an excellent chance of him coming after you," he said softly. "I posted a letter to your former headmistress, telling her you'd decided to accompany me on a little pleasure cruise. If he's as loyal to you as you are to him, he should be waiting at the levee when we return to St. Louis."

"He won't even hear that I'm gone. There wouldn't be—" She stopped. "You'll be disappointed if you think you can use me to draw Dominic to you."

His gaze centered on her face. "You seem very certain." He shrugged. "No matter. Then you'll remain on the *Rose* until you tell me where he is."

"You can't keep me here."

"Oh, but I can. Shall I tell you how?" Nicholas's long, shapely hand reached out and smoothed her hair back from one temple, his touch as delicate as the brush of the wings of a butterfly. "There is no one to help you here. This boat belongs to me, and you'll find no one interested in any plea for aid. Mikhail and my friend Valentin are completely loyal to me. And the crew would lose very lucrative positions if they displeased me."

So she would be alone in her struggle. For a moment she felt a tiny *frisson* of apprehension. She dismissed it impatiently. Her struggles had always been faced alone, except when Rising Star had been there to support her. This was no different. "I don't need help. I'll still get away from you."

A flicker of admiration crossed his face. "No tears? No pleas? I can almost see why Mikhail has developed a fondness for you."

"I never cry." She met his gaze. "And you will never hear me plead."

"Oh, but I will." Passion flared in the darkness of his eyes. "And it will be my very great pleasure to grant those pleas."

GOLDEN FLAMES

by Kay Hooper

Victoria was waiting for him in the lobby of her hotel, and Falcon paused for a moment just inside the doors to gaze at her before she saw him. The black velvet cloak she wore hid a part of her gown from him, but he saw with a feeling of triumph that she had indeed worn red, as he'd asked her to do. The gown was obviously tulle, and the red was a deep, rich color which, along with the black cloak, set off her fair beauty strikingly. Her hair was up in an intricate style, made curiously fragile by a black satin ribbon woven in among the gleaming strands. She had fastened the cloak at her throat, which prevented him from seeing if the rubies dangling from her delicate ears were matched by a necklace, lending fire to her creamy breasts. Fortunately, his imagination where she was concerned was vivid.

He approached her on cat feet. "Beautiful. Just beautiful."

She looked up at him, startled by his silent approach, and a faint color swept up her cheeks. But there was something new in her eyes, something half shy and half excited, and he knew his seductive efforts had borne fruit. He offered his arm with a slight bow, and amusement rose in him when she accepted the arm, her sidelong glance showing a rueful appreciation of his gentlemanly manners.

The lady was no fool; plainly, she found his publicly donned courtesy quite definitely suspect.

"Why do I feel I'm being led into the lion's den?" she murmured as he guided her out to the waiting carriage.

Falcon laughed softly. "I can't imagine. Are you afraid of me, Victoria?"

She didn't answer until they were inside the closed carriage and moving. "Afraid of you?" She seemed to consider the matter, gazing at him in the shadowed interior. "I think it would be unwise of me to pretend you aren't a dangerous man."

"Not dangerous to you, surely," he said in a silky tone.

Her green eyes were serious. "Western men are a peculiar breed, a law unto themselves. Sometimes their gallant manners would make a European nobleman cringe in shame at his own lack, and at other times they're as rough and raw as the land that bred them. Dangerous to me? To any woman, I should think."

After a moment, he smiled. "I was born in Ireland."

"Were you? But you're a Western man nonetheless. A Texas Ranger, didn't you say?"

"Yes, for several years."

"And a Union soldier before that." Her tone was thoughtful. "And before that—a scout, perhaps? An Indian fighter?"

"Both," he confessed, oddly pleased by her perception. "And the scar?"

He lifted a hand to finger the crescent mark on his cheekbone. "This? When I was a boy, my brothers and I often rode through Apache camps near our ranch, borrowing the Indian custom of counting coup."

"Trying to touch as many braves as possible? I've heard of it. Is that how you were hurt?"

He smiled. "In a way. My half-broke mustang took exception to a raid one night and threw me. I landed on a sharp stone. A battle scar, of sorts."

She smiled in return, thinking of a young boy cursing his temperamental mount.

"Did I tell you how beautiful you are?" he said suddenly, huskily.

Her smile faded slightly, leaving only the curve of delicate lips. "Yes. Yes, you did. Thank you."

Falcon reached out to touch her cheek gently, and then his hand dropped to toy with the fastening of her cloak. "Is this to keep out the cold? Or me?"

Her gloved fingers tightened around each other in her lap, and Victoria felt her breath grow short. "The dictates of fashion," she said finally.

He unfastened the cloak slowly, holding her eyes with his, very aware that her breath, like his, was shallow and quick. And some distant part of him marveled at these incredible feelings. She felt it too, this aching fire, and he was delighted by her swift response to him. "Fashion can go to hell," he muttered.

Victoria made no move to stop him, though she knew she should be ashamed of her wanton desire to have him see her, touch her, kiss her. What she felt was excitement.

He opened the cloak completely, pushing it back over her shoulders, and caught his breath at what he saw. The gown was cut low, baring her luscious breasts almost to the nipples, and against the creamy flesh a ruby necklace gleamed with dark fire. The lanterns hung outside the carriage sent a part of their light into the shadowed interior, playing over her exposed flesh with the loving glow of pale gold. Her breasts rose and fell quickly, each motion suggesting that the gown couldn't possibly hold the full mounds captive a moment longer.

"God, you're so beautiful," he said hoarsely, and his hands were on her bare shoulders, turning her toward him. He was inflamed even more by her instant, pliant response.

Victoria didn't even try to resist him. She had invited this, she realized dimly, invited this by agreeing to accompany him tonight, by wearing the provocative gown. And why couldn't she feel ashamed of that? Why did she feel only achingly, vibrantly alive and incredibly excited? Why did she want to feel his hands on her, his lips . . .

One of his hands slid down her back, finding the swell of her buttocks and pulling her as close as possible, even as his other arm surrounded her, crushing her upper body against him. He could feel the firm pillow of her bosom pressed to his chest, feel as well as hear her soft gasp, and an urgent sound escaped him just before his lips captured hers.

She was prepared for the shocking possession of his tongue this time—as well as she could be prepared for a sensation so devastating—and her body responded feverishly. Against his hard chest her breasts swelled and ached, and her arms slid up around his neck of their own volition. He was easing her back into the corner, and she could feel his arousal against her hip, bold and demanding.

When he released her lips at last she could only gasp, and her head fell back instinctively as he plundered the soft, vulnerable flesh of her throat. Her fingers twined in his thick, silky hair, and she wanted suddenly to remove her gloves so that she could feel his hair, his skin. And then his lips moved lower to brush hotly against her straining breasts, and she forgot everything except sheer pleasure.

"So sweet," he whispered thickly. Her low moan sorely tested his control. "Victoria . . ."

She had never known such pleasure existed, and the only coherent thought in her mind was the desire to feel more. She was hot, cold, shaking, her body a prisoner of the sensations sweeping over it with the relentless rhythm of an ocean's waves. The hot, wet caress of his tongue seared her skin, and his hand gently squeezed her breast until she thought she'd go out of her mind, until the stiffened nipple thrust free of confining silk and his mouth closed hotly around it.

All her senses were centered there, drawn by his pleasuring mouth, burning with a hunger she had never known. Something inside her, some dimly perceived barrier, melted in the heat of his caress, and she couldn't even find the breath to cry out her astonished delight.

She was hardly aware of his hand sliding down over her quivering belly, but a sudden touch at the vulnerable apex of her thighs jerked an instinctive, shocked protest from her lips. "No! Falcon, don't!"

"Shhh," he murmured against her skin, his hand rubbing gently through the layers of clothing while his mind vividly imagined the soft, damp warmth too much material hid from him. He wanted to draw her skirt up, find his way through the delicate feminine underthings until he could touch that heat, caress the womanly core of her. His entire body ached with the need to feel her naked and passionate against him. His tongue teased her nipple delicately with tiny, fiery, hungry licks. "Don't stop me, sweet. So sweet. You taste so good."

Victoria wanted to protest again, but the heat at her breast had sent a part of its fire lower, deeper into her body, and the hot clamoring inside her became a hollow, bittersweet need. "Falcon . . . you shouldn't . . . I can't . . ."

He lifted his head slowly, his darkened eyes intent on her flushed face. She looked thoroughly kissed, heart-breakingly beautiful in her innocent awareness. Her lips were red and swollen, her eyes sleepy with desire and dimly shocked. He slid his hand back up over her belly, cupping her breast gently and briefly before easing the silk upward until she was decently covered again. Then he surrounded her flushed face softly in one large hand and kissed her, vaguely surprised at the surge of tenderness he felt.

He brought them both upright, drawing the cloak back over her shoulders as she slowly lowered her arms, and fastening it again. And when she was sitting demurely, gazing at him with huge eyes, he leaned back into his own corner and sighed softly. "No one at the party will doubt that I want you," he murmured. "A man can never hide what a woman does to him."

Her eyes flicked downward to the straining evidence of his arousal, and then skittered hastily back to his face in confusion. Between the plantation of her childhood and Morgan's thriving ranch, she could hardly have avoided learning of the physical evidence of male sexuality, but his soft, bold reference to his body's response to her was both shocking and—in some part of herself she didn't want to acknowledge—exciting.

He chuckled softly. "Making love in a carriage is an awkward business," he offered. "If there had been a bed nearby, sweet, a loaded gun wouldn't have stopped me."

BANTAM BOOKS
GRAND SLAM SWEEPSTAKES
Win a new Chevrolet Corsica . . .
It's easy . . . It's fun . . . Here's how to enter:

OFFICIAL ENTRY FORM

Three Bantam book titles on sale this month are hidden in this word puzzle. Identify the books by circling each of these titles in the puzzle. Titles may appear within the puzzle horizontally, vertically, or diagonally . . .

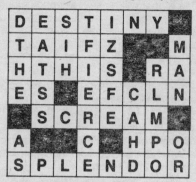

D	E	S	T	I	N	Y	
T	A	I	F	Z			M
H	T	H	I	S		R	A
E	S		E	F	C	L	N
	S	C	R	E	A	M	
A			C	H	P	O	
S	P	L	E	N	D	O	R

This month's Bantam Books titles are:

DESTINY

THIS FIERCE SPLENDOR

THE SCREAM

In each of the books listed above there is another entry blank and puzzle . . . another chance to win!

Be on the lookout for these Bantam paperback books: INDIAN COUNTRY, SOMETIMES PARADISE, and BE HAPPY YOU ARE LOVED. In each of them, you'll find a new puzzle, entry blank and GRAND SLAM SWEEPSTAKES rules . . . and yet another chance to win another brand-new Chevrolet automobile!

MAIL TO:　　　GRAND SLAM SWEEPSTAKES
Post Office Box 18
New York, New York 10046

Please Print

NAME _____

ADDRESS _____

CITY _____ STATE _____ ZIP _____

OFFICIAL RULES

NO PURCHASE NECESSARY.

To enter identify this month's Bantam Book titles by placing a circle around each word forming each title. There are three titles shown above to be found in this month's puzzle. Mail your entry to: Grand Slam Sweepstakes, P.O. Box 18, New York, N.Y. 10046

This is a monthly sweepstakes starting February 1, 1988 and ending January 31, 1989. During this sweepstakes period, one automobile winner will be selected each month from all entries that have correctly solved the puzzle. To participate in a particular month's drawing, your entry must be received by the last day of that month. The Grand Slam prize drawing will be held on February 14, 1989 from all entries received during all twelve months of the sweepstakes.

To obtain a free entry blank/puzzle/rules, send a self-addressed stamped envelope to: Winning Titles, P.O. Box 650, Sayreville, N.J. 08872. Residents of Vermont and Washington need not include return postage.

PRIZES: Each month for twelve months a Chevrolet automobile will be awarded with an approximate retail value of $12,000 each.

The Grand Slam Prize Winner will receive 2 Chevrolet automobiles plus $10,000 cash (ARV $34,000).

Winners will be selected under the supervision of Marden-Kane Inc., an independent judging organization. By entering this sweepstakes each entrant accepts and agrees to be bound by these rules and the decisions of the judges which shall be final and binding. Winners may be required to sign an affidavit of eligibility and release which must be returned within 14 days of receipt. All prizes will be awarded. No substitution or transfer of prizes permitted. Winners will be notified by mail. Odds of winning depend on the total number of eligible entries received.

Sweepstakes open to residents of the U.S. and Canada except employees of Bantam Books, its affiliates, subsidiaries, advertising agencies and Marden-Kane, Inc. Void in the Province of Quebec and wherever else prohibited or restricted by law. Not responsible for lost or misdirected mail or printing errors. Taxes and licensing fees are the sole responsibility of the winners. All cars are standard equipped. Canadian winners will be required to answer a skill testing question.

For a list of winners, send a self-addressed, stamped envelope to: Bantam Winners, P.O. Box 711, Sayreville, N.J. 08872.